A Little night Mischief

Emily Greenwood

sourcebooks casablanca

Design by Anna Kmet/Shannon Associates

Published by Sourcebooks Casablanca, an imprint of Sourcebooks, Inc.
P.O. Box 4410, Naperville, Illinois 60567-4410
(630) 961-3900
FAX: (630) 961-2168
www.sourcebooks.com

Printed and bound in the United States of America
VP 10 9 8 7 6 5 4 3 2 1

For Michael, with love

One

A pox on Lady P-S, Felicity Wilcox thought as she tugged extra hard on a patch of watercress growing along Yardley Stream. It came loose easily, almost sending her backward into the water.

The Wilcox family did not need—she assaulted a fresh patch of watercress—any help. They would manage this difficulty on their own. Anyway, Felicity knew perfectly well that Lady Pincheon-Smythe's visit earlier that morning hadn't really been motivated by a desire to help. She'd come to see whether the rumors were true.

Felicity's stomach, unsatisfied with the meager breakfast she'd eaten, rumbled loudly. The watercress was to be part of lunch.

The warm June morning was quiet, without so much as a cart passing on the road just above her, which ran parallel to the stream and led toward Longwillow village. But that changed a moment later as she was curling her fingers around a final bunch of greens and she became aware of the sound of thundering hooves. In the next instant a rider dashed by on the road above, sending a shower of mud down on her.

She yelped and lurched in surprise. Her feet slipped and she fell backward into the stream. Cool water immediately began seeping through to her undergarments. Above her the racing hoofbeats slowed abruptly and came nearer again. They stopped somewhere over her, though the high banks of the stream prevented her from seeing either the horse or the rider.

She struggled to stand up as the fitted bodice of her antiquated gown constricted her with its new weight of water. Straining to get a deeper breath, her empty stomach churning queasily, she had just taken in the sight of a tall gentleman striding toward the stream when her vision clouded and she fell backward again.

A muffled curse drifted in the air above her as strong arms caught her and tugged her upward. The sun shone blindingly behind her savior, and she closed her eyes against it. He held her for a moment clutched against him, so that she inhaled a masculine scent: rich, woodsy, with a spicy, surprising note of… orange? He let go of her with one arm and jerked at his coat. Then he laid her on the ground and she opened her eyes to blue sky.

Her bare arms felt not grass below her, but the satiny smooth, wonderful-smelling lining of her rescuer's coat. She turned her head and there he was, squatting next to her with a look of concern on his face.

"So, you'll live," he said, one of a pair of elegant black brows drifting upward with the hint of jest, a lightness for which she was absurdly grateful. She'd never in her life swayed or swooned, and she had no intention of becoming a vaporish miss now.

"Apparently I will," she said as her wits reassembled.

She pushed herself up to a sitting position and blinked, focusing her gaze on the stranger. The dramatic whiteness of his crisp shirt was creating a startling contrast with his skin. But no, it was not the shirt. He was remarkably tanned, darker than any Englishman she had ever seen. His hair was glossy black, short but with a wave to it, and his deep brown eyes—they were as dark and rich as chocolate—held an intelligent light. His face was all planes and angles and well-modeled bones.

He was darkly, astonishingly handsome. And, from the richness of the fabric on which she lay and the cut of his clothes, a wealthy gentleman.

The man's gaze lingered on her face, and she grew aware that her bonnet was hanging about her neck by its strings and that her wavy gold hair was now barely held by the bit of ribbon she had tied around it that morning. Her bodice and skirts were well splashed with water and mud, but his faint smile said, if anything, that he approved of her. The breeze danced a loose strand of hair against her cheek as she gave him a dry look.

"You've undone all my efforts, you know. The cress was going to be part of lunch."

They both glanced in the direction of the stream, where a spreading patch of watercress could be seen in the distance downstream.

"Forgive me." He grinned ruefully at her, an expression that projected confidence that he would be forgiven. He probably always was.

"I had no idea you were in the stream," he continued, "or I would have checked my pace. Although," his eyes twinkled, "here it was, my very first time causing a female to swoon, and it was through clumsiness. Mortifying."

She laughed and reached for the hem of her skirt, squeezing out the excess water. And thought, with a flutter, that she'd been rescued by a fabulously handsome rogue. A stranger, someone who couldn't possibly know anything of her family's recent misfortunes. He wouldn't know anything about the rumors, or care that they were true—that some crony of her uncle had won Tethering, her beloved home. How wonderfully refreshing to talk to a new, unknown person. She couldn't think when that had last happened.

"I'm sorry to disappoint you," she said, "but I'm sure it was not a proper swoon. Doubtless it was just the heat of the day."

He tilted his head. "Was it? Perhaps, then, you would like a drink."

"Thank you. That would be welcome."

He stood up spryly, towering above her for a moment before he turned toward his horse and began rooting around in his saddlebags. He was tall and slim in his white shirt and dark breeches that hugged well-muscled legs, and the spread of his broad, angular shoulders made her stomach do a little flip.

Having apparently found some water, he turned and came back toward her, holding out a silver flask of unusual design. Sitting on his haunches near her, he watched her lift it, as though he wanted to be certain she was well enough. When she put the flask to her lips, she was startled by the thought that this man's lips had been there too—or would be.

He handed her a small packet.

"What's this?" she asked.

"Some jam sandwiches pressed on me." He chuckled. "I was staying with my cousin, who is accustomed to carrying food about with her. She assures me that her young daughters will turn into tiny trolls if allowed to become too hungry, though, disappointingly, I have never witnessed the transformation."

Jam sandwiches sounded divine.

He sat down on the grass across from her, and she opened the packet and wondered if she should get off his coat, but he didn't seem concerned about it. He was watching her with light dancing in his eyes, and she liked that.

And then she reminded herself that she no longer had the right to flirt with him, or any man. That her days of such spontaneous fun were in the past. The girl who'd laughingly bested all the village gentlemen in ring toss at the fair and never gone unpartnered at any dance had put all of that away.

But. He was a stranger. It was not as if her contact with him would last any longer than the few minutes they were in each other's company. Before the hour was out, she would certainly be back at Blossom Cottage, the dower house, darning socks and pulling weeds. What would be the harm in enjoying his admiration for this little bit of time? It had been so long since she'd allowed herself to feel anything toward a man.

She held out a sandwich to him. "Would you like one?"

"No, thank you. I am not far from my destination."

She took a bite. Heaven. When had she last tasted anything so good? They weren't exactly starving at home, but they had run out of jam and sugar ages ago.

"The color has come back into your face," he said. "It suits you."

"Well, I must certainly look pale next to you," she replied.

She was being bold. Flirtatious. *How did she dare?* a little voice whispered. She'd trained herself over the last three years not to consider men and the fun and playful times she'd once enjoyed. And with all the work she had to do at Tethering, she'd been able mostly not to care, or at least, to forget. But if a man like this one lived in Longwillow, she'd be tempted. Someone like him wouldn't live in a small village like hers, though. His whole demeanor spoke of sophistication and affluence, of a confident readiness for challenge.

"Well, anyone who'd just returned from Spain a few weeks ago would be tan." He cocked his head. "Do you live nearby?" His eyes flicked toward her dress. "Or perhaps you work on one of the estates. I will guess that you are… a governess, yes?"

"A governess?" she repeated. Ah, but of course she looked like a servant, because who else would wear such old clothes? Her dress must be a good four decades old. When Uncle Jonathan had died unexpectedly—and ignominiously—a few weeks earlier of a stroke after losing their estate in a London gaming hell, there'd been no money for mourning clothes. Felicity had found some gowns in the Tethering attic that had belonged to a departed relative who shared her medium height and dyed them black. They looked acceptable. Mostly.

She was not well dressed, but the intensity of his gaze told her that he found her attractive. A seductive feeling. Prettiness hadn't been on her mind for ages.

"I live close by," she said vaguely. She consumed the rest of the first roll and started on a second.

Apparently he was content with her answer. "And have you had much practice gathering watercress in the wilds of this roaring stream?" His eyes teased hers.

She leaned over her bent knees and nibbled on the roll. "I normally have no trouble at all, when gentlemen aren't dashing about startling me. And the stream is swollen with the recent rains. It's not as simple a matter as it might look."

He flicked a glance toward the stream. "Is that so? I believe I might vow to gather three times the amount you had without getting so much as a drop of water or mud on myself."

A ripple of pleasure traveled through her. "Oh, really? I should like to see such a feat. But the rocks are all covered over with moss and water, and I've already gathered all the watercress within reach."

He merely lifted an eyebrow and sprang to his feet—he seemed taut, like a bouncy spring, full of energy and strength—and disappeared over the side of the stream bank. She came up on her knees for several moments to watch him unobserved as he picked his way among the stepping-stones, hopping as surefootedly as a twelve-year-old boy.

She sat back down and finished the second roll and told herself that when the third was done, she would get up and leave, before this fascinating stranger discovered anything of substance about her.

The last sandwich was almost finished when the black top of his head reappeared, then his face, wearing a boyish grin in irresistible contrast with his manliness. The stranger put an arm on the top of the bank and hopped neatly up. He came and knelt down next to her and presented the watercress with an elegant flourish, as if it were a bouquet for his lady. She laughed and accepted the enormous handful he'd picked. Oh, she'd forgotten the fun that gentlemen could be.

"Well done, noble sir," she said, continuing the tone he'd set.

"You are most welcome, my lady."

She put the last of the jam sandwich in her mouth, pressing a finger to her lower lip where a sticky crumb rested and pushing it in, and saw with a shiver that his eyes were drawn to her finger. He was close enough that she could, in that quiet moment, feel the heat coming off him and hear the sound of his breathing. His deep brown eyes were focused solely on her. He might be a stranger, but he was also real—a flesh-and-bone man, not some dreamed-up Galahad on a white horse—and he must have plans and responsibilities of his own. She closed her eyes and imprinted his features on her mind for later, so that his face might be like a flower brought home and pressed after a happy meadow picnic.

Desire for all the things she'd given up surged

within her, but she pushed it back down. Opening her eyes, she dusted her hands off. "I must be on my way."

A look of disappointment crossed his face, just a flash. She was glad, though she shouldn't be.

"Of course," he said affably, standing up and holding a hand out to help her up. She took it, and it was warm and strong as he tugged her easily upward. Oh, what would it be like to have the right to hold the hand of a man like him?

He leaned over and picked up his coat, giving it a brisk shake to knock off the bits of grass that clung to it, and put it on. It was a particularly vivid claret color, unusual like him.

"I can't offer you a ride, can I?" His lips quirked up in a wicked half smile that said he would enjoy sharing a horse with her. "I must stop in Longwillow on business before completing my journey."

She looked up at his enormous white horse and flattened together lips quivering in a returning smile. No more. She shook her head.

The sound of carriage wheels approaching could now be heard from behind them, and he said, "Ah, that will be my accoutrements. I had planned to precede them."

"Then you must be off."

"Yes. Though I'd rather stay and find out if I might render you any other service, my lady."

"No!" she said, too sharply, so that he looked quizzical. But she needed to rein herself in, or she'd be tempted to ride right off into the sunset with him, if only he would ask her.

"Might I beg the favor of your hand to kiss?"

She hesitated, wanting to agree but knowing she had already indulged herself too much here. She'd probably dream about these moments on the stream bank for years.

"Very well." She held out her hand to him and he took it and, bowing over it, brushed his warm lips once against the back of her hand, then more slowly a second time, until she burned with the pleasure of his mouth and breath against her skin. He dropped her hand and, looking at her now with eyes that were no longer laughing, bid her good-bye.

He hopped jauntily onto his horse and was away down the road.

As she stood watching him, the carriage that had been approaching rolled past her and disappeared where the road curved ahead. She licked her lips and caught a lingering taste of jam sandwich, the best food she'd had in ages, though she knew its ambrosial quality had mostly to do with him. Her hand still held the watercress he'd gathered for her.

She started down the road. A host of everyday tasks awaited her, and the moments on the stream bank were as gone as a dream dreamt.

A fifteen-minute walk took her to the shoulder-high stone wall that marked the beginning of the Tethering property. Behind the wall, a line of apple trees created a pretty screen between the road and the estate. The tall wrought-iron gate stood open, as she had left it earlier. She cast a yearning glance up the sloping gravel drive to Tethering Hall, her ancestral home, which stood atop the hill like a friendly sentinel. Even more—a member of the family.

Biting her lip, she experienced a familiar fury at her uncle Jonathan, who had always promised that the Tethering estate would belong to Felicity's family when he died. Jonathan had never been interested in running the estate and had left that task to his sister Caroline, Felicity's mother. When Caroline died three years ago, the tasks she and Felicity had been sharing fell solely on Felicity's shoulders. Felicity had been happy to take them on, even though her uncle's gambling problems meant that most of the estate's proceeds disappeared on the gaming tables. She'd become a master at making a household budget of nothing into something by making economies, even selling off small pieces of furniture when necessary. She'd made it work, successfully kept things running—and now Jonathan's foolish weakness had taken that all away from her.

She turned away from the path to Tethering and walked instead toward the dower house. Blossom Cottage was a pretty stone dwelling that stood among a scattering of fruit trees several minutes' walk from the drive. She liked the cottage, though like Tethering its roof leaked and its furniture was old. But it would do for now, and more importantly, it belonged to her family, which could not at the moment be said of Tethering.

But she had hope. Already, she had written to a lawyer, although she'd not yet mentioned this to her father. Whoever this gambler was, he was not going to find a warm welcome when he arrived.

Two

Well, James Collington thought as he neared the wrought-iron gates of the Tethering estate, he was a long way from a sun-drenched Spanish vineyard. One week he'd been immersed in the intricacies of the Palomino grape and its profitability, the next he was staking everything he had in a London gaming hell. And now the foreseeable future involved an estate he'd won from someone he barely knew. At least he would have a home for the time being, however temporary.

Tethering was worth about three hundred pounds a year, Jonathan Beresford had said when he staked it. James had seen right away that if he won the estate, he could sell it—and solve his problem.

Raising his eyes, he caught sight of the manor house in the distance, at the top of the hill that gradually sloped up from the gate. Were those *turrets* poking up near its roofline?

He passed through the gate, which was, unhappily, rather rusty. Something to fix. Already James had an interested buyer, and he wanted the property to be irresistible. The carriage with the few provisions he'd bought in the village followed him onto the estate.

He wondered if Beresford's old family retainers had moved out, as James's lawyer had suggested they do in the letter he sent, in case they were upset about their master losing the manor.

To the left, not far from the drive, stood a small stone cottage with some washing hanging from a line in the back. Ah, doubtless the new location of the servants. Who would, he hoped, have the key to the manor, and maybe the name of the bewitching young woman he'd just met. He would go there first.

Felicity put the watercress in a bowl in the kitchen and discovered a line of ants crawling up one of the legs of the work table. Martha, their lone servant, was at work in the cellar, so Felicity investigated the ant problem herself. A piece of bread had fallen outside the kitchen door, attracting the ants, and she got rid of it.

The kitchen once again secure, at least until the next invasion, she made her way to her father's study, stopping in the doorway to greet him. Deeply immersed in work on his latest book of poems, he did not at first hear her.

Like Felicity, Mr. Wilcox was wearing clothes from Tethering's attic. A leaky roof had spoiled much of his more recent attire, and so he was dressed today in a gaudy gold and emerald coat from the Georgian era. She smiled to herself at the picture he presented amid his books and papers. He looked up at her over his spectacles.

"Here you are, my dear," he said warmly. His tufty white eyebrows, which matched his thick white hair, rose upward as he took in her damp and muddy appearance. "It looks as though you've been busy."

"I was getting some watercress for our lunch and slipped in the stream," she said, deciding not to mention the stranger.

Just then a sharp rap sounded at the front door, startling them both. As she knew Martha couldn't have heard it, Felicity went to answer it herself.

She opened the door and before her stood her handsome gentleman from the stream bank.

He blinked at her in evident surprise, then his mouth turned up in that familiar crooked grin.

"Well, hello again," he said.

"But how did you find me?" she asked in a voice filled with the pleasure she was feeling because he'd come to find her, never mind that she'd been able to enjoy herself with him because he *was* a stranger. Out of the corner of her eye she caught sight of a mud spot on her bodice and wished she'd changed already. The stranger looked very smart with his claret coat buttoned neatly, the sunlight gleaming off his tall black boots.

"Ah." He hesitated. "I did want to see you again, though I'm surprised to find you here."

She tipped her head quizzically. "But whom did you expect to find?"

"I didn't think I could be so fortunate," he said with a merry twinkle in his eyes, "that coincidence would send you my way twice."

"Coincidence?"

"Here I am, looking for a key, and I find you again, my enchanting young lady of the stream."

Unease pricked at her. "A key? To what?"

"To Tethering Hall, of course. You must have guessed by now who I am."

A sick feeling stole over her. "No," she whispered.

He bowed. "Mr. James Collington. My lawyer sent a letter about the change in ownership of the estate."

"You're Mr. Collington," she said in a voice dead of emotion.

He gave a rueful shake of his head, unaware of her reaction. "We have started off on something of a wrong foot, but not in a bad way, of course."

No. It couldn't be. Her head felt as if it were being squeezed. "Very much in a bad way," she said.

Her words and tone made his friendly expression disappear.

"Believe me, sir," she continued, "that I had no idea you were the gambler who has taken my home."

His face darkened at her words. If he had been dangerously handsome before, now he looked plain dangerous. "You must be greatly deluded, miss, if you consider that you are to be consulted as to the ownership of the manor. But as my being here does concern your work situation, you may want to have a care in how you speak to me."

"Work! What on earth are you talking about?"

His black eyebrows now drew down over eyes heavy-lidded with displeasure. "If you cannot keep a civil tongue in your head, you may soon find yourself without a place to stay."

"I certainly shall not! This house belongs to my family."

"Come, come," he said with haughty impatience. "The dower house belongs to the estate and therefore now to me."

"You are wrong." She met his eyes with her chin up. "Tethering belonged to my uncle Jonathan, but the dower house is the property of the family of Caroline Wilcox, who was my mother."

His brows shot together. "What the devil? Beresford said there were only two old family retainers in residence. No family."

She stilled. "So you didn't know about us. There's been a mistake."

"Unfortunately," he agreed, his expression growing grim.

"More than unfortunate," she corrected in milder tones. He hadn't known about the Wilcoxes! Hope stirred. She'd been living on hope ever since that dark day when they'd closed the door to Tethering behind them and walked down the hill to Blossom Cottage.

"Tethering rightly belongs to my family," she explained. "I've—my father and I have run the estate in recent years. We've taken care of everything while my uncle has lived in London, and there has always been an understanding among us that the estate would be ours on my uncle's death. He simply had not yet made the necessary arrangements with his lawyer." She paused. "So you see, now, that we have moral claim to the estate."

Mr. Collington sucked his teeth. "Miss…?" he began.

"Wilcox," she supplied, finding it bizarre to be properly introducing herself to the man with whom she had spent such carefree moments on the stream bank. She could feel a grin spreading over her face, and probably she looked extremely silly, but she didn't care because the wrong that had been done them was going to be righted. "I know that as a gentleman, you'll act with honor and revoke your claim to the estate."

He inhaled abruptly and said nothing for several moments.

Why wasn't he agreeing with her? He was a man of honor—she was sure of it from their meeting on the stream bank. She reminded herself then that this was all coming as a surprise to him, and probably not a very welcome one. But still, fair was fair.

"Miss Wilcox," he finally said, "I'm sure you are well aware that the property belonged freehold to your uncle. I saw the deed myself."

"Yes," she said. "My uncle has acted reprehensibly in this affair. I am speaking of to whom the estate belongs morally, setting aside such things as wills and deeds. How can the turn of a card be allowed to change the fortunes of an entire family? I know you see what is right, not as a matter of law but as a matter of justice and honor."

His eyes flashed with a fiery light that startled her, though when he spoke his tone was icy. "I do not care for your insinuations. Your uncle wagered the Tethering estate to me and lost it, Miss Wilcox. The circumstances are regrettable. We have both been misled by your uncle. But the facts are indisputable. The estate now belongs to me. There is nothing else to say on the subject."

The unyielding quality of his voice shocked her. She'd been so certain that this man who had rescued her by the stream with lighthearted chivalry and even gathered her watercress would agree with her. How could he possibly be meaning to behave in such a heartless, unfair manner?

"Surely you jest."

"Surely I don't."

He was very, very serious.

She couldn't have been more disappointed in him. She had believed in him so much for a few foolish minutes.

But that was all over now. She straightened her shoulders.

"There certainly is more to say, Mr. Collington. You *know* that very well as a gentleman, regardless of whether the deed was properly emended." Her gaze flicked over his fine clothes. "Tethering is not even very large. You wouldn't like it. It won't be approaching the grandeur to which you are no doubt accustomed."

His hard eyes were unreadable. "As a matter of fact," he said, "I like it already."

He regarded her steadily with an expression that told her he would be as moveable as a mountain. "If I might have the key?"

His eyes flicked behind her then, and she heard a shuffling noise, her father coming along the corridor. He came to stand next to her in the doorway.

"Good afternoon," he said to their visitor with polite interest.

Her father seemed not to notice the tense atmosphere prevailing in the doorway but looked cheerfully untroubled, and unaware, too, of the bizarre look of his clothing. Mr. Collington's eyes briefly widened at the sight of him.

"Good afternoon, Mr. Wilcox," their visitor said before Felicity could speak. "I am James Collington. You have received a letter from my lawyer."

"Ah. Well, then," her father said with a rueful smile, "we must welcome you to Tethering."

"Thank you," Mr. Collington said, ignoring Felicity's intense look. "Most kind of you, sir. I was just about to have the key from your daughter."

"Oh, yes, of course," Mr. Wilcox said, casting a glance at Felicity, who had not moved. He nudged her slightly with his arm. "Felicity, we must not keep Mr. Collington waiting."

Her face flaming with anger and frustration, she stood there for several tense moments as both men looked at her, waiting. Finally, teeth clenched, she dug in the pocket of her gown for the key that she had kept with her every day like a talisman since leaving Tethering and placed it in Mr. Collington's outstretched hand.

"Thank you." He dipped his head in farewell and went over to his white horse. He swung himself deftly onto its back and set off for the manor house, which lay uphill from them, several hundred yards away. His carriage was just arriving, and it followed him up the hill.

Felicity's father turned toward her with a heavy sigh. "Well, that's that, my dear. But at least we can be grateful that our new neighbor seems a good sort, considering the kind of people with whom your uncle sometimes consorted."

"A good sort!"

She supposed she shouldn't be surprised if her father liked Mr. Collington—she'd liked him at first, too. And she'd been so convinced for a few hope-filled moments that her playful Galahad would undo the injustice of what her uncle had so stupidly done. "Nothing could be further from the truth. He's a gambler just like Jonathan, and not to be trusted."

Mr. Wilcox raised one eyebrow skeptically. "Actually, my dear, I suspect our Mr. Collington is not in the least like Jonathan. For one thing, he won. From the looks of him, he is a successful man."

"But, Father," she insisted, "it isn't right! Tethering cannot be lost to us."

Her father sighed. "Felicity, nothing could seem more true to me than that my brother-in-law, with all his disreputable doings over the years, finally succeeded in losing everything he had to lose." He turned and went inside.

She watched as the distant figure went up the hill toward the manor house. In that moment she knew that she'd do anything to get Mr. James Collington to go back from whence he came.

James muttered dark imprecations as he rode up the sloping, rather weedy gravel path to Tethering Hall. Damn that Beresford! The man had clearly been weak and dishonorable, and now James had no choice but to cling to what he'd won from him, and in so doing put a family out of their home. Two old family retainers, bloody hell.

His mouth pressed in a grim line, he considered the manor house as he drew closer. It looked like a tiny French castle shrunk in size and condensed together. What would have been towers with pointed turrets were set instead against the front of the house like impossibly fancy columns, establishing a trim contrast with the steeply angled roofline. The effect wasn't fussy but neat, partly due to the boxlike size of the house—it was like a tidy package. Its modest appearance, perched at the top of the hill with the orchard sloping gently away behind it, was handsome and welcoming. He could see why Miss Wilcox wasn't ready to surrender it. The estate looked to be well worth the risk he'd taken when he'd staked his sherry vineyard against it.

He left his horse with Fulton, his personal servant and factotum, who was unpacking the carriage, which James had borrowed from his cousin Josephine. As he approached the manor, he thought of how the Wilcoxes must have been living in it until a few weeks earlier and cringed. Devil take it, if it hadn't been for his brother, Charles, he wouldn't have been in this troubled little corner of Hertfordshire at all.

He should have known better than to have trusted his brother and signed for that debt. It was supposed to have been for a thousand pounds—a grand enough sum as it was. It wasn't until after Charles was killed that the matter of the missing zero came to light. An acquaintance of James's had bought up the debt—and bought James some time. But now the man was dead and his heir had given James until the end of August to repay the entire debt, or he would forfeit the collateral: Granton, his ancestral estate.

Pushing away thoughts of Charles, he arrived at the front door. After turning the key in the lock, he took hold of the battered, chalky doorknob and pulled. It promptly came off in his hand. He looked at it in surprise, then shrugged. A doorknob was easily fixed. He mentally added it to the list with the rusty front gate.

A quick inspection of the rooms revealed water damage in several places, two chimneys that, to judge from the stains around the fireplaces, smoked when lit, and a host of other maintenance chores. All the rooms were surprisingly bare of furnishings, rather as if someone had decided to keep only those things that were truly needed. The library, however, was well stocked with neat volumes. A handsome pair of large windows spanned the room's back wall, but the view they offered of a rose garden beyond was obscured by pieces of brown paper standing in for missing panes. Several large curls of wallpaper hung from the walls.

With a sigh, James reached into an interior coat pocket and removed the small, folded sheaf of blank paper he always carried with him. He took it over to the library desk, where he found a quill and a thickened store of ink. He made notes about the rusty front gate, the doorknob, the windows, and the wallpaper, and then went out of the library to survey the rest of this house that Jonathan Beresford had assured him was in "perfect" condition.

The end of his ramble found him in the drawing room, which had an unusual but handsome balcony with high, decorative sides that ran the entire span of the room. He stood on the well-worn carpet and calculated. With several weeks' effort, the manor could be fixed up into something very nice indeed. A modest investment in repairs would yield a large return when he sold the house—large enough so that, combined with the proceeds from the pending sale of the bodega's first batch of sherry, he would be able to pay the debt. He would contact his interested buyer, Mr. Dover, and begin making arrangements.

Fulton was finishing unpacking his master's personal effects as James entered what was to be his bedchamber. Dust motes wafted freely in tiny beams of sunlight that were coming in through holes in the conical ceiling above one window, where the roof of one of the decorative turrets was obviously in need of repair. More notes to make.

The manservant looked up from a pile of folded stockings and raised a wry eyebrow at his master. James grinned. He really did feel very optimistic about this undertaking.

"It's charming, isn't it, Fulton!"

Fulton's other eyebrow went up. "Indeed, sir," he said, casting his eyes up at the water stains radiating from the ceiling holes, "though one would probably be more protected in a tent."

"Nonsense, you old hen," James said good-naturedly. "This is a wonderfully strong old house. It has great bones. I love it."

James walked over to the front window, which had a view down the lawn to the dower house. He could see Miss Wilcox scampering around the front of the cottage, running in a low crouch, apparently chasing a chicken. Despite everything, he couldn't help but chuckle. She was a very attractive woman, regardless of her tart tongue and her inability to corner a fowl.

"Take heart, Fulton," he said without turning. "We won't be here long. If all goes according to plan, at the end of two months I'll have this place fixed up and sold and we'll be moving back into Granton Hall for good."

Fulton, who was well acquainted with his master's business affairs, merely grunted.

James pondered the eccentric appearance of Mr. Wilcox and his daughter. Her gown had no doubt once been all the crack—at the time of Marie Antoinette. She had obviously abandoned whatever huge underclothes the dress must originally have been worn with. Her very appealing figure, while perhaps a shade slender, was nonetheless rounded in all the right places, as he knew all too well from having held her against his chest.

She was quite a beauty. He closed his eyes and recalled carrying her out of the stream, the spread of her lashes dark against her delicate cheek. She had been charming then, light and free as the summer day, and he'd very much wanted to kiss her. That was out of the question now. Even if she weren't a gentleman's daughter, she was doubtless well on the way to hating him by now.

They were of very minor gentry, of course, and they gave new meaning to the phrase "genteel poverty." Losing the estate would have been a terrible blow to their standing in the community, never mind the changes it must have brought to their daily life. Miss Wilcox's appeal to his honor had stung. He'd been forced to make so many compromises these last few years since he acquired the debt—it had changed his life. Taking the estate of another family, however legally it belonged to him, was, he hoped, the very last compromise he'd have to make.

He and Aunt Miranda would enjoy living here while he fixed it up. He was glad, anyway, of a chance to get her away from London. He'd come back from Spain to find that she'd used a large portion of her small income on charitable enterprises for the poor. And while that was laudable, if she didn't stop, she'd soon be one of them. He cocked his head, pondering an idea.

"You know, Fulton, I think I will have a small house party here in a few days when Aunt Miranda arrives. It will put the fire in our efforts to make this place more habitable."

Fulton coughed at this announcement. There was a pause before he said, "Very good, sir."

James decided to go down to the dower house, to see if the Wilcoxes might recommend a housekeeper for him, and perhaps someone for the orchard. The first thing he needed was more staff. As he walked down the hill to their cottage, he resolved that he would be especially patient and polite with them to try to smooth things along. After all, they were to be neighbors for the summer.

Three

As she rushed about the yard after the wily Spots, trying to encourage an entirely free-roaming hen into a new pen, Felicity brooded angrily on Mr. Collington. How could she have smiled and flirted with the man who was even now installing himself in her house, possibly even napping in one of her family's beds?

Despite her father's untroubled stance, she knew that they had to find a way to get the smooth, infuriating Mr. Collington out of Tethering Hall. She had been wracking her mind this last hour, trying to find a way to get rid of him—or more to the point, make him want to give up Tethering for good. The less happy he was with his new property, the less likely he was to make any trouble about keeping it when the time came. She hoped the family lawyer would not be long in responding to her letter, because though Mr. Collington was currently just up the hill from them, what she wanted was to never see the man again.

At least she knew the enemy a little. He was confident, quick-acting—hadn't he hopped into the stream without a second thought for his fine clothing?—and no fool. Getting him to relinquish Tethering would require some focused thought. Or rather, crafty plotting, and very likely sneakiness. She felt a martial thrill.

Spots put on a burst of speed and headed for the trees at the back of the yard, near the wall. But just that morning Felicity had finished making a pen out of old crates for Spots, and it was time for the hen to try it. She set her chin in determination and, holding her skirts wide, made a rush and caught the bird up in them. Spots was outraged but trapped.

Satisfied with her triumph, she turned around, ready to bring the now squawking, writhing hen over to the pen some dozen feet away. She froze. Mr. Collington was standing behind her with an expression of wicked amusement on his face. She blinked at him, her skirts bundled up at her waist with their squirming burden and the late-afternoon breeze teasing at her now exposed, stocking-clad calves. His amused regard took in her legs, and she lifted her chin. He smirked.

She moved past him without a word on her way to the pen, where she deposited the enraged hen. Straightening up from her labors, she ignored Mr. Collington and brushed out her skirts. She had not changed her clothes yet, and now the already rumpled, muddied gown had dirty chicken claw prints on it.

He approached and cleared his throat. "Hello again, Miss Wilcox," he said in that warm, deep voice that had made her want to melt not a few hours earlier and, drat it all, still made her want to melt. She pushed the awareness away.

"Well?" she said.

He started at her greeting, but almost instantly his features assumed a pleasant expression.

"I was hoping," he said, "that you might give me the recommendation of a woman to be housekeeper."

"At Tethering?" She was almost speechless at his brazenness. "You want me to help you hire someone to keep house for you in *my* house? Mr. Collington, my father may be reconciled to your presence here, but I assuredly am not."

He absorbed her words and pressed his lips together, as if keeping himself from speaking. Bringing a glossily booted foot up to rest on one of the crates, he leaned an elbow across his thigh and peered into Spots's pen. She didn't care for his skeptical expression, which suggested this was a feeble-looking pen, though it certainly was.

"We must agree to disagree, then, on my presence here," he said. "And as to my household staff, I simply thought you might prefer to choose the person," he said in a reasonable tone. "Consider it an olive branch."

"Nonsense." She folded her arms in front of herself. "You simply don't know anyone else around here to ask."

He laughed, white teeth flashing in his sun-bronzed face and amusement dancing in his brown eyes. "All right, that is also true."

He was clearly hoping to win her over with his charm, and she'd have to watch out that he didn't. Already she could not ignore his now-familiar, long, well-muscled legs, displayed almost right below her chin. That unusual reddish-brown coat—the coat she'd been lying on not long ago—hugged his broad shoulders. Her heart skipped a beat.

She drew herself up straighter and tried not to notice the chicken prints on her skirt. Time to get started on her efforts to drive him away. Fortunately, his request had given her an idea: she could harass him through his household! She just needed someone she could rely on to be unsuitable.

"Perhaps the local murderess would do," she mused aloud as she considered candidates.

He guffawed. "Come, come, Miss Wilcox. I highly doubt that you would know the local murderess, if there even is such a person."

"Oh, there must be three or four, at least. Longwillow is a very rough village, you know, and there is quite a bit of crime in this area."

He raised an eyebrow. "Funny. It seemed such a charming place. Flowers everywhere."

"Yes, well, you don't want to go there after dark."

"I'll keep that in mind," he said with laughter in his voice.

Just you wait, she thought, having finally determined the perfect housekeeper for someone who looked as neat and efficient as Mr. James Collington.

"All right then," she said in a tone of surrender that she hoped sounded genuine, "it happens that I do know a housekeeper who is available. And I can recommend a cook, too."

"Thank you, Miss Wilcox. That is most gracious."

She indulged in silent feelings of satisfaction, pleased with the idea of him suffering. This might even be a bit fun. "You can send over to the village. Mrs. Withers for housekeeper and Mrs. Bailey for cook."

He then gave her such a heart-stopping smile in thanks that she almost regretted what she was setting him up for. Almost.

"There's just one more thing," he said. "Can you tell me who has had the care of the orchard?"

"I have."

"You? But surely your father…?"

She crossed her arms. "My mother grew up on this estate, Mr. Collington. She taught me everything I needed to know, and I have cared for it the last three years."

"I see." He did not look pleased by this information. "Then it seems that you are the person I am seeking. Would you consider continuing to oversee the orchard for a stipend?"

Ah. She should have seen that coming, since he was obviously determined to settle himself in on the estate. Well. She loved that orchard almost more than any other part of the estate. The chance to get back to it—to spend some of this blackguard's money returning it to its proper state—was so, so tempting. But that would be helping him.

"No," she said.

His eyebrows went up. "No? I'm surprised that you would not want to see it well tended." When she said nothing to this he said, "Well, if you should change your mind, let me know. The stipend will be twenty pounds for the summer."

She swallowed hard. Twenty pounds! Money like that could make a difference for the Wilcoxes.

It would eliminate, for one thing, the burden of worrying about how they would pay for her brother Simon's school fees.

Her father appeared just then, coming out the back door.

"Oh, good morning, Mr. Collington," he said warmly, coming to stand next to Felicity. "I thought I heard voices."

Mr. Collington greeted her father politely.

"Perhaps you might like to come inside for a sherry, sir?" her father said.

"Sherry?" Mr. Collington said, looking as if her father had just said something amusing.

"Father," Felicity broke in, "excuse me, but you haven't forgotten that the church garden party is today? Crispin will be expecting us. I thought we might leave right after luncheon."

"Oh," her father said slowly. "Er, no, not exactly. That is, I thought that you might go without me, dear. You know I am not much for that sort of thing."

She tried not to feel exasperated at what she knew was coming. Her father disliked social events. When her mother had been alive, her father had gone gamely along to parties and functions. But since her mother's death three years earlier, he'd declined any invitation. However, this was an event they could not in good conscience miss. And she really wanted her father's company today, in case this first meeting with Crispin was awkward.

"Father, I'm sure he will want to see you, and so will all our old friends. We have yet to welcome him back, and this is his first church social as our vicar."

Mr. Wilcox turned to their visitor. "The Reverend Mr. Markham, our newly installed vicar, is a local young man and a family friend." A light came on in her father's eyes. "I have it! What would be better than for Mr. Collington to go in my place? Everyone will want to meet our new neighbor."

Argh. What a terrible idea.

Apparently Mr. Collington didn't agree. He looked pleased. "Well, if you don't think anyone would be unhappy with the substitution, Wilcox, I would welcome the opportunity to meet some of the neighbors."

"No, no, not at all." Her father was almost gleeful at the escape he was arranging for himself. "It will be an improvement—new blood, you know."

"Why don't I pick you up in the carriage, then, Miss Wilcox?" Mr. Collington regarded her with what looked suspiciously like amused triumph. "When were you planning to leave?"

"In about an hour and a half," she grumbled.

"Perfect." He cocked his head at her father. "Say, you're not Wilcox the poet, are you?"

Mr. Collington read enough poetry to be familiar with her father? Felicity thought her father's work was brilliant. But his name was hardly on everyone's lips.

Her father smiled broadly, a sight she had not seen in some time. "The very same. Are you a poetry reader, Mr. Collington?"

"I am, sir. I must compliment you on your last collection. It was a masterwork."

"You are most kind. I admit I am happiest among books. That's the only thing I have missed—" He stopped abruptly and the cheer faded from his face. He took off his glasses, which seemed suddenly to need a speck of dirt wiped off.

Their visitor watched him, his dark brown eyes unreadable. "You must come up to the manor tomorrow, sir," he said, "or at your earliest convenience, and make use of the Tethering library. Indeed, I insist you regard it as at your disposal."

What was Mr. Collington doing, Felicity thought, making overtures to her father? And what kind of hospitality was this, anyway, offering her father the use of a library that was rightfully theirs?

Mr. Wilcox put his glasses back on, an expression of cautious delight on his face. "My good sir, that is a very generous offer."

"And a sincere one," Mr. Collington replied. "You must make as free with it as you always have." All affable pleasantness, he was the embodiment of an admirable gentleman. Felicity could hardly expect her father not to be charmed by him. And then, before she could bat an eye, he and her father had arranged for the Wilcoxes to dine with him at Tethering the following night.

Mr. Collington took his leave of them. *Enjoy your peace now, sir,* Felicity thought as she watched his tall, muscular form stride confidently out of the garden. And then she savored some delicious thoughts as to just how helpful his new cook and housekeeper would be. Mrs. Withers had never worked more than half a day put together in her life, although she was known to have an amazing talent for always looking as if she were busy. And Mrs. Bailey really was reputed to be a fine cook, but no one had tasted anything good from her hands since she had taken up with the bottle some ten years earlier. Tee hee.

The Wilcoxes' midday meal consisted of the water-cress bouquet, which Felicity consumed while refusing to allow it to remind her of how she had come to have it, plus two eggs each and some now very hard three-day-old bread.

"A fine meal, my dear," her father said, wiping his mouth after taking a final sip of water. They had in the interest of saving for Simon's school fees and clothes decided to forego ale and wine. "You do very well with what we have."

"I wish it were more," she replied with feeling.

Her father regarded her from across the small, round table. Blossom Cottage had a pleasant dining room of cozy proportions, with large windows that looked out on mature lilac bushes.

"I've had a letter from Simon," he said. "Brief, such as boys of fourteen are wont to write." He cleared his throat. "I'm afraid he's gotten into a scrape. He and some friends borrowed a horse from a local farmer as a prank. Apparently," he continued, squinting in bemusement, "they were going to dye its coat and return it a different color, to confuse the farmer." He shook his head. "But in the process, they managed to lame the horse."

"But that's terrible!"

"Yes, I am afraid it's rather serious. I received a letter from the headmaster as well. The farmer has been paid for the horse, but each of the boys will have to contribute ten pounds to its replacement."

"Oh," she said, "so much."

Her father looked uncomfortable. "Is it too much to hope that our economies will have yielded such an amount?"

"I'm afraid so," she said, unable to keep the dismay out of her voice. This was a blow. Ten pounds! For a stupid prank. "I could wring Simon's neck."

Her father gave a wry, halfhearted smile. "Yes, I could too, but I'm afraid that won't help. For what it's worth, his letter was abject. He'll not do something like this again."

"Well," she said, "this puts a different light on Mr. Collington's offer."

"Offer?"

"He has offered me a stipend of twenty pounds to oversee the care of the orchard."

"I see," her father said, surprised. "That is a generous amount. But would you feel comfortable doing such a thing?" he asked. "Surely something else could be arranged." He stared off into space as if a solution would come to him.

As the person who kept track of household finances, Felicity knew there was no other way they would get such a sum. And really, she didn't want anyone else looking after her orchard.

"I don't mind. And this way, if we get Tethering back, the orchard will still be in good condition."

"Get it back?" Mr. Wilcox sighed. "My dear, life is good here in Blossom Cottage."

"Yes, it is," she replied carefully. "But it's not where we belong."

"Nonsense, dear, it is a family house."

"But it's not Tethering."

"No, it's not," he agreed, fixing her with a steady gaze, which was a rare look from her head-in-the-clouds father. "Tethering was your mother's home, and it is a fine house."

"It's our family house, Father!" she said. "If Mother were here," she began, but stopped. A lump rose in her throat as she thought of her lively, giving mother, whose companionship and wisdom she still missed.

As she lay dying of the fever that had claimed her, Caroline Wilcox had smiled weakly and said to her daughter, "Don't fret, dear. I'll always be with you in spirit. Especially here at Tethering, where our family has always been. Just remember not to let anything happen to the estate. Take care of Tethering, and it will take care of all of you." She had passed from consciousness before her daughter could reply, but Felicity could never forget these words, or the unspoken promise they called from her.

"My dear," her father said gently, "of course I have many fond memories of Tethering Hall, and most precious are the years spent there with your mother." He sighed. "But that's what they are—memories of a time gone by. Life is change, Felicity. Tethering is no longer ours, but we have the cottage. And," he said in a firm tone, "we shall make a very nice life here."

When she didn't reply he fixed her with a shrewd look. "We must make Mr. Collington welcome, my dear."

"I will try," she said, with a pang at this necessary duplicity.

He smiled. "Thank you. I know this is a hard burden

to bear, especially for you, who were mistress of Tethering from a young age. And a fine mistress you were. And still are! Why, think of how much more fully your talents might blossom here in our little household, now that Jonathan, God rest his soul, is not among us to drain away money."

"Yes, Father."

He put down his napkin. "I'll be off to my study now."

She rose and gave him a fond kiss, feeling a tug of conscience about duping this honest, trusting man who thought he had now convinced her to accept their lot in life. Fortunately, it was a small tug since she knew she was going to do what was best for the Wilcox family.

Four

Felicity fixed her hair into a simple knot and changed into a fresh gown, if fresh was the right word for a gown that had started life decades earlier as a dainty yellow frock and was now a vague grayish-black. It had fitted half-sleeves and a scarf collar that had taken the black mourning dye differently, which she hoped might pass as an intentional accent. She wrapped up a loaf of bread in a tea towel and stood by the door to wait for her unwanted escort.

Mr. Collington arrived outside Blossom Cottage in his handsome open carriage with a driver. He got down to hand her in, then sat across from her on the fine leather seat. The carriage started up with a gentle jerk, the luxurious cushions and well-sprung seats of their conveyance creaking softly with a sound that indicated a lot of money had been spent to ensure a smooth ride. They pulled onto the road to Longwillow, which was about a mile away.

As they drove through the open gates, Felicity said, "I had planned to make a stop on the way."

"Before your father extricated himself and sent me

in his place, you mean?" he asked with laughing eyes. She refused to share his mirth and tipped her chin at an angle away from him.

"Certainly we can stop," he said good-naturedly. "Where do you want to go?"

"A cottage up ahead," she said, "around the bend."

He got the driver's attention and conveyed her directions, then turned to face her. "And who will we be visiting?"

"Nanny."

"Yours?"

"And my mother's."

"Ah," he said, "the recipient of your package?"

"Yes."

"Are you going to speak to me only in monosyllables?"

"Ideally."

He grunted. He didn't try to make any more conversation, and they drove on in silence for several minutes. Finally, she said, "I've changed my mind about the orchard. I'll do it."

"You will?"

"Yes. But I'll want half of the stipend before I start."

He raised an eyebrow. "Oh you will, will you? But if I pay you beforehand, Miss Wilcox, how can I be certain you will do the job?"

She made a shocked sound, allowing her eyes to rest on him long enough to glare. "Obviously, you will have to trust me. I am hardly a trickster. *I* am not the gambler."

"Or you might do worse," he mused, ignoring her, "now that I have time to reflect on it. How do I know you won't undermine my efforts?"

That brought her up short. Did he suspect something? "What do you mean?"

"You might practice some creative gardening technique that leaves me with damaged trees, a poor harvest." He pushed his lips outward in a shrug. "Something diabolical."

"Oh, really," she said tartly, waving a dismissive hand, "that would be ridiculously childish. I love the orchard. Why should I do such a thing?"

"Why indeed?" he said. "Perhaps because you cannot stand that I am here?"

"That is hardly a secret."

"True," he said lightly. "But it puts things in a certain light."

She allowed herself a small, sincere smile. "You have my word, Mr. Collington, that I will not undermine your efforts in the orchard." Elsewhere, definitely, but she'd never harm the orchard.

"Good. Then we have a bargain, and you shall have your ten pounds tomorrow."

James was pleased. This should work out well. He wanted the orchard to be in the best possible condition when Dover came to see the property. Not that he would let Miss Wilcox know he planned to sell the estate. She'd doubtless find a way to have his meals poisoned before she let him dispose of it as he saw fit.

A few minutes later the coach paused at the turnoff for the cottage, which was perhaps a hundred yards off the road. The coachman turned around and said that the wheels would get stuck in the mud if he drove up the rough path to the house, so James got out first to hand his passenger down, stepping wide of the soft mud that surrounded the carriage. He reached up a hand to her where she stood on the top step, but she ignored it, making as if to sail by him unassisted. But as she came onto the second step and saw the quantities of mud below, she checked herself mid-stride and lost her balance. She fell forward against him. He clasped her to him, and her flailing arms encircled his neck.

Their faces were suddenly mere inches apart. Their eyes locked.

"Put… put me down," she breathed, her hazel eyes dark and unfocused as they looked into his.

"Is that really what you want?" She was light in his arms. Distractingly curvy.

"I—I," she began, her brow furrowing.

Behind her the carriage jostled briefly as Tom talked to the horses.

Her brows snapped together. "Put me down this instant, sir!" she said firmly.

He did.

"Oh!" She fairly growled at him as her feet hit the muddy ground.

"But you said…" he remarked innocently.

Her lips pressed together, Miss Wilcox stepped over the mud into a patch of grass, where she wiped her shoes before making her way toward the cottage, chin high in the air. He drew into step beside her, though she did not acknowledge him.

The cottage was cheerful-looking, with a thatched roof and flowers blooming in neat rows bordering the path that led to the front door. To one side were a small stream and a scattering of trees. As they drew closer, the door opened and out came an older woman dressed in a neatly tailored gray frock. Quite obviously, Nanny. When she appeared, James could have sworn he heard a shriek from somewhere behind the house, but glancing around he saw nothing.

"Miss Felicity!" Nanny boomed. His eyes widened at Nanny's remarkable presence. She was short and stout with a thick-featured, ruddy face and unusually large teeth. Her hair was pulled into a bun so tight that she looked bald. She was as like to a man as a woman could be, especially one who was so immaculately gowned.

"Nanny dear," Miss Wilcox said, her face lighting up in a charmingly sweet smile the likes of which James had not seen since their moments on the stream bank. She was wearing a dress of washed-out black, another relic of bygone days. Her funny, drab clothes had the remarkable effect of drawing attention to her prettiness, as if to underline that her beauty depended not at all on what she was wearing. Feeling uncomfortably warm, he turned his gaze to the quelling vision of Nanny.

Miss Wilcox approached Nanny and placed a kiss on the plump, ruddy cheek. He squinted. Was that a hairy wart on the old woman's chin? Nanny stood back from Miss Wilcox and scrutinized her.

"Heavens, child, whatever are you wearing? That might have been your great-aunt's tea gown."

Nanny turned her gaze on James. "And who is this swarthy young man?"

Miss Wilcox's face assumed the irritable look he recognized as being reserved for him. "Nanny Rollins, this is Mr. Collington. The one who has taken Tethering."

He ducked his head politely. Nanny looked scandalized. "The gambler! Lady Pincheon-Smythe was right!"

James remembered his pledge to himself to be indulgent with the Wilcoxes. He could see that not just Miss Wilcox but her friends too were going to test the limits of his patience. "The very same," he replied pleasantly, "recently returned from sunny Spain. Although I must point out that I do not gamble frequently."

Nanny waved an arm dismissively. "That's just the kind of thing Beresford would have said. Gamblers never want to admit how deep in they are."

Miss Wilcox interrupted this line of conversation. "Nanny, I brought you some bread baked this morning." She handed over the wrapped bundle. "Were you saying I had arrived just in time for something?"

The ferocious look disappeared from Nanny's strong features. "Yes, dear, it's Twinkle. He's been stuck in a tree since last night, and I've no way to help him down."

"Twinkle?" said James.

"My cat," said Nanny.

Ah, the origin of the strange cry he heard earlier.

"Oh," said Miss Wilcox sympathetically, "not again."

"Yes," said the nanny-troll, shaking her head, though obviously charmed by her cat's behavior. "The naughty fellow loves adventure. But he's getting old and he will sometimes overestimate his abilities." She gestured toward the stream several yards away. "He's in one of the lower branches over there."

They went as a group toward the tree in question, and

Twinkle had obviously noticed their approach because he began wailing more furiously. They stood at the base of the tree and looked upward to where the cat was, on a branch about a dozen feet above. There was one thick branch below it, about six feet from the ground.

"All right," Miss Wilcox said. "I'll go and get a stool."

"What are you doing?" he said as she turned to go. "You're not going to climb up there."

She gave him a scornful look. "I certainly am. I got him down last time."

"Well, I'll get him today," he said, pulling off his jacket.

"You are not needed," she said firmly. "I will take care of it."

But he was already pulling himself up to the lower branch. In a few moves he was standing on it and staring into the wild eyes of an enormous yellow tabby. Twinkle did not look as though he trusted him. Muttering a hope that Twinkle did not spook easily, he pulled him off the branch, tucking him under one arm. Then he leaned down and, grabbing the lower branch, swung out of the tree. As soon as James's feet hit the ground, Twinkle flexed his needlelike claws into James's side and jumped away, running into the house.

"Poor thing," Nanny said, shaking her head in sympathy for the cat, "he'll want a lie-down now." She looked at James. "Thank you, young man. I'm glad to see you're good for something. I don't hold much with gamblers."

He thought of correcting her again, but decided it was not worth his breath, and wondered instead if there was any blood seeping through to his shirt from Twinkle's claws. At least his coat was red.

Nanny looked at Miss Wilcox. "And your brother, Miss Felicity! What a scrape he's gotten into now!"

Miss Wilcox reddened and brushed impatiently at a strand of hair that had come loose from the bun at her pretty nape. James watched her, thinking that since he'd met her she'd continually been the classic damsel in distress—the fall in the stream, the plummeting family fortunes. While she was obviously very capable, what she really needed was a good man. As pretty as she was, why wasn't she married?

"I'm sure we needn't—" Miss Wilcox began. But her old nanny was not deterred.

"That prank with the horse. What a fool idea."

"I don't see how you could have heard—"

"Timothy Brooke's mother told me." Nanny shook her head. "Whoever thought some old farm horse would be worth thirty pounds?"

Ah. The reason why Miss Wilcox had changed her mind about helping him with the orchard.

Nanny continued. "I won't say I'm not worried about you in all this, Miss Felicity. Your mother always carried more than her share of the Wilcox family's responsibilities, with your father off forever in his study, and I can see that's what will happen to you."

Miss Wilcox glanced sideways at James, clearly not happy to have the family business aired. "Nanny," she said warningly.

Nanny ignored her. "Your father's too dreamy to say anything, but I'm not. You need a husband. Preferably a rich one. That would resolve so much."

Miss Wilcox gasped. "Nanny!"

The old troll was completely unbothered by Miss Wilcox's dismay, and James quite liked her for it. "It's always 'Oh, Nanny, don't bring that up.' As if the idea of your marrying were preposterous."

"Nanny," Miss Wilcox's voice was steely, "we are fine. Father's poetry sells well, and..." her eyes drifted toward him, and she dropped whatever she was going to say. "You needn't worry about any of us." For being a young, slim, and pretty *señorita,* there was something surprisingly commanding about her.

Nanny pressed her lips with displeasure. "Things have come to a sad state since I was nanny for the Beresfords, that's all I'll say."

Miss Wilcox closed her eyes and took in a deep breath. "We have to be going now. I promised Crispin I would attend the church garden party."

"Dear Crispin," Nanny said, glee lighting her face. "Now there's a fine young man. And he's more than fond of you."

But here Miss Wilcox cut her off by leaning in for a parting kiss. "Good-bye, dear. I will stop in again soon."

Nanny enveloped Miss Wilcox in what looked like a crushing hug.

"Good-bye, Nanny Rollins," James said with a grin. Her eyes widened as if she sensed he was being saucy. He was, but fortunately he was no longer in short pants.

They returned to the carriage, James wondering just how many family responsibilities Miss Wilcox carried.

"So, the infamous Reverend Markham," he said,

once they were seated. "A suitor?" he asked, not wanting to notice that he felt a particular interest in her answer.

"No," she said in the general direction of the puffy clouds beyond his shoulder.

"Nanny seems to think so."

"Nanny, God bless her, has opinions on everything."

He chuckled in agreement.

Felicity couldn't wait to get to the garden party, simply because she was itching to get away from Mr. Collington. She should have known Nanny would say whatever she was thinking. She always had. But did she really have to say all that in front of Mr. Collington?

He had behaved admirably with Nanny, despite her rudeness, and between that and his general surfeit of manliness, she could feel herself being pulled toward him. She had already had to spend an effort resisting the dreamy thought of what it might have felt like if he'd kissed her when he helped her down from the carriage.

The party was being held, as it was annually, in the Bishop's Garden, a plot of land to the side of the church that was very prettily laid out with curving, shrub-lined paths, generous plantings of flowers, and weathered old statues. Almost as soon as Felicity and James arrived, Crispin spotted her and came over.

It had been almost three years since she'd last seen him, and she saw now that he had matured from the young man of nineteen he'd been when he left for university. He was handsome in his new black vicar's clothes, with his fair hair and the muscular physique of the university rower he had been. She was still getting used to the idea of him being their vicar.

"Here you are, finally," he said, and gave her a friendly embrace. And she thought, *good, yes, we can be friends now.*

"I was afraid you wouldn't come," he continued. "I only had your note to say you'd be here, and it's been so long."

She smiled. They had gone down a difficult road together right after her mother died, but seeing him now, she felt no grief over the past. Healing time had covered over their mistakes.

His eyes slid sideways toward Mr. Collington with a flicker of irritation, but he quickly smoothed it over into a look of polite inquiry. She chuckled to herself, thinking such skills would serve him well as vicar.

"This is Mr. Collington," she said, intending to introduce him, but finding that she was unable to frame his presence in a way she could accept. "He is… that is…"

"I arrived in the area only today," he said, "and the Wilcoxes encouraged me to come and meet my new neighbors."

"Ah," Crispin said. "Then we must welcome you." His voice held a loyal, faint hint of reluctance. As they were talking, Felicity could see Mrs. Rossiter bearing down on them, and she could guess that the woman was bursting with curiosity about this newcomer to their village. A new face in a place as small as Longwillow was something of great interest.

Felicity barely had time to perform the introductions before Mrs. Rossiter was carrying Mr. Collington off with her, like a trophy to be displayed to the other villagers.

As soon as they were alone, Crispin said low, "So Collington is the gambler who won Tethering from your uncle."

She sighed. "Yes. Father insisted I bring him in his place."

Crispin, who was familiar with Mr. Wilcox's reclusive ways, pressed his lips together. "That was thoughtless of your father. I can believe he doesn't mind about the family losing Tethering, or care about your family's standing in the community, but he might be more aware of how you are being affected. Instead he sends you off with the man who has taken your family's home."

"No, Crispin, don't. It's all right."

He looked at her with a serious expression. "No, it isn't. This is a very awkward situation. And I don't in the least like the idea of that man," he glanced in the direction of Mr. Collington, who was standing in the midst of what looked like the entire Ladies' Garden Guild, "living on the estate with you. He looks like a fast sort. I don't believe he can be trusted," he said with an unvicar-like lack of charity.

She frowned thoughtfully as she watched the tall, tanned Mr. Collington conversing with a bevy of older ladies, who looked to be hanging on his every word. He was moving his arms neatly, describing some large, rounded object with his hands, and the sun shining against the smooth fabric of his coat was picking out the long contours of his muscles. "Yes, he is rather jarringly different."

Crispin took her hands, startling her. "Why don't you go and stay with my mother for a while at Stonecroft? I know she'd love to see you. And I'd feel better knowing you were being properly cared for."

"Oh—thank you," she said, surprised. "But Blossom Cottage is perfectly fine. For the moment. And I couldn't leave Father in any case."

"But I'm worried about you." His eyes fastened on hers, and with a pricking of unease she saw an intensity in them that conveyed a deeper meaning to his words. "How could I not be? I've worried ever since that night, when we shouldn't have..."

She tugged her hands away and clasped her fingers tightly in front of her skirts. "Yes, Crispin, we shouldn't have," she agreed firmly. "But that's in the past. And there it must stay." Her own memories of that night were locked away, and she had not the smallest wish to probe them.

He crossed his arms, his eyebrows lowering. "You can't just dismiss what happened, Felicity."

"But I have. There's nothing to say about it."

"Oh yes there is," he said insistently with a look of growing resolve. "Something important." He glanced around them, frowning. "But this isn't a good place."

She didn't like the sound of that. "I don't want to remember that time in my life. I want to focus on the present. Mr. Collington has offered me a stipend to oversee the care of the orchard, which will take care of our financial needs for now. And I've written to a lawyer to have the wager that lost Tethering examined. I firmly believe that before long we will have Tethering back."

His eyes shot open. "What?" he cried, drawing a few stares their way.

She could sense Mr. Collington's eyes on them, and she glared at Crispin.

He returned her look with his chin lifted, not backing down, though he spoke in moderated tones. "This is just the sort of thing you *should not* be doing. What you need—" he began.

But at that moment, to her intense relief, Mrs. Rossiter called for everyone's attention. The annual vicar's tour of the garden would begin in five minutes. Would the vicar please come forward?

He pressed his lips together. "We'll finish this conversation later. I have to see to the tour."

He made his way to the head of the group that was forming, and Felicity watched him talking with the garden ladies, his features softening into a congenial look. Feeling herself relax, she realized how tense she had grown during their conversation. It was not as if she didn't trust him—he was a vicar, for goodness' sake, and moreover a thorough gentleman. But that was the problem. The last thing she needed was for Crispin to be determined on doing his gentlemanly duty.

They'd grown up together, their families being close, and Crispin, being two years older, had been the leader on many a childhood adventure and buried treasure hunt with Felicity and her brother, Simon, and Crispin's younger sister, Susannah. But Felicity didn't need Crispin to guide her now. Nor did she want him worrying about her, telling her what young ladies ought not to do, or trying to help. She would take care of things herself.

She found a seat on a stone bench behind which a tall row of arborvitae created a natural wall. The lemonade table was on the other side of the shrubs, in the shade of an overhanging tree, and as she sat peacefully contemplating the garden, she could hear the pleasant sounds of people filling cups of lemonade, like a sporadic fountain. Presently she realized that someone on the other side was discussing James Collington.

"Yes, my dear," a woman's voice trilled, and Felicity recognized Augusta Tulkingham. "Our new neighbor will be quite an addition."

"I do agree," sighed Miss Pimble. The spinster's soft, girly voice sounded dreamy. "I envy Miss Felicity, living so close to him."

"Jemima!" Mrs. Tulkingham scolded. "Miss Felicity deserves our pity but certainly not our envy. The Wilcoxes have never done things properly, and now they're in a right state. Their standing has utterly plummeted, and that can mean nothing good for a young, unmarried lady, pretty or not. Her father should have seen to her marriage long ago."

"Quite right, dear," Jemima Pimble agreed meekly.

Felicity's eyebrows snapped together. She didn't want anyone's pity. Pity! When she had capably managed an entire estate for years.

But even as indignation burned in her, a lump was forming in the back of her throat. Why did everyone have to be going on about marriage today? She never thought about marriage.

On the other side of the arborvitae, Jemima Pimble

gave a sigh, her little girl's voice making it come out high and thin. "She's such a pretty thing, and she used to be the toast of the village. I suppose she could have had any fellow she wanted. But she just sort of disappeared into that house, didn't she?"

Unexpected tears burned at the back of Felicity's eyes. She squeezed them shut furiously. She never cried. She hadn't even cried when her mother died—she'd simply been numb. Nor had she wept even once since the day she'd taken that vow—her vow never to marry.

And what did she need from a man anyway, she told herself angrily, trying to force the lump in her throat to go away. She took several deep breaths, and that steadied her some. Three years ago she'd put away attraction and fun and flirting and replaced it with meaningful work, and she hadn't looked back to see what she'd missed. Managing Tethering had been a deeply satisfying challenge. A worthy life's goal.

But without it…

No! She couldn't even entertain the idea that the estate might truly be lost. She couldn't, because beyond that thought lay a wasteland of emptiness and meaninglessness. Without her work at Tethering, she wouldn't know who she was.

She really had no choice: she couldn't rest until she found a way to get Tethering back.

She patted the skin under her eyes, where a little moisture had escaped, then pinched her cheeks lest she'd gone pale or splotchy. Thank heaven no one had come by. She'd get up in a minute, as soon as she was sure she looked normal. If there was going to be any more gossiping about her, she clearly couldn't afford to hear it.

On the other side of the hedge, Augusta Tulkingham said, "Ah, Lady Pincheon-Smythe, how nice to see you."

"I have only just arrived. Mrs. Tulkingham, Miss Pimble, you remember my nephew, Mr. Godfrey, the schoolmaster."

Both ladies muttered expressions of welcome. Mr. Godfrey's voice could be heard greeting them and making bland comments about the garden, and Felicity was struck by its remarkably nasal, methodical quality. She could easily imagine him lecturing on hypotenuse angles. Leaning close to peer through the bushes, she saw a very pale man with an oval head that had sparse, long, dark hairs spurting from the scalp to lie lankly against his head. He must have been about fifty.

"Have you met Mr. Collington, our new neighbor, Lady Pincheon-Smythe?" Miss Pimble asked.

"Hmph," Lady P-S replied. "Not yet. But the name rings a bell. I believe he had a brother who was an MP." A pause. "There was something about the brother, but I can't remember what."

So, thought Felicity, Mr. Collington was rich *and* important.

"Well," said Mrs. Tulkingham, "our Mr. Collington is not an MP, but he is all one might wish in a gentleman. And he owns a sherry vineyard in Spain."

"Charming, I'm sure," Lady P-S said. "Now, have you seen Miss Wilcox? I wish to introduce her to my nephew. Such a nice young lady. I am quite determined to take her up as a cause."

Felicity jumped up and made her escape.

An hour later, she and Mr. Collington were on their way back to Tethering. She was a quiet passenger as she stared unseeingly at the countryside and tried to think of ways to get him to give up on Tethering and go away.

"Well," he said abruptly, breaking into her thoughts. "You and Markham certainly seemed to have quite a bit to say to each other."

"I'm surprised our conversation was of any interest to you."

He crossed his arms. "I could hardly fail to notice the intensity of your discussion, and I can't have been the only one. You should have a care, Miss Wilcox, how you bestow your attentions. In a place as small as Longwillow, such marked attention to a young vicar could be easily misconstrued."

The nerve! "How dare you give me advice on how to conduct myself in my own neighborhood? You, an unwanted interloper."

He leaned back against his seat, one black eyebrow arching upward mockingly. "Unwanted? Why, I must say, my very first encounter in the neighborhood, with a hazel-eyed damsel on the banks of a stream, led me to believe I would be very welcome here indeed."

She was momentarily speechless. "You are insufferable! I would never have been friendly to you if I had known who you were."

His eyelids lowered lazily over his dark brown eyes. "But you *were* very friendly," he said.

"And never shall be again."

"Never is a long time, Miss Wilcox."

But she refused to say another word to him. Instead, she looked away and thought harder on how to get him to give up Tethering.

Five

FULTON STOOD IN THE DRAWING ROOM EARLY THE next morning and sighed as he pondered what to address next in this godforsaken manor. He was fairly dismayed about his master's plans to have a house party so soon after moving into what Fulton privately called "the old heap." And this with practically no staff in place yet, save for the footman and stable boys Lady Josephine had lent them. The idea that anyone from London was going to shortly be in residence in rooms whose windows were currently festooned with bird droppings made him want to swoon.

Jarvis, the footman, was coming along the hallway carrying a small end table, and he paused in the doorway on his way past.

"You wanted this fer the chamber where t' master's aunt is to stay, sir?"

"Yes, that's right, Jarvis. At the moment there's not even a shelf to set a candle on in there, and I think we can all agree it would be best to have a candle handy in Miss Claremont's room."

Jarvis cast a furtive glance down the hallway. "'Tis true, then, sir, what I heard?"

Fulton gave him a sober look. "Jarvis, as I have made clear to you, I do not condone gossiping about our master or his circle." He paused. "However, I would prefer that, should any of the new staff hear rumors, they understand that Miss Claremont was unwell at the time, grieving the death of her sister."

Jarvis was enthralled. "It's just, sir, that she seems a practical lady, like, and not one who might carry on."

Fulton sniffed. "Miss Claremont *is* a practical, eminently respectable lady, as I can assure you. And Mr. Collington takes the best care of her. She's like a mother to him. It was a heartrending scene that night—I can still see her quivering on the bed and Master sitting beside her, comforting her."

~

Felicity was just passing by the side of the manor, having sneaked into the orchard to watch the sun rise as she had every day since the Wilcoxes had received the letter about losing the estate. It was the place in the world where she felt most at peace, and she needed that peace now more than ever. Today, though, she hadn't found as much solace as she craved.

As she came within hearing distance of the window, she caught some words of a conversation being carried on inside.

"Master was up all night," she heard a man say, obviously from his speech one of Mr. Collington's servants. "I never would have believed that someone so practical and confident could be brought to such a state."

She was instantly intrigued. What had the confident, practical Mr. Collington done?

"A state, sir?" said another, even less cultured male voice. "What sort a state?"

A pause. "It was dreadful. The rocking, the tears, and all the time wailing about ghosts."

"Ghosts!"

Ghosts? She blinked. Mr. Collington was afraid of ghosts? This was very interesting news indeed!

"Yes. You cannot believe the trouble we had that night trying to restore peace. Calls for extra candles to light the room up as bright as a summer's day. And demands to open all the windows to show that the moaning sounds had only been the wind. It took some time to put those fears to rest, I can tell you."

Shuffling sounds told her someone was moving around in the room. She quickly stepped away from the window and, crouching over so she would not be seen passing, made her way into the trees that ran along the property and toward Blossom Cottage.

So, Mr. Collington was deathly afraid of ghosts! Who would have guessed that so virile a man… But this was a very useful piece of information. In fact, as she drew closer to the cottage, an idea was forming in her mind. A brilliant idea of how to get Mr. Collington to renounce his claim to Tethering. She would *scare* him away!

She even had an idea already for who her ghost could be—it was perfect, really. And she would begin that very night, at the dratted dinner to which her father had agreed. Dinner would give her a chance to sow the seeds of trepidation in one so fearful as

Mr. Collington. She almost felt sorry for the grief she would have to cause him, but she steeled herself. Needs must.

Felicity stood looking at herself in her bedroom's small, murky mirror, wearing the one fancy gown she had dyed, a rich ivory satin that had taken the black color well. The house was quiet in the dusky early evening; her father had not returned from Tethering's library, and she doubted it had occurred to him to dress for dinner. But then, he was already wearing a mustard silk waistcoat with faded poppy embroidery, along with his black mourning armband.

She smoothed her gown's unfashionably fitted waist against her curves, the rich cloth a lustrous black in the fading light. Its half-sleeves and low, scooped bodice looked dressy. Couldn't a person just look good in something, even if it wasn't the style that everyone else was wearing? She *felt* finely enough turned out—rather pretty actually. The fashionable Mr. Collington would probably think her a very odd bird in the gown, and that made her like it even more. She grinned, thinking that no one would ever guess that under the fine satin she wore a tatty old chemise.

Opening the top drawer of her dresser, she took out a little box. Inside was a simple pearl necklace her mother had given her, a family heirloom that Felicity used to wear all the time when she went to parties. Once she'd taken her vow not to marry and taken on the running of Tethering, she'd simply stopped going to parties and balls. She might have met someone, might have been tempted, and that would have been wrong.

But she wasn't afraid of being tempted tonight. Even though she was just the tiniest bit fascinated by James Collington, the way she supposed women always were by handsome rogues, her heart and her vow could not be in the smallest danger from such a blackhearted scoundrel. There was, however, much to be said for being well turned out when dealing with a man. *That* was something she'd not forgotten. She put the necklace on, and it settled against the hollow of her throat, a lucky charm that pulsed with her mother's love.

She gathered her thick, dark gold hair in a low, loose knot at the back of her neck. On her way up to the manor, she picked a creamy sprig of summer jasmine and tucked it in her hair near the nape. Perhaps it wasn't totally appropriate with her mourning gown, but did Uncle Jonathan really deserve "appropriate"?

Standing quietly outside the familiar front door of Tethering Hall, she gently rubbed her forefinger against its weathered wood, the grain as familiar to her as her own skin. The door was warm from the day's sun, and she pressed her cheek against it, feeling the answering embrace of a stationary member of her family.

Stifling a fierce urge to simply let herself in, she knocked and was received by a smartly dressed manservant, who told her that Mr. Wilcox was still in the library, but that Mr. Collington awaited them in the drawing room. She went to the library and fetched her father from behind an enormous stack of books piled on a table.

"Father," she chastised him gently as they walked, arms linked, toward the drawing room, "you are as one starved who is gorging. I must urge moderation. Mr. Collington has, after all, given you free access. You do not have to commit all the books to memory."

Her father laughed, sounding giddy, and his eyes were alight with excitement. "Oh, my dear, it is good to be back among the books! And Mr. Collington is the most thoughtful of hosts. He had a luncheon brought in to me in the library and has been most obliging."

She groaned. Her father was completely in Mr. Collington's camp.

Her father's white hair was standing up in tufts around his head where he had probably been clutching it in the midst of deep concentration, as he was wont to do. She reached out and tenderly smoothed it down as they stood outside the drawing room, a place where she hadn't ever before waited in her life.

Butterflies stirred in her stomach in anticipation of what she was going to set in motion. The servant opened the door, and they walked in. Mr. Collington stood at their arrival.

She had forgotten how tall he was, or maybe now that she stood with him indoors, his height was more evident. His coat of sea blue hung wide from his shoulders before tapering in toward his waist. Fine as he was, he looked as out of place as a peacock among chickens.

When he greeted them, his brown eyes registered a momentary look of surprise at her polite response. He cocked his head consideringly, a smile playing at the corners of his lips. She smiled serenely and reminded herself that she must set the right tone with him, appear to be reconciling herself to his presence.

The drawing room no longer looked as it had when they left a month earlier. It had been immaculately cleaned, their shabby old furniture replaced with a few new things, and every polished surface now reflected the gentle dusk light coming through the tall windows. Even the rickety old staircase that led up to the walkway near the ceiling looked refreshed, as if it would creak less under its new coat of polish. Dismay stabbed her. She would have loved to make Tethering shine, but there had never been enough time or money to do it.

He was watching her as she looked around the room, and she turned a steady regard on him where he stood a few feet from her. His eyes, fixed on hers, held a brightness, an alertness that gave him an air of someone ready for anything.

A servant arrived bearing a tray with a bottle of sherry and three glasses, and their host offered them each a glass. The first sip was startling. The liquid tasted unlike any sherry she'd ever had, not necessarily in a pleasing way. Mr. Collington watched them drink.

"What do you think of my sherry?" he asked.

Her father looked unsure. "It is… that is," he began hesitantly, finally leaning over to examine the bottle's label, which Felicity could see was unhelpfully written in Spanish. "I say," he said, his eyebrows knitting, "but are you certain this is sherry, sir?"

Mr. Collington chuckled, a deep, masculine sound.

"Oh, but I assure you it is. The sherriest of sherries, that which is drunk by the people of Jerez themselves. Jerez being the town that gave us the English name 'sherry.'"

"Ah," her father said, and she guessed he was hoping Mr. Collington would not ask how he liked it. The wine was not in the least sweet, as sherry was supposed to be. Instead it was like pale, dry fire on the tongue.

"I think you mentioned that you are especially fond of sherry?" her father said.

Mr. Collington looked from Felicity to her father, neither of them having drunk beyond the first sip, and laughed, his white teeth a striking contrast with his tanned face. "Yes, I do like sherry very much. In fact, that's one of my favorites in your glasses, though I realize it is not the usual style of sweetened sherry to which the English palate is accustomed. It is *fino*, one of the wines produced at my vineyard near Jerez."

"Ah yes, you own a vineyard, don't you?" Felicity said, remembering what she had overheard at the garden party. She was curious; she would have thought he spent most of his time gambling and going to parties, not contending with the business of a vineyard. Of course, owning a vineyard didn't mean he spent any time there.

"Yes," he replied. "A few years ago I bought an established sherry bodega, as the Spanish call a vineyard, in the south of Spain. The Bodega Alborada is poised to supply a good portion of the English market. With English-style, sweetened sherry, of course. What you have in your glasses is what the Spanish prefer.

I've come to like it very much myself, but it is an acquired taste, as I suspect you'll agree."

When he said "Jerez" and "Bodega Alborada" the Spanish words *sounded* foreign, not like foreign words being pronounced as part of the King's English. He almost looked foreign, too, with his black-as-night hair and eyebrows and his tanned skin and chocolate eyes. He was looking at her father, and she allowed herself a moment to study him.

Mr. Collington looked every inch the gentleman in his fine clothes, but his muscular grace was that of a man who used his body. She could imagine him striding up vine-covered hillsides or even, astonishing that this should occur to her, swimming in the blue waters of some exotic coast, the sunlight glinting off athletic, tanned shoulders.

What on earth was she doing, thinking about the bare shoulders of a man she hardly knew? Thinking about a man's body? It was as if a strong wind from Spain—hadn't she read of such a thing, a *sirocco* or some such?—had come with him into their drawing room. And blown through her mind as well, sending it down startling paths.

She forced her gaze into her sherry glass and reminded herself firmly that, however much his manly presence gave it the lie, this man would quiver at the thought of ghosts. That was, thank heaven, a fairly quelling thought. What was the point of fabulous shoulders if the man they belonged to was, well, not manly?

"Er…" began her father, twisting his lips about as he struggled, she guessed, to say something polite about the unappealing drink.

Their host held up his hand with a rueful chuckle. "No, no, it's all right," he said, going over to pull on the bellrope, "I'll have some sweet sherry brought."

"Actually, Collington," her father said, putting his glass down on the table, a slightly guilty look creeping over his features, "if you don't mind, might I just nip back to the library for a moment? I've remembered something I wanted to look up."

Mr. Collington waved his hand. "But of course, Mr. Wilcox, I encourage you. We shall await your return."

Felicity nearly groaned. Her father never "just nipped in" when books were concerned. Once in the library he could unwittingly forget everyone and everything else for hours.

"And perhaps while you are gone," Mr. Collington continued, turning an innocently vacant host's expression on Felicity, "Miss Wilcox would be so good as to provide a tour of the walkway. I confess a curiosity as to what is up there."

"An excellent idea," her father said.

She smiled weakly in agreement, and her father left the room, abandoning her to the company of the enemy.

"It's just some old family paintings," she grumbled.

"If they are half as fascinating as their contemporary offspring, I shall feel richly rewarded," he said as he gestured toward the narrow mahogany stairway.

"Just what do you mean by that?" she asked, then realized she didn't want to have such a personal conversation with him. She turned and stepped up the stairs.

The curving, rounded railing was smooth under her

hands and as familiar to her as her father's glasses or the gnarled trunk of their oldest apple tree. The balcony had always been one of her favorite places; woman and girl, she'd never felt so content and comforted as when she sat on its worn carpet, her back to the wall and her feet against the high sides that hid her from view.

Mr. Collington's deep voice drifted up from much too close behind her. "Your father is a published poet and you are unique," he said. "Your style, for instance, is…" he paused, "unusual."

"Hmph. I suppose you must know all about style. You dress like a peacock."

His response was a deep chuckle that made the hairs on the back of her neck stand up.

Six

James watched Felicity step briskly ahead of him, as if she couldn't put distance between them fast enough. Where on earth *did* she get her strange supply of gowns? And when had the smell of jasmine become so intoxicating? She had a sprig in her hair whose fragrance was teasing him maddeningly. As he walked behind her, he imagined fitting his hands around her waist, so well-delineated in her last-century gown, and stopping her one step above him, at a perfect height to press his lips to that spot just where her neck met her partly bare shoulder.

He'd found his thoughts straying to her all too often in the last twenty-four hours, conjuring up the image of her lying in his arms after he'd pulled her from the stream. It had been such an uncomplicated encounter, sweetly erotic for him, and her too, he was certain, though she'd never admit it now.

As he stepped onto the balcony behind her she moved forward to stand in front of a painting hanging at eye level. He supposed she preferred it to looking at him.

"Have you ever gone to London, Miss Wilcox?" he asked her, suddenly curious how she would like it. She was so unlike the women he met there.

She turned to look at him. "No." She cocked her head, considering. "Not that I have minded. I don't think I'd like it. I've heard it's smelly and crowded."

He laughed. "It sometimes is. But don't you ever crave excitement?"

"You know," she said with a sigh, "I don't need your pity, Mr. Collington. I like my life perfectly well."

They walked along looking at the paintings of her ancestors and the knickknacks that stood on recessed shelves. As she answered his various questions, he noticed how she trailed her hands along the walls and railings—lightly, almost affectionately, like one might stroke a favored pet.

They came to a picture of her Uncle Jonathan.

"I suppose your uncle gambled away most of the estate profits?"

"Jonathan was one of the most unlucky people you could imagine," she replied. "He was weak. As, I believe, all who gamble for large stakes must be."

He was weak, was he? He leaned back against the side of the balcony and rested his elbows on it, looking at her. Her eyes drew his attention, though he did not want to be caught staring at her. But they were a beautiful dark green-brown, the colors of forest moss and rich earth. Something about her spoke of the quintessential beauty of nature. She was different, singular, astonishingly lovely in her black gown, with a simple pearl necklace and a jasmine flower her only adornments. And she was regarding him with undisguised contempt. He shouldn't want to laugh, but he *did* want to. Though, he thought, mirth tickling the edges of his mouth, that he did not dare.

"You know, Miss Wilcox, if you were a man, I would have had to call you out several insults ago. But of course," he paused lazily, his gaze sweeping slowly over her body, "you are not a man. And maybe you dislike gambling simply because your family never won. Winning, I can assure you, is deeply satisfying."

"I don't respect gamblers," she said, crossing her arms, her eyes looking at him from under disdainful eyebrows. Very pretty, elegant eyebrows.

"Someone always has to lose. It's a waste."

"Some gambles are necessary, Miss Wilcox. Much of business is a form of gambling. A good businessman informs himself, then trusts his instincts."

"And you are a man of business?"

"Of sorts. I have the bodega and a few other interests."

"Do you gamble with your affairs?"

"I take risks, yes. That's the only way to increase profit."

She shrugged, unimpressed. "Well, I hope those risks will beggar no one but yourself if you are wrong."

"And the people who work for me," he pointed out. "But I don't risk more than I can afford to lose."

"As my uncle did."

He shrugged. "Ultimately, one must be in control of one's passions."

Felicity's face burned at the word "passion." The balcony was narrow, not much more than a yard wide. The two of them were close enough together that she could smell faint whiffs of his scent, familiar to her from sitting on his coat. It was creating little thrills in her as she inhaled it. Was that hint of citrus something from Spain? Oh, why did he have to be her handsome stranger? No one half so exciting had ever crossed her path, even if he was a man afraid of ghosts. The illusion of manliness he presented was incredibly beguiling, and she could have dreamed harmlessly of him and their time by the stream for the rest of her life. But now he was here, and far too real and troublesome. She couldn't dream about him now.

She turned away from him and looked back at the portrait on the wall behind her, the last one.

"And here is Great-Great-Aunt Isabella," she said blandly. The portrait showed a stout woman, firmly upholstered in brown with not a speck of jewelry. Felicity and Simon had spent happy times as children addressing inappropriate comments to the portrait, delighting in imagining how shocked the real woman would have been to hear such naughtiness.

"Of course," Mr. Collington said, looking amused.

"What do you mean 'of course'? Do you have a Great-Great-Aunt Isabella?"

"No, but I did have a Great-Great-Aunt Isophine." He laughed, then tilted his head reflectively. "But aunts can be nice as well. My Aunt Miranda is a singular woman. She took care of me and my brother from the time I was orphaned at twelve."

He sounded like just the sort of good son any woman would be pleased to have adopted. But then, hadn't he humored bossy Nanny Rollins when he could have put her in her place? She couldn't afford, though, to think of him as being kind and good.

"You have achieved a drastic change in the manor in one day," she accused. "At least in the drawing room."

Mr. Collington drew closer to where she had stopped, by a small, round window that had been opened to let in the fresh air. "I have great hopes for Tethering Hall," he said. "With care and work, it could be as magnificent as a tiny jewel."

"What do you mean?" she demanded. "Tethering already is a jewel. I doubt there's another house like it in England." She waved her fingers in a dismissive gesture. "Maybe you have had it cleaned and replaced some worn furnishings, but that's all it needs."

"You are obviously fond of this house, Miss Wilcox," he said. "But perhaps, being as close to it as you have been, you haven't seen all of its needs. Like… here," he said, glancing at the window behind her. She turned and looked at the place he indicated, a large area of damp rot in the wood of the frame.

She reached out and tenderly touched the soft, crumbly area, then looked up at him defensively. "It's just a little water damage. A carpenter can fix that easily."

He shrugged. "Maybe it will be easy to fix, and maybe when the frame is removed for repair, other problems will be revealed. The point is, this is just one frame in a house that is very much in need of repairs."

"Which you can provide," she said.

"Tethering will benefit from what I can offer it," he said.

"Money," she said contemptuously, turning so that her back was to the window and crossing her arms. The breeze coming in gently ruffled a curling strand of her hair, tossing it against her neck and cheek.

"Yes, money," he said. "It takes money to accomplish things."

She realized, after a moment, that neither one of them was speaking. His dark brown eyes were resting on her intently. He reached out and tucked the breeze-blown strand of hair behind her ear. She stilled, startled by his touch.

"I can't forget the beautiful young woman I met by the stream."

Her cheeks warmed at his words. She stood unmoving, listening to him, her eyes looking up at him under half-lowered lashes. What was he doing? What would he say?

He brushed his thumb against the warm skin of her cheek, then let his hand fall. She had not moved. She could not. This was what it meant to be fascinated.

He bent his head and took one of her hands. Holding it up, he turned it over and traced the palm with a fingertip. He rubbed his thumb lightly along the row of calluses that gardening and other labors had made on her palm, a part of her that she had not known until now was yearning for a gentle touch to unlock its hidden sensation.

"A useful little hand."

He lifted her hand and dragged his lips along her palm toward her wrist. She caught her breath at the feel of him against her.

Not just her cheeks but her lips were warm now. "You," she said at last, almost just a breath. As if she were surprised to see him standing there.

"I've wanted to do this from the first moment I met you," he said huskily.

James Collington bent his dark head toward her, his deep brown eyes holding hers. And then he was kissing her, his warm, moist lips against hers. His tongue stroked against her mouth, making prickles shoot along the back of her neck, and she opened to him. And loved it, the feel of his mouth on hers, and the sense she had through his sure movements of his leashed strength and firm body. A gathering rush of desire spread through her.

He deepened the kiss, bringing his hands up to press along her exposed nape and hold her close for his lips even as she at first tentatively, then with more sureness, pressed her hands against his taut waist. How firm and alive the contours felt under her palms. She was amazed.

His tongue gently explored inside her mouth, and she explored back. His lips traveled down along her neck, and the rasp of his late-afternoon bristles against the tender skin of her neck gave her thrills. She thought she would sink to the floor with the pleasure of it.

He crushed her to him, her breasts pushing upward as they came against the hardness of his chest. With a shock she felt the evidence of his desire pressing into her inner thigh.

The sensation of his hardness penetrated her haze of pleasure. She gasped and pushed against his waist. He dropped his hands and stepped away, looking at her, his breathing labored.

"What," she demanded raggedly through passion-tender lips, her senses still racing, "do you think you are doing?"

He crossed his arms and looked at her with darkened eyes. He seemed dangerous now, haughty and dark with his foreign tan and hard male beauty. "Nothing we haven't both wanted to do. And you were hardly a reluctant participant."

"Oh!" she burst out, turning her back on everything she had just experienced. She had to. She might have lost her mind for a few minutes, but she knew what was what. "You are the most arrogant man I have ever met! You think you can just waltz in anywhere and do whatever you want."

He raised a sardonic eyebrow. "Unrelated issues aside," he drawled, "you can hardly deny that there is an attraction between us."

A gust of warm wind blew in through the open window at her back and bounced her hair against her cheeks, and she pushed it roughly away from her face. "There is no such thing as an unrelated issue in regard to you and your presence here, *Mr.* Collington. And—and I don't call what just happened attraction. It can't have been anything but temporary insanity!"

He leaned his hips back against the railing and gave her a lazy look that made her blood boil in more than one way. "Take it from someone who has seen quite a bit more of the world than you, Felicity Wilcox. That was attraction. Deny it all you want. It won't just disappear."

From below them came the sound of the library door opening.

"Felicity? Collington?" Mr. Wilcox's voice drifted up to them.

Giving Mr. Collington a furious glare, she turned

away from him and called out, "Here, Father," in an uneven voice. She cleared her throat and, without a backward glance, rushed along the walkway calling, "Just finishing our tour of the balcony."

Seven

Felicity silently berated herself as the three of them walked toward the dining room. That had been a disaster. She needed to keep James Collington at arm's length, not melt for him. She'd surrendered the minute he'd touched her—and loved every second of it, before she'd come to her senses. Insanity, she'd called it, and she knew it had been some kind of madness. She'd tasted desire once, three years ago, and had dismissed it as a pale substance easily avoided. But then, it hadn't felt like that intense, impossible-to-resist urge that had overwhelmed her in the balcony.

Obviously she'd lied when she'd said she wasn't attracted to him. He drew her. Some deep part of her had consented to be captivated by him on the walkway. And why should she be surprised? He'd ridden into her life on a white horse and been her gallant, playful rescuer, the sort of thing of which every young woman dreams while knowing it won't ever happen. But he *had* come along, handsome as the devil, and done something to her—it was as if he had lit a candle inside her that she could not blow out.

But she'd find a way to extinguish this flame. She'd managed these last three years to simply forget about men, about attraction and companionship. And marriage. And babies.

A sob started low in her chest and she pushed it down, hard. What on earth was wrong with her lately? She'd been fine all these years, not thinking about any of what she'd given up. The choice for a family of her own was not for her anymore. Tethering had been her choice—and her reward. And she wasn't going to let this man take it away from her.

Thank heaven she had a plan. While it was perhaps a little daft, it just might be the way to make Tethering a place James Collington wouldn't be able to stand.

They took their seats at the table. She and her father sat next to each other, across from Collington. Felicity hated like anything to admit it, but the dining room looked handsome. Their old table had been thoroughly polished and was now gleaming richly in the glow of a generous number of beeswax candles, and a handsome centerpiece of fruits and flowers gave the table an air of plenty it hadn't had for years.

But Mr. Collington obviously hadn't gotten to everything yet, she thought as she sat down and experienced the familiar wobble in her chair. She felt his eyes on her and looked up, steeling herself against any look that might claim intimacy. But his face was unreadable. She looked away.

His servants began bringing around the food, some kind of steaming meat pie that practically made her eyes roll back in her head with its wonderful, rich scent.

"A simple repast bought in town, I'm afraid. The household is in the process of acquiring a cook. But I trust that the Longwillow shops will not have let us down."

They had not, and every bite was heaven.

She waited until about halfway through dinner, when there was a lull in the conversation, before setting her plan in motion.

"Mr. Collington," she began after taking a fortifying sip of wine, "surely you will want to know some of the fascinating history that goes along with Tethering Hall." She smiled in what she hoped was a believably sincere manner.

Her father looked at her quizzically. "What's this, my dear? Have you come upon some story of a past king or queen who stopped for a visit?" His eyes twinkled merrily at the idea.

"No, Father, something much more exciting." She paused for effect and looked directly at Mr. Collington, who was regarding her across the candlelit table with interest. "I'm speaking of Lovely Annabelle."

Her father grimaced. "Felicity, I'm sure Mr. Collington doesn't want to hear about that."

"Lovely Annabelle?" Mr. Collington said, his eyebrow lifting with interest. "I am intrigued already. She sounds like a heroine in a tragic ballad." His eyes with their intelligent lights focused on her, although she thought she caught a glint of humor in them. Well, the story she was about to tell should sober him right up.

"Your guess is close," she said. "Lovely Annabelle was one of our ancestors who lived here at Tethering

Hall about seventy years ago." She paused again for dramatic effect. "She was a woman who, family legend tells us, had always been certain she would not marry unless it was to a man she truly loved. Unfortunately, having arrived at the age of thirty-eight, she still had not found anyone."

"And was she lovely?" he interrupted.

"Yes, she was by all accounts lovely but also very determined. And then she finally met a man she could love. She was preparing for the wedding—"

"But Miss Wilcox," he broke in again, and grinned. "You're telling this all wrong, jumping to the wedding when you haven't even said who the man was. Surely the groom is important."

She ground her teeth. He was making this needlessly difficult. But they'd see who would have the last laugh. "Well, who he was is not important for the purpose of the story, but if you must know, the man was some nobleman new to the area. I forget his name."

"Lord Butterfield, my dear," her father supplied with a sigh.

"Yes, that's right. Thank you, Father."

"Yes, thank you, Mr. Wilcox," said Mr. Collington. "For my part I know that, should my fiancée become the heroine of family lore, I should certainly like to be remembered for my role in being her beloved."

"As I was saying, sir," she said, just managing to keep the exasperation out of her voice, "on the day of her wedding, just before the ceremony, Annabelle passed too near to the fireplace in her beautiful, gauzy wedding gown. Her skirts caught on fire, and when she bent over to put them out, her hair fell in the flames and ignited. She was burned to death right in front of all the guests."

"Well, that is certainly a sad story," he said, his lips curving into a grimace of dismay that she was sure he meant to look ironic. She, of course, knew how he must really be feeling upon hearing of someone actually dying in this home. Ah, how such a story must affect a person who had been brought to hysterics by the ghostly keening of the wind!

"Poor Lovely Annabelle," he said. "Perhaps a flowering bush should be planted in her honor."

"A fine idea!" Mr. Wilcox interjected, clearly wishing to move on.

Mr. Collington was certainly putting up a brave front, but then, he must be used to it. After the spectacle he'd made of himself among his servants, he'd doubtless become an amazing actor, so that his virile appearance might give the lie to any rumors. She hurried to finish her story, fixing Mr. Collington with a penetrating look.

"But that's not the end of my story. Legend has it that Lovely Annabelle haunts Tethering Hall at night, unable to rest because she was never able to be with her love after all those years as a lonely spinster."

"Well, a ghost at Tethering!" Mr. Collington finally exclaimed, glancing from Felicity to her father. He was holding up marvelously, she had to admit. "And have either of you ever encountered the ghost of Lovely Annabelle?"

"No," said Mr. Wilcox firmly.

"Yes," said Felicity just as firmly. Her father gave her a quizzical look. She smiled weakly.

"What is she like, then, Miss Wilcox?" Mr. Collington asked with what sounded like a note of indulgence in his voice. In the candlelight, she could have sworn she saw sparks of amusement dancing in his eyes. Really, he was a very good actor.

"W-e-l-l," she began, thinking quickly. She had not planned out Lovely Annabelle's look yet. Best to describe something unpleasant—she did not want to create a romantic figure. "We saw her as children. Unfortunately, she was not a pretty sight. She was burned, of course, so her head and hair are charred, and she still wears her white wedding gown."

That should do it, she thought. She spared a glance to see if he was weakening and was disappointed that he looked in no way aghast, but she understood that was to be expected. Now was not the time she was concerned about. No, all that mattered would be the dark of night when, with no one to see him and the darkness to raise his fears, he realized that a ghost was roaming the house.

"Felicity," her father said, a warning note creeping into his voice, "perhaps you've entertained our host enough with such fanciful children's stories."

"Of course, Father. I just thought that our host might like to know a little of this history of his… newest acquisition."

"Thank you, Miss Wilcox," he said pleasantly, giving no sign that he noticed her little dig. "I shall be sure to keep an eye out for Lovely Annabelle."

Mr. Collington stood soon after, signaling the end of dinner. He invited his guests to return to the drawing room for coffee, but Mr. Wilcox declined for them, pleading fatigue. And so Mr. Collington, after arranging with Felicity to tour the orchard together in the morning, saw the Wilcoxes on their way.

❧

It was well after midnight that same night, a cloudy evening, which was perfect. Felicity had already put on a stained and tattered old white gown. She stood before her mirror now, a candle lit on the table beside her and a mug full of soot in her hand. In for a penny in for a pound. She lifted the mug and dumped a generous dash in her loose hair and began rubbing it in. Very quickly she looked like something bad had happened to her. Perfect for Lovely Annabelle.

She kept working until all her hair was covered. The mass of chalky blackness now surrounding her face made her look as pale as a corpse. She made some random smears on her face and neck and stepped away from the candle-lit reflection. She looked appalling, and certainly unrecognizable, at least from a distance.

Blowing out the candle, she grinned, thinking of Mr. Collington's likely horror. It was time. She ignored the last-minute rush of panic, the voice that reminded her that the consequences if she were discovered wandering the home of a gentleman at night would be dire. The choice between doing this and that wasteland future of emptiness without Tethering was no choice at all.

Gently she eased her door open and crept downstairs. Fortunately, her father was a heavy sleeper. Once outside she kept to the line of weeping willows and maples that bordered the lawn leading up to

Tethering Hall. Even her careful footsteps and her excited breathing seemed very loud in the stillness. She had never been out alone in the middle of the night before. It was daring and irresponsible—and exciting.

Drawing near the house, she made for the back. Getting into the manor would be easy because she knew something that the efficient, house-fixing James Collington couldn't possibly have discovered yet. She crept over to a large flagstone set in a line with others that formed a path through the small decorative garden directly behind the mansion.

Grass and weeds had grown across the stone over the last years, and she pushed them away. Once the surface was clear, she slid her fingertips underneath the stone and lifted it up on its hidden hinge. And then she was descending the few steps into the underground tunnel that led into the house.

The tunnel's original purpose was a mystery, and its existence was a family secret. She and Simon and Crispin had used it frequently as children, though she had not been in it for years. It was part of the quirky charm of Tethering that she loved so much.

Inside the tunnel was utter darkness, and she made her way by feel, crouching over because the ceiling was low. The tunnel's air was stale, but the smell carried familiar notes that triggered memories, most very happy. The tunnel led her downward, and in a few minutes she was pushing gratefully against the small door at the end that led into the cellar of the manor.

Stepping down to the cellar floor, she gathered her thoughts. She needed to get upstairs, close to where

Mr. Collington would be sleeping on the second floor. But she didn't want to wake up any servants who might surprise her before she could get his attention and haunt him, briefly and from a distance.

She slipped off her shoes and stepped noiselessly onto the stone basement stairs leading up to the first-floor kitchen. All was quiet as she passed through the kitchen and continued down the hall toward the stairs to the second floor, though the sound of her wildly beating heart filled her ears. She hugged the wall as she went so as not to make the heavily worn wood in the center of the hallway creak. Once on the stairs, she kept to the sides again and reached the second floor hallway without making a sound. A candle burning in a sconce cast a low light over the corridor.

Her target must be in the master bedroom, since it was the largest and had the nicest views. She crept forward to stand just outside the door, took a deep breath, and moaned.

The sound startled her in the quiet, killing her courage for a moment, and she stopped abruptly. But then she gathered her wits to her task and moaned again, a mournful, feminine sound. Putting out a tentative hand, she gently rattled the doorknob. She moaned again for good measure, then decided as panic rose in her chest, that would have to be enough to get his attention.

Quickly, and keeping to the walls again, she crept toward the end of the corridor, where a panel was set in the wall at hip-level, cleverly hidden as part of a large section of carved wooden trim work. Just as she released the tiny catch on the panel, a door opened down the hall. Someone—it had to be Mr. Collington, since the servants wouldn't be sleeping up there—stuck his head out.

She executed what she hoped was a ghostly movement by raising her arms and waving them. Then she gave one last mournful "woo" for good measure, quickly hopped up into the secret opening, and swung her legs to stand on the small shelf inside. As she quietly guided the door back into place, she heard footsteps racing down the hall. She turned and grabbed hold of the pole that she knew ran from the attics to the cellar and was away downward.

Perfect!

She landed in the cellar with a shocking thud and stinging hands that reminded her she hadn't slid down a pole in years. As she grabbed her shoes, she paused a moment to listen to the footsteps above her. Surprisingly, he seemed to have found the courage to run after the ghost, but doubtless it was a reflex and he was even now being overcome with horror. Huzzah, but that had gone well!

Giddy with her night's work, Felicity slipped out through the passageway to the garden. She replaced the stone, quickly pressing the disturbed grass back into place, and was off again, down along the tree line.

Once outside Blossom Cottage, she dunked her filthy hair in the rain barrel and made use of a bar of soap she had put there earlier, along with a cloth for drying herself. She scrubbed her face and neck, dried off, and then slipped quietly back in the house. In a matter of minutes she was lying damply in bed, mightily pleased with her cleverness and stealth.

That hadn't been bad at all. Actually, doing the haunting—and getting away with it!—had been a thrill. When had she last felt thrilled? Well, if she had to answer truthfully, it had been when she'd been in James Collington's arms. But she wasn't going to think about that.

A few more nights of haunting should reduce him to a quivering heap. She drifted off to sleep more hopeful than she had been in weeks.

Eight

From his front bedroom window James stood in just his breeches and watched the strange dark figure pause outside the dower house for several minutes. Probably trying to do something about whatever she'd put in her hair.

So, "Lovely Annabelle" had decided to pay him a visit. If he hadn't stopped to put on his pants, he would have gotten into the hallway in time to apprehend her. But what would he have done with her? Certainly not what he would have liked to do, though perhaps her luscious appeal would have been somewhat muted by the coating of soot or whatever it was she had applied.

Apparently Felicity Wilcox was now going to scare him away from Tethering Hall, he thought with a wry twist of his lips. Well, good enough. He couldn't remember the last time he'd played a game that wasn't cards, and this one looked to be unusual at the very least. He wondered how she'd gotten in and out of the house so easily. Very possibly the house had a secret passageway or two.

He returned to bed. But, aroused as he had been

since the kiss in the balcony, sleep did not come. His mind kept supplying images of her in her ridiculous old-fashioned clothes. Not the ghost costume, but her black satin dinner gown, and even the muddy, faded gown from the first day they met. How did she manage to look so alluring in such odd clothing? She had a glow, like a fresh peach whose ripeness and lush color beckon you to sink your teeth into it. Though it wasn't his teeth he wanted to sink into her.

She affected him, as though she were some sort of sneaky enchantress insinuating her way into his thoughts. Or an imp, more likely. Something about her was doing things to his control.

He flopped and turned on his lumpy mattress for an hour, edgy and yearning. Hades, but it had been a long time since he had been with a woman. But the bucolic, ramshackle Tethering estate was not the place to indulge himself. Felicity Wilcox was a penniless, overworked gentlewoman who wished him all the worst. And he had a goal to accomplish from which he must not be distracted. Getting involved with her in any way would send him wildly off course, and that was something he could not allow.

The next morning he awoke early as usual and was grateful for a clear head and a vigorous desire to attack the tasks of the day. He was still keeping farmer's hours, but then, he had been a farmer for the last three years.

The Bodega Alborada had been in declining condition when James purchased it, but it had good land and a large store of maturing sherry casks. With the design of increasing its value so that he could sell it before the time given to pay the ten-thousand-pound debt his brother had saddled him with, he had fixed up the caverns where the sherry matured and purchased new equipment, all under the advice of Old Pedro, his foreman. James had been more than happy to lose himself in the exhausting work. Anything was better than reflecting on the shambles of his life in England, where his beloved estate, Granton, was threatened by debt and scandal clung to the Collington name.

In Spain he'd taken up hoe and scythe to work alongside the dark-haired peasant men. He'd gained a deep knowledge of the grapes, and found that work as satisfying as the time he spent among the casks planning for the maturing and bottling of the different sherries. The last three years had been fulfilling in their way, but he fully expected that the future would hold so much more. Starting with the return of Granton.

When Fulton brought his breakfast into the morning room, James asked after the progress being made on renovations at Tethering Hall.

"The workmen have arrived, sir," Fulton replied, setting down James's coffee cup and pot. "They are ready to begin with the roof. They estimate it will take them a few days to repair it."

James poured himself some coffee, wishing it were the thick, darkly roasted brew he drank at the bodega. He had used up precious time in London settling the importation details for the sherry, though of course that time had also netted him the Tethering estate. Now he had only two months left to get Tethering fixed up and sold to Dover so he could meet the terms of the debt. Still, the time remaining was adequate. He would invite the man down in perhaps a month, by which time the house and orchard should be in good shape, with a staff installed and running things smoothly so that Dover would be eager to assume ownership.

"The workers will be done before the guests begin arriving, correct?" James asked.

"Indeed, sir," Fulton replied. "The men are eager to receive the promised bonus on finishing."

"Very good, Fulton. And the staff?"

"Several footmen and housemaids have been engaged, sir. And the women recommended by Miss Wilcox—Mrs. Withers and Mrs. Bailey—arrived early this morning. They both seemed eager for the employment."

"Good, good." James nodded his head, pleased that his plans were all proceeding briskly. "You know my philosophy on staff, Fulton."

"Indeed I do, sir. A happy staff is a happy enterprise."

"Exactly," James said with a smile of satisfaction. He glanced sidelong at the manservant, who was busying himself removing crumbs from the table with a cloth.

"Fulton, did you hear anything last night, any unusual noises? Around midnight, perhaps a little later?"

Fulton paused in his wiping. "Noises. Yes," he cleared his throat. "I heard the floors creaking and assumed you had gotten up. Also, there was a moaning sound." Fulton looked uncomfortable. "If I may add, sir, apparently the stable boy saw a 'ghostly figure' near the trees late last night. He says he heard from the locals that there's some sort of"—he cleared his throat, a man who disliked repeating silly gossip—"lady ghost who is supposed to appear and haunt the property."

Damn, James thought, she'd been seen. That was just what he didn't need—unwanted attention. He didn't need rumors of strange doings at Tethering reaching Dover. And after the last time his family was in the news, he couldn't afford for more gossip about the Collington family to start up. He'd have to force Felicity Wilcox to stop this silly business before she did it again. He'd have to put a little fear in her.

Fulton was looking at him. "Sir, you don't think this might be distressing to Miss Claremont, when she comes to stay?"

"No. Not in the least. The other time… she'd had a very distressing dream about her dead sister. It was simply a very difficult time in her life."

His aunt Miranda would be fine, of that James was certain. She'd recovered now from the death of her beloved sister. But Miss Wilcox was indeed stirring up a delicate situation at Tethering. Doubtless her purpose was to accomplish his discomfort and departure. He couldn't afford for her to know she was having some success, if only because he couldn't allow any hint of scandal to surround the estate. Well, it shouldn't be too difficult to spur her into a little sense.

"Who did the locking up last night?" James asked.

"I did, sir. Though the locks on one or two of the windows are not in good condition."

"Well, perhaps you will let it about that a cow got onto the property last night, and that must have been what the stable boy saw."

"A *cow*, sir?"

James pressed his lips together. "Yes, I damn well know a cow doesn't look like a ghostly woman, but it was dark and how can anyone be sure of what was seen? We need to create a logical explanation. I can't afford to have the least hint of anything unseemly going on here."

Fulton looked sober. He was fully aware of what was at stake. "Of course, sir. I understand."

"Good." James wiped his mouth and stood up from the table. "I'm going to call on the Wilcoxes now. Miss Wilcox is to accompany me on a tour of the orchard." He pulled out his pocket watch and glanced at it. "I imagine Mr. Wilcox will be along shortly to use the library."

"I shall see that he is brought lunch."

"Thank you, Fulton. You are essential."

"Yes, sir," Fulton said as he focused his attention on removing a bit of wax from the tabletop, his normally impassive features momentarily altered by a pleased look. Like his master, the indispensable Fulton liked nothing so much as a job well done.

On his way down to Blossom Cottage, James passed Wilcox on his way up to Tethering. They did not speak beyond a greeting—he could see that the man was eager to get to the library.

A sharp rap on the front door of Blossom Cottage called forth a stout, graying servant somewhat long in the tooth. She led James to the sitting room and went to fetch her mistress.

Felicity was sitting at the breakfast table distractedly pondering a note from Crispin. He was writing to invite her, in a rather insistent tone, to attend an assembly in town in a few days, but her thoughts were not on dancing. She was instead savoring the gossip Martha, their daily servant, had just repeated to her: one of the stable boys had seen Lovely Annabelle! Felicity was indulging in optimistic scenarios of James Collington's distress. Had he lain awake all night, worrying about what was going on at this country house? Would the gossip of the servants help create a desperate atmosphere? And had his new cook and housekeeper arrived to wreak havoc yet? With any luck, he was already having grave doubts about the Tethering estate.

She was just dashing off a reply to Crispin, to thank him but decline, when Martha came in to announce the arrival of Mr. Collington. Felicity blanched. She'd momentarily forgotten their appointment to inspect the orchard. Or maybe he was here to say good-bye! Quickly she drank the remainder of her tea, gave Martha the note for Crispin, then stood and neatened her appearance before striding into the sitting room.

Mr. Collington, standing by the window in his smart breeches, gleaming black boots, and the vivid garnet tailcoat, seemed too much for the small room, with its homey tatting on the tabletop and its simple furnishings. Too smart, too manly, too exotically handsome to be standing in the faded cream and mauve sitting room at Blossom Cottage. He turned at her entrance, those chocolate eyes steady under their dark, neat brows, though she thought the corners of his mouth twitched momentarily. And there was something else about his regard, something that wasn't funny at all.

Strange. She would have expected some signs of trepidation. But then she reminded herself of the acting skills he had displayed at dinner.

She lifted her chin.

"Good morning, Miss Wilcox. I hope you are well today," he greeted her, his deep, now-familiar voice sounding perfectly normal.

"Good morning, Mr. Collington," she said, ignoring the flip-flopping sensation starting up inside her at the sound of his voice. "I trust that your ill-gotten home is proving comfortable." If only he would reveal some discomfort or inconvenience resulting from Lovely Annabelle's visit. He looked, however, well rested.

"I thank you for your kind consideration." His eyes glinted at her. "Although, astonishing as it is to report, I had a visitor near my bedroom late last night."

Oh, good, he *had* been disturbed by Lovely Annabelle. Time to pretend utter ignorance. "Mr. Collington! Surely that is not an appropriate subject for us to discuss."

He chuckled and moved closer to her. Suddenly the sitting room seemed not just small but tiny. How had she and her father spent so many nights reading quietly together in this place? The room was practically a closet.

"Of course you would be right, Miss Wilcox, if I were talking about anything but a visit from the very same Lovely Annabelle that you described to me not a few hours earlier."

"No!" she said in what she hoped was a shocked tone. With James Collington standing so near, looking down at her with those lights in his eyes, she was not at all sure what she was doing or how she sounded. He was doing it again, working his charm on her as he had in the balcony.

Inching backward away from him, she came up against the sitting room wall. He followed her and rested his bent arm against a built-in shelf near her head, managing to look relaxed and menacing at the same time as he stood at the outside edge of a polite distance from her. Though she needed more space between them, she would not give him the satisfaction of watching her slink back.

She tipped her chin up and found his dark brown eyes focused intently on her. Was she blushing? Her face, and especially her lips, felt hot. *Stop this*, she wanted to yell at her body.

"Yes!" he said. "Astonishing, isn't it? Why, you had just mentioned her at dinner, and then she appeared."

"Well, um," she said. Her voice came out irritatingly breathy, and she cleared her throat. "She perhaps heard us talking about her at dinner. Or maybe she's been lonely. No one has slept in Tethering Hall since your nasty letter arrived."

One of his eyebrows arched. Really, the man looked astonishingly devilish at times, with his dark hair and eyebrows and those shrewd eyes. Was he suspicious? Nothing about him at the moment looked like someone who fooled easily.

"Must be a lonely life, being a ghost in a house when no one is living there," he said.

"Yes, that's the point, isn't it?" She was glad to get back to the subject. They were talking about Lovely

Annabelle, but there was a separate current flowing under their conversation that she needed to squash. "Ghosts are lonely and unhappy. Things haven't worked out well for them. They want other people to suffer too."

He chuckled, a rich, canny sound. "So that was why she was moaning outside my bedroom door and rattling the doorknob."

"Well, it must be, mustn't it?" She forced herself to focus, to forget about the exciting feelings his nearness was causing. This was a chance to push home her reason for the haunting. "You know, Mr. Collington, Lovely Annabelle never moaned and rattled my doorknob."

"She didn't?"

"No. I only ever saw her sitting in the chair in my room. Sometimes she sang me a little song, then she would sort of disappear."

"A little song? How sweet."

Sweet? Heavens, but the man was hiding his fear well. For a panicked moment she wondered if she could have made a mistake in what she overheard. But no, James's servant had clearly been talking about his master.

"Yes, well, the point is that she liked me being there and she doesn't like you being there. I would not call moaning a sign of welcome."

"Some people would."

Her face flamed at his words and his sultry tone. She pressed her lips together primly, crushing their warm eagerness.

His eyes narrowed. "Well, since you seem to be

on such friendly terms with her, you may give her a message from me."

"Oh?" He wanted her to give the ghost a message?

"Yes." He drilled her with an intense gaze. "Tell her that, charming though she is, I will tolerate no more visits from her."

"And just how do you think I might relay this message?"

He shrugged. "If she's sung you songs in the past, I have little doubt that you'll find a way to get in touch with her."

She was bewildered. Mr. Collington seemed so different from what she would have expected of someone in mortal fear of ghosts. But he must be accustomed to masking his terror, and he was doing so now, very effectively, with his arrogance and his wicked ways. Clearly, if he was trying to push her to contact the ghost, he was desperate. She had to admit that it was brave of him to seek a solution for his problem.

"Well," she said, "I will see what I can do."

He leaned fractionally closer to her. "See that you do, Felicity Wilcox," he whispered.

She had to put some distance between them before she crumpled under the force of those dark eyes. In a quick move, she scooted away along the wall then strode over to the door.

"Hadn't we best be going, then?" she called over her shoulder.

She caught a glimpse of his satisfied grin out of the corner of her eyes. He thought she was going to solve his problem. She allowed herself a secret grin. *Au contraire.*

"Yes, of course," he agreed, striding over toward the door. She had opened it and was out of the room before he could come any nearer, but still she was fairly certain that she heard him give a low chuckle.

A gray horse stood tethered outside the house, along with his own handsome white mount.

"Do you ride, Miss Wilcox?" he asked.

"Of course," she replied, hoping she would not disgrace herself—Tethering hadn't had horses for years. He helped her up into the saddle, and they set off on a path that led around the side of the manor to the orchard.

Nine

They kept their horses to a slow pace as they moved among the rows of apple trees that ran in a wide swath away from the house. On either side were hedgerows that allowed occasional views of the estate's few tenant farms. The warm, fresh air held the scents of honeysuckle and roses, and the morning light filtered softly through the leaves all around them. The only sound was that of the horses' hooves brushing the tall grass and the occasional buzz of a pollinating bee.

James cast a glance at his companion, who was staring intently at the trees, her eyes roving over them in an assessing manner. Her thick golden hair was gathered at her nape and tied in a knot with a tattered, colorless ribbon. She was evidently not aware of the telltale smudges of black soot along her hairline in back.

"The grass is high," he observed as their horses picked their way along a section where weeds brushed the riders' feet in the stirrups.

"Mmm-hmm," she replied, not looking at him.

"But the trees look well-maintained," he continued. "I don't see much dead wood, and the dense blossoms bode well for a good harvest."

Still focusing on the trees, she said nothing as they rode along. They came eventually to the far southeast edge of the orchard, an area that apparently had been neglected. Several of the trees were leafless and weather-beaten enough to have been dead for some time, and others had broken and dangling branches. Although the grass in most of the orchard was high, in this area it was thicker and overgrown with weedy bushes. It would take laborers days to clear the area.

"What happened here?" he asked.

She sat silently staring at the dead trees, though not, he would guess, in surprise.

"This isn't going to work," he said finally, "you being the orchard overseer, if you refuse to talk to me about it."

She turned to him. "What do you know about orchards anyway? I could tell you that all the trees need to be cut down to the ground every year to give a good harvest, and what would you know differently?"

He guffawed. "It is true that I don't know a lot about fruit trees, which is why I have engaged your services. But I do know about growing things. I have just spent three years cultivating grapes for my sherry vineyard."

"You?" She rolled her eyes. "Gentlemen don't do farm work."

"Not all gentlemen are alike, just as most gentlewomen would not be having a conversation with me about how to maintain an orchard."

She pressed her lips in reluctant admission of the truth of what he said.

"So, what's going on in this corner? Why is it so neglected?"

She looked back at the trees. "Apple canker. I was too busy last year and was never able to get back this far. The canker took over, and heavy weeds settled in. It was too much to tackle on my own, so I left it."

"You did all the orchard work?" he asked incredulously.

She shrugged. "Most of it. Once in a while, if my uncle hadn't overspent too badly, we'd hire a laborer to help."

"That must have been a lot of work," he said, remembering the calluses on her small hands, so unusual for a gentlewoman. That they were capable, skilled hands had fascinated him in a faintly sexual way, as if they knew what they were about.

"I did what was needed, and I didn't mind. And you needn't worry that I won't do my part now. I don't want to see the orchard go to ruin. But I don't have to like that it is, for the moment, yours."

"For the moment, eh?" He chuckled.

Her eyes flashed. "You find this a lark, don't you? That someone else's estate has fallen into your hands by a roll of the dice. You're like a child with a new toy."

"I hardly consider this estate a toy, Felicity."

"Miss Wilcox," she corrected.

He arched an eyebrow at her, a reminder that he knew her in ways that she didn't want to admit. "And I am very serious about restoring the orchard and the house to excellent condition."

"Fine," she said in a small voice. She began again, her voice bolder. "And you need have no doubt that I will do my utmost to fulfill our bargain about the orchard. We'll need at least a half-dozen workers for pruning and clearing."

"Good. Fulton has already arranged for some laborers to come tomorrow. You can instruct them as to what needs doing." He looked at her for a moment. "You know," he said, "I do want what's best for the estate." He had a strong urge to reassure her that this place she loved would be cared for, even though it would never be hers, no matter how much she hoped. He didn't want her to see him as a threat to the estate. And it irked him that she wouldn't allow that he might be an honorable man.

She fairly glared at him.

"You have to admit," he said, "that I've made nothing but improvements since I arrived."

"I grant you I've noticed that," she said grudgingly. "You are perhaps not as much of a wastrel as I had thought."

"Hah, a fulsome compliment from Miss Felicity Wilcox."

Her lips twitched in answering mirth, and she turned her horse along the back edge of the orchard. He followed her and they picked their way along the path to the western part of the orchard.

He was struck with the thought of how young she must be, perhaps twenty to his twenty-eight, and yet she'd known great responsibilities. She would make a very capable overseer, he thought as he watched her ride ahead of him, her head bobbing about as she inspected the trees and land. The thought that he was concealing his plans for selling Tethering from her gave him a twinge of conscience, but he ignored it. He couldn't afford to have a conscience about it, and anyway, there was nothing reprehensible in what he was doing. The estate was his, and he was paying her a generous amount to oversee the orchard.

The day was warm and it was past noon by the time they were done with their inspection. Leaving the rows of trees, they came upon the stream that ran along the property and stopped to let their horses drink. Doubtless the same stream on whose banks they had sat that first day, though here its banks were almost flat.

As they sat in silence while the horses drank, he dug into his coat pocket and pulled out two apples he had brought with him and reached over to offer one to Felicity. Her navy gown had seen better decades, but still he noticed how it hugged her curves. The ride had brought a pretty blush to her cheeks and loosened some of her hair—one piece waved artlessly along her cheekbone, and his fingers drummed against each other, wishing to push it behind her ear. And more.

Damn it all, he thought as she looked at him quizzically. What was he doing with this kind of daydreaming? Already he was far too warm.

She took the apple he was holding out and raised a skeptical eyebrow. "An apple. How appropriate," she said, accepting it.

"This one came all the way from London."

She examined the red fruit. "It's probably dry and

fluffy then." She took a bite. He knew she couldn't wait to pronounce it disgusting.

She chewed and swallowed, then grudgingly acknowledged, "It's better than I thought it would be."

"High praise indeed."

She scowled at him, but he could see the corners of her mouth tugging upward. "Well, it must be from last year's harvest, and the storage conditions can't be good in Town. I hear it is very dirty and crowded there."

"Perhaps more for people than apples," he said, laughing. He was struck with the thought that he had laughed more since he met this woman than he had in quite some time. "What an idea you have of life in Town. Tell me, have you ever been farther than Longwillow?"

"No, I haven't," she said. She looked away from him, over the banks of the stream, to a brilliant green meadow beyond dotted with trees and sheep, and he turned to gaze, too, upon a scene of bucolic perfection.

"I love the country," she said with surprising passion. "Beauty is everywhere I look. Why would I seek a change?"

"You know," he said, "if you cast your eyes farther beyond Tethering, beyond Longwillow, you might find something new you liked, new people."

She shook her head, and he wondered why the devil he was suggesting she meet new people. He certainly didn't mean for her to change her life by marrying some wealthy yahoo or, God forbid, the young vicar. She was far too much of a prize for that. And too much of a handful.

Felicity watched Mr. Collington as he sat astride his horse, all capable good cheer. Tethering was obviously an engaging challenge for him. He liked challenges. She wanted him to be worthless, a useless dandy, but she couldn't anymore tell herself that he was. He was knowledgeable, he made plans, he took action. All attributes she respected. All enormous obstacles in her way.

"You obviously savor travel and town living," she said. "I wonder you should want a small, provincial manor like Tethering at all. You can't be planning to live here."

"No," he replied, his expression turning sober, "probably not beyond this summer."

He pulled his horse away from the stream then and directed it up the hill toward the back of the house and the stables. She squeezed her horse onto the narrow path beside him.

"Well, what will you do with it then?" she persisted, looking intently at the side of his forward-directed face as their horses carried them up the hill toward the stable. "The estate will go to ruin if you just leave it empty."

Still looking ahead, he replied, "I am not certain. There are several possibilities. I may offer it to my Aunt Miranda."

Her heart sank at this news, and she looked away, to the overgrown currant bushes that bordered the path on her side, biting her lip to force down emotion. She realized that she had been softening toward him, just a tiny bit impressed by his capability and seriousness in dealing with the estate, and undeniably dazzled by his charming, handsome self. She had presumed that he didn't really have a plan for Tethering, that he wouldn't miss it if something induced him to give it up. Had some foolish, feminine part of her thought she might charm it out of him? That would never happen. He had a whole universe of plans that she couldn't know about, and in some of them Tethering figured.

The Reverend Mr. Crispin Markham turned away from the door of Blossom Cottage and returned to his horse. According to Martha, Felicity was accompanying Collington on a tour of the Tethering orchard. With a frown, he mounted and made his way up Tethering's drive.

He hated that the Wilcoxes' fortunes had declined so dramatically. Grimacing, he recalled the bizarre gown Felicity had worn to the garden party. At the same time, though, her reduced circumstances might just be the way to help her see sense, because it had been clear at the garden party that she was going to be difficult.

With a rueful snort, he reminded himself that she'd never been what one would call tractable. But ever since he'd been man enough to notice, she had gotten his attention. From laughing playmates they'd grown into friends, but by the time he turned eighteen he'd known he wanted them to be more. The challenge had been getting her to see him amid all the other gentlemen who vied for her attention at parties and balls.

And then her mother had died, and everything had changed between him and Felicity.

After that night, she had refused to talk about what had happened. She kept to the house and refused all visitors, including him, and what could he say? Her mother had just died, and she was grieving. And he was supposed to be going off to university. It was what his family expected, and what he had to do. So he'd left her to the solitude she'd wanted then.

He'd written to her several times from university, but she always kept the tone of her responses casual. He hadn't liked it, but he'd had the pressures of university to engross him. And what else could he have done then?

Now, however, he was back to stay. And he wasn't going to let Felicity dictate how things would be between them. Not only did he want to erase the sense that he had done wrong by her three years earlier—he wanted her. He could take care of her now, take her away from the shambles her life had become, and he meant to do it.

As he drew close to the manor, he heard the sound of voices from behind the house and directed his horse around the side. Felicity and Mr. Collington were coming up the hill toward the manor on horseback. Crispin grunted in irritation. Collington's presence and his willingness to hire Felicity to oversee the orchard were only making things worse.

At the sound of his hoofbeats, they turned to see him approaching. Calling out a greeting, he came toward them. He nodded briefly in Collington's direction and stopped his horse alongside Felicity's.

"Crispin, this is a surprise," she said. "I just sent you a note not two hours ago."

"Yes, I got it." He waggled his eyebrows playfully. "I've come to change your mind."

She frowned slightly. "I'm sorry you've come all the way here, but I'm afraid I really do have to decline the invitation."

"Why?"

She glanced sideways at Collington, who was watching their conversation with a dark expression.

"Crispin," she said in a low voice, "I don't *owe* you explanations."

"I think you do," he said in a stubborn tone, "considering what—"

Her brows snapped lower in warning.

He pressed his lips together in frustration. "Of course." He rubbed his eyes with the fingers of one hand, then sighed and forced a smile. "Of course you don't owe me an explanation about the assembly. I was just looking forward to seeing more of you. To having a chance to really talk."

She gave him a smile, and though it was only small, it sent a jolt of pleasure through him. "I do look forward to visiting with you at greater length, Crispin. Soon. But right now, things are very busy."

"They are indeed," Collington intoned from over her shoulder. "And I'm afraid we're not done here yet, sir," he said, sounding not in the least regretful, "and so Miss Wilcox and I must bid you good day."

Felicity glared at Collington. Crispin wasn't happy about how this meeting had gone, but he would speak with her later. It was not as if she would be going anywhere. He ducked them a stiff farewell and took himself off.

As soon as Crispin had left, Felicity turned on Mr. Collington. "That was incredibly high-handed of you. You practically dismissed him."

"So I did," he replied haughtily and urged his horse upward again toward the stable. "If you and Markham want to have a lover's quarrel, do it on your own time."

"How dare you. Crispin Markham's behavior has always been that of a gentleman," she said, though something hitched inside her at these words. "What a sordid mind you have."

"Do I?" he murmured with a sly curling of his lips. "Forgive me."

As they entered the stable, her spirits sank lower and lower. Things just kept getting more complicated. The efficient James Collington was at the moment legally entitled to do what he wanted with her family estate—the estate her mother had given into her charge on her deathbed—and now Crispin was pressuring her to let herself be courted, when marriage was the last thing she needed.

A stable boy appeared to see to them as they entered the stable, and James came over to help her off her horse. She reluctantly accepted his help, pulling away the instant her feet touched the ground. He seemed not to notice but took the reins to lead her horse into a stall.

She watched his tall, expensively dressed form disappear into the stall and felt a violent surge of frustration. If only Jonathan hadn't been so weak, none of this would be happening. But he had brought this man into her life, and she was not going to surrender to him in any way whatsoever. Tonight she would haunt him again, and she'd find a way to make it far more disturbing for him than it had been before.

And she was absolutely not going to allow herself to think of him in any way, except in terms of how to get rid of him. No thoughts lingering on the memory of a kiss, no wondering how he felt about her, and absolutely no yearning.

She was at the stable doors without having said so much as good-bye when Mr. Collington caught up with her.

"Just a minute," he began pleasantly, taking her arm. "I wanted to ask you something."

"What?"

His smile was tame, as if he were not holding her there against her will, but his grip was a restraint. "I am having a house party here at Tethering. A few friends and family members, nothing too large. I would like you and your father to join us."

She narrowed her eyes. "What do you mean, join you?"

"I mean I'd like you to join us at dinner, and perhaps luncheon, and for anything else."

"Anything else?"

"I don't know," he said impatiently, waving his free arm vaguely, "picnics, excursions, that sort of thing. Lighthearted country fun."

"No," she said, and tried to pull her arm away. He held on. His blackguard's eyebrows shot up.

"No? Just no?"

"Right," she said, pushing down the huskiness threatening her voice. Why should she feel betrayed that he didn't understand things at all? "My answer is 'No, I don't want to be part of your gathering of people come to see the quaint manor you won.'" She tugged firmly on her arm. He let her go.

"I'm trying to help you as well as myself. You need to get comfortable with the way things have changed."

"Anyone with a modicum of feeling would see why I—we!—wouldn't want to come."

"Oh, do stop being melodramatic." He sighed. "This situation is simply one of life's gray areas. It's unfair, but you resisting won't make it go away."

"You going away would make it go away," she said, and marched out of the stable.

Ten

James had an unreasonable urge to punch his hand into the stone back of the house. Felicity Wilcox was nothing if not infuriating. Usually he was good at letting other people's displeasure slide off him, and he was ready for her to hate that he was there. But he didn't want her to hate *him*.

Well, he would not let her be the thorn in his side that she so wished to be. She would get over her anger. And he would get over caring what she thought. He began to whistle, thinking he would go inside and satisfy himself with the degree of progress being made in the house. Few things were so gratifying to him as work proceeding apace. The sight of all the guest rooms thoroughly cleaned and prepared neatly for his houseguests would surely drive all thoughts of Felicity from his mind.

Miranda was to arrive the next day, along with his cousins Hal and Josephine, and Josephine's family. James wanted things as perfect as possible. Even more so since he'd received a note that morning from Hal informing him that Thomas Block, the powerful local

MP and a friend of Hal's, would join the party briefly. James would take advantage of this opportunity to start laying the foundation for his future. Collingtons had always been MPs, and he was the last of the Collingtons at the moment.

He had planned on seeing to some of the preparations for the guests himself since he had sent Fulton into town on several errands. At the bodega, Old Pedro often teased James that no detail was too small for his notice, and it was true. But all his work was paying off now, because the bodega was finally becoming profitable.

He walked along the upstairs hallway and stopped outside the room that would be Miranda's. The room had been covered in cobwebs and dust when he arrived, the bed badly needed a fresh mattress, and copious bird droppings had decorated the outside of one window. Nonetheless, the room had a very pretty view out over the orchard, and he knew it would suit his aunt nicely when clean, and he had emphasized that this was the new housekeeper's first priority. He opened the door and stepped in, expecting to find a fresh, pleasant country room.

Nothing had been done. Not a blessed thing, he thought furiously, looking around. The place was as filthy and unfit for his aunt as ever.

He stomped out of the room and yanked open the door to the chamber next to it. The same sort of sight met his eyes.

He went down the hallway and looked in on room after room of neglected filth, his jaw growing tight. He was ready then and there to dismiss the new housekeeper, that Mrs. Withers whom Felicity had recommended. She was clearly the worst sort of slattern. Which was no doubt why she had been recommended to him.

But.

He reined in his billowing temper.

Guests were arriving and he must have a clean, presentable place for them.

And good help was not easy to find. Clearly, he hadn't found it yet in her case. But perhaps he could mold it, he told himself as he turned to stride purposefully downstairs. He had a party of visitors arriving the next day and he could not afford to have a too-spare staff here to help. The staff who were here would have to make do.

He went in search of Mrs. Withers.

He found her sitting in the drawing room, ostensibly sewing a hole in the drapes, but her dreamy gaze was directed out the window. He cleared his throat. She glanced up immediately, a defensive look on her face. He smiled charmingly and came toward her.

"Mrs. Withers," he began in a pleasant voice.

"Sir?" she replied, managing to look as though she couldn't bear to stop work long enough to talk to him.

"I just wanted to let you know, myself, how pleased I am to have you here at Tethering."

Her jaw dropped in astonishment. He had by now guessed that his new housekeeper did not have a reputation for hard work. Rather, the latter, he expected. Fortunately, she looked vigorous enough.

"You are pleased, sir?" she finally managed to say.

He poured honey into his smile. "Very much. I

myself was told by numerous individuals," he lied blithely, "that you have sometimes done the work of three women."

She made a choking sound and fluttered her hands around her throat. "Really, sir?"

"Truly. So of course I had to have you here at Tethering, where there is so much to be done."

Here was a topic a lazy woman could agree with. She nodded earnestly. "That is true, sir, there is a great lot of work to do here, the house bein' neglected for so long."

"Exactly so," he said deferentially. "And I cannot but be glad that the care of this home will be in the hands of someone as capable as yourself."

"As myself," she mumbled, her eyes taking on a bemused, faraway look.

He hoped that would do to light a fire under her. He'd found that most people, once they believed others thought well of them, would work very hard to make sure that good opinion held.

He winked at her for good measure and saw her plump cheeks blush. "You will not be disappointed, sir, I believe."

That was one problem likely solved. And a good thing, too, since he was extremely hungry for his lunch. Although, as he walked toward the dining room, he remembered that Felicity had recommended the cook as well. He wondered with a sinking heart what Cook would have in store for him, if anything. Probably something burnt. He shuddered to think of what his guests would say if the food were disgusting. And more serious, what if she poisoned someone?

But he was pleasantly surprised by his luncheon of poached turbot in butter. It was, in fact, delicious. He even had one of the footmen send his compliments to Cook. And he thought with satisfaction that Felicity Wilcox had not been so clever as she thought.

Dinner changed his mind. The meat with its Madeira sauce was burnt to a leathery state that resisted his knife like wood, the bread managed to be both blackened and gooey, and the amount of salt used in the vegetables would have served to preserve an entire ham. Fulton, back from town, was serving him.

James threw down his fork in disgust. "Fulton, what the devil is the matter with Cook? Lunch was splendid but this meal is inedible. We can't offer food like this tomorrow."

Fulton looked uncomfortable. "I was afraid of that, sir. When I went into the kitchen to begin serving, Cook seemed rather the worse for drink."

James cleansed his appalled palate with a sip of wine. "But luncheon was superb. Can she only be relied upon to cook early in the day?"

"Allow me to investigate," Fulton said, disappearing. He returned several minutes later.

"It appears that your luncheon was not cooked with any spirits."

"Ah," James said. "And dinner was. The Madeira."

"Yes, sir," Fulton said. "I believe that she consumed at least two bottles while cooking your meal."

"Two bottles!" James exclaimed, his eyes wide. "That argues to someone with a formidable tolerance for drink."

He groaned. Felicity strikes again. Clearly the cook

was an established lush. Still, luncheon had been excellent. Cook had talent.

"Right," he said. "Tell Cook no more meals cooked with wine or spirits of any sort for now. Then for goodness' sake make sure all the bottles are locked up."

"Very good, sir," said Fulton. He cast a glance at his master's plate full of nasty food and went to get him something else to eat.

As James tucked into his cold, puny supper of bread and cheese, he thought about Felicity Wilcox. She was causing him no end of trouble, but then, that was her goal—she obviously wanted to get rid of him by making it unpleasant for him to stay. Except she wasn't having that effect at all. He liked her more than ever now, as if she were an acquired taste. Like preferring a complex, rather nutty sherry over a sweet one. He'd laughed more since he'd met her than he had in all the last few years put together.

She touched some part of him that he couldn't name and didn't want to think about, and she was unique. If the beautiful women he'd met in London were diamonds of the first water, she was an opal, soft and fiery.

Her constant nearness was driving him to lunacy, for it was lunacy to imagine doing what he wanted to do with her, a young gentlewoman under his protection on the estate. Even now the thought of her was making him quite stupid with desire for her. He'd been just about to kiss her, *again*, in the sitting room at Blossom Cottage—and he knew she would have responded.

She would make some country gentleman a good wife someday, he thought with a twist of his lips, probably Markham. There was something between them, obviously. But what?

He drummed his fingers on the table. Markham had been gone for the last several years, from what he had been told. So whatever it was between them must surely be from an earlier time. Had there been stolen kisses in the orchard or some such? Surely not, he thought irritably. That would have been totally inappropriate. And difficult. Young gentlemen and ladies were not allowed such opportunities. Parents and neighbors kept a close supervisory eye on them at all times.

He thought of Felicity's family and felt a stab of something he didn't want to name. Her family for the last several years had consisted only of her dreamy, distant father, someone who seemed hardly to have noticed that his own house had been changed out from under him. James could easily imagine the sort of chaperone and parent he had made.

He glowered at the candles on the table, which were flickering in the gentle breeze coming through the window. Why should he care, he demanded of himself, as his wicked mind alternated images of her disheveled in his bed with images of her sitting at a sedate country breakfast table, sipping morning tea with the vicar. It wasn't as if he were wanting a wife. And certainly not one who thought he was a useless cad. His whole life lay ahead of him, and he intended to use it in pursuit of challenges. Marrying was something he would do someday, he thought as he downed the rest of his wine in one swallow and poured another glass, but it wasn't anything he need think about for years.

Dammit, he knew what this was—frustrated lust. They hadn't finished that kiss on the balcony properly. That was the problem—unfinished business, something he hated. What he needed, he realized, was one proper kiss, and then he could be resolved that there would be no more. Then it would be a simple matter to put this attraction behind him. After all, she was working so hard to annoy him. Once he'd gotten over thinking about that kiss, he could just let his irritation take over, and that should finish things off between them.

He drained his wine in several large swallows and, figuring that now at least he could look forward to the oblivion of sleep, went upstairs to bed.

Eleven

Several hours later, Felicity paused in the dark hallway near Tethering's master bedroom, waiting to make sure that no one was awake. She was satisfied that she had made not a sound as she crept into the manor in her bare feet. It was after midnight and she was again disguised in her Lovely Annabelle costume, preparing to disturb the sleep of James Collington. The day spent in his company had only made her more certain she had to get him to leave as soon as possible, before she did something foolish, like throwing her arms around him and kissing him. Already Lovely Annabelle had gotten a reaction out of Mr. Collington. She'd been seen by the stable boy, too, and the gossip of servants would increase the tension in the household. With any luck, tonight would accomplish her goal of making him believe he couldn't bear to live at Tethering.

Outside, a cloud passed over the moon, dimming her only source of light, and she approached the master bedroom blindly, slowly, with her arm thrust out. Before she could reach the doorknob, which she intended to rattle, her bare toes banged into something very hard, like a statue or an urn, which hadn't been there before.

"Ow!" she said much too loudly before clapping a hand across her mouth in horror.

Searching with quiet fingers, she found the knob and gave it a brisk jiggle. Then, hoping she was not pushing her luck, she moaned once and, reaching into her pocket, extracted a generous handful of soot, which she dropped in his doorway. Then she quickly made for the hidden panel at the end of the corridor. As she crept along, the sound of heavy footsteps rushing on creaking floors sent her flying.

Someone was stirring in that bedroom!

She was through the panel and down the pole in a trice. Once in the cellar, she heard footsteps on the floor above her. Quickly, panic racing through her, she made her way to the hidden secret door. She slipped out and upward along the tunnel. Several heart-pounding minutes later, she was pushing aside the paving stone that led into the garden.

Having replaced the stone, she crouched in the bushes a moment, catching her breath, calming her racing heart, and listening. No one emerged from the house, so she trusted that her pursuer would be searching inside for her, at least for the few minutes it took for her to complete her mission outside.

Now for the second part of tonight's plan: the stables. The outdoor servants were the ones who had seen her before, so she'd give them another scare tonight.

She made for the orchard tree line, which would provide cover and a means of escape if anyone should emerge. Creeping silently from tree to tree on her bare feet, she planned to get close to the stables and make her ghostly presence known before disappearing into the orchard and returning to Blossom Cottage.

Tonight was darker, with the clouds thick over the moon, and though she knew it was silly, she felt skittish. Maybe some of her jumpiness came from knowing James Collington was on the other side of Tethering's walls. But he would be cowering and quivering. He had to be.

She was perhaps fifty feet away from the stable doors when she heard the sound of a twig snapping about twenty feet behind her.

She froze.

What had that been? Her heart knocked in her chest. She stood still, listening for several moments. Nothing but the sound of her own breathing.

She gave herself a stern shake. It had doubtless been a small animal, or maybe a branch had fallen from a tree. Nonetheless, when she started moving again, it was at a faster pace. Shortly she stumbled on a root and fell forward onto her hands and knees in a pile of crackling dried leaves and sticks.

"Who's that?" called a voice from the stables. "Who's out there?"

Someone was stirring in the stables! She stopped behind a tree, heart pounding, thinking that she'd done enough haunting for one night. The seeds of fear had been planted. Though she could dash past the stable to make Annabelle's presence distinct, the stable boy was on the alert and she might be apprehended. Better to go back to the cottage.

A twig cracked again, much nearer this time, making her already pounding heart jump. And then she heard something far worse.

"Lovely Annabelle." A whispering man's voice.

Horrors! Someone was calling for Lovely Annabelle. The ghost of Annabelle's lover?

Felicity was not going to stand around to find out. She took off like a shot, running full tilt back the way she had come, toward the corner of the house and the far-off safety of Blossom Cottage. Sticks and pebbles cut her bare feet and branches from the trees slapped and caught at her, but she flew on.

Until she ran into a tree.

"Oof," she gasped into the night stillness.

But it wasn't a tree she had collided with. Though it was hard, it was not scratchy with bark. No, it was the broad, firm, familiar chest of a man. James Collington. His arms flew up and imprisoned her against him.

She looked up at him from under her lashes, breathless, her heart thudding wildly in her chest. In the weak moonlight, his eyes flashed at her and he looked dangerous. His black hair was tousled from sleep, but he didn't look silly. Instead, with his tan skin and the dark shadow of a beard forming on his strong jaw, he looked like nothing so much as a sleeping bear awoken too early. She swallowed hard.

"Lovely Annabelle," he said quietly, and now it did not sound soft and spectral. It sounded deep and ominous and very much as if it were coming from a live man. "So, you like to play with fire?"

She stood frozen, unable to say a thing.

The voice sounded from the stable area again.

"Who's there? Who's out there?" it demanded. A shuffling sound indicated someone moving toward them from the stables.

James looked down at her. "Should I say I've caught our ghost?" Devilish lights crackled in his eyes. "Or perhaps I should say nothing and see if whoever that is can find you. Or us."

Oh, dear heaven! Would he expose her?

"Please, not?" she croaked hopefully.

He leaned away from her. "It's Collington. Out for a walk," he called. His voice rumbled in his chest and vibrated into her body where she pressed against him.

"Oh, sir. Sorry, sir," came the voice. "Good night."

"Good night," James called back. And then he returned his full attention to her.

"Well, Annabelle. You owe me a forfeit," he said. He shook his head, a lazy, menacing motion. "You are nothing if not persistent, woman. I thought I told you there was to be no more haunting."

"But why are you here? You're afraid of ghosts!" she blurted out.

"What on earth gave you that idea?"

"You did ask me to contact Lovely Annabelle for you…"

"Because I knew I was speaking to her then. And I told her in no uncertain terms that the haunting must stop."

"But I overheard your servants talking about your fears, when you thought one night that the moaning of the wind was a ghost!"

His eyelids lowered. "And you assumed they were talking about me."

"I—" she began, then realized anything she said would only make things worse.

"Foolish of you."

His thumb came up and rubbed across her bottom lip. Shivers tingled along her neck and shoulders. She waited, in fear mixed with anticipation, for what he was going to do next. He turned his thumb and examined it in the weak moonlight.

"Good. I don't think black lips would look as good on me."

He leaned forward and brushed his lips against hers gently, and she caught a whiff of wine and that manly, intoxicating scent that was James. Then he crushed his warm mouth against hers, and, sanity forgotten, she opened to him. She kissed him back and he pulled her more tightly against him.

It felt like heaven, just as she'd dreamed. The heat and hardness of his body came to her through the thin fabric of Lovely Annabelle's gown. She wrapped her arms around him and squeezed him to her.

He groaned and moved his hands to her sides, where they clasped her hips and drew her roughly against him. This time when she felt the evidence of his desire she was not shocked, but thrilled.

His hands moved upward to mold against her breasts, and she knew herself to be melting inside, her defenses, her reason, turning to mush, slipping away. His tongue stroked inside her mouth sensuously, the pleasure making her quiver. He moved his lips below her ear, his dark hair and whiskery cheek tickling her skin, and murmured some foreign words.

"*Qué bella espectra.*" His voice was husky.

Espectra. Spirit? Ghost? Her thoughts swirled dizzily. *Bella*… beautiful?

He kissed her again, and she moved her hands to tangle in his hair. The heat of his hands traveled through the fabric of her gown as he ran them up her waist and over her breasts, where they stopped to make slow, beguiling circles.

"You really, really shouldn't have come out tonight," he said, his lips right under her ear. It sounded less like an admonition and more like someone stating an unfortunate fact.

"Yes," she whispered. "I… see that clearly now."

She should pull away, but no part of her wanted to separate from him. Instead, she explored upward, skimming her hands over those shoulders that had so often drawn her attention. She buried her face in his chest and breathed in his scent that she loved.

With a quick movement, he slid his hands below her bottom and scooped her up. Their breath sounded loud in the night stillness.

"Oh!" was all she had time to whisper before he set her on a tree stump. He knelt in front of her and kissed her with gentle insistence, and she knew such a surge of being treasured, of being cherished by this man. An irresistibly good feeling.

Tentatively, she moved her hands along his sides, over the width of his ribs and inward along his waist. He shivered, as if she were tickling him, only not in a funny way.

He pushed one shoulder of her gown down her arm and her freed breast fell loose. She should have been shocked, but she wasn't, because she knew he wanted her. He pressed his lips to the base of her neck and slowly, draggingly, kissed downward along the tender skin. Both of them were breathing hard, and she heard him growl low. As his moist lips moved closer to the tip of her breast, she shuddered. And all the while, her heart was beating out a thrill: *he wanted her, he needed her, he must care about her.*

Her mind was nothing but rich, incredible sensation, urgent desires that she'd never known before and that she never wanted to come to an end. But then she became aware, with crashing disappointment, that they *were* coming to an end. He had taken his mouth away from her bosom and now, disorientingly, only cool night air lingered over the moist trail his lips had left. And then he was tugging her sleeve back onto her shoulder.

He sat back on his haunches, away from her, and looked into the darkness beyond her.

"What?" was all she could manage. How could he just stop?

"This isn't going to work," he said.

"Work? What are you talking about?" And why was he talking? Why had he stopped? She jerked at the shoulder of her gown, which was threatening to slide back down, and knew she had let herself go too far. Was he playing some kind of game with her?

"Once we had a proper kiss," he said in a gloomy tone, "I thought it would solve the problem of this attraction between us."

So. It had been a trick of sorts. It hadn't been something genuine that had arisen between them, something of the moment, but calculated for his own purposes. She should have known. He always had a plan.

He rubbed his eyes with a hand. The moonlight fell in shadows on the hollows of his cheeks, giving him a haggard look. "It's this—this thing between us. The attraction."

She crossed her arms, squeezing them tightly to her. She couldn't let him know how deeply connected she'd felt to him just now. How she'd thought for a minute, and deeply welcomed the thought, that he cared about her.

"Attraction, pooh! I'd have to be crazy to be attracted to the man who's stolen my family estate."

"Obviously neither of us would have chosen this. It's inconvenient—"

"It's impossible!"

"Admit it or not, it doesn't change what's true."

"All right. So there is some physical… force between us," she said, grateful for the cool tone she'd been able to summon when her heart felt wrung. "But what happened tonight is the end of it. Period."

James lifted an eyebrow at Felicity. She was furious at him, and probably equally with herself for succumbing, but she'd never admit any of it, and he had to admire the strength of her spirit. "Agreed. But will it be as easy as that?"

The feeble moonlight fell like silver mist on her ridiculous disguise as she sat there on the stump. Her normally pretty features looked silly with their soot smudges, and she'd be scrubbing forever to get the stuff out of her hair. Funny though she looked, he'd take her back to his room right then if he could.

"We'll just make sure that it is," she said in that cool

tone so different from how they'd been addressing each other only a minute before. Felicity Wilcox was *fun*. She'd brought him something he hadn't known in ages: delight. Along, of course, with passion. By God, the passion.

"It's as simple as this," she said. "We don't touch each other."

Simple. Right. "Very well, I won't start anything if you don't."

"Hah! You can count on that. Me starting things was never the problem."

"No?" This from the woman who'd been wandering his home and grounds at night. Whether she wanted to admit it or not, she liked to play.

"No." She turned to go then, but he caught her arm.

"You and your father will come to my house party," he said.

She didn't turn around. "I've already said no."

"Oh, but you will come," he repeated.

She turned around, her eyes sparkling angrily at him. "We certainly will not."

He let his eyes run over her disguise. "I don't think you're in a position to argue about this."

Her pretty mouth pursed in frustration. He smiled thinly.

"That's not in the least gentlemanly of you, Mr. Collington."

"It's James," he said, fixing her with a look that forced her to acknowledge all that had so far passed between them.

She crossed her arms in front of her. "Didn't we just agree to stay away from each other?"

"We agreed not to touch one another. But I won't have people thinking there's ill will between us. And anyway, how do you know your father wouldn't want to come?"

"He doesn't like parties."

"Maybe he'll surprise you. Is it right to make other people's decisions for them?"

"I know him very well. He's not interested in the kind of people likely to come to a party hosted by a fashionable gamester."

"Well, I doubt he would be happy to hear what his daughter is getting up to in the evenings."

He waited. She pressed her lips together unhappily.

Finally, she said grudgingly, "Very well, Mr. Collington, we'll come to your party."

"James," he said firmly.

"*James*," she said, as if the word itself were reprehensible.

"Thank you, Felicity," he said, enjoying using her name. Felicity—happiness. Felicity, who could make him feel so giddy, even though she also made him want to tear his hair out. "It will be my pleasure having you both as my guests. My visitors will arrive tomorrow, so you'll join us for dinner."

He narrowed his eyes at her. "And I believe I can count on Lovely Annabelle staying away during my house party? This is a game I can't allow you to continue."

Her reply was only a grunt, but he took it for assent.

"Good, because I won't have my guests being made uncomfortable by rumors or visitations."

Despite her protests that she knew very well how to get home, he walked her all the way to Blossom Cottage.

"Go away," she said, when he would have stood as she washed the soot off herself with a bucket she'd left outside the cottage.

It wasn't until the next morning that James discovered that Lovely Annabelle had left him a calling card in the form of a pile of soot outside his door that he had unknowingly tracked all over his carpet and into his sheets. He groaned and rang for a maid to clean up the mess.

Twelve

Felicity awoke the next morning to the unhappy knowledge that her haunting had been a miserable failure. Worse, she and James had *kissed*. She threw the covers over her head. She'd failed in her plan to haunt him, and only succeeded in pulling back the door to her heart that she'd kept shut for three years. Now, when she could least afford to open it even a crack, and to this man of all men.

Wonderful. She was uncontrollably drawn to the man who had taken her family's estate, a man as handsome and charming as any devil sent to tempt a poor mortal.

All these years, attraction had been something she'd had no trouble doing without. Had passion lain in wait, to ambush her? Because being attracted to James was the worst possible thing that could happen. It would undermine her efforts to get Tethering back, first off. And anyway, because of what she and Crispin had done, she could never marry. She'd vowed that she would never either explain herself to a man, or trick him into thinking she was pure. Marriage was closed to her.

James is a different sort of man, a voice whispered. *He's unconventional. He might understand.* But she knew this was nonsense. He might be attracted to her—very well, he was—but to look beyond her transgression of three years ago would take love, abiding love. And that was not what was between them.

A foolish, dreamy part of her wanted to spin a fantasy that a very grand love might grow between them, but she crushed it.

She hid under the covers from the bright sunlight streaming in her window. It was a fresh new day and she felt horrible. On top of everything last night, no one save James had even seen Lovely Annabelle. The stable boy might have thought he did, but James had confirmed his own presence, and no one would think the ghost had been there too.

Maybe, she thought dispiritedly as she got out of bed and cringed as her scratched and battered feet met the floor, she could haunt again, but this time only in the servants' quarters. Servants were a superstitious group. If she scared them enough so that they left, he would have no staff. No one would want to work at Tethering if it was said to be haunted.

She sighed and dipped a cloth in the pitcher that stood on her dresser and peered into the mirror, then began scrubbing at the traces of soot she had missed last night. She was having trouble summoning the verve, the hopeful, playful energy that the thought of haunting James had previously brought. It had all gotten so complicated.

She made a face at her still-sooty likeness in the mirror. What about haunting his houseguests? That would be quite a victory, if she could pull it off. And maybe worth the danger. He thought she'd agreed not to haunt, but she hadn't actually said she wouldn't. And Tethering had more than one secret passageway.

She pulled on a gown of dingy dotted swiss that she had dyed black all those weeks ago. It was riskier than she had originally thought it would be, tangling with James. If he did catch her again, what was to prevent him from exposing her as the strange, unchaste woman who was invading the home of a gentleman by night? She would become the local madwoman, and who would want to associate with her or her family then? What a feast that would be for the gossips. While she could stand being considered a bit odd in her old gowns, she couldn't allow her family to become pariahs. Even worse would be her father's shock and disappointment.

She didn't want to take chances, to pin her hopes on anything besides what was solid, she thought as she pulled a brush through her hair, which was rebelling against the soot and soap treatment with prodigious frizz. But she still had heard nothing from the lawyer. So she had no choice. Tethering was her life. She had to get it back.

At breakfast her father squinted at her as she bent to kiss him.

"My dear," he said, putting down the roll he was buttering as she took a seat, "you have a dark smudge by your ear." He leaned across the table, peering at her over his glasses. "It almost looks like… soot?"

"Oh." She gave a light laugh and pushed down a splash of hysteria. "I… er… dropped my hairbrush in the cold hearth this morning. Some ashes must have gotten in it."

His eyebrows shot up in surprise. She hated fibbing to him, but it was in the service of something good.

"I see." He took up his roll again. "My dear, I don't think you need to tell Mr. Collington any more stories like the one about Lovely Annabelle. We wouldn't want him to think we were trying to poison his pleasure in his new home."

"Oh, of course," she said as she put her napkin in her lap. She clutched it there, forcing her hands to stop shaking. She took a quiet, steadying breath.

"Felicity," he said, clearing his throat, "I received a note this morning from Lady Pincheon-Smythe."

"You did? How surprising."

"Yes, I was surprised. She was not my favorite of your mother's friends, but she does have a point."

"And what is that?" she said, picking up her knife and buttering her bread.

Her father cleared his throat. "She reminded me of my fatherly duty to see my daughter well married."

She put down the knife. "Really! How appallingly interfering of her."

"No, don't be upset, dear. She is right. I have been selfish these last years, enjoying having you here with me. I would be failing in my duty to you, though, if I didn't guide you toward a good marriage. Your mother and I were so happy during our years together, and I could wish nothing less for my daughter. I saw how your mother bloomed when you children came along."

He couldn't know how his words pricked her,

raw as she felt. She wasn't strong enough just then to withstand dreams of a happy family life and children.

"Father, you loved one another," she said, carefully keeping the emotion from her voice. "There is no one I care for."

"Is there not? Be that as it may, she is right that you will never meet eligible men if you don't go about in society more. She has invited you to join her at tea with her nephew, and I would like you to go."

"Oh, Father, no. Mr. Godfrey is an awful bore."

"You have met him?"

"Well, no, but I observed him at the garden party."

"Come, my dear, that is no way to get to know a person. You must give these things a chance to develop."

"But I'm so happy here with you." He had left her to herself all these years, never interfering in her social life, or rather lack of one, and that had suited her perfectly since she was not going to marry. Now was a terrible time for him to start feeling remiss.

He shook his head. "You are a vibrant young woman, and I am a contented recluse. Poetry is my life now. You must have the chance to pursue your own happiness."

"But Tethering—"

"Is no longer ours," he reminded her firmly. "That doesn't mean you cannot still be very happy and fulfilled. Lady Pincheon-Smythe will expect you next week," he said in a tone of finality. "And I want you to consider Mr. Godfrey seriously as a suitor."

"Yes, Father," she replied morosely.

They continued the meal in silence. As they were finishing, he asked, "Have you any pressing plans for today, dear?"

She put down her teacup. "I must set the workers to their tasks in the orchard, but I should be done by late morning," she said, pouring herself more tea, needing the extra jolt it would provide. "Was there something you wanted?"

"I could use your help in the library, taking notes while I review what I've written as you usually do."

Oh, help! The last thing she wanted was to spend more time at Tethering—in possible contact with James—than she had to. But she could hardly deny her father this simple request. "Of course," she said, "I would be glad to."

"Thank you, my dear," he said warmly. "You are a good daughter."

If he only knew. "Nonsense, Father," she said, "you are the best of parents. You know I always enjoy helping you with your work."

He blushed at her praise. "Why don't you come and find me in the library when you are done, then?" he said.

She nodded, then remembered her promise to James. "Mr. Collington is to have a house party and has invited us to dine with them. The guests are arriving today."

"How very kind of him!" Her father was pleased. "And maybe there will be some young gentlemen there. I have even thought that perhaps young Markham—"

"Oh, Father!" she broke in. "Truly, the role of matchmaker doesn't suit you at all."

"Needs must," he said firmly. "And we will want to be gracious to his guests, to show that we are happy to have Collington as a neighbor."

"Yes, Father," she agreed, even as she knew she'd

likely have to do her best to make James Collington and his guests uncomfortable.

Crispin wanted to have a serious, uninterrupted, and private conversation with Felicity. He found her in the Tethering orchard later that sunny morning, amid a party of laborers who were clearing and bundling brush. She was pruning a dead-looking tree with a D-shaped saw, wearing one of those shabby dresses that he hated seeing on her.

She looked up at the sound of his footfalls and stopped sawing. Putting down the tool, she dragged the back of her hand across her forehead.

"What brings you here today?" she asked with a smile.

"I was just visiting with Nanny Rollins, and I thought I would stop by and see how you were faring." He raised an eyebrow. "When you said that you would be overseeing the orchard, I didn't think you were going to be one of the laborers as well."

"I need to be in among the trees so I can see and feel how they're doing."

Hmm, he thought, how to say this without offending her? "It's not your fault, Felicity," he began, "if you don't see that it isn't appropriate for a young lady of your standing to be sawing away at tree branches. Your father does not guide you as he might."

She gave him an impatient look. "Crispin, my mother and I planted this tree together as a sapling, along with that entire row behind you. I believe she—and my father—would be happy to know that I'm seeing to its care."

"People know about Jonathan and his gambling," he said bluntly. "Everyone can see how the Wilcox fortunes have declined. And now you're working on the estate for pay, and doing the labor too. You'll have the complexion of a farmer."

"Do the town gossips think I should just sit in the dower house in meek acceptance of whatever fate delivers to me? I will apologize to no one for what I deem necessary."

He clenched his teeth in frustration. She picked up the saw again and placed it against a thick branch.

"Here, let me do that," he said, tugging it. She let it go and gave him a look. He took off his round black vicar's hat and black vicar's coat and rolled up the sleeves of his white shirt.

"Which branches do you want taken down?"

"The whole tree," she said, crossing her arms, the corners of her pretty mouth curling. Her hair was gathered at her nape in a loose knot. She was even lovelier now than she'd been three years ago. He guessed that she was unaware that crossing her arms right under her bosom as she was doing framed her breasts and pressed them upward.

He dragged his attention back to their conversation and frowned. "You weren't going to cut it down yourself, surely?"

"I was just making a start. The workers would do the heavy labor." She watched him sawing away for several moments. "If you put too much effort into that, when the branch gives you'll end up with the saw in your leg."

Pressing his lips together, Crispin shifted his position. Having been away for so long, he had forgotten how maddening Felicity could be. He sawed for several minutes until the branch came away.

He glanced around them, then leaned the saw against the tree trunk. The workers who had been toiling nearby had moved on to another group of trees some distance away, out of earshot. He turned to Felicity, gathering his thoughts.

"I know you've said you don't want to talk about what happened between us, but we must."

"No."

"We were intimate," he persisted, looking into her hazel eyes and reading her shock at his blunt words. "I compromised you thoroughly that night three years ago. We did what we should not have done. But now I want to make things right."

Silence. Finally, she responded. "Crispin, I am grateful for your gentlemanly impulse, but it is not necessary."

"Gentlemanly! I've felt at times these last three years that I could hardly call myself a gentleman."

She put a hand on his arm. "We were young, foolish, distressed. But no one suffered any consequences. We will simply never speak of it again, as if it never happened."

"No one suffered? I took your virtue! Sullied you. How could that not affect you as a marriageable young woman?"

Felicity shook inside as she listened. Lost virtue. Sullied. The words were true, but no one else except Crispin could say them to her. She herself had long ago put the whole memory from her mind.

She'd had to, for how could she dwell daily on this thing that had determined her future?

But now he was forcing her to recall that night three years ago when, with everyone overwhelmed by grief over Mrs. Wilcox's death a week earlier, the two of them had been sent to the orchard to pick apples for the overburdened kitchen. There'd been guests at Tethering then, with many people's needs to see to, and no one was watching over the conduct of two young people who already knew each other well—and surely knew the rules.

But rules had been far from her mind that early autumn night, when mortality and grief hung heavy in the air. The reality of her mother's death, of the death that awaits every human, had overwhelmed her, so that life seemed suddenly pointless. All she had wanted was an escape from her pain, and the comfort of human contact. A comfort her distraught, private father couldn't offer.

When she had turned to Crispin as they stood among the apple trees in the gloaming, an embrace meant to comfort had turned into much more. He was grieving too, needing too, like her, something that was purely of life. She had responded almost frantically to his kisses, and their touches had only grown more urgent. They'd slipped through the hidden door in the garden and lain together on his coat on the dirt floor of the secret tunnel that led to Tethering's cellar.

Afterward, she'd refused to speak of what happened, save to let him know when time had passed that there had been no consequences. She knew he hadn't been happy about her refusal to discuss it, but it had been for the best. And though she had lost much that night—her virginity, her chance for marriage—she'd also gained so much, because what happened had shocked her into taking up the mantle of responsibility that her mother had left behind.

Thinking of that time now brought back a ghost of that long-ago despair, along with confirmation that she'd made the right decision in moving past what had happened with Crispin. She hadn't loved him, and she had discovered so much as she learned to manage Tethering. Now she just needed to convince him that the past must not have any bearing on their future.

"It hasn't affected me and it won't," she said, "especially since I don't intend ever to marry."

His eyes flew open wide. "Don't be ridiculous. Marriage is exactly what you need."

"No," she said firmly. "I have Father and Simon and Tethering to look after."

He gave her a hard look. "You don't. Collington has Tethering. You're just the gardener."

She flinched.

He frowned. "I'm sorry. I didn't want to have to speak so bluntly to you, but I know you can be stubborn." He reached out and took her hand. "The truth is that I care very much for you." His voice deepened. "I think about you all the time."

She was speechless. Here was Crispin, her vicar now, a man grown. Handsome, young, strong, the late-morning sunlight glinting off his golden hair. He dropped to one knee and her heart fell.

"Felicity, darling, would you do me the very great honor of becoming my wife?"

Weighted seconds passed. She so wished he hadn't said any of this. "Oh, Crispin," she said, squeezing his hand.

"Before you answer," he broke in, his voice husky, "know how much joy it would bring me to take you away from all this." He swept an arm wide, indicating the orchard, Tethering—her whole life. Or at least the life she had had until a month ago, the life she had chosen.

And found so compelling. What did she really have at the moment? Now, without Tethering, she had that terrifying future of a too-quiet life at Blossom Cottage. There would be her father, but he mostly wanted his books, and Simon, who would come home on vacations but before long would leave to make a family of his own. Without the estate, she would have no challenge, nothing meaningful. She didn't know how she would survive the stillness and the empty days.

All right, Crispin could be an escape from that. He was the one man she could in good conscience marry. But she didn't really need to consider his offer. She hadn't loved him years ago, and she still didn't. And she didn't want to be taken away from her falling-apart life—there was still hope. All might still be righted, and she wasn't going to give up yet.

She tugged on his hand to urge him upright and looked into his earnest, handsome face. "I thank you for the honor you do me, Crispin. You are all that is generous and good. You have ever been a good friend to me, even if we have not always been wise."

His brows lowered at her tone and he looked about to speak. She pressed on. "But no, I thank you, I can't marry you."

"Felicity," he said urgently, pressing her hand with his, "you speak as though we were merely friends doing favors for one another. Nothing could be further from the truth. I was in love with you three years ago, and I—I love you now."

Her stomach lurched at his words. She respected and cared for him, then as now. The last thing she wanted was to hurt him.

"You will forget me," she said gently to him. "You must." She pulled her hand from his. "We were different then, younger, less formed. Thrown together often and not well guided. It is no wonder we formed attachments."

His face darkened. "It is not attachment I feel! It is something far earthier and more real."

"I understand what you are saying. But you deserve the wholehearted love of a good woman, and I cannot give you that."

"How can you be so sure of that?" he demanded. And she did wonder at herself, because she had no doubt about how she felt. And she knew why. Her assurance came from what she'd been experiencing since she first met James. With him, she'd felt things she'd never felt for Crispin or any other man.

He ran a hand roughly through his hair. "I've surprised you," he said in a shaking voice. "I see that. Don't give me an answer now."

"But—"

He held up his hand. "Just give yourself a chance

to consider this carefully, the advantages, and… everything we have talked about."

"Crispin," she began just as a twig snapped nearby. They turned in that direction and there was James, coming from behind a group of trees. Oh God, how much had he heard?

"Well," he said as he drew near them, his long, black-clad legs eating up the short distance, making her heart beat faster with every step, "it doesn't look as though much work is getting done in this corner."

Crispin glared at James as he came to stand among them, and James returned his look with a hard one of his own.

"Collington," Crispin bit off. "This is hardly appropriate, expecting Miss Wilcox to do actual labor. It's bad enough asking her to oversee the orchard. She is a gentlewoman."

"I don't notice Miss Wilcox complaining," James said, lazily turning a glance toward Felicity, a look freighted with something dark.

"Besides, she handles her responsibilities admirably. Why shouldn't I hire her to do *whatever's* needed?"

At the suggestiveness in James's words and tone, Crispin's eyes shot open and his eyebrows slammed together. James remained cool, though she sensed that for some reason, he was deliberately antagonizing Crispin.

"Crispin," she said quickly, "you must remember how much I love the orchard. I want to be here. It reminds me of Mother as nothing else can."

Crispin focused on her, his jaw square with clenching. He inhaled sharply, and then, nodding abruptly at her, said in a tight voice, "Felicity, Collington. Good day," and strode out of the orchard.

"Well, that was interesting," James drawled.

She crossed her arms tightly. She really didn't need to see James again so soon after all that had happened the night before. "Just what are you up to?"

He held up his hands innocently, though with his dark beauty, he could hardly have looked more like a devil. His brown eyes held a dangerous glint.

"Why, nothing at all. The young vicar seems touchy about matters concerning you, my dear. I wonder why that is?"

"If he is, it's no business of yours."

"Ah, but I do want to know what's going on between you and Markham." It was not a request.

"You don't have any right to know."

"Don't I?" His eyes dropped to her bosom, leaving a trail of heat meant to remind her of what she'd allowed him to do only hours before. "After all, as the owner of this estate, I am responsible for the welfare and protection of those who live on it. That includes you, Felicity."

"Well, don't include me. I don't need—or want—your protection."

He looked at her, his eyes hooded. "He's too young for you, you know. What is he—twenty-two or -three? But a callow, romantic youth. Probably fancies himself in love with you."

She clenched her teeth. "You are without a doubt the most arrogant man I have ever met."

He smiled in wicked satisfaction, as if she'd complimented him.

She marched off up the hill, wishing with all her might that she hadn't promised her father she would help him in the library that morning. What she really needed at the moment was several hours alone in a quiet room.

Thirteen

When Felicity reached the library, her father was of course already at work. If Oliver Wilcox was in the midst of composing poetry, he thought about it nearly every moment, and she hid a small smile when he greeted her with an abrupt "Good morning" and immediately handed her a sheaf of poems to read back to him. Having her listen to his poems was an essential part of Mr. Wilcox's creative process, and she was always pleased to play this role. This morning even more so. She needed the distraction from her racing thoughts, and focusing on words with her father was just the thing to provide it.

They got down to work. At lunchtime a servant arrived with trays of food for them. She looked with mingled appetite and dread at her portion of game pie, knowing that she had recommended the unsuitable Mrs. Bailey to James. She poked at the pastry with her fork. Her father, who was already tucking into his own lunch, glanced at her.

"Aren't you hungry, my dear?"

"I'm not sure I am, actually."

"Well, that's too bad. All the meals I've had here have been delicious, and this pie is no exception."

She had to admit the pie did smell good. But it might still be terrible. Her father did not have the most discerning of palates, especially when he was immersed in working. Well, she might as well taste it anyway, if only to have the satisfaction that her plan to ruin James's meals was going well. She took a cautious bite.

She might have known. The pie was excellent.

What had happened to the drinking problem that had gotten Mrs. Bailey dismissed from her last three jobs? The pie bore no evidence that its preparer was too drunk to cook properly. The vegetables were diced in perfect cubes, the pastry was tender, and the sauce delicious. Maybe Mrs. Bailey had simply not found the spirits yet. Well, there was always hope. In the meantime, she thought, sighing, no sense in letting a good lunch go to waste.

As she ate, she looked around the library. It slowly dawned on her that the room was exceptionally tidy. All the books were put away with their spines neatly lined up, and there was not a speck of dust to be seen. She frowned. She'd anticipated at the very least to see signs of neglect today. She had even dared to hope for a domestic crisis, perhaps ruined laundry or angry accusations of laziness. Something.

Dismay stabbed her. Was this part of her scheme not going well either? Bother it all! None of her plans had worked so far.

But she would not give up. She had no choice. Though she was going to have to think up some additional means of troubling the waters here. Something different that would have more certain consequences.

She had her chance soon after lunch, when her father asked her if she would go out and pick him a bouquet of wildflowers to contemplate.

As she was emerging from a copse by the stream in front of the manor, where she had been looking for wild roses, she caught sight of James and two guests, a fashionably dressed man and woman, and realized his visitors must have arrived. They were standing about twenty feet away, on the grassy hill leading up to the house, talking. Felicity ducked behind a weeping willow and thought. An idea quickly formed, and before she could surrender to caution, she crept down to the stream and began dabbing her dress with mud.

She would make him look bad in front of his guests. That would give him the feeling that he would never be able to trust his neighbors at Blossom Cottage—who knew what they might do? She needed him to feel unsure, uncomfortable, unhappy at Tethering.

For now, she would create for his guests a picture of James's country lover. She pulled out her hair ribbon and shook loose her hair, arranging it to hang across one side of her face, then undid the top buttons of her gown. Spying a small piece of bark loose on the ground near her feet, she picked it up and pressed it in front of her left front tooth.

She suffered a brief attack of hysteria at the insanity of what she was doing, before finally emerging from behind the tree. Tormenting James was leading her into the most bizarre and unseemly behavior imaginable. But needs must, she told herself, and marched out boldly toward where he stood talking with his guests. They were facing away from her, toward the dower house, and James was sweeping his arm out expansively, as if gesturing at his domain. They couldn't see her coming, so she called out as she approached.

"Oy, James, love," she began. They all turned at the same time, obviously startled. She came briskly toward them swinging her arms in as unladylike a manner as she could.

As she drew closer, she noted a satisfying look of astonishment on his features. His companions, a handsome, auburn-haired gentleman who looked to be in his thirties and an older lady with salt-and-pepper hair, appeared very surprised as well. A good start.

Felicity came to stand next to James, much closer than was appropriate, and smiled broadly. His eyes widened as he took in her "missing" tooth and unbuttoned bodice, and he scowled at her before glancing at his companions, who were regarding her with interest.

"Yes?" he said impatiently.

She winked at him, feeling like the comic relief in some awful small theater production. "Don't you remember me, sir? Poor Mirabelle what was so good to you yesterday?" She glanced at his guests and was both gratified and horrified by their silent watchfulness. They were definitely interested in what Mirabelle and James had been doing. Stirring up her courage, she asked, "Ain't you going to introduce me to your friends?"

Silence. His eyes had thunder in them.

"Yes, do, James," the gentleman said with an eager smile.

James sighed. "All right. Thomas Block, may I present Mirabelle…?" He was waiting for her to fill in a last name.

"It's just Mirabelle, sir."

"Right. Mirabelle. You'll want to remember Mr. Block. He's the MP for Longwillow area."

Oh, heavens! What had she done?

Mirabelle curtsied in an exaggerated manner as Felicity struggled to stay in character.

James cleared his throat. "And may I present Miss Miranda Claremont, Mirabelle," he continued, finishing the introductions. "My aunt."

His aunt. The nice one. Aaagh, she thought, weakening with panic, she would probably see these people at dinner tonight. Well, she'd just have to do this right, so that she would not seem at all the same person later when they were introduced properly.

Mirabelle curtsied again. She smiled excessively. "You didn't say last night, James—when I saw you late last night," she said as cloyingly as possible, "that you was to have real quality here."

"Didn't I? How remiss of me."

His aunt spoke. "I'm pleased to meet any friend of my nephew," she said, without the least hint of anything but polite interest. Her eyes were friendly.

Felicity wanted to run off right then and abandon her absurd plan. But she kept a hold of herself. This was all in the cause of getting Tethering back. She couldn't quit now, even if this aunt was the nicest woman ever to walk the earth. Felicity's panicking mind raced, thinking up more inappropriate behavior for Mirabelle.

"James," she said in a wheedling voice, leaning over to rub her upper arm against his, "you haven't forgotten about the present you promised me, have you?"

She didn't look up at his face, not wanting to see his expression. He was probably horribly angry by now—she was embarrassing him in front of his aunt and an MP, for goodness' sake—but that was just as well.

But his voice, when he replied, was cool enough. "Remind me, Mirabelle dear, what it was I promised to give you." She glanced upward quickly and saw that his chocolate eyes held a wicked light.

"Jewelry," she said outrageously, figuring that was a likely enough gift for a doxy.

"Ah, yes," he agreed in a smooth, deep voice. "A reward."

Her face flamed at the suggestiveness of his tone. She knew very well that he intended to remind her of their passionate kiss the night before.

Mr. Block coughed once and said, "Jewelry. My word."

"Some of the gentlemen what I have known is not as generous as my lord. They doesn't keep their promises."

His aunt was nodding. "That's true, my dear. You must look out for yourself and make sure that gentlemen," she cast a stern look at James, "keep their promises."

He held up his hands in surrender. "Of course.

Mirabelle knows that she will definitely get what's coming to her."

That did not sound good. She'd done enough here—it was time to leave.

"Well, now that that's settled, I'll be going." His aunt said good-bye to her and wandered off to inspect a heavily blooming pink rose bush. Mr. Block, on the other hand, was now regarding Mirabelle with entirely too much interest.

"But you're not going to run off, are you, dear girl, when we've all just met?" he said. "Perhaps you'd like to give me a tour of your neighborhood. I'd be pleased to meet with more of my… constituents."

Her stomach flipped over at this disastrous idea. The eager look on Block's face suggested he wanted to get to know her in a most unsuitable way.

"Yes, Thomas," James said, "that sounds like an excellent idea. I'm sure Mirabelle would be glad to… entertain you."

Mr. Block grinned at Felicity.

"Oh—er," she stumbled, looking to James for help.

He smiled innocently, as if he had no idea how she was squirming. "Shall I give him your direction?" he asked her.

"No—no thank you," she said hurriedly, blinking and smiling like an idiot. "Must be going. Good-bye, then."

"You're not going to leave without a farewell kiss, my dear, are you?" James asked.

"Oh—" was all she could reply before he grabbed her arm firmly and planted a kiss right on her lips. The bark on her tooth poked a bit as his mouth came against hers, and she could feel him smiling evilly against her lips.

"You'd better run fast," he whispered against her mouth before releasing her.

"Good-bye, Mirabelle," he said louder, giving her backside a surreptitious squeeze and a brisk shove as she turned. Already almost running, she waved good-bye to his bemused guests over her shoulder and fairly sprinted into the woods, her heart racing.

She didn't stop until she was well away and hidden among the trees, where she could lean against a large maple and catch her breath.

Dear heaven above, had she really just done that? Her chest heaved with exertion and excitement. How on earth had she, a nice gentlewoman, had the nerve to be doing things like that in broad daylight? What would her mother have thought of the lengths Felicity was going to in order to regain the estate?

And could she truthfully tell herself that scene had only been about Tethering?

The pull of James enticed her. Something about him invited play and risk.

But she hated risk, she reminded herself.

And yet she felt so alive.

Unseen behind a tree, Crispin stood with his mouth dropped open in astonishment. He had come back, wanting to talk to Felicity again but not sure what to say, and stopped among the trees to think. And, hidden from view, he had come upon the scene he had just observed.

What on earth was she doing dressed like—like some kind of tart!—and showing herself to Collington and those other fashionable people? He hadn't been able to hear what was going on, but he could see that she had let her hair down and unbuttoned her gown quite low. Collington might have been able to see down her gown, he thought with an angry twist of his lips, never mind that the man had kissed Felicity and, from the angle where Crispin stood, seemed to have groped her bottom. What the devil was going on?

He knew himself to be at that moment a sham vicar, because he wanted to stride over and plant Collington a facer. And more!

A calm voice of reason whispered to him that Mr. Collington could hardly have asked Felicity to dress in such a manner—she had done that on her own. And maybe Collington didn't recognize her, since she looked different with her hair down across her face. And she seemed to have done something to her teeth.

She had told Crispin she meant to get Tethering back, and he knew she was deeply attached to the estate. But had she decided to sacrifice everything—her very respectability—in pursuit of it? She certainly had the capacity to be whimsical, which he knew from experience did not always work out well. But this—this—charade was taking things too far! Didn't she realize what she was doing?

Crispin strode in silent frustration among the trees toward the front gate, knowing he wasn't ready to talk to her now. He needed time to think.

She'd been carrying too much responsibility for too long, and now she was taking wild chances. He was beginning to wonder if she could be trusted at all not to do something totally reckless. He knew one thing. He wouldn't sit by and watch her ruin herself.

James watched Felicity escape into the woods. Damn. She was going to cause real trouble at this rate. Ever unjudgmental, Miranda wouldn't care a bit about Mirabelle, but Block was an MP. What if he noticed there were strange doings at Tethering—if he realized that the gentlewoman living in the dower house was pretending to be James's lover, or heard about Lovely Annabelle—and made a news item out of it? Though from what James knew of Mr. Block's powers of concentration, he was hopeful that when Block did meet Felicity, he would not recognize her. But he couldn't count on it.

"Eh, James," Block said, shading his eyes as he searched the trees for Mirabelle, who fortunately had disappeared effectively. "That's one your brother Charles would have appreciated. Take after him, do you, heh, heh? Just hope you don't share all his traits, heh, heh, or the funds might not be safe."

James closed his eyes as irritation surged, but he said nothing. Catching Block's eye, he looked pointedly at his aunt, trying to shame the man into dropping this line of conversation. Block was apparently slow in taking hints.

"Know any more like her, do you? Wouldn't mind a tour of the area, I say, not at all."

James clenched his teeth. Thomas Block was a successful fool, well-spoken when he needed to be, affable, and powerful, but lacking in any discernible moral conviction. A politician of a stripe not unfamiliar to James, who had grown up around politicians, some he respected and some he plain disliked, but all of whom had to be tolerated and treated well. He had never liked many of the aspects of politics that his father and brother so clearly enjoyed—the jockeying for position, the glad-handing, the negotiating of compromises with devilish people. James could succeed in politics—he knew what he would have to do, and he was personable enough. He only wished he felt more enthusiasm for the undertaking.

He sighed. He was going to have to find enthusiasm for an MP's life somewhere if he was going to repair the image of the Collington family that Charles had left in people's minds. Meanwhile, he could only hope that the honorable Thomas Block could not stay long at the all-too eventful estate of Tethering.

When Felicity returned to the library and her father, her hair was secured neatly at her nape and she was somewhat collected, though her gum was still throbbing from the bark. Her father was seated at the table where he had been all morning, though her view of him was obscured by several tall piles of books.

"If that's you, Felicity dear," her father's voice called out, "could you bring the flowers over to me?"

"Yes, Father," she said, grateful she'd remembered his request on the way up to the house. Glancing down at the pale pink roses in her hand, her eye was caught by the sight of her still-unbuttoned gown. She had just finished hastily doing the last button when he stuck his head around the pile of books.

The sunlight caught a smudge of dust in the corner of his spectacles, and his white tufty hair, too, looked the worse for having been clutched with dusty hands. He must have been looking into some of the older, infrequently used volumes.

"Wasn't that Crispin I saw out there, in the wood?" he asked.

"Crispin? No, I don't think so."

"I think it was, dear," he insisted. He moved the pile of books slightly to his left so that he could see her better and leaned across the desk, steepling his fingers. "You know, I believe he admires you."

She merely blinked at him, astonished that her oblivious parent should have noticed such a thing.

Mr. Wilcox hesitated, cleared his throat. "In fact, I didn't want to say anything earlier on—I have never liked to pry into others' affairs—but I see now how very remiss I have been in not doing so."

"Oh, no, Father, really."

He held up his hand. "No, my dear, these things must be discussed. I have a fine view of the estate from here, and, well, I noticed earlier today, while you were in the orchard, that Crispin took your hand rather urgently."

"Goodness, Father," she said, feeling creeping panic, "I'm sure it would have been hard for you to see anything from the library."

Her father gave her a look. "You forget that I am a poet, my dear. Reading the meaning behind a man clasping a young lady's hand is child's play. He has proposed to you, hasn't he?"

"Well," she began, still trying to adjust to her father's sudden and growing interest in her romantic life. While Felicity's mother had sometimes talked about marriage and the future with her, when she died, any discussion of such things stopped, because Mr. Wilcox never said one word to Felicity about men or marriage. He'd never shown any interest in her social life or desire to interfere, and that had suited her perfectly. Oh, why, now that things were getting so complicated, must he start to show an interest? Drat that Lady P-S!

Her father waited patiently for her to answer. He was wearing a black and gold striped waistcoat over a white shirt trimmed in red, doubtless put on at random that morning, as usual. Oddly, his garish clothes never detracted from a quality of dreamy sincerity she associated with her father. She couldn't outright lie to him.

"Yes," she admitted. "He has proposed."

"But that is wonderful news, my dear!" he cried. "Why didn't you say so?"

"Because I don't want to marry him."

Mr. Wilcox's brows drew together in astonishment. "But whyever not? I would be pleased to see you married to such a fine young man!" He gave her an encouraging look. "And I don't mind telling you that having your future secured would be a weight off my fatherly shoulders."

She hated the idea that she might be a burden to her father. When they had had Tethering, she hadn't been. If anything, *she* had been supporting *him*.

"I truly have no wish to marry, Father," she said. "But I will see about helping out at the village school in the fall."

His face clouded. "What's this? Not marry? But you might have your own house and children. I'm certain I should love some grandchildren. Crispin Markham would make you an admirable husband."

She mutely shook her head, her heart sorer by the moment.

"Surely you don't want to be an old maid? You are lively. You should be around other young people." He shook his head. "This is my fault. I have allowed you to take on far too many tasks in recent years. Lady Pincheon-Smythe was right."

"Oh, bother Lady Pincheon-Smythe!" she exclaimed in exasperation.

"Felicity!" her father said sternly. "She is right. You ought to be married. You've had one offer now, and a good one it is, and the chance of another offer, if I don't miss my guess, from Mr. Godfrey, Lady Pincheon-Smythe's nephew, whom you are to meet at tea. Lovely though you are, I am afraid that not many eligible young men are likely to be found around Longwillow village, and as we cannot afford to journey anywhere, you'll have to pick from either of them."

"Oh, Father, no!"

"Oh, my dear, yes. I am afraid I must be firm on this subject, for your own good." He paused, oblivious to her horrified expression. "Of course," he mused, staring into space, "there could be the possibility of an offer from Mr. Collington."

She could take no more. "Father, I beg you will say nothing further."

"All right, my dear. But you have heard me. You will have to make a match, and soon."

Fourteen

Felicity took extra care dressing for dinner that night, and not just to ensure she looked very different from Mirabelle so that Mr. Block and Aunt Miranda wouldn't realize they were the same person. Even if she and her father were outside of what was fashionable, they could still present themselves well.

She put on the nice black satin gown again, liking the weight and fit of it as it hugged the curves of her waist and bosom. She twisted her hair into a neat, upswept style at the back of her head, leaving several strands to fall gently against her cheeks and neck, and tucked a few tiny pink roses into it. Her mother's pearl necklace again sat at the hollow of her throat.

Mr. Wilcox was waiting for her in the cottage foyer, looking handsome in his dark evening clothes, which fortunately had very little ornament on them. The only sign of the dated origins of his attire were the charming little red heels on his evening slippers, which made her smile. The red heels were meant to be the final detail for a man who wanted to be at the height of fashion. In 1760.

When she and her father entered the drawing room at Tethering, James and his guests were already standing about, talking and drinking sherry. She was surprised to see Crispin there, but then she remembered that James had invited him to the dinner party when leaving the church garden fete. With a sinking feeling, she realized that Crispin's deciding to come likely had more to do with her than any amicable feelings toward his host.

James stood near the door with his aunt and a very fashionably dressed woman, whose dramatic gown looked out of place in Tethering's unostentatious drawing room. As he made introductions, Felicity's heart pounded with fear that his aunt or Mr. Block would recognize her. But Aunt Miranda showed no sign of having seen her before, save a brief initial wrinkling of her forehead. And Mr. Block, she soon realized, was a person of scattered attention.

The lady with James was Mrs. Lila Pendleton, a widow. She had raven-black hair and exquisite alabaster skin, and her slender figure showed to perfection in her very low-cut gown of crimson. Felicity noticed, much to her displeasure, that Mrs. Pendleton stood close to James's side and frequently touched his arm.

The other guests were James's cousins: Lady Josephine Dunlop and Viscount Roxham. Lady Dunlop's husband, Sir Robert Dunlop, a baronet, was also present, and the couple had two beautiful little girls, Lydia, who was five, and Alice, seven, who were taken away by a maid after they had been presented. For being aristocrats, James's family was remarkably unstuffy. Quite the opposite, in fact;

Viscount Roxham winked at her when they were introduced, and Lady Dunlop smiled warmly. Her husband seemed shy.

Felicity found herself in a group with Mr. Block, James, and Mrs. Pendleton.

"And how is business at the bodega, James?" Mrs. Pendleton asked. She held herself in a composed, erect manner, as if she would not be induced by anything to smile too much, laugh too loudly, or ever allow a dab of gravy to cling to her lip.

"It's going very well, actually," James replied. "I just received a note from my agent in London to confirm that shipments are moving as they should."

Mrs. Pendleton looked at him rather as though she wanted to do something with him; kiss him perhaps, consume him in some way. Instead, the lady said, "Well, when you are back at Granton Hall, you must give a ball. It will be the best way of announcing your intention to stand for Parliament."

"Parliament?" Felicity repeated.

Mrs. Pendleton turned to address her with a look that said *she* was well established in James's inner circle. "James is going to be an MP. Isn't that right, Thomas?"

Mr. Block was nodding. "He's just the sort of fellow we need in Parliament. Great political lineage and all that. Gets things done."

"Yes," purred Mrs. Pendleton. "Just like his brother and his father before him."

Felicity was watching James. So, more plans. An MP. Of course. He would do very well in Parliament. It took no effort to imagine him steering policy and making deals and speeches. She guessed he would find that supremely rewarding. Only he didn't look at all pleased by the discussion of his future. His face held a tight, closed-off expression.

He'd do well as MP married to someone like Mrs. Pendleton. They'd be two perfect people. They could revel in one another's perfect company and have some perfect children.

She looked away and pushed down a memory of the vulnerability she'd heard in his voice the night before, when he'd told her she shouldn't have come out to haunt. There'd been so much more than admonishment behind his words. But none of that mattered at all. She could see that so much clearer now.

Viscount Roxham turned to Felicity. "You must come and look out the window with me, Miss Wilcox," he said.

"Must I, my lord?" she replied, but she let him take her by the elbow and lead her over to the window that gave onto the front lawn. They stood together gazing out over the hillside, down to the stone facade of Blossom Cottage, which was gradually being obscured as dusk gave way to evening. The window was open, letting in the heady scent of the rose bushes blooming just outside.

"Mr. Collington's family must be very well known and respected," she said. She was watching a moth crawl along the windowsill, making its way into the house.

Beside her, the viscount shrugged. "They have at times been important members of Parliament. But James's brother was very far from the eminent personage Lila presents. Lila likes what she thinks is going to be fashionable, and she wants to get her hooks into James. He's been out of circulation for a while, off in India and then Spain."

The viscount was very, very handsome in what struck her as an exceptional way. He had wavy, short blond hair and a freckle off to the side of his mouth, and his blue eyes were speckled with green and gold so that they looked lively. And full of mischief—there was a slant of teasing wickedness there that she expected women of every age must find irresistible. It made her want to smile; she liked him already. She rather supposed it would be impossible for her, as a woman, not to.

He smiled back, creating devilish little sideways dimples—clefts?—behind his mouth. "But never mind about them, Miss Felicity Wilcox," he said, his blue-green eyes twinkling. "How is it that I have never seen *you* in London?"

"Quite simply because I have never been there, my lord," she said. She smiled in spite of the dull feeling in her stomach.

"You must call me Hal, lovely girl, or I shall think my dear departed father is standing behind me."

He spoke of his dead father so cavalierly and so lightly. "Heavens, what on earth sort of son are you, sir?"

"Oh," he said cheerfully, "the very worst sort, I assure you. Went in for all the naughtiest of boyhood pursuits: snipped little girls' pigtails, scandalized the maids by putting frogs in the beds and swapping Dr. Pitt's loosening draught for the treacle. An awful tease, I'm afraid."

She laughed, scandalized and amused at the same

time. Here was a careless rogue indeed. "I'm sure the household must have been relieved when you grew up and matured."

"I'm afraid not," he said, shaking his head. "Unfortunately, young men can get into quite a bit more scandalous behavior than boys." He arched an eyebrow suggestively, and she found herself laughing more.

"Oh dear. Whatever did your parents think of you?"

"Couldn't stand me, of course." His glance wandered to a spot behind her a second before she heard James's voice.

"Quite right they were, too," James said, coming to stand next to her. She glanced at him and was pleased that the glamorous Mrs. Pendleton was not with him.

The viscount excused himself to go speak to Aunt Miranda. As soon as he was gone, James leaned in close to her so that, with their backs to the window, only she could hear him. His words came out in a tone of dark honey.

"You had better behave yourself tonight, Felicity, if you know what's good for you. No visits from Mirabelle, and let me remind you that Lovely Annabelle is not to make an appearance either while my guests are here. I'll have every reason not to keep your secret if you cross me on this."

She couldn't ignore the threat in his tone, though scared was not exactly how she felt. His warning touched her somewhere deeper, in the part of her that liked to play too much.

His hand stole around behind her and skimmed up her back before coming to rest, hot and large, on her bare nape, just staying there. His threat of exposing her was real—she saw it in the intensity of his dark eyes.

All right, he was deadly serious about not being made a fool of in front of these people. But this was James, and his hand still felt like forgotten heaven, and she wanted to press against it and be enveloped by it.

"I want you to promise me you won't haunt while my guests are here," he said low.

"I, um, I," she said. Trying to think with him so near, and with that hand on her neck that made her want so much more that she couldn't have, seemed impossible. She forced herself to focus, and to step to the side so that he had to drop his hand or risk being seen touching her. She was sorry when his hand fell away, but also grateful.

Why was he so very concerned about her disturbing his guests? She glanced around at them, skipping over his aristocratic cousins, who seemed to be on very amicable terms with him. Her gaze came to rest on Thomas Block. An MP. James wouldn't want to have something happen while an MP was there. And Mrs. Pendleton, too, she thought as she caught some strains of Mrs. Pendleton gossiping. Felicity's gaze returned to James, who was watching her.

Ah. He didn't want his guests bothered because he didn't trust some of them not to make a public story of strange doings at his house.

"Felicity?" he said with a warning note, his brow lowering.

She scowled at him. "I understand what you want," she said.

His features relaxed and he leaned near her ear to

whisper, "Thank you, sweet witch," the soft wisps of his breath tantalizing her ear and neck.

Hal was coming back toward them then, and James moved discreetly farther from her. She watched him laughing at something his cousin had said, his white teeth flashing in a boyish grin that brought out those crinkles at the corners of his eyes that *did* something to her. By the stars, but he made her heart flutter. His touch, even the feel of his breath, made her senses sing.

She had to be honest with herself. She loved jousting with him, loved disrupting his plans. If he left Tethering, he would take all the fun with him. And if he stayed much longer, it was easy to imagine making herself ridiculous over him. He was a very wealthy gentleman who enjoyed taking risks and having adventures. He was going to be an MP and marry someone like Lila Pendleton. Felicity was the daughter of an impoverished member of the very minor gentry whose clothes weren't even from the current century. Her family had fallen in stature to almost nothing. And why was she even allowing herself a fantasy of truly being with James—of marrying him? She knew she could never marry. In a saner moment, she had taken that vow to remain unmarried. It had been the right and honorable thing to do, and it still was.

James leaving Tethering was the best thing for the future of her family, and for her heart. She had all but agreed not to haunt while his guests were there, but as soon as they were gone, she must redouble her efforts. Her shoulders sagged slightly. She had just about lost her taste for Lovely Annabelle's antics.

A servant came by with a tray of food to nibble.

Felicity and James declined, but the viscount selected something and popped it in his mouth.

"Excellent!" he pronounced. "I must compliment you on your cook, James. For a bachelor, you are setting up a household well."

"But you must give your compliments to Miss Wilcox, Hal," he said, turning toward her. "She is the one who recommended Cook."

She blushed at this undeserved praise. "Um..." she began as she glanced at his eyes and read there that he knew what she had tried to do. He must have experienced something awful from Cook's hands. Well, a small victory. "I am glad you have found that she suited."

"Doubtless you are," he said, and something flickered in his eyes that said *touché.* "And you'll be pleased to know how delighted I am with the talents of my diligent new housekeeper as well."

"You are?" She couldn't help her shocked tone. Mrs. Withers was being praised as a virtuous worker?

"Very much so, but surely that's not surprising to you, Felicity, since you recommended her as well."

She smiled as guiltlessly as possible and was saved from the necessity of a reply by the arrival among their group of Mrs. Pendleton, Mr. Block, and Crispin.

"There you are, darling James," the widow drawled, linking her arm with his. He gave her a smile full of charm.

"Say," Mr. Block said to Crispin with a dawning grin, "you're the local vicar, aren't you? Don't suppose you know that minx Mirabelle? I've a mind to pay her a visit before I leave."

Felicity blanched.

Crispin looked quizzical. Before he could speak, Mrs. Pendleton asked, "And who is Mirabelle?"

Mr. Block winked at James. "James knows her. Introduced us this afternoon." He turned to Felicity, his head cocked. "Funny thing is, she looks a bit like Miss Wilcox." He bobbed his head contritely. "Begging your pardon, miss, if you know her. Different sort of person. Not a lady."

"Oh, ah, no, I don't know her," she stammered. Was Mr. Block playing a game with her? But the look in his eyes was completely sincere. "Perhaps she's from one of the farms."

"I don't know her either," Crispin said tightly, giving Felicity a surprisingly stern look, as though he knew what she'd been doing. But how could he?

"Well, I don't know why we're talking about her if she's not of good society," Mrs. Pendleton said. "Is she, James?"

"Ah," he began. Felicity stole a glance at him. Would he give her away?

"She is from a good family that has fallen on hard times," he continued. His eyes shot little sparks at Felicity. "But I am sure she will soon put her feet on the right path, if she knows what's good for her."

"Well, let's speak no more of her, then," Mrs. Pendleton said, and Felicity, as much as she disliked the woman, could have kissed her.

Mr. Block and Crispin were called away then by Sir Robert Dunlop. Crispin gave Felicity a look as he left that seemed freighted with meaning, but she could not guess what he was trying to intimate.

Mrs. Pendleton's gaze fell on Felicity. "So, Miss Wilcox, have you been to Town this season?"

"Miss Wilcox does not like Town," James said, watching Felicity with a smile teasing at the corners of his mouth.

"What? Not like Town?" Mrs. Pendleton regarded Felicity with particular scrutiny, no doubt, Felicity thought, taking in the odd cut and color of her gown and her simple hairstyle. Felicity tipped her chin up proudly. "When were you last there?" the woman demanded.

"Indeed, Mrs. Pendleton, I have never been to London."

Mrs. Pendleton's eyebrows shot up in astonishment. "And yet you declare that you do not like it!"

"Actually, it was Mr. Collington who said so."

Mrs. Pendleton glanced at James, who shrugged. "Well, do you or don't you like it?" she demanded of Felicity.

"As you yourself have suggested," she replied, trying to keep from giggling as she caught James's laughing, conspiratorial gaze, "I can't say I don't like it, never having been there. I am fond of the country, though."

Mrs. Pendleton smiled in satisfaction. "Just so. You certainly have that country air about you." She looked pointedly at Felicity's attire, frowning. "Your modiste seems to be very old-fashioned," she pronounced. "You might do with something more current, Miss Wilcox, even if you are never to go anywhere."

Felicity couldn't help laughing outright at Mrs. Pendleton. "I suspect the tailor who made this gown has been dead for some years. It belonged to my late Great-Aunt Matilda, who loved balls and parties when she was young."

Mrs. Pendleton's eyebrows shot upward another fraction, and Felicity enjoyed a moment of wicked glee, knowing she had thoroughly appalled the woman. She was clearly at a loss as to how to reply to the idea of wearing the outdated clothing of long-dead relatives.

Aunt Miranda moved to join their party just then, and she apparently heard Felicity's statement.

"Miss Wilcox, how charming, that you are wearing a relative's gown! That argues to a wonderful appreciation of family. And it does look splendid on her, doesn't it, James?" she said, putting her hand on his free arm. Mrs. Pendleton still held on to the other one.

"Miss Wilcox always looks charming," James said, looking intently at Felicity. The merriment was gone from his eyes now. "She has a fashion all her own."

Felicity burned with pleasure at his words but was afraid to look at him for more than a moment, lest he see how his compliment made her want to beam. Instead, she smiled at his aunt. "Thank you, Miss Claremont. You are most kind. I enjoy wondering what my great-aunt might have been doing when last she wore this. Perhaps it was to a ball."

"Well, if she was half so pretty as you, my dear, I am certain she would not have wanted for partners," Aunt Miranda said warmly.

In the next moment, a look of delight broke over the older lady's face. "But, my dear," she said, her eyes bright with excitement, "why don't we just ask her?"

Felicity's brow furrowed. "I don't understand, Miss Claremont, ask who what?"

"Why, your Great-Aunt Matilda, of course. You can ask her if she ever wore that dress to a ball. And anything else you want to know."

"Oh, Miss Claremont," Felicity said, comprehending. "You must not have heard me. My great-aunt died years ago."

"But I do realize that."

Felicity was unsure. Was Aunt Miranda playing some game with her? But the older lady looked sincere. Very sincere, and very eager. Mrs. Pendleton, however, wore a disgusted look, and Felicity noticed that James's face was queer. The viscount merely looked amused.

"We can contact her through my medium!"

Fifteen

Felicity and Lila looked suitably astonished. James hoped he himself did not look aghast. Hal, of course, thought it was a lark. Devil take it, Miranda had always been one to give credence to odd mystical ideas, but this was too much. Was she going senile? Talking to the dead? What on earth had she been getting into in his absence? Clearly he'd been gone too long.

"Oh," Felicity said slowly. Then she smiled at Miranda, with a genuine look of pleasure that was not in the least condescending, and James could have kissed her for it. "Ah, thank you, Miss Claremont. That would certainly be fascinating, if ever I am in London."

Miranda's eyes were alight with excitement. "I've already communicated with my dear sister Louise, who died several years ago."

"Oh, really, Miss Claremont," Lila said impatiently, "don't you know that this communicating with the spirits business is all a load of rubbish? I am astonished you give it any credence at all."

Miranda blinked, her gray-blue eyes vulnerable. James was at a loss as to how to intervene—he didn't want his aunt's feelings hurt, but he couldn't have agreed with Lila more.

Felicity filled the heavy pause. "That must have been a great comfort to you, Miss Claremont." She placed a kindly hand on Miranda's arm.

Miranda was pleased. "I believe I should like being in London with you very much, Miss Wilcox."

Lila was just turning a harshly skeptical eye on Felicity and no doubt preparing a comment when Fulton appeared to let James know that dinner was served, to James's great relief. He didn't want his guests engaged in a conversation that could only make Miranda look ridiculous. But later he must think more on this problem of Miranda and the trouble she might get into. She was strong in so many ways, but unfortunately susceptible to charitable pleas and brave new ideas. He meant to bring her to live at Granton Hall, but left alone there when he traveled, he could see her turning it into a meeting place for wayward spirits and a refuge for orphans.

Crispin appeared by Felicity's side to lead her into dinner, his mouth set in a grim line that made her nervous.

"I saw you today," he said in a low, urgent voice. "When you were pretending to be that—"

She bit her lip. Oh dear. How much had he seen? Well, it had all been harmless, after all.

"Mirabelle," she whispered. They were the last couple in line approaching the dining room, several feet behind the viscount and Lila.

"I want to know what's going on between you and Collington."

"What do you mean?" His harsh tone startled her.

"There's something between you two. I can see that."

"That's—that's not true," she said. "There's nothing between us. I hate that he's here and I'm trying to get him to give up Tethering by making him uncomfortable."

"I don't believe you. You're tending the orchard for him, acting out crazy charades, and laughing into his eyes every chance you get." Crispin's lips met in a tight line. "Did he know that was you today or not?"

"Yes, of course he did," she replied angrily. He was slipping into full big brother role, and she wouldn't have it.

His eyes shot wide. "But this is outrageous!"

"Since you are outraged," she snapped, "you can just leave me alone. You needn't watch."

The other guests had entered the dining room, leaving Felicity and Crispin alone in the hallway. She quickened her step toward the doorway, but he grabbed her arm, keeping her from entering, and pulled her back a few steps from the door.

"Just a minute," he said, his eyes narrowing. "You don't by any chance have anything to do with rumors I've heard about a ghostly lady at Tethering Hall?"

Rumors had reached Crispin? But that meant she was having an effect! This was good news.

He was watching her. "You do, don't you?"

"Crispin," she said, tugging her arm away from him, "just leave me be."

"No." His chin stiffened in that bossy way she remembered from childhood. "I won't stand by and watch you ruin yourself. As your friend and your vicar, I'm telling you now that if I hear of any more crazy antics at Tethering, I'll bring this before your father. He'll know how to make you see reason."

No! Not that. Her father was too good. He trusted her, and she couldn't bear him knowing how she'd disobeyed his wishes. He wouldn't see what was practical and fair here. He wouldn't understand how she'd needed to do what she did—he'd only push her harder to get married now that he had the idea she needed a husband.

"If you do," she said, forcing her voice not to shake, "I shall never speak to you again." And she turned away and made for the dining room doorway.

From where he stood at the head of the table, James could see Felicity and Markham in the hallway. What the devil were they muttering about out there? Markham was looking at her in an intense, totally unsuitable manner. What *was* between them? It had damned well better not be something like a secret engagement.

What the devil? Now Markham was grabbing her arm! James was just making for the door when Felicity entered looking flushed.

"Miss Wilcox," James said, "here you are at last. Your seat is next to me." He indicated the chair to his right. Before Markham could move, James had stepped behind her chair and pulled it out for her.

James smiled with secret nastiness at Markham. "You're at the other end, Markham. Next to Mrs.

Pendleton." The vicar, who looked for a moment as if he wanted to run James through, scowled deeply and went toward his seat.

Felicity sat down, and before James could even say a word she was talking to Hal. The servants appeared and began serving soup, and James watched with growing irritation as Felicity ignored him for his disgustingly handsome cousin. What could they possibly have to say to each other in such quantity?

Eventually, keeping an ear tuned to Hal and Felicity's conversation was taking up so much of James's attention that several times he found Robert jabbing him in the ribs and saying, "Isn't that right, old boy?" James merely agreed with Robert each time since he had no idea what was being discussed between him and Mr. Wilcox.

Now Hal was telling Felicity exaggerated tales of his daring. To be truthful, James had to admit that the tales were not really exaggerated. Hal *had* done heroic things during his military service. But James could not stand the look of admiration that had settled onto Felicity's face as she listened to him.

Finally, Hal began to speak of his mastery of foreign languages. This James definitely could not stomach.

"Come now," he broke in, "what is this faradiddle you are peddling to Miss Wilcox? You most certainly do not speak French like a native. Why, I am certain that innkeeper in Paris is still trying to understand why you asked God to wound him when he sneezed."

Hal winced and Felicity laughed.

James wished mightily that he and she were alone. Then he could raise a hand and touch her sweet lips with his fingers, and brush them against her satin cheeks. Her laughing eyes made him yearn to possess—there was no other word for what he wanted—the creamy skin of her shoulders and bosom, so richly alluring in the flickering candlelight. It would be like fragrant satin, he guessed, and as intoxicating as he found her every time he'd touched her. He almost regretted that she had agreed that Lovely Annabelle wouldn't make an appearance while he had guests. He yearned to tussle with his ghost, bedamned to propriety, fairness, and every other limitation.

Felicity could feel James's eyes on her. She turned her head to look at him and with a jolt saw the raw desire in his eyes. His gaze felt hot—at least, it was making her feel hot, as if he were kissing her with his eyes. She sensed them on her, warming the bare skin of her shoulders and bosom. Her lips and skin hummed with the memory of his kisses.

"And how is your Spanish these days, cousin?" Hal asked James.

James pulled his eyes away from hers and chuckled. "*Touché*, cuz. Not good, but adequate for talking with my staff at the bodega. And I have engaged a master to begin lessons on my return in August."

"What's this?" Mrs. Pendleton demanded from across the table, where she sat between Crispin and Mr. Block. "You're not studying Spanish, James?" She coughed scornfully. "Surely you have people there to deal with the natives."

"I prefer to handle things myself," he replied. "Though Hal is right. I spent so much time learning the sherry business that I haven't taken the time to learn written Spanish. But I will correct that this autumn, when I make a visit."

Mrs. Pendleton rolled her eyes theatrically in a thoroughly English expression of disdain for lesser peoples. "What can you possibly learn from the Spanish?"

"The local people have much to teach me about sherry production."

"I hope they'll have helpful advice when you are poisoned by the food and contract some vile local disease," she said.

He laughed. "All at once, Lila? That would be quite a feat."

Felicity fixed him with a gimlet eye. "The first time *I* encountered *you*, sir, I ended up covered in mud."

He looked surprised by her mention of their first meeting, and embarrassed too, at the suggestion her words carried that he had done something ungentlemanly. The idea that he was squirming delighted her.

"What's this?" Crispin asked in a tight tone.

"Yes, it sounds like the devil of a story!" chimed in Mr. Block.

Felicity regarded James archly. "The first time I encountered James Collington, he startled me into Yardley Stream."

"But I didn't know you were there at the time," he protested.

"You fell into the stream?" Mrs. Pendleton asked with a scandalized expression that said ladies didn't fall into streams.

"Yes, I was picking watercress at the time."

"Really!" Mrs. Pendleton was aghast. "Don't you have servants for that?"

Felicity knew delicious mischief was dancing in her eyes at James's discomfort, because she could feel it bubbling up inside her. He scowled at her, though his eyes were merry, and she almost giggled. She couldn't stop herself from teasing him, playing with him, tormenting him.

Her father looked at her. "So that was the cause of your mud-splattered clothing that day, my dear."

James looked pained.

"James!" scolded Miranda. "I am horrified that you caused this young lady to be covered in mud."

Felicity almost felt bad for him.

"I have already apologized, as Miss Wilcox is well aware," he said, sending Felicity a meaningful look. "But I will do so now again."

He bowed his head apologetically. "I beg you will accept my deepest apologies, Miss Wilcox." A lock of his black hair had fallen forward to curl above his eyebrow, and in the candlelight the masculine planes of his face were even more defined. He was far, far more handsome than any man ought to be. His cousin the viscount might be equally handsome, but James held a special appeal for her, something that went far deeper than the way his features were arranged.

As he looked at her, his lips wore a wry expression but his eyes smoldered, demanding she remember all that was between them.

"Accepted," she said. "It was, fortunately, a very old dress."

"Do you have any that are not?" Mrs. Pendleton asked.

"Lila, dear," Hal said, "weren't you going to tell me all about the Manderly affair?"

The party broke up not long after dinner, with most of the guests pleading fatigue after their travels. As James was seeing Felicity, Mr. Wilcox, and Crispin to the door, Mr. Wilcox recollected something in the library that he needed, and he left them all standing in the entry hall.

Crispin's hand was on the doorknob and he looked from Felicity to James with a dark expression that worried her.

"Well, good evening, Markham," James said. "Thank you for joining us this evening."

Crispin, tension written in the stiff line of his posture, did not look as though he wanted to leave, but he could not reasonably do otherwise.

He compressed his lips firmly for a moment, then abruptly said, "Thank you for the invitation, Collington," in a voice devoid of gratitude. "Good evening." He gave Felicity a pointed look, sketched a bow, and departed without another word.

They were left standing alone by the door. James lifted an eyebrow to her in silent commentary, but she made no reaction.

A candelabrum on the narrow hall table cast shadows on the pale green-painted walls. The night was growing cool, and she wished she had brought a wrap. She hugged her arms.

From above them, sounds of the guests moving about in their rooms filtered down. But the first floor was quiet, and intimate, with James standing not two feet from her.

"It seems your father is either among books or thinking of books," he said, breaking the silence.

She sighed. "Yes, and the Tethering library is probably his favorite place of all. You have been generous. Thank you."

She looked at him steadily, at the now-familiar face of the man who was living in her family's home. She could no longer conjure the anger and resentment she had first felt toward him. Her heart sank. She was losing her fire—in fact, it had almost entirely faded. Her ferocious feelings against James had been replaced with warmth, affection, and desire. Despair crept in.

He shrugged, his broad, capable-looking shoulders in his dark evening coat making her heart turn over. How good his shoulders had felt under her hands the night before.

"You are both welcome here. And I do value your contributions to the estate and the orchard. Although," he said, fixing her with a shrewd look, "I don't think I shall ask you for any more staffing recommendations. My palate has barely recovered from Cook's first assault."

Felicity laughed softly, thinking of him eating whatever foul meal Cook had prepared. However, her efforts in that area had ultimately had little effect. Despite what may have happened initially with the cook and housekeeper, the house and food bore witness that James had obviously brought the staff around to wanting to please him. Just as he was doing, with the magic of his charm, to her. Was there anything this man couldn't accomplish when he set his mind to it?

"There's to be a picnic outing tomorrow," he said. "You and your father will come, of course." He said it pleasantly, but he was not offering her a choice.

She knew she most certainly could not spend the day at a country picnic with James and his guests. That would surely be the end of any resolve she had left to get him away from Tethering. And get him away she must.

"No, thank you," she said. "We shall not be coming."

He lifted an eyebrow. "We had an agreement, Felicity."

"Yes," she said, and forced coldness into her voice, "but we've done enough tonight to create for your guests the illusion that there are no hard feelings between us."

Felicity's words stung James. Had they only been creating an illusion that night? That wasn't what it had felt like. He regarded her unflinchingly, allowing the silence to drag out, so that she felt forced to continue.

"I've already played the friendly neighbor!" she said in a tighter voice, as if she were very tense. "What more do you want from me?"

His eyebrows shot up at her mention of playing the friendly neighbor, which could only remind them both of Mirabelle's visit earlier that day. Her hazel eyes grew stormy.

"We do *not* need to come."

He wanted to growl in frustration. Where was his laughing temptress of earlier, who had teased him in front of his guests? He wanted her back, the smiling minx who laughed and flirted, not this woman who only refused him. He wasn't going to do anything to her, not any of the things his fantasies had already supplied. But he needed her to be as she had been. They could at least enjoy one another's company. He wasn't ready to give that up.

"But you will," he said in a voice that would brook no argument. "It's Miranda's birthday tomorrow, and I want it to be a special day for her. She has taken a liking to you and your father, I can see that, and she would be very disappointed if you didn't come."

Her face registered a struggle between warring impulses, no doubt between wanting to tell him to go to the devil and not wanting to hurt his sweet, kind aunt. James was fairly certain he could count on her essentially good nature winning out. He really hoped he was right. Funny how the idea of a picnic without Felicity now sounded like a day without sunshine.

"You're fond of blackmail, aren't you?"

"I do whatever it takes to achieve my plans. I hardly think you have grounds to complain, Mirabelle-Annabelle. And there'd better not be any other 'belles' lurking about."

"Oh, very well," she grumbled, looking down at where her hands hung clasped against her black gown, "we will come."

"Good," he said, and his hand lifted to brush against her soft cheek even before he'd willed it. She looked up, startled, and he experienced a small victory in her look of astonishment mingled with pleasure as he pulled away. In the next moment Mr. Wilcox's footsteps could be heard approaching the entryway, and they stepped abruptly apart. But not before she shot him a terrific scowl.

James and Miranda were the only two down early for breakfast the next morning, and he was glad for some time alone with her. Looking at her as she sat across from him, a smallish, trim, older woman with graying hair and wrinkles where once her handsome face had been smooth, James was acutely aware that she was of an age when health began to decline. Miranda had been like a mother to him, and the thought that he might be out of the country when she needed him worried him. Catching his eye, she smiled at him, bringing out the crow's feet that added life to her gray-blue eyes.

Was it right to leave her without a family member while he was gone? She was in good health, vigorous even, but she was getting older. Maybe he should decide now, before leaving, to limit how long he would be away.

"You look pensive, my dear," she said, regarding him over her teacup.

He smiled. "I'd like you to come to live at Granton as soon as it's back in my control."

"Why, thank you, that's a delightful idea. I've always loved Granton."

He knew that familiar anger that surged whenever he thought of his brother and the endless troubles Charles had caused. "I'm sorry that you haven't been able to be there these last three years."

"Don't worry," she said.

"Well, once I pay off the debt and we can return to Granton, I want to see you happily settled there. But I will also have to be gone sometimes."

Her eyes narrowed into a shrewd look. "And you're wondering how this aging old aunt of yours will get along without you to look after her."

He frowned. "Miranda, you are as vigorous as a young lady, but I do worry about leaving you without family for months at a time."

She put her cup down and smiled confidently. "Well, you can put your mind to rest, dear. I'll never be entirely alone again. Josephine has become a good friend to me, and Louisa will always be with me in spirit, which is a great comfort."

He cleared his throat. This was a delicate subject to approach. "As to that, Miranda, I am a bit concerned about this medium of yours, this Madame Lottie."

"Why should you be? She's done me a great service in helping me to communicate with dear Louisa. I am grateful to her."

"Yes," he said slowly, considering how best to proceed. "I'm delighted if she's brought you happiness. It's just that, well, to be frank, people like Madame Lottie have been known to accept a great deal of money from their clients. I want to be sure that she is not one of those people."

She gazed at her empty cup, not meeting his eyes. When she spoke, her voice was very quiet. "I don't expect you to understand this, James. You're all about reason and logic, and this has to do with the heart and the spirit."

Damn, he'd gone at it wrong. He didn't want Miranda to feel he was judging her.

"Yes, I do give her money," she continued. "It's small compensation for what she offers me."

She looked up at him then, and he knew they would not discuss the matter any longer just now. But he was no more at ease with it than he had been when he raised it. He didn't like the idea that, once they had regained Granton Hall, she would be alone there with just the servants for company when he was gone to Spain or London. What if she *were* going senile, as he had feared when she first spoke of speaking with Louisa? Though she seemed lucid enough now. But she was too trusting—more trusting than he could ever be—and that might lead to her being taken advantage of. Older people were not infrequently abused by servants. But he saw that he couldn't express any of these concerns to Miranda. She would be insulted and hurt.

They ate in silence until she spoke several minutes later. "Tethering Estate is a very nice property."

"Yes, isn't it?" he grinned. He was pleased with his success at Tethering. The house was shaping up nicely, and the crew of workers Felicity was directing had the orchard in healthy condition. He still had much of the five hundred pounds he'd won at hazard left, and he had received word yesterday that all was going according to plan for the sale of the sherry. The receipts from the sherry, along with the five hundred pounds and the proceeds from the sale of Tethering, would pay off Charles's debt, though James would not have much left in the end. But once the debt was cleared, he could begin receiving the rents again, and the bodega would keep producing. All would be well. Although, now when he thought about selling Tethering—leaving it—the idea held less dazzle and charm than it first had when he won the estate and saw how it might solve his problems. He didn't want to think about why. He couldn't afford to.

"I almost like it more than Granton Hall," Miranda said carefully, watching him as she spoke.

He didn't like hearing her say that, but he had to acknowledge that his own affection for Tethering had grown. Granton Hall was not charming or intimate, but a statement of a family's excellent lineage. The Collingtons were an old family that had for three hundred years been respected landowners and members of the House of Commons. Now, thanks to Charles, that respectability was tarnished, but James was going to see it righted.

"And how do the Wilcoxes feel about you being here?" she continued. "It must be a bitter pill, though they handled themselves admirably last night."

He tugged at his shirt collar, which was annoyingly tight. Fulton must have shrunk it. "I don't think Mr. Wilcox minds much at all, but Miss Wilcox is not happy about it." A gross understatement, but Miranda did not need to know the details. He shrugged. "That's fate for you."

"Fate?" she repeated. "Hmmph."

"I'll have to sell it to pay off the debt. And then we can return to Granton Hall, where we belong."

"Ah. I see." She paused. "James, do you care about securing Granton Hall because you love it, or because you're angry with Charles?"

Her words startled him. For the last three years, he'd been unable to think of Granton without a sick feeling because of what Charles had done. Very well, truth be told, perhaps he did not so much pine for its familiar buildings and land at the moment as yearn for it not to be tainted. "Both, of course."

"The scandal was three years ago. So what if people then gasped in delighted dismay about Charles Collington's downfall and savored the gossip they heard about the estate? I doubt anyone remembers now, or cares. Except you. Charles was always a thorn in your side, wasn't he? Too loud, too undisciplined, too emotional. He was excess while you are quite the opposite. He must have been an embarrassing sibling."

James didn't want to dredge up anything to do with his brother. He simply wanted to go forward. "The Collington name is a good and old name, and it deserves to be respected."

"You can't forgive him for what happened, can you, James?"

"I can hardly forget. He saddled me with a huge debt!"

She sighed. "You're right, James, but being right won't make you happy. Charles is dead, and he cannot offer explanation or apology. We can't even be sure that he didn't just make a mistake about the amount, or that he wasn't convinced he would soon have the money to pay the debt."

"Yes," James said drily, "with the hospital funds he took."

Miranda grimaced. "Charles was doubtless more grandly flawed than many of us. Too inclined to work deals and exaggerate his own capacities. But it doesn't matter anymore because now he's gone. And the only one who's suffering is you."

"I am not 'suffering,' as you put it, but I would like

to point out that I am hugely out of funds still, thanks to my brother."

"Nonsense, James. Even without Granton Hall, you now have a fine home here at Tethering, plus the proceeds from your bodega. I'd say you've done very well for yourself." She paused. "I hope you won't undervalue what you've already achieved."

"On the contrary, Miranda, I am quite satisfied that things will work out as well as I might have hoped."

She sighed and reached over to caress his cheek with a gentle stroke. "James," she gave a half smile, "you always did have wonderful things you were going to do. And now you *have* done some good things. Why not let go of the past and stop to enjoy what you've accomplished?"

He could only smile quizzically at her.

Sixteen

The day of the picnic outing was quite glorious, a quintessential English summer day. The sun shone in a soft blue cloudless sky and the air was light and fresh, carrying with it the teasing scents of myriad blossoms. A breeze gently lifted the leaves in the trees now and then. All nature seemed to be in harmony.

By late morning the carriages that would take the picnic party on their outing were being loaded. Felicity stood waiting in the drive with her father and watching Lydia and Alice, Sir Robert Dunlop and Lady Dunlop's young daughters, flitting about in their yellow frocks like two butterflies. The little girls were eager to get going, and they circled their parents insistently and badgered the servants loading hampers with their questions, and unknowingly charmed Felicity all the while. It was a bittersweet feeling, because giving up her hope of marriage all those years ago had meant saying no to children. And while that hadn't seemed such a sacrifice at seventeen, now it truly did. She couldn't allow herself to consider this now, she knew, or she'd be lost to tears, emotion, foolish behavior. Envy was wrong, it was poison to the spirit, she reminded herself.

She decided then that she would treat the picnic day as if it were outside of time. She would allow herself to enjoy whatever pleasures presented themselves. Today was a gift. She might as well have one full day of freely enjoyed pleasure in the company of James and his family. He would be gone soon, apparently, off to be an MP and see to his other business. And all their time together would simply be part of the past.

"Aren't you done yet, Fulton?" cried Lydia in her high little voice, dancing around at the man's feet. His arms were full of a large picnic blanket.

"Not quite yet, miss," came the muffled but patient reply.

"Lydia, leave Fulton alone," scolded her older and much wiser sister. "You're going to make it take longer to be ready."

"Oh, do sit down, girls," Lady Dunlop implored her children. With reluctance they seated themselves under a tree and began pulling up violets.

Finally it was time to go and the party set out in two carriages, with the Wilcox and Dunlop families riding together in one and James and the rest of his guests in the other. Mr. Block was apparently going to conduct some local business during the day, and so did not join the picnic.

They drove for perhaps half an hour, to a spot among a low sequence of hills where the first raspberries of summer were growing in large patches on the sunny slopes. The little girls escaped happily from the carriage, bubbling over with plans to pick as many berries as possible.

Hal announced that he wished to stroll along the stream at the bottom of the hills and then climb them for a view of the surrounding countryside and issued a general invitation. Lila Pendleton, James, and Aunt Miranda agreed to come along, and Mr. Wilcox declined politely and sat down with barely concealed eagerness to read peacefully under a tree. Felicity volunteered to go berry-picking with Lydia and Alice, while their grateful parents rested on a picnic blanket. The servants began unpacking lunch.

Felicity followed along behind the little pastel butterflies as they rushed excitedly from clump to clump of ripe red berries, shouting whenever they saw a cluster and eating as many as they put into their baskets. She had been picking for about a quarter of an hour when she became aware of a rustling sound several feet from her. Lifting her head to see what it was—perhaps a rabbit she could point out to the girls—she realized that it was coming from behind an enormous, thickly overgrown patch of raspberry canes that was hopelessly intertwined with a stand of forsythia bushes. But it wasn't a rabbit after all, she realized as she drew closer. Someone, no doubt one of their party, had strolled over that way and was speaking.

Not wishing to eavesdrop, she was about to make her way closer to the children, who were begging her to come see how many berries were in their patch, when she heard Mrs. Pendleton's sharp voice from the other side of the bushes.

"James, what are you up to here?"

"What do you mean, Lila?" came James's voice. "Aren't we just taking a walk? You were the one who wanted to come this way."

She made a sound of exasperation. "I mean at this piddling little estate, Tethered Up or Dithering or whatever it's called. It's practically a hovel compared to Granton Hall. Why spend a whole month here when you could settle things and be off to Granton?"

Felicity's blood started to boil at such dismissive treatment of her beloved home, but then she reminded herself that she did not really care about the opinions of Lila Pendleton, fashionable snob. And that people who listened to others' conversations heard things they did not like. But now she could not move. She had to hear what James would say.

"I like Tethering," he replied. "I find it charming. And I need to see to some renovations."

"Really, James, you must have done just about all that can possibly be done to that little manor already. Fulton can see to the rest. Why don't you come back to London with me tomorrow?"

He laughed. "Actually, you'd be surprised at what could go wrong at a place like Tethering Hall."

Felicity blushed as his words.

He continued, "Anyway, I quite like it there. It's peaceful."

"Peaceful! Ha!" scoffed Mrs. Pendleton. "What's keeping you there isn't peace, James Collington. It's Felicity Wilcox."

Felicity strained toward the bushes, trying desperately to lean closer without making any movements that would cause sound. She had to hear his reply.

"Miss Wilcox," he said, "is an unusual and interesting woman. Rather a funny little country mouse, I grant you."

A funny country *mouse*? Had he really just called her that?

"I've seen the way you look at her when you think nobody is watching," Mrs. Pendleton said. "There's something between you."

A sharp cry from up ahead suddenly drew Felicity's attention, and she turned to the direction where the girls had been picking berries.

"Miss Wilcox!" Alice was shouting and waving her arms. Alarmed, Felicity rushed over to the girls and discovered that little Lydia had tumbled into the raspberry patch. Felicity's face was still flaming from the conversation she had overheard even as she gently extricated the tearful child and inspected two small scratches.

James and Mrs. Pendleton arrived a few moments later, having heard the commotion. When it became apparent that Lydia was all right, James suggested that they all rejoin the group for lunch. Felicity watched Mrs. Pendleton and James walk in front of her. They had been lovers, she guessed, and maybe they still were. That was why Mrs. Pendleton talked so freely with him of his affairs. But this hard woman shouldn't be James's type, Felicity thought, pressing her lips. The widow was all snobbish *ton*, concerned with nothing but fashion and society, while James was noble, devilish, playful—and far too good a man for Mrs. Pendleton. Felicity was horribly jealous, and also more than a little disgusted with him for liking Mrs. Pendleton at all.

Felicity took her seat on one of the picnic blankets next to Lady Dunlop. The luncheon offering looked delicious; Cook had clearly maintained her sobriety and outdone herself. But Felicity wasn't hungry. She nibbled halfheartedly at a thin piece of cold beef and watched James talking to his aunt and her father. The sunlight was dancing in his wavy black hair and he was grinning at something Miranda had said. Did the man, in addition to being a dutiful nephew, have to be kind to Felicity's father and hardworking and smart? Couldn't the man who won Tethering have been nasty and boorish with buckteeth and a paunch? Couldn't he have been like Lady Pincheon-Smythe's nephew, whom, God help her, she was meant to consider a suitor?

She swallowed a piece of beef that might just as well have been a wad of stocking for all that she tasted it.

"Well, Miss Wilcox," Lady Dunlop said, breaking into her thoughts. "It must be awkward having my cousin owning your family home."

Felicity almost choked, so startled was she by Lady Dunlop's frankness. Swallowing with difficulty, she glanced at her father, to see if he had heard, but he was deep in conversation with Aunt Miranda.

She thought to dissemble but caught the steady look in Lady Dunlop's eyes and decided she would answer truthfully. "It was awkward at first, but James has been… considerate. A good neighbor."

"I see," the other woman said in a way that suggested she had a good enough imagination to guess how Felicity might feel. "James has always been both lucky and able to make the most of what he had."

Felicity said nothing.

"He lands on his feet," his cousin continued. "But then, he makes his own luck."

Lady Dunlop considered Felicity. "Had you never heard of the Collingtons before he came here?"

"No," she replied drily, "but apparently I should have."

Lady Dunlop chuckled. "The family has been entwined with the running of the country for generations. About three years ago there was a notorious family scandal that provided entertainment for the gossip sheets for several weeks. His brother Charles, an MP, was unfortunately killed while making off with a large amount of money entrusted to him for a hospital building fund. Once Charles was dead, it came out that he'd ruined the family fortunes. That was why James went to Spain."

Felicity was astonished. James wasn't rich? "He ran away to Spain?" she asked incredulously.

Lady Dunlop laughed. "Of course not. He went there to make his fortune in order to clear the debts. That's why he bought the bodega."

Felicity blinked. "So he's not wealthy?"

"Wasn't. But he's on the way up again. Because of the success he's made of the bodega." Lady Dunlop looked rueful. "Acquiring your home was, I'm afraid, a valuable coup for him."

"I see," Felicity said. Everything was so much clearer now. Tethering wasn't anything like a new toy for James, or simply a challenge. The estate's rents would be the means to remake his future—no wonder he was putting such effort into its workings. "He never said."

Lady Dunlop gave a wry half smile. "Well, he wouldn't, would he?"

No, of course he wouldn't, Felicity thought as her companion's attention was claimed by Lydia. James needed Tethering, she thought. It had never occurred to her that he *needed* it at all.

She had a sudden urge to give up her whole plan to get back Tethering. Knowing he needed it, she suddenly found she actually wanted him to have it. She felt a rush of forgiveness toward him—he was no longer her adversary at all, but someone who needed Tethering, just as she did. Well, not quite as much. He was still much better off than the Wilcoxes, obviously. But now she felt compassion for him. He'd had troubles too, though he gave no sign of them.

She tugged wretchedly at a patch of weedy grass growing near her edge of the picnic blanket, her heart rioting. What would happen if she gave up trying to make Tethering unpleasant and embarrassing for him?

He might stay.

She couldn't have that. She would be just down the hill from him, at Blossom Cottage, inescapably close. He was too fascinating. Completely irresistible.

Oh, how had things come to this? She hadn't been yearning for someone to come along and change her life. All right, she'd had her silly moments of wishing for a fairy godmother to fix all their money troubles and cure Jonathan of his gambling. And maybe she had, once or twice, allowed herself to wish she'd never made that mistake with Crispin, that she might be able to marry. But that kind of thinking turned too easily to pity, and she had been so fulfilled by what she did for Tethering that it had been easy to let those kinds of thoughts go.

James was so different from anyone she had ever known. She flushed hotly, remembering how wonderful, how magical it felt to be in his arms. Truthfully, she wanted to be there now. And she knew he wanted her there too.

Clearly she'd allowed herself to get too caught up with him. Her life wasn't about thrills and adventure, even if some foolish part of her seemed to crave it. She was a girl who liked to be busy with something meaningful, the way running Tethering had been meaningful, even if the meaning had been in small things, like creating the right environment for an apple tree to fruit, being a caring mistress to her servants, and sharing a meal with her father from the produce of their estate. James Collington was a confident risk-taker, blithe adventure-seeker, and heart-palpitation-inducing charmer whose world was filled with powerful, glamorous people. Not what this "funny country mouse" needed at all, even if she could have had him. Which she couldn't.

Oh, what did it matter who he was anyway? One way or another, he would be gone at the end of the summer. And, she very much feared, he would be taking a little piece of her heart with him. It must only be a very little piece.

Lady Dunlop was still talking. "I think," she said, "that what James needs is the adventure of marriage and parenthood, which I am here to tell you must be infinitely more jaw-dropping than anything he's yet encountered."

After this astonishing statement, she smiled kindly at Felicity. "I'm afraid I am more outspoken than is proper, but as you have no doubt noticed from my cousin Hal, it is a family failing."

The other woman's frankness left Felicity breathless. But she quite liked her. "I prefer plain speaking myself."

After that, Lady Dunlop was apparently pleased to move on from discussing James, for which Felicity could not have been more grateful.

She was surprised to notice, as she ate her lunch, that her father had abandoned his solitary reading and seemed to be conversing very animatedly with Aunt Miranda. Felicity couldn't hear what he was saying, but he looked so happy and engaged, gesticulating occasionally as Miranda nodded and talked, that Felicity realized her father might have been lonely for the company of people his own age. Of a woman his own age. She certainly couldn't be surprised if he was enjoying Miranda's company; Felicity liked her very much herself.

When lunch was over, Felicity allowed Alice and Lydia to lead her over to the little stream that ran at the bottom of the hill. She sat talking with them and let them undo her hair and thread violets and buttercups in the loose strands. The girls named her Fairy Queen Felicitania and made her a ring and bracelet of braided clover flowers.

Alice and Lydia had each brought a doll, and soon the dolls were the fairy queen's devoted handmaids, who were to go to a fairy ball Felicitania was holding that night. The three whiled away the afternoon making leaf dresses for the dolls and fancy shoes of braided grass, and they laughed and imagined together. Away from the adults and talk of things that could only distress her, Felicity felt happy. Carefree, as she had wanted to be that day.

The afternoon shadows were growing long when James came and scattered them, growling and moaning, pretending he was the ghost of the stream. The little girls jumped and shouted and giggled hysterically and ran about, with a grinning James running after them. He "wooed" and waved his arms at them, chasing them among the trees and hedgerows for several minutes, until the girls and their pursuer collapsed in a pile near Felicity.

When they had caught their breath, Alice sat up.

"Uncle James," she said, her small, light brown eyebrows set in a serious line, "ghosts don't come out during the day. You are silly," she pronounced.

He was lying on his side in his white shirtsleeves with his long body stretched out, his head propped up on his elbow and his black hair tousled from chasing the girls. He put on a look of disappointed astonishment, and Felicity couldn't help giggling.

"No!" he said in mock seriousness. "But how can we know what ghosts might do? Don't they have free choice about when to haunt?"

"Of course they don't," said Lydia soberly in her high little girl's voice.

Alice agreed. "Everyone knows that ghosts only come out at night. They like the darkness."

"But what if they are thirsty?" James queried seriously. "Can they have tea?" His laughing dark brown eyes were now all concentration as he considered the problem.

"Nooo!" wailed both girls, giggling and rolling in the grass with glee at the delicious ridiculousness of this adult. When they had recovered their seriousness, Alice said, "They can't eat and drink or pick up things, except haunting things, like chains."

"So they wouldn't, say, dump a pile of soot on your floor?" He flicked a glance at Felicity, raising his eyebrows. Her lips twitched at his teasing.

"W-e-e-l-l," said Alice thoughtfully, "I suppose they might, but it doesn't sound much like a ghost thing. Just messy. Sounds more like something a naughty goblin would do."

"I see," James said, nodding seriously. "A naughty goblin. I think we must have one of those at Tethering."

"Oh yes, probably," agreed Lydia. "Mummy says we must have naughty goblins at home because our clothes always end on the floor and our toys aren't put away and we're sure it's not our fault."

James glanced at Felicity, one eyebrow quivering upward in mirth. "What do you think, Queen Felicitania? Can ghosts do whatever they like?"

His eyes were dancing with laughing light, and she threw a handful of violets that she had absentmindedly picked at him. She should have known he would be good with children; he had been happy enough to play games with her.

"I think," she said, getting up and shaking out her dress, "that it's time for tea. And Aunt Miranda's birthday cake." Her hair was still loose, and she realized it was well sown with dainty weeds, but she would not have dislodged them for the world, no matter how wild she now must look. Leaving James to bring the girls, she made for the clearing, where the tea table had been set up under the shade of a tree, as if her life depended on it.

Seventeen

James watched her go, her flowery golden curls bobbing and her skirts whipping as she walked briskly away. Almost as if she were escaping from something, which was ridiculous, since they'd been having a perfectly pleasant time here with the girls. Quite a bit more fun than he'd had all day, actually. He'd forgotten how pleasant and easy life could be in the country; he really hadn't taken any time to smell the roses these last three years. In general, perhaps, he forgot about rose-smelling. But Felicity made him remember. She was so easy and fun to be with, at least when she wasn't trying to be disagreeable. Apparently today she had put her dastardly schemes aside—she hadn't said or done anything to torment or embarrass him all day.

Yes, he thought, helping the girls up and escorting them, one on each arm, to where the tea things were set up, he liked this part of the country. For a moment he wished he could forget all his plans and just stay at Tethering. Life was so pleasant here, airy and light and fun, yet strangely compelling. He allowed himself to imagine the delights of late summer and fall, when there would be the festive doings of the orchard harvest. And the pleasure of Felicity's company.

He shook his head, wondering at himself as he deposited the girls with their parents and collected a cup of tea and some cake from Fulton. He sat down alone under a low-branching, leafy tree near where the blankets were arranged and reminded himself that the subtle, sweet pleasures of Tethering would surely be fleeting. After all, the beautiful Felicity Wilcox could not remain unattached forever. But James didn't want to think about the future, when she'd probably marry the damned vicar. And if she didn't, there'd be someone waiting behind him. James even suspected his own cousin Hal of wishing to deepen his acquaintance with her, for all she was of such minor gentry.

Felicity was sitting some yards away from him, on a picnic blanket with Hal and a petulant-looking Lila. The sunlight was shining in Felicity's long, loose, dark gold waves. He was struck with a desire to bury his face in its beautiful, silky mass. She was wearing another one of her funny, home-dyed mourning dresses, and he found himself wishing he could see her in a pretty gown for once. She was laughing at something Hal must have said, and even from where James was sitting, he could see that her hazel eyes were merry and bright. She was so lively, so lovely.

Lila caught the direction of his gaze and smirked at him. He suddenly wondered how he could have ever been attracted at all to Lila. She was a beauty, but that was all. Underneath, what did she have but the manners and interests of every other woman of the *ton*: fashionable clothes and the latest entertainments? He was suddenly glad he would soon be in Spain again and away from fashionable people. And away from Tethering Hall and Felicity Wilcox, which were beginning to take on far too much meaning. Because the only meaning she could possibly have if she were going to be in his life would be as his wife. Being with her even today and not being able to touch her was already enough of a torment for him.

Watching her now as she sat in the dappled sunlight, he imagined kneeling behind her, pulling her to him, exposing the angle of her neck and kissing all along it. In his mind he placed his hands on her round breasts, allowing their fullness to expand his fingers.

Her loose hair, the freed golden waves, bounced in the wind as he watched, teasing him. He must not touch her, yet his fingers and lips itched to discover everything about her.

With a muttered curse he looked away from the party, toward the stream. He would discover nothing further about how Felicity might feel in his arms because she was an innocent young lady, and getting leg-shackled was the furthest thing from his mind. As appealing as she was, he must make sure there were no more kisses. He pushed thoughts of her from his mind and addressed himself firmly to his tea.

After tea was over, the adults began to make noises about its being time to return to Tethering. Lydia and Alice, however, were crestfallen at the idea of leaving.

"But Mama," Alice said in as reasonable a voice as she could muster, no doubt aware that whining was guaranteed to put her mother in an ill-humor, "we haven't been all the way up the big hill yet." She smiled angelically, and James was certain *he* would not be able to resist such an entreaty. "We did so want to see the view from the top."

Lydia's round child's face looked very sad. "Papa," she said softly, "I want to climb the hill, too."

Robert and Josephine shot one another long-suffering looks. They began gently to hush their daughters, explaining that the party had been there long enough and everyone was tired.

"I'm not tired, Josephine," James announced, standing up and drawing in an exaggeratedly deep breath. "This fresh country air invigorates me." He grinned. "I'd be happy to take the pixies up the hill."

His cousin smiled at her daughters, whose faces now looked hopeful. "Why, thank you, James. That would be kind of you, for the girls' sake."

"Yes, good idea, James," added Miranda, looking up from her conversation with Mr. Wilcox.

"Cousin James," piped up Alice, "can Miss Wilcox come?"

"Of course, if she wants to."

Alice and Lydia glanced pleadingly at Felicity. "Please come, Miss Wilcox," the two little girls sang out together. "You want to see the view too, don't you?"

Felicity looked startled and flicked a glance at James. He shrugged helplessly. Seeing the girls' enthusiasm, she obviously didn't want to deny them. "Of course I'll come." She looked around at the rest of the party, sitting on their picnic blankets. "Would anyone else like to join us?"

No one wished to, though the party climbing the hill was encouraged to have a good time.

"Very well," said James, winking at her and taking each girl by the hand. "We shall have to have all the fun ourselves."

As they climbed the hill, Felicity fell into step beside Alice, who reached for her hand. It was late in the afternoon now, and all seemed warm and lazy. Even the bugs were chirping less often. The big hill that the girls wanted to climb was just beyond the smaller hill where the party had picnicked. James, Felicity, and the girls went over the top of the smaller hill, down the short grassy slope to its bottom, and then began to climb the larger hill behind it. The grass on the taller hill was higher, probably because there were no raspberries there, and so no reason for anyone to have walked on it or cut it back.

The little girls laughed and took exaggeratedly high marching steps to move their legs through the grass and wildflowers that were as high as James's knees. Near the top a few fruit trees grew in clusters.

Finally they reached the summit and the view of the surrounding countryside was before them. The girls cried out happily and rushed to talk over one another, trying to find the best word to describe it.

"It's so beautiful," Felicity said, and he felt a foot taller for having shown it to her.

"Yes, isn't it?" he agreed. "Have you never been here before?"

She stared out over the scene of hills and bright fields, many dappled with different colored spots of wildflowers, that rolled away as far as the eye could see under fluffy white clouds. It was not just that the scene was the epitome of pastoral beauty, but that they stood at just the right height to see the details along with a wide view, as if they floated above it.

She shook her head. "I don't remember coming here before. It would be rather a long walk from Tethering, of course, and we haven't had horses for years."

That blasted Jonathan and his gambling. He felt fiercely that he would have shaken Jonathan Beresford until his head rung if he had known him then—he would have shaken some sense into him. But then, if Jonathan hadn't gambled away Tethering, James never would have come here. He would have never met Felicity.

Alice's voice piped up as she came to stand by the two adults. "May we roll down the hill please, Cousin James?" He looked down the hill, the one side having few trees, and thought it probably would be great fun to roll down. He chuckled, knowing Josephine would doubtless not allow such a thing because it would not be ladylike. Fortunately, he could not be expected to preserve the proprieties.

"Certainly, my dears," he said cheerfully, "go right ahead."

Alice and Lydia squealed with glee and positioned themselves along the rise. Their dresses really were rather fine. Felicity raised an eyebrow at him and he held up his hands in mock helplessness. "What can you expect from a bachelor cousin?"

The little girls launched themselves then, shrieking and laughing as they bumped and tumbled. Her eyes on their little rolling forms, Felicity said, "Little girls need to tumble about almost as much as little boys until a certain age."

"And what about young ladies?" he could not resist asking in a teasing tone. "Do they have some of the same needs as young men?"

She turned to him and he saw that she was blushing, and very prettily too.

"James," she scolded, "that is hardly an appropriate comparison."

"Isn't it?" he asked innocently, ignoring the warning voice that sounded in his head. "But even you are not always concerned with propriety, are you? It's one of the things I like best about you."

She looked surprised by his frankness. And truly, he was not sure what was tempting him into it. Ah, but that was not true. He knew very well what was tempting him, as much as he meant to remain impervious to her charms.

Her expression turned dark then, her fine eyebrows drawing together. "Yes, you find me unusual, don't you? 'A funny little country mouse' were, I believe, your words."

"Ah," he said. "You overheard my conversation with Lila."

Her pert chin tipped upward. "It was hardly in private, after all."

He reached out and cupped her warm, soft cheek. "There is nothing in the least mousy about you, my sweet, except perhaps," he chuckled, "that you sometimes scurry about at night."

"Hmph." She looked away over his shoulder.

"What would you have had me say to her?" he asked

softly, seeking, and capturing, her gold-flecked gaze. "That I quite like Felicity? That I find her charming when she is not tormenting me, and even sometimes when she is?" He shook his head slowly. "Lila would have it all over Town in a trice, and the next thing we knew the gossip sheets would have us engaged."

She stood still, watching him, her eyes no longer defiant but unreadable. From the bottom of the hill came sounds of shouting and playing as the girls rolled in the high grass somewhere out of sight. The rest of the party must be busy packing up, but the smaller hillside separated them from view.

He took a step closer and caught the heady scent of her, of the flowers in her hair and her sun-warmed skin. She was beautiful, so desirable. So very much herself. He was weak, he freely admitted to himself. Later he would remember why standing on an Elysian hill with Felicity was a terrible idea. Later he would call himself all kinds of fool. Young gentlewomen were not to be trifled with. There was no future for them together.

But now was all he could think of. Now Felicity was here, Felicity who was far too often on his mind. Felicity, who had been trying her best to drive him away but had succeeded only in gaining his respect for her pluck and daring and sense of fun. And for her uniquely creative, if sometimes devious, mind.

He didn't just admire her, though. He wanted her. Her luscious figure was driving him to distraction. The day was warm, but that was not the reason he was burning.

"You know," he almost whispered, "you owe me something from yesterday."

"I do?"

"Yes, Mirabelle owes me a kiss, a forfeit from her game."

At the mention of Mirabelle, she looked wary. She leaned away from his hand and he let it fall.

"You already kissed Mirabelle," she said, her hazel eyes regarding him suspiciously.

"That wasn't a proper kiss," he replied. He leaned toward her until he was close enough to feel the warmth of her outward breath against his lips. "This," he whispered against her mouth, "is a proper kiss."

❧

The instant his lips touched hers, Felicity let every thought of "no" float freely away.

His flesh was against hers, warm and soft. She opened to him and his tongue drew her response, as if she even needed coaxing. His hands, warm and large, came up to trace the length of her neck and the curve on each side where it met her shoulders, an area bared by her frock. She kissed him back eagerly, urgently, and her arms went across the breadth of his ribs and came to rest against the flexed muscles of his back, which she could feel under the fine cloth of his coat.

Oh, if she had ever allowed herself to dream of a Galahad, James—with his dark male beauty, his charm and confidence, his ability to turn everything to a success—would have fit exactly.

He coaxed her backward, their steps matching each other's, so that they came to stand under an old cherry tree. The low-hanging branches surrounded them, creating a sun-dappled green alcove. In the distance below them, the little girls' laughter pealed faintly.

"Sweet heaven," he murmured against her mouth, then pulled gently away. Before she knew what was happening, he was standing behind her, kissing her neck with a sensuousness that trickled and rushed down to the core of her. His hands rubbed inch by snug inch up her sides, molding themselves along her waist and stopping to cover her bosom, one hand on each breast. Languorously he rubbed his flexed fingers over the cloth where her nipples had grown hard. A small cry of pleasure escaped her. His desire pressed firmly against the back of her, discernible through the worn, softened fabric of her gown.

"Oh, James," she exhaled shakily, leaning back against him, sure she would slide to the ground if she didn't.

"Felicity," he whispered back raggedly. "Your curves are driving me to madness," he said against her ear. He groaned, a soft growling sound. "Stop me. Walk away."

"But I don't want to." She closed her eyes. Her limbs were weak with desire as he continued to swirl his fingers and palms over her breasts.

He stepped around in front of her now and stood against the tree trunk, looking at her, his dark brown eyes crackling with energy and heat. He reached out toward her, and she put her hand in his warm, large one, feeling deep trust. He tugged her to him, so that she fell gently to him with her hands pressed against his muscled chest, her face tipped up to his.

Reaching up, he tangled his fingers in her hair, and

she was startled to notice that his hand was trembling. As close as they were, she could read passion in his darkened eyes.

"You *are* a fairy queen, who has bewitched me. I'm mad with wanting you."

She was delirious, drunk with pleasure. "I feel the spell between us," she whispered.

She gave in to the urge to explore the contours of his chest through his shirt. He shuddered and dropped his hands behind her to pull her fully against the length of him, a groan of deep satisfaction escaping him. Her senses sang dizzily as he tugged her to stand between his legs. How long and hard his thighs were—dear heaven but it felt good to be imprisoned by him like this.

He pressed himself to her, low against her belly. How very hard he was there. With a rhythm that was new but somehow familiar, as if it were written on her somewhere inside, he rubbed himself against her. Pleasure and wildness spiraled through her, made her breathing ragged and her mind empty of any thoughts save of him and what he was doing to her.

And then—shockingly, and so disappointingly—he pulled abruptly away. He was panting, and his eyes were so dark, almost black. "My God, we can't go on like this. At this rate we'll have to get married."

His words acted like a blast of cold water, and though she had wanted only to pull him back against her, she pushed away from him. "No," she said vehemently.

He looked startled at her tone. Almost hurt, but that was impossible. He had only been joking about marriage, she knew that. This attraction between them—they both knew it was there, and it was powerful. But, at least for him, it was not love. And it didn't matter anyway what it was, because marriage could never come of it. She'd made her vow.

Her face burning with shame and frustration, she nonetheless forced herself to look unaffected. "All right, so we find one another—"

He crossed his arms, his mouth tight. "Yes? Can you admit it?"

"Irresistible! I admit it. I do find you irresistible. But attraction is all this is or can be. We're adversaries, for pity's sake."

"I don't feel like an adversary," he said in a low, smooth voice, his dark eyes pinning hers. He didn't look like he was joking.

"What do you want from me?" she whispered, all topsy-turvy. Nothing made sense anymore.

But before he could answer they heard a little girl's voice pipe up with "Lavender's blue, dilly dilly," and another followed it with, "Lavender's green."

"The girls are coming," she whispered urgently, stepping farther away from him and looking out toward the hillside. The next moment, Alice and Lydia came into view. Behind her, Felicity heard James exhale heavily.

The children were obviously tired from the long day outdoors. Lydia sat down on the ground at James's feet and began to rub her eyes and fuss. James patted the top of her head absentmindedly, then swung her up onto his shoulders amid her shrieks of delight. Alice, who looked as if she wished she were young enough for such a ride, turned to Felicity and took her hand,

and they all walked quietly down the hill. Felicity was still so stirred up inside, and so disappointed that she had not gotten to hear what it was that he wanted. Maybe he wouldn't even have said. But she had so wanted to stay on that hillside and explore with him all the things they were feeling and hoping.

So foolish. She'd only get her heart broken.

She could see him out of the corner of her eye, his long, firm legs jauntily descending the hill with Lydia on his shoulders, a hearty grin spreading over his tanned face as the girls giggled over something. He had moved on from their encounter. Her eye was caught by the flexing of his muscles in his close-fitting tan breeches, and an image filled her mind of him working among the vines at his Spanish bodega, bent over with a bright sun shining down on his dark head. His exotic lapis-blue tailcoat only made her imaginings more real. He was telling the girls about his travels as a younger man, talking of Rome's Coliseum and giving them gory details about the Christians who had been fed to the lions there.

She swallowed hard, reaching for an inner strength to bear the knowledge that she loved this man. He was good and he was sweet, and funny, and brilliant, and he made her senses sing. He was everything she loved and wanted. She loved him so.

There. She'd admitted it to herself. She was dealing in truth now, though it didn't matter to anyone but herself. Because what was between her and James could never come to anything at all.

Even if she and Crispin had never done what they had, even if she felt free to marry, Felicity knew James was not in love with her. In lust, certainly, but not love. James, next in line in a family of MPs, cousin to a viscount, was important and significant in a way the Wilcoxes were not and did not even want to be. With all his plans and energy, he was like a muscular hummingbird who would flit from his various projects, to the houses he owned in England, his vineyard, to Parliament. A busy, important man. He was many things that Felicity wasn't and didn't even want to be.

Needing to steel herself, to stiffen her spine so she could endure the rest of this day together, she reminded herself harshly of his words about her to Lila Pendleton, ignoring what else he had said to her on the hilltop. She was unusual, a funny little country mouse. Not the words of a besotted lover. And he was right; they were from two different worlds.

She was deeply grateful to find, when they reached the picnicking area, that the carriages were all packed and ready to depart. She had never craved the familiar, plain comfort of Blossom Cottage more.

When she arrived home, a letter was waiting on the hall table. It was from their lawyer.

Eighteen

With a gasp, she swept the letter off the small pile of mail that Martha had put on the hall table in their absence. Her hope mounting, she tore it open immediately.

Mr. Blake wrote to inform Miss Wilcox that according to his investigation, there was absolutely nothing illegal about the transaction between the late Sir Jonathan Beresford and Mr. James Collington.

Tethering Hall and the estate lands were, in fact, legally and irrevocably the property of Mr. Collington.

Hardly knowing what she was doing, she wandered blindly to the back garden and slumped onto a bench. She let her head fall into her hands.

A weight of doom settled on her. Everything was a disaster. All her hopes and dreams for Tethering—and for her future—were truly dashed. She had failed in the task her mother had set her. She had lost the estate that had defined her, that had given value to her life and hope to her future.

And now, too, there was this: James would be

always connected to the estate, close by when he visited, but as unattainable as Tethering itself.

She looked out past a cherry tree, barely registering the beauty of the summer evening's gloaming through the blur of tears that for once she didn't stop. Her thoughts turned over likely futures, none of which could she bear. James would be away often, in Spain and at his other estates, and she would have the memory of caring about him and the constant reminder that he was about in the world and away from her. When he returned to Tethering, he might well come with a wife. And what could Felicity do but sit at the dower house and watch? She shuddered at the image her mind cruelly provided of James with his arm around a beautiful, fashionable wife, strolling through the orchard in bloom.

Tears slid unchecked down her face as they never had since she'd been grown. Hot and messy, they rolled in unrelenting streams down her cheeks, and she let the sobs that she hadn't known lurked within her out, uncaring of the ugly sounds she made in the quiet garden. There was no one to hear.

And there was more quiet desperation to consider, more of a future that broke her heart to envision: she might, pressed by her father, end up married to someone she didn't love. It would have to be someone like Mr. Godfrey, because she couldn't bear to involve Crispin in a marriage that, out of honor and romantic notions, he felt compelled to offer. How long would her father give her before he pressed her into making a choice? She couldn't remain forever with him as a burden, when another man would take on her care. Even if that man would be taking a ruined woman.

She didn't know how long she sat thus, weeping. Despairing. Perhaps the weeping was something of a release, as if, at least, she would no longer have to hide her feelings from herself. She would no longer ignore how she felt. She would face and accept her feelings, even the ones she didn't want. There was something healing in that, even if it meant admitting the pain of knowing her love for James was not returned.

Time slid by and the tears gradually came more slowly, as though they'd exhausted themselves. She became aware of the sounds around her, of the chirping of a robin a few feet away and the light scent of the roses across the garden coming to her on the breeze. She sniffed a few times and took a very deep breath against the heaviness in her chest and wiped her wet cheeks with the inside of her sleeve.

A practical action, tidying herself up. It made her aware that while tears might release a little of her pain, she couldn't sit and pine her life away. It wasn't who she was. She had to do *something*. It was possible—just possible now—that she could still make Tethering such an unpleasant place that James would want to leave and not return. He owned it, but she could make it into a place that he didn't want to visit. That would be better than having him there.

But she would have to do what he'd asked her not to do, what she knew would hurt him the most. She would have to haunt his guests, to create a scene that might damage his chances as an MP. To create a spectacle that would make his guests believe there were ghosts and other strange doings at his house.

Though the last thing she wanted to do was hurt James and betray his trust in her, she had no choice. She had to make Tethering into a place that he wanted nothing to do with.

And, with Crispin angry and threatening to expose her, she would have to make her move that very night, or risk losing her chance.

She sat quietly staring out of the window in her room at Blossom Cottage that night, dressed only in her chemise, watching the quiet night grow darker. Finally, with the moon high in the inky sky, she stood and pulled on a dark blue silky dressing gown she had rescued from the moths several months earlier. She didn't plan to be seen that night, so she would not bother with Lovely Annabelle's costume—she only needed something dark to provide some cover. The blue gown was daintily embossed about its low bodice with pale blue forget-me-nots, and its insistent femininity cheered her.

She sneaked out of the house, closing the side door silently behind her, and set off for the tree line, but this time she didn't feel the same excitement as before. Then, she had been angry with James, and tormenting him had filled her with naughty glee. Now her feelings were closer to sick and sorrowful panic.

Life was change, her father had said—after all, her mother had died and life had gone on. They'd have to think about things less grandly than she had hoped.

Simon would likely not be able to go to university. Her father would be happy enough with his lot, of course, and would have his poetry, which, good though it was, could not be relied upon to provide much in the way of funds. Maybe she could find work at the village school, or perhaps as a governess—maybe that would dissuade her father from the idea of her marrying. The final loss of Tethering would mean change for them all, but they would muddle along.

The night was cloudy, and the back of the dark hall was only faintly lit by the obscured moon, but she didn't need light, the way being so familiar. Quietly she lifted the stone that hid the entrance to the secret passage, her breath catching with relief that it had not been discovered yet and sealed up. She had other, less appealing plans that she could have resorted to if this entry had been no longer available, but the passage was the best way to get into the house unnoticed. As before, she crept along the tunnel and was soon in the basement. This time, however, she did not go to the stairs but instead made her way in the darkness along the wall, feeling with her hands until they finally discovered a tall shelf.

It took quite a bit of force to move the shelf away from the wall. The shelf had likely not been touched since she and Simon and Crispin had, in the course of poking about in the basement one summer day years earlier, discovered something thrilling behind it. What it concealed had captivated them for that whole summer.

The shelf finally pushed aside, she ran her hands along the wall behind it until she found the ring she was looking for, about the height of her hips. The iron circle was perhaps four inches in diameter, and when she grasped it and pulled it, twisting her hand at the same time, it gradually began to move, taking with it the panel to which it was attached. The mechanism was old and a little rusty, so it took several minutes to quietly work the small door free. But once it was rotated upward, she could feel with her hands the good-sized opening in the wall that she remembered.

Bracing her arms on the inside, she hopped up to sit on the edge of the opening, then pulled her legs and skirts inside. Running her hands along the far interior wall, she soon touched the ladder. She gathered her dressing gown over one arm and began to climb up, staying alert as she went for another small door on a floor above.

A few minutes' hard work brought her up to the second floor, where the bedrooms were. With her hands she reached beyond the ladder for the outline of the trapdoor that led into a second-floor room that she guessed was either empty or housing one of the guests. It was not, fortunately, the master bedroom, so she knew James wouldn't be in there.

Now that she was so close to executing her plan, panic begin to rise in her breast. Before when she'd haunted, she'd been in the hallway or outside, public places with a relatively easy escape, or at least the possibility of hiding if necessary. But tonight there were many more people present besides James, and it was a great deal riskier. While she wasn't dressed as Lovely Annabelle, if discovered, she couldn't imagine how she would begin to explain what she was doing.

She took a deep, steadying breath and steeled herself. Now that she knew where the door to the second floor was, she could find the narrow walkway that led along behind the second-floor rooms. She gingerly put out a foot to the side of the ladder and probed for, and found, the floor rail. Letting go of the ladder, she began to creep along the walkway, going several feet before stopping at what seemed like a good place.

She and Simon and Crispin had never told anyone about the secret passageways they discovered, not wanting their fun to be taken away from them, so they had never been able to ask why the passageways were there. Thinking about them now, she supposed they had been put there so that lovers could meet secretly.

She began tapping softly on the wall and moaning. She stopped to listen, but no sounds of arousal came from the other side of the wall. Her plan would come to naught if no one awoke and heard the ghost. She knocked more loudly and moaned insistently.

This time, her efforts produced results. A startled feminine shriek sounded from the other side of the wall. She knocked and moaned once more, then quickly made her way back to the opening by the ladder. She had decided that, to make her ghost seem more ethereal and mysterious, she would enter the room on the other side and make some noise there before leaving. It was a good plan because the opening did not give onto the room directly, but to the inside of a large wardrobe, where she could be concealed for the few moments she was making noise. She would then make her escape.

From the other side of the walls she could hear muffled yelps and cries and someone moving about. She experienced a moment of worry, realizing that Lovely Annabelle might also be scaring Alice and Lydia. Felicity didn't mind in the least giving the adults a fright, but she would not for the world have scared the girls. She would get this over with and hope they would not awaken. Weren't children supposed to be sound sleepers?

Now she was in front of the ring attached to the door for the wardrobe exit, and she quickly tugged and twisted the ring so that the flap slid upward. It gave out a low grating noise, but that couldn't be helped. She could only hope no one heard it above the woman's squealing.

Another few inches and the door was up and away from the opening. With the slot open, she could better hear the sounds from the next room. The shrill voice belonged to Lila Pendleton.

"Help!" she yelled. "There's something in my wall!"

From down the hallway, rapid footsteps sounded, stopping, no doubt outside Mrs. Pendleton's room. Felicity heard someone knock softly on what must be her door. Mrs. Pendleton squealed anew, perhaps surprised this time by the sound of the knocking.

Felicity allowed herself a moment of wicked glee, then worked herself through the opening and into the large wardrobe it gave onto, glad for the clothes hanging there that were muffling her sounds. She noticed that the clothes smelled familiar, but it was a passing thought, her mind being much more occupied. She must be here only a few moments, then she must leave. The longer she stayed, the greater the chance she would be discovered.

Her bare feet touched the bottom of the wardrobe without making a sound, and she pushed at the clothes to make room for herself. She was standing in a deeply crouched position among the clothes, just about to moan, when the door to the wardrobe suddenly flew open.

"Ah!" she yelped in astonishment and fright, then clapped her hand over her mouth.

Her view of the outside was obstructed by the clothes around her, but she could perceive the glow of candlelight in the moment before a strong hand took hold of her arm and yanked her from the wardrobe. She fell forward, stumbling against a familiar hard chest before she stood on her own feet.

Oh, heck!

Before her stood an angry James. He held a candle to one side and peered at her under harshly lowered brows, his mouth tense, his eyes alight with something she did not want to consider. His chest was bare; in fact, as she stood there frozen before him, the sounds of voices and movement increasing in the room next door, she noticed that he wore only a pair of breeches. His dark hair was disheveled, as if from sleep, and his eyes were black pools. She swallowed as, under his ferocious glare, she knew herself to be in the presence of a dark and wicked rogue unleashed from the bonds of civility.

"Felicity," he ground out, his teeth wolf-white in the candlelight, "what the devil are you doing here?"

She tugged her arm where he held it to get him to

release his tight grip, but he only increased the pressure. Giving up, she demanded, "What are *you* doing *here*? This isn't the master bedroom."

"Felicity," he said in a voice heavy with warning, "you're not the one who's going to ask the questions." His eyes bored into her. She resisted an urge to squirm.

Before he could continue, a knock sounded at the door.

"James?" a woman's voice asked urgently in a loud whisper; it sounded like Lady Dunlop.

"Yes, what is it?" he asked as if he didn't know, continuing to stare at Felicity.

"Lila has heard… noises in the walls of her room. She wants you to investigate."

He looked conflicted for a moment, as if he wouldn't take his eyes from Felicity, then said, "All right, Josephine, I'm coming."

Felicity's heart surged with gratitude for the interruption. As soon as he left the room she would slip back out through the wardrobe. She tried to keep the relief from showing on her face.

His lips, however, curved up in a smile that could only be called fiendish. "Don't even begin to imagine that you will be leaving until I've dealt with you," he said. He tugged her forward and grabbed her other arm. "You'll wait right here until I return."

Holding both her wrists with one of his large, strong hands, he put down the candle and thrust his other arm into the wardrobe, emerging with a neckcloth. Her eyes gradually widened as she saw what he meant to do. It took him only a few moments to deftly tie her hands together behind her back. Ignoring her shocked, angry whispers, he tied her bound hands to the tall bedpost.

With her arms thrust back behind her, her breasts were pushed up, and they strained against the low, forget-me-not neckline of her silky dressing gown. She felt as if she were presenting herself to him like a molded custard on a platter and was wildly dismayed. How had things gone so terribly wrong so quickly?

He cast a glance at her plump bosom, then grunted in exasperation.

"Almost you tempt me not to leave."

"Oh!" she gasped in horrified outrage.

"The time for maidenly scruples is gone, Felicity. I will deal with you when I return."

Pulling a shirt on, he took the candle with him and left.

Nineteen

Striding down the hallway, James could only hope that Block, who was staying in the room across from Lila's, had not heard anything. Thank heaven the man was leaving tomorrow.

Lila's door was open and he knocked quietly on the doorjamb and went in, his mind unhelpfully dwelling on images of Felicity tied to his bed with her breasts straining erotically against her bodice. He now had a huge erection that he was grateful the darkness would hide.

Lila was pacing and running her hands through her loose hair, clearly distressed, and Josephine was making soothing noises at her. They both looked at him as he entered.

"James, thank heavens!" said Lila, sounding more than a bit hysterical. "Something was making noise in the wall," she said dramatically, gesturing with a handkerchief toward the rear wall.

"It moaned, I am certain!" she continued before he had a chance to act. "It must be some sort of specter! Or some fiend! Oh!" she wailed and he cringed, wishing she would be quieter. Not only was Block only across the hall, but the Dunlops' room was next door, and Robert was something of a stickler. So far, though, there was no sign of him or the children.

"Or an intruder," she continued, her eyes widening further, "bent on stealing my jewels!" She buried her face in her handkerchief and allowed as how she never should have left the safety of Town. They would probably all be murdered in their beds by spooks or brigands.

James sighed. Felicity could not have picked a more perfect victim to convince of the dubious safety of an old country manor. As he drew closer, his cousin shot him a questioning look.

"Actually, James, I believe I heard something as well," Josephine said in a low, reasonable voice. "Just as Lila describes, some knocking or bumping sounds in the wall, and a moaning sound."

He nodded sympathetically, a very embarrassed host. And one who was ready to strangle a certain country lass.

"I'm terribly sorry you've been disturbed, ladies. No doubt I should have mentioned this before, but we have had one or two problems with animals trapped in the walls."

Josephine's eyebrows shot up at this statement, and Lila pulled her handkerchief away from her face and made a ferocious sound of disgust. "Animals!" she burst out, astonishment making a scary mask of her sharp features in the candlelight as he winced at her volume. "In the very walls of my room? Well, I never, in all my life!"

More sympathy was called for. "Yes, it's appalling, I agree. The house was unoccupied for a month or so, and apparently a family of—of badgers made a nest in the walls. I'm afraid some babies were born and it has been difficult getting them all out. Of course, they're nocturnal animals. I'm sorry they've bothered you both."

Josephine looked as if she didn't entirely believe him, but she also did not seem to be distressed, for which he was grateful.

"Well," Lila said huffily, "I can only say that I am glad I had planned to return to London tomorrow. I have certainly had enough of the pleasures of the country."

"Of course." James bowed his head in contrition for having been the provider of this less-than-satisfactory experience. "I apologize for the inconvenience."

He and Josephine left a sour Lila some minutes later, the latter having announced she would surely not sleep another wink knowing there were vermin in the walls near her, despite assurances that there was no way for the animals to get to her.

Josephine paused in the hallway before returning to her room.

"James, it's funny," she said, "but I thought I heard your stable boy gossiping with my groom this morning about some ghost that was believed to inhabit here." Her eyes screwed up as she thought. "A 'Pretty Anne' or something like that, who is supposed to have been seen here recently." She gave him a shrewd look. "You don't suppose this incident tonight had anything to do with this purported ghost, do you?"

Blast! Felicity's efforts to stir up trouble were having

a widening effect. He could only pray that tales of strange doings would fail to reach Dover's ears, at least until after the sale was complete. Which meant, also, that he must get Felicity quietly out of the house.

Maintaining outward calm, he bent to bestow a cousinly kiss on Josephine's cheek. "Of course not, cuz, there are no such things as ghosts, as any rational person knows."

"Of course not, cuz," she returned, "but people have been haunted by more than spirits." With a small smile, she turned and disappeared into her room.

Mr. Block's door opened. "Eh, Collington, what's all the ruckus?" he asked, looking bleary.

Damn. "I'm afraid Mrs. Pendleton heard a few scurryings in her walls. Animals. Country living, you know."

Block grinned. "I'm a dab hand with critters," he said, stepping into the hallway. "Be glad to help."

"No!" James said much too forcefully. "That is," he continued reasonably, "I thank you, but that won't be necessary." He cast a glance at Lila's closed door. "She has gone back to bed, as I think it would be best for us all to do now."

"Eh, right, see what you mean, Collington. Do let me know if you want any advice on the problem. Had rats m'self."

"Thank you, Block. Good night, then."

Block went back into his room and the house grew quiet again. Heaving a deep breath, James made for his own room and a certain ghostly woman who deserved every dastardly thing he decided to do to her.

He entered his bedroom and in the dim light of the candle he held approached the figure at his bedpost.

Felicity watched the candlelight—and James—come closer. Ever since he had left her, tied up in the dark room, her outrage and fear had been growing in equal parts.

How could he have tied her up like this, the evil man!

And what in heaven's name was he planning to do with her?

If he wanted to have his wicked way with her, she would be unable to resist, and not, she had to admit with a sinking heart, just because she was tied up.

He went over to the bedside table and put the candle on it, then came to stand before her, his expression enigmatic.

"Felicity, Felicity," he began in a scolding tone that held a definite edge of anger, "we had a bargain that Lovely Annabelle wouldn't come while my guests were here."

"I did what I had to do," she said, looking at him defiantly.

"Is that all you have to say for yourself? Do you realize the trouble you are causing me?" He sucked his teeth, his lips tight. "But of course, trouble was your goal, wasn't it? Well, there is a price to be paid for deceiving the master of Tethering."

"But—" Her eyelids shot fully open as she watched him move closer. "You can't—"

He ignored her and leaned forward to press his lips to the skin of her upthrust breasts. He groaned and buried his face.

Ohhh. He felt so good against her. His whiskery

face and the heat and moistness of his mouth sparked a rush of desire within her. She sucked her breath in sharply and tried to hold herself in check, to stop herself from responding—or from begging him to touch her more. Deep in her body and low, a warm hum stirred. She wished her arms were free so they could curl around him and squeeze him against her, even as she instinctively knew that being tied to the bedpost made what they were doing more exciting.

James smiled against Felicity's breasts. She was trying not to respond, but he could hear how her breathing had quickened, and now he could feel her pressing just a little bit toward him in spite of herself. By the stars but he wanted her, ached for her. His breeches were growing tighter every moment.

He kissed the inner swell of one breast moistly, then dropped lower to kiss the hardened nub of her nipple, which presented itself so appealingly through the thin fabric of her gown. She couldn't help herself—she moaned.

"I am thinking of penalties," he murmured as he moved his mouth to the other tip and hovered in front of it. She was still trying to pretend she wasn't responding to him. He breathed on her, close up, dampening the cloth of her gown with his breath, and that did it. She arched toward him. With a grunt of satisfaction he captured her nipple in his mouth and playfully nipped it.

"Oh, James." She squirmed against him. Her leg brushed against his erection and a jolt of pleasure and wanting ran through him.

He brought his hands to either side of her slim waist

and followed her curves slowly up, taking the fabric of her gown with him. She wore nothing beyond a shift under the thin gown, and she felt like absolute heaven. The sound of her restrained panting poured heat on his desire.

He was just working his way upward along her neck toward her beautiful mouth when there was a soft click and the audible sound of a gasp.

His fogged mind supplied Felicity as the gasper, and why shouldn't she gasp? But wait, something was wrong, because now she had stilled.

"James," she hissed, moving her shoulder to hit his arm repeatedly.

"What?" Why was she suddenly so stiff?

He looked up at her face and was disconcerted to see her gaze trained on the door. With a sinking heart, he turned his head and beheld Lila in the doorway, a look of triumph on her face.

"Well, my goodness," she addressed them in a sugary tone that did not hide her glee at finding them. "This is quite a position to find you two in!"

"Er," began Felicity weakly. James flicked a glance at her and knew a stab of remorse. She looked either like a desperate victim of something dastardly, or the willing participant in something naughty.

Blast. Blast! his mind yelled. What had he done?

He'd compromised her thoroughly, that's what he'd done. Now there was nothing for it. The decision was made in an instant, and a secret part of him welcomed it.

Draping his arm around Felicity's waist, he stood next to her to face Lila. He could feel Felicity's frantic regard against the side of his face.

"Well, Lila," he managed a chuckle, "you've caught us at a private moment." And one the likes of which she herself had engaged in before, he was well aware. "This was not how we were planning to make our announcement, of course, but now you will be the first to know. Felicity and I are to be married."

"What!" Lila gasped, obviously astonished. And probably disappointed too, that she would not have a juicy gossip item for her return to Town. It was one thing to suggest you had come upon an unengaged couple and compromised them. It was another entirely to report on exactly what an engaged couple were doing. That smacked of voyeurism, and Lila would be too embarrassed to relate gossip about finding Felicity tied up.

Beside him, Felicity inhaled sharply. He glanced down into her face and read, under her outraged eyebrows, astonishment, among other things that did not suggest she was a besotted fiancée. Fortunately, Lila was still in the doorway and the dim candlelight would not allow much nuance to be revealed. He dug his elbow sharply into Felicity's ribs and gave her a ferocious look that demanded cooperation in what he had begun.

"Well," Lila said, looking from James to Felicity, "I suppose I am to congratulate you both."

"Thank you," he said, and was seconded by Felicity's almost inaudible thanks. He shot a sideways look at her, hoping she wasn't about to faint. She seemed all right, although her out-thrust chest was going up and down very rapidly. He wished Lila would disappear instantly so he could free Felicity.

Or rather, calm her, since he didn't actually want to free her.

"We'll say good night then," he said firmly. "Felicity was just about to leave."

Even across the distance of the room he could see Lila's skeptical eyebrow shooting upward and her lips pursing.

"Good night." She faded from the doorway and James was there in three strides to close and lock it.

"James!" Felicity hissed, the moment he turned around. "What have you done?"

"Saved you from your own foolishness, that's what," he said, coming to stand in front of her with his hands on his hips.

"What!" She struck him with her shoulder and he stepped back a foot. "You're the one who tied me to the bed and started… started doing things. Untie me at once!"

He leaned his shoulder against the other bedpost, crossing his arms. "Is this the thanks I get for saving you from being the talk of the town? Your reputation would never have survived being found in my bedroom."

Her eyes shot sparks in the candlelight. Hades, but she stirred him to the point that he felt a little out of control. More than a little, actually, because what he really wanted was to torment her and himself into delirium and *then* untie her. And do other things.

"I never would have been found at all if you had not tied me to the bed like a madman!"

He shook his head back and forth. "It's useless to go round and round like this when you know very well you are not supposed to be here to begin with." He arched an eyebrow. "Not that I mind seeing you this way, of course. But coming here was far from wise."

She closed her eyes and clenched her teeth. "I wasn't trying to be wise."

He lifted an eyebrow at her and she stamped her foot, though quietly. "I demand you untie me immediately! This is horribly demeaning. I feel like a masthead."

"You don't look demeaned. In fact, you look delectable."

"James!" she began again, although her pleading sounded tinged with desperation that had nothing to do with perhaps feeling like a masthead. She wanted him, but she didn't know what to do with the wanting.

They would have to have a quick wedding, he decided as he stepped forward to untie her hands. She snatched them away as soon as he had undone the cravat and stepped away from the bedpost.

Twenty

Felicity rubbed her wrists and breathed deeply. What had just happened? She'd been so caught up in what she and James were doing, more caught up in desire than she could ever have dreamed. And their wicked play… her body was still humming everywhere he had touched her. But now there was the disaster of Lila Pendleton's arrival.

What on earth was James up to with this engagement business? Was it some sort of joke? She couldn't bear it, not from him.

"This is all just a game to you, isn't it?" she said.

One corner of his mouth tipped up in a half smile, and his eyes flicked toward the wardrobe she had emerged from earlier. "You seem to enjoy games well enough."

She ground her teeth in frustration. "No, I don't. This isn't me," she insisted.

A raised eyebrow mocked her, and she made a sound of exasperation. "Oh, fine, it is me, obviously, but I never do things like this." *Anymore*, she thought. Once upon a time when she was young, she'd been so game for fun.

"They seem to come to you naturally enough."

"But I don't like risk!"

"Don't you?" he asked, his voice seductive, as if the idea of her taking risks interested him. "Creeping about in a gentleman's home after dark is certainly a risk."

She was grateful for the darkness that hid her flaming face. She wasn't like him. She would never have bet her future on the turn of a card. But a little voice was insisting she had loved the risk of playing games with him.

"If I could have gotten you to leave, it would have been worth it," she said.

"Ah, so you *are* a gambler." He paused. "Felicity, aside from the fact that we really have no choice now that Lila has seen us in my room like this, is it such a terrible idea to marry?"

Her jaw dropped. "You are serious."

"Of course."

"But I'm not going to get married."

He looked as if she had just said she was going to visit the moon later that night. "What are you talking about?"

"Exactly what I said."

His mouth compressed angrily. He crossed his arms, and it seemed like the line of his jaw had suddenly gotten harder. "I knew it! You're secretly engaged to Markham. Damned sham of a vicar!"

"I am *not* engaged to Crispin," she said, feeling exasperatedly as if she was destined to have a conversation about being engaged to Crispin every twelve hours. "I mean I'm not going to get married, ever."

His eyes squinted in disbelief. "What is this about then, some kind of vow?"

He saw her eyebrows flick upward in surprise. "That's it, isn't it? You've made some kind of strange vow. What is it, eternal chastity? You're a daughter of Artemis, something like that?"

She pressed her lips together in embarrassment. Chastity was the one thing she couldn't claim. "I vowed when I was seventeen that I would never marry."

He rolled his eyes. "Oh, for pity's sake. What does seventeen have to do with now? You can just forget about this silly vow."

"No, I can't."

"You have to. Unless you prefer Lila Pendleton's brand of gossip, because if we aren't engaged, she's going to be very busy spreading rumors, and she won't even wait until she's gone—she'll start with Josephine, and then move on to dropping hints among the servants. It's too juicy a story."

She sank back against the bedpost, feeling ill.

"So, that's settled," he said, taking her posture as surrender. "We're engaged."

"I can't," she whispered.

"Why the devil not?"

But suddenly she'd had enough. She'd carried this wretched secret for three years, and instead of fading over time, it was causing her more trouble by the day. She was sick of its weight in her life. It had been part of what had made her so willing to make Tethering her life, but now Tethering was no longer hers. Let someone else look at this secret for a while—she was tired of tending it.

"You want to know why, James Collington? Fine. I'll tell you. Because I'm not a virgin."

His head jerked as if she'd struck him.

She'd managed to shock him. Well, fine, she was angry now, angry about how she'd told herself three years ago that it didn't matter what the secret would cost her, angry that he'd pushed her to speak of it, and she didn't care what happened now.

"Felicity," he said, his voice a warning, "if this is one of your charades—"

"It's not. I am entirely serious."

His hands tightened into fists at his side and his eyes flashed at her in the candlelight. "So, you are having an affair with Markham. How long has this been going on?" His voice was icy. "And I warn you, you'd better not lie to me again."

"I have not lied to you about Crispin," she said coldly.

"But it was him, wasn't it?" His nostrils flared. His jaw had grown hard and stern. With each moment he looked more tightly wound. Dangerous. She crossed her arms, as if that would protect her from him. Her anger would protect her.

"Yes!" she said acidly. "It was him. It happened once, three years ago, and he feels even worse about it than I do. I vowed afterward that I would never marry, because then I would have to explain myself, as I am doing now."

"Are you in love with him?" he snapped.

"No! I never was. And that's all I'll say."

His dark eyes bored into her. "And you expect me to believe you?"

"Believe what you want, but it's the truth," she said,

returning his gaze unflinchingly. "And now you see why I cannot marry."

She was astonished to find that suddenly she felt strangely lighter. The truth had been spoken and the earth hadn't swallowed her up. She was almost...proud?

But she *did* feel that—she was proud of herself for releasing the hold of that secret. There would be consequences—starting, of course, with James's disgust and renouncing of the engagement. But speaking the truth out loud had brought release, and she knew suddenly in her bones that she would find her own path in life, one that was not dictated by what happened one night when she was seventeen. Probably she would have to leave the area, once Mrs. Pendleton spread her gossip. But she'd go somewhere and start a life for herself—maybe she'd even find a way to travel to a distant land where no one had ever heard of her.

For a time he merely stood where he was, his lips grim, the sound of his breathing pronounced, as if he were gathering himself. If she had ever imagined such a scene, she would have painted herself cringing, waiting for cruel words from him. He was doubtless preparing them now, but she knew that however much she wanted his respect and love, she would not deny who she was to have it.

James watched Felicity, feeling as if the world had just been stood on its head. Jealousy burned hot in his chest and made him want to smash his fist against the heavy oak bedpost. Why had she done this thing? Had she been so attracted to Markham—God, the name made him feel sick—that she couldn't stop herself?

And yet she said she was never in love with him. How could he trust her?

A swirling miasma of dark feelings rushed about in him, demanding answers that he didn't even want. It tried to supply visions of the two of them together, whirling images of the orchard, a hay cart, the back of a market stall—there were acres of places where two willing young people could sneak. They could have been together easily.

But he could not look at those imagined scenes.

He *would* not.

Slowly another part of him was struggling to gain his attention. He was angry—furious—about something Felicity had done when she was seventeen, it whispered. What was it he had just said to her—*what does seventeen have to do with now?* He hadn't even known her then. But he knew her now, *knew* that she was honorable—and hadn't she just proved that, with this painful confession, when she could easily have agreed that they would be married and left him to be surprised on their wedding night?

He respected her. Which meant that he believed her, believed that there was nothing between her and Markham beyond this one—encounter.

As James stood before Felicity in silence, his face registering dark emotion, the tension in the room grew by the moment. Just when she was certain she couldn't stand the silence a second longer—when she was about to make for the closet and run as fast as she could back to Blossom Cottage—he spoke.

"All right," he said.

"All right what?"

"So you are not a virgin," he said with a heavy sigh. "We are still engaged."

She blinked, unable to believe what he was saying. "But—but don't you care?"

"Yes," he said darkly, "the very thought of—"

He closed his eyes and clenched his jaw a moment, then opened them and ran a hand roughly through his hair, making his already wild locks more crazed. "Done is done. What I am interested in is now." He reached out and traced a warm hand along her shoulder toward her neck and rested his hand in the curve. How she wanted, right then, to melt into his strength. "And now we are engaged."

Had she really just confessed her secret fault to him? Yes, and she'd been prepared for his disgust, hatred even. But she could never have thought he would still want to marry her.

"But why?" she asked, her heart starting to beat loudly in her ears. "Honor does not compel you now."

"It damned well does. And even if it didn't," he said, his eyebrows giving the barest sizzling wiggle, "I find I quite have to have you."

Her heart dipped low. He wanted her, was prepared to marry her, but he did not speak of love now, at this time when lovers would. But, then, hadn't she known that was how things stood?

"This is nothing to make a game of," she said in as haughty and emotionless a voice as she could manage. "This isn't piquet or vingt-et-un. These stakes can't be recouped."

He sighed and closed the distance between them. "I

am playing no game, sweet. I have stated in all seriousness that we are engaged."

She lifted her chin. "I haven't agreed," she said.

"I don't see that you have any choice." He crossed his arms and stood there looking extremely arrogant.

She wanted to give in and have what she wanted, even if it wouldn't be wise. She loved this man. With all her heart. She came alive when they were together. The thought that he was drawn to her only because of passion was painful.

But maybe, just maybe, he might in time come to love her too.

"Very well, then, we'll get married." It wasn't the way she might have allowed herself to dream of becoming engaged to him, but the fact was she was going to be married to him. He cared about her, liked her, and definitely wanted her. She allowed herself a tiny, cautious smile.

He chuckled quietly and reached out to pull her into his arms. "Not exactly the way a man imagines his fiancée accepting his proposal of marriage, but coming from my sweet tormenter, a gentle, seemly response."

She looked up into his dark, now lightly mocking eyes and hoped that she had made a wise decision.

"One kiss," he said, "and then we must get you home."

"All right," she whispered back, already yearning for it.

He bent toward her lips and lingered just next to them for several moments, so that they were each inhaling their mingled breaths. Then lightly he brushed his mouth against hers, his lips soft and firm, his whiskers prickly. Her skin lit with sensation where he touched her, and she opened to him, wanting him to come in.

The kiss had started slow and controlled, a quick taste before she must leave, but all thoughts of departure fled as the kiss consumed them both. He groaned against her, pressing her tightly against him so that her breasts, covered only by her chemise and the thin material of the dressing gown she wore over it, were pressed flat against his chest.

He left her lips to drag his mouth along her cheek toward her ear and whispered there, fairly panting, "Hell's teeth, woman, shouldn't you be wearing something more structured out in the world?"

"Ah," she said as his warm breath against her ear sent shivers down her back. "I didn't..." His mouth opened against her neck, and he began gently sucking an area that seemed connected to some internal chute that sent a bolt to where she was already slick with moisture. Her knees trembled.

"I didn't," she began again, not sure what she had been meaning to say. Something about her clothing. Why *was* she wearing this tatty old dressing gown? Oh, yes. Lovely Annabelle.

She moaned as he pressed his hands against her waist, fingers splayed. He pushed his hands up slowly, snugly molded against her, describing her shape even as he pushed her thin gown and chemise up along with his hands to gather under her bosom. His hands came to rest under her breasts, which felt full, pendulous, impossibly sensitive to every movement of the cloth against them, cloth that was alive with the penetrating warmth of his hands. He made her feel worshipped, and she loved it.

"Your shape is so beautiful," he was murmuring, head bent as he watched his hands take possession of her breasts. He groaned.

Her own curious hands had found their way into the opening of the shirt he had hastily donned and were now tracing the tautness of his skin, feeling the lean muscle and bone of his hips. She explored upward, where his torso branched out widely at his ribs. Her mind flashed to Greek myths, to stories of handsome, flawless gods come down to frolic among mortals, and she thought, *Ah, I see what all the fuss was about.*

"James," she whispered breathlessly, feeling amazement at the strong beauty of his perfect male form. "You are rather magnificent."

He exhaled a shaky laugh. "Rather?" he teased. "Not entirely?"

She glanced up at him, his head still inches above hers even bent over, and saw his dark eyelashes against his cheek, his eyes closed in what could only be pleasure. Feeling her gaze, he opened his eyes, arched an eyebrow, and with a naughty chuckle, deftly unfastened the three little front buttons molding the dressing gown to her bosom and flicked the gown off.

Twenty-one

James knew he was completely lost to gentlemanly impulses. Actually, he should have known better than to even have kissed her at all, now, in the middle of his bedchamber, in the middle of the night. After the exquisite torture of Felicity tied to the bedpost.

He tossed her onto the bed, and she propped herself up on her elbows, managing to look waiflike and sensuous at the same time in her tatty chemise. The chemise would have to go immediately, and he never wanted to see the unworthy thing on her again. Blood was rushing through his veins, pounding in his ears with passion, and he dropped onto the bed next to her and pulled off his gaping shirt.

Her eyes grew wide, though she did not exactly look fearful. He grinned. Her lips looked happily full with kissing, her eyes dark with desire as she gazed at him.

"Um," she whispered, "is this a good idea?"

Whatever gentlemanly part of him might have asserted that no, it was not a good idea to tumble his secretly engaged fiancée in his bedroom with a house full of guests was not speaking loudly enough to be heard above the rushings and yearnings of his body. His only answer was a passionate kiss that pressed his naked chest against her chemise and let him feel her firm nipples veiled by the cloth.

Enough of the cloth! He leaned away and grabbed it where it was gathered, just below her bottom, and briskly worked it upward, pausing when he got it below her breasts. Her slim, pale legs and beautifully rounded hips were exposed, and he was harder that he could ever remember being. He looked at her face and reached for a modicum of sanity.

"Felicity, sweet Lis, do you want to do this?"

Leaning back languorously on her elbows, her lower half bared and the roundness of her breasts well suggested by her thin chemise, Felicity looked to him like some Italian painter's ideal of the goddess of pleasure. Innocent as any man could want, sensuous as any man could desire. Her head rolled slowly to the side and her lips parted, and a bolt of desire shot home.

"Mmm," she said, her breathing shaky, her eyes closing, "we are to be married. Must be all right."

"Right!" he gasped, and worked the chemise under her arms. She fell against the bed and he tugged the gown the rest of the way off her relaxed arms and gazed at her, drinking her in. Surely she *was* some sort of goddess. She had him completely under her spell.

Through her lowered eyelashes Felicity watched James push off his pants and caught her breath at the startling male item before her eyes. He grinned and came toward the bed.

He lay down next to her, propped up on his elbow, his nude body warm and so much harder and larger than her own. She reached out in wonder to trail her fingers along his upper arm, and saw the muscles flex as, with a wicked smile that created tiny wrinkles at the corners of his brown eyes, he captured her fingers and kissed them.

He proceeded, kissing, along the back of her hand, down her wrist and along her forearm, every press of his lips against her heightening her senses more. He kissed her breast lavishly and captured her nipple in his mouth, so fully hot and wet now without the cloth between them.

"Oh, James, that's..."

"Really good?" He sucked her gently. Made her whimper. "Amazingly good?"

He moved to the other breast. "What you always needed but didn't know?"

She laughed a little, a low, moaning sound. "Heaven."

"Almost," he murmured. "Just wait."

She pushed her fingers through the hair above his ears in a way that was half need and half blessing. He slid his hands down along her body, tracing the width of her naked hip, cupping his hands around her bottom.

She ran her hands over his chest, loving the leashed strength of his taut muscles. Her hands wandered farther down, to touch him tentatively where he was so hard.

His breath caught and, with a shy smile of feminine satisfaction, she explored him with her fingertips, lightly because she didn't know how it felt for him, whether a stronger touch might hurt him. He groaned and fell back against the mattress and allowed her to stroke him for what seemed like a very short amount of time before his hand captured hers.

"If you do that one second longer," he ground out, but didn't finish. Instead, he pushed her gently back to the mattress and came up over her. He ran his hand along the tops of her thighs before slipping it between her legs. She let her legs fall apart, and he stroked lightly upward along the tender flesh of her inner thighs. She shivered as she felt the confidence in his fingers as they worked upward to touch her in that secret place where she was now… wet. She might have felt embarrassed, but he moved surely against her there, rubbing her tenderly but confidently in a way that told her he expected this, wanted it this way—and that made her delirious with pleasure.

Both of them were breathing raggedly, the sounds deeply intimate in the quiet room. A breeze gusted in from the open window, its cool freshness playing along their heated skin. He brought his leg across hers, and the hairs that covered it brushed, lightly rough, against her. Pushing his leg between her thighs, he gently nudged them farther apart. She relaxed and let him settle himself between them.

She was breathless with desire that was like a tangible substance she'd inhaled, which was now rushing and curling along inside her, winding her up and unfurling her at the same time so that she wanted to lay herself open to James's whims.

He paused at her entrance. His face was above hers, his eyes gazing into hers.

"Are you sure?" His voice was raspy.

"Yes," she said, her own voice little more than a groan.

He moved against her but did not enter, driving her pleasure higher without going any further to releasing her.

"Truly sure?" he asked, but this time she knew he was merely teasing her. His erection played against her swollen flesh, deepening the ache in her almost unbearably.

"Yes, please. James."

He closed his eyes and with one firm thrust, plunged into her.

He stretched her astonishingly. She was impossibly filled with him, and it was as if she had never before had an experience like this. Anything that had happened to her in the past was nothing. She'd never felt before what she was feeling now with him. He began a slow, exquisite rhythm, and with that any lingering memories she had of another time diminished into wisps and floated away.

He plunged deeper and rubbed against her inside, winding her up, taking her with him, up, higher and higher until a burst of exquisite pleasure finally released within her. It *was* heaven, a little piece of heaven here on earth.

The twisted-up feeling unfurled slowly and deliciously, like filling her body with liquid pleasure. She heard his deep groan of release and his body went slack atop her.

Her arms had twined about his back, and she hugged him to herself. His whiskers tickled her cheek and she sighed, her lips creeping up in a smile silly with love. She was grateful for the darkness.

They clung together for quiet minutes, she, at least, listening to the intimate sound of their breathing in the still room. After a time she realized he was drowsing against her. She'd never known such happiness.

Twenty-two

Someone was shaking her awake.

"Felicity? Lis? O Felicitania, Queen of the Fairies."

Astonishingly, it was James's voice she heard. And then she was awake and she remembered, and smiled.

His voice near her ear grew quietly urgent. "We've got to get you out of here, sweet. It's past four and the servants will be up soon."

She blinked, feeling the newness of lying naked with him in a bed in what used to be her family home. And soon would be again! she suddenly realized, now that she was to marry him.

She realized in that moment what had not sunk in hours earlier: she had won Tethering back after all!

Though, amusing to think of it now, it had certainly happened in a way she would never have imagined. She smiled at the thought and turned on her side, the already pushed-down sheet sliding from her belly so that it draped part of the rise of her hips, and she was happily uncaring to be almost naked because James had so clearly enjoyed her body. He was looking at her now, a lingering glance at her body and then her face, his expression mysterious in the predawn light.

James thought that Felicity could not have been more beautiful then, tangled in the sheets, giving him a guileless, sweet smile such as he'd wanted to see directed at him again since their first meeting by the stream. Her body was pale and fresh in the gathering summer light, and he was honored by the trust she'd placed in him. He seemed truly to have won some victory with her, and he now felt powerfully that he never wanted to disappoint her.

She reached out a hand and touched his cheek gently, her hazel eyes sparkling. "Mmm. I feel dreamy."

He rolled his eyes at her and couldn't keep his lips from turning up. Felicity after lovemaking was bewitching. "Well, you'll have a rude awakening to reality if we don't get you out of here soon. Never mind Lila—Miranda and Josephine would make a hideous fuss. They're both very rigid on the subject of young ladies being married before they find themselves in the beds of gentlemen."

He sat up and tugged at her lax arm, grabbing her by the hand and pulling her upward. Once he had succeeded, she leaned into him and wrapped her arms around his neck, resting her head of mussed and curling silk against his collarbone.

"It feels freeing to admit that I quite like you, James Collington. Lovely Annabelle was getting to be such a desperate burden. Especially when what I really wanted was to be happy with you. Happy like we were that first time we met by the stream." Her soft lips pressed a precise kiss against his skin.

Well, he thought with delighted amazement at her pliancy, she was more than a little taken with him. Good, very good. He congratulated himself. Marrying Felicity was the best idea he'd had in a long time.

A small, niggling voice reminded him that she would certainly be very angry when she discovered that Tethering was to be sold. But there was no need to tell her now, when she was so happy with him. She was so delightful, so sweet, and his entirely now, save in name, which would come in only a short time. The marriage must be as soon as possible. That way, no matter how angry she was with him about Tethering, she would have to get over it at some point.

From the darkness of the house, the chime of a grandfather clock sounded the quarter hour.

"You must go," he said, standing up and bending to get his shirt and breeches, which had been tossed on the floor hours ago. "We'll go back the way you came—we can't risk someone finding you in the hall."

Felicity got off the bed to root around for her chemise and dressing gown, which were both in lumps on the floor, and she smiled to herself as she sensed James's eyes on her bare backside. She truly would look ridiculous if anyone saw her about in these private clothes, she thought as she did up the buttons on the now very wrinkled dressing gown.

"You needn't come," she said as she turned toward the wardrobe, whose door still stood open. "I'll be fine on my own."

"I'm coming with you," he said firmly, following her to the cabinet from which she had emerged that night.

She paused in front of the door and turned to him,

her head cocked. "What were you doing in here, anyway? Aren't you staying in the master bedroom?"

"Foiled your plans, didn't I?" he chuckled with satisfaction. "At first I was in the master bedroom, but it needed painting. I haven't moved back yet." He looked at her shrewdly. "And a good thing too, else how would I have found out about this secret passage?"

He stretched beyond her to peek into the wardrobe.

"You can't know," she said firmly, standing with her arms wide to block his view of the opening beyond the clothes. "It's been a closely kept secret for years."

He put a hand on either side of her waist, carefully picked her up and, ignoring her muffled squawk of outrage, moved her to the side. "Ah, but now that I am going to be part of the family, what better initiation than a trip along the secret passageway?"

And with that, he climbed into the wardrobe and disappeared, leaving her to follow him. He found his way deftly in the darkness ahead of her, with no need of direction until they emerged in the basement. He chuckled in admiration as she made for the opening in the wall that led to the outward passage.

"There are *two* secret openings in the wall down here?" he asked in astonishment as he stood behind her while she climbed in.

"Actually," she replied from inside the tunnel, her voice muffled by the thick surrounding walls, "there are several more."

James shook his head in amazement and followed behind her to emerge in the garden outside the house. He never would have guessed this was here, though he thought that perhaps he would have found the secret passages if he lived in the house longer. They were probably among the particularities of Tethering that especially pleased Felicity. He would have to see about having something similar installed at Granton Hall. Then the master and his lady could sneak out at night for moonlight escapades. He would make up the loss of Tethering to her. He *would* make her happy.

James took her hand and led her briskly among the cover of the trees. Their bare feet made only small sounds against the twigs and leaves, and in a few minutes they had worked their way around to the back door near the dower house garden. James pulled her into his arms for a quick kiss, and then she disappeared quietly into the cottage.

Felicity managed only an hour or two of sleep after returning to Blossom Cottage, and was out walking at mid-morning when James arrived at Blossom Cottage to seek permission to marry her from Mr. Wilcox. She returned, not long after he departed, to find her father fairly babbling with happiness. Mr. Wilcox gave her an enormous hug and congratulated her several times, and she knew that she too wore a very silly smile.

She went out to the garden after lunch and was trying to focus her mind—which insisted on reminding her that happy though she might be, the marriage held love only on one side—on pruning rose bushes when she heard the sound of an approaching horse. She turned giddily, thinking James must have returned. But it was not James—it was Crispin. Her heart sank at the sight of this good man who had always been a friend to her.

He waved and dismounted. As he came toward her, she knew that he knew nothing yet of how her life had changed overnight. How little did she wish to speak of it with him. But she would not be a coward.

"Crispin," she greeted him, putting down her shears. "Shall we go and sit in the garden?" She gestured toward the old stone bench that sat at some distance from the house, shaded by a cherry tree.

"Yes, I'd like that," he said with an air of purpose that made her stomach twist.

As soon as they sat down, he took off his black vicar's hat and blurted out, "I've come to see if you've made up your mind."

"I did say before that I could not accept," she reminded him gently. Even though he had often been like an older brother to her, today she felt the elder.

"But you've thought about it further? I know we would be good together. I would do everything to see that you are happy."

His words only made what she had to say harder, but it had to be said. "Crispin, I've accepted a proposal of marriage from Mr. Collington."

"What?" His face tightened, his handsome features screwing up. She was so sorry to cause him pain.

"That damned, no-good gambler! That smug bastard. He's too fast for you—he's tricked you."

"No, don't. He is a good man, regardless of how he came to own Tethering."

"You said there was nothing between you," he

accused. The anger and hurt in his eyes were hard to face, but he deserved to understand.

"There wasn't anything between us then—nothing like there is now."

"How could you have lied to me?" he demanded angrily.

"Stop it, Crispin. You've never had a right to know the details of my private life."

"I blasted well do have that right! I've known you almost my whole life. We were meant to be together. Dammit, Felicity, we *have* been together."

"Crispin, that was one night three years ago. I was grateful then for your comfort, and I still am. We shared a… a connection, affection. But there was no result from it that would have forced us into marriage, and much as I appreciate your gentlemanly impulses," she said, taking a deep breath before saying hard words, "I have never wanted to be your wife."

He stilled. His familiar blue eyes grew hooded, and his voice was harsh as he said, "You barely know him. And I don't believe," he scoffed, his mouth twisted in a sneer, "that your father has given this his blessing."

"He has."

He stood up abruptly, doubtless unaware that he was crushing his hat in one large hand. "Well, then, let's see if he rescinds it when I tell him just what you've been up to."

"Crispin!" Felicity gasped. "Listen to yourself."

"You can't see that Collington's a scoundrel! I'll have to—"

"Listen," she broke in, wishing it hadn't come to this, "all other considerations aside, we have to marry. Mrs. Pendleton happened upon us in his room last night."

He stood silent a full minute staring down at her. She held his gaze.

"I see," he finally said. "You surprise me." Though his face was twisted in bitterness, he had schooled his voice into neutrality. "I would not have thought," he began, but stopped, his hand coming up to cover his face, obscuring his eyes. He took it away after a few moments and looked at her, and it was as if he were a different person, or suddenly older.

"I'll wish you happy then," he said in that neutral voice.

She stood up even as he turned to leave. "Crispin, wait. Cannot we part friends?"

"No," he said, not turning around. "I don't wish to see you for a very long time."

And with that he strode out of the garden. She slumped back onto the bench and knew a sense of sorrow that their embrace in the garden that night had led to so many consequences. It had left wounds in them both, but the wounds had been washed with salt water now. They were clean, and in time surely they would heal.

A note arrived from James after lunch, via Fulton.

Dear Felicity. It was all very properly written, a suitable note that any engaged man might write to his fiancée, giving no indication of the passionate night they had spent together. Felicity felt smug at their secret knowledge of each other.

I have just received news of a pressing business matter that must take me to London tomorrow. My aunt and my cousins will be returning then as well, and I invite you to join our party. We will be staying at Sir Robert's London townhouse, where she and Miranda will be able to act as your companions.

Yours most affectionately,
James

P.S. My cousin Josephine has offered to make some of her own mourning clothes available, should you require something of a different fashion for Town.

London. She leaned back against the hallway wall and stared into space while Fulton awaited her response. Well, why not? She had not thought to go there. But now that a visit was offered in the company of James, the city beckoned like a gift waiting to be unwrapped.

Yes, she would join the party with pleasure, she scribbled back in a note for Fulton to take, and gratefully accepted Lady Dunlop's tactful offer of mourning clothes. Felicity had only a few weeks left in her mourning term, and she was heartily sick of her drab, self-dyed attire.

Fulton left with the note and she stood in the doorway, watching him make his way up the hill to Tethering. She was astonished at herself, at the changes that had come over her in so short a time. True, her feelings for James had been growing for some time. What had changed was her acceptance of them.

She and he were to be married, and a whole realm of possibilities was opening before her. She needn't be at Tethering every moment now—they would share in managing it. And she so wanted, for the first time in years, to get out into the wider world. It was as if a flock of rushing birds that had made a home in her had suddenly been released into the wind.

Closing her eyes, she twirled around once on the doorstep of Blossom Cottage, her heart light and free. Then she went inside to begin packing for London. With a chuckle, she thought she must send a note to Lady Pincheon-Smythe, letting her know that she would not be able to make it to tea after all.

James put his pen in the ink pot and sat back in his chair with his hands behind his head, looking out the windows of the Tethering library. He'd had a busy morning of correspondence since receiving word from his London agent that business there required his presence. Additionally, he'd received a note from Dover saying that he would shortly be in Hertfordshire and was hoping to visit the Tethering property, after which, if it was all that James had described, he would be prepared to discuss the terms of sale. James had written him immediately, inviting him to stay in James's absence.

And then, of course, it had been necessary to make sure that Felicity would be gone while Dover was there. Affairs between them were still too new to reveal his plan of selling Tethering to pay off the debts against Granton Hall, and he wanted her more firmly in his camp before he broke the news to her. So he had written the note inviting her to London, not sure how he would proceed if she chose not to come. Fortunately, she had accepted cheerfully. Not that he liked the idea of misleading her about his plans for Tethering. But really, it was merely an omission rather than a lie.

She was in his thoughts constantly, and memories of their night together had been tormenting him sweetly all morning. That had been the most magnificent episode of lovemaking he had ever experienced, and he was eager to expand upon it, which would likely not be easy in London with Miranda chaperoning. Maybe if they were very careful in Town, he mused, allowing his thoughts to wander along possible scenarios for further seducing Felicity.

They must set a wedding date, he decided, pulling out a calendar for July. In August he would have to leave for Spain, but now he no longer felt concerned about what trouble Miranda might get into with him gone, because by then he and Felicity should be married, and she could look after Miranda for the months he would be away. Things were working out very well indeed.

Twenty-three

Felicity sat at the vanity table in her richly appointed room in Sir Robert Dunlop's elegant London townhouse. She was already dressed, and the maid James had engaged had just left after arranging Felicity's thick hair in a high, regal coronet with a few strands curling teasingly around her face. She was wearing a beautiful ball gown of Lady Dunlop's, of lavender silk for mourning, but such a rich, blue-purple color that it was almost pale hyacinth. It was a good color on her; she knew she looked her best. All of the clothes Lady Dunlop had lent her were cleverly designed to fit the idea of mourning while still looking fashionable and flattering.

A knock sounded at her door.

"Come in."

James stepped inside her room and closed the door. He focused on her and a slow smile spread over his face, the candlelight dancing in his eyes. He looked the very quintessence of a noble English gentleman in a bottle green coat and crisp white cravat, someone whose ancestors had surely contributed materially over the centuries to the prosperity of the country. His Spanish tan had faded now, under the weak English sun, but his dark looks were no less intensely appealing.

He would always have the power to take her breath away, she thought as she took in his dark, masculine presence, his broad shoulders that seemed ready to bear any weight. She loved him, though he did not know this. He didn't need to. And the past week in London—a week filled with parties and trips to the theater and sightseeing with Miranda—*had* been wonderfully, dazzlingly fun. If it had also been tinged with the bittersweet knowledge that however much he wanted her, he did not love her, well, that was her own business.

She watched him in the mirror as he came to stand behind her, and he bent to press a kiss where her bare shoulder met the rise of her neck. He rubbed his lips slowly there, gently exhaling, all the while enveloping her in a cloud of Jamesness, of his intoxicating scent and the force of his energetic self.

He had something behind his back—one arm was behind him—and now he brought it forward and held it over her shoulder for her to see. It was a flat box, like one used for jewelry, and she looked up at him, feeling her throat constrict with pleasure.

He smiled. "Open it."

She took it, the dark wood a luxurious weight in her hand, and slowly undid the clasp and opened it. Inside was a pendant of a large, jewel-cut amethyst set off with tiny diamonds. She gasped in pleasure.

"Oh, James, it's beautiful."

Looking pleased with her response, he took the necklace out and fastened it around her neck. It hung low, nestling near the top of her décolletage, a sparkling dark counterpoint to the lighter purple of her gown. His hands, done with their task of fastening, flattened against the tingling skin of her bosom and slowly crept downward to tease the exposed tops of her breasts.

Shivering with pleasure, she cleared her throat. He lifted his head to look at her in the mirror, and she said reluctantly, "We really ought to leave. The others may be waiting to go."

James screwed up his lips in frustrated desire. Living in the same house as Felicity for the past days had been an exquisite torture that was leaning more toward just torture hourly. He desperately wanted to throw her on the bed immediately and ravish her, then do it again at least five more times, in five different ways, to make up for all the blasted curbing of urges he'd been forced to do since they had arrived at the Dunlop home.

"Right," he said abruptly, trailing a hand up along her neck and cheek, then dropping it and stepping back. "Let's go then. The delights of the Wilkington soiree await."

She stood and took the arm he presented, and they walked out into the hall. "But I do want to mention, my dear fiancée," he said in a ridiculously sober tone, "that you must be certain to save me more than one dance tonight."

She turned to look at him, one eyebrow raised irreverently. "Oh?"

They started down the marble staircase that led to

a handsome foyer. "Yes, my sweet, innocent country miss. Or rather," he lowered his voice seductively, "not so innocent." She blushed furiously and he chuckled. "Anyway, there's no need for you to be quite so accommodating to the young bucks. You'll give them the idea they have a chance of engaging your affections."

They had arrived at the bottom of the stairs. She stepped off and turned to look at him over her shoulder. "And don't they?" she teased.

"They had better not even consider it if they don't want to find themselves facing a dawn appointment," he pronounced in his haughtiest tone.

She laughed. "Even I, country mouse that I am, know it's perfectly acceptable for young ladies and gentlemen, married or not, to flirt more outrageously than we do in the country. I have just been getting used to it."

"Well, then, get unused to it," he ordered gruffly. "I don't fancy my wife having a collection of suitors while I am off in Spain."

"But we'll be married then," she said. "We'll be together."

"Well, yes. But you'll have to stay here, while I go. I'll need you to look after Aunt Miranda."

Felicity stilled at James's words.

So. He planned to leave her in England while he was in Spain. She knew that he was to go to Spain at the end of the summer, but she saw now that ever since that one night they had shared, and through all the happy times they'd had since in London, she'd assumed they would not be parted. *She* couldn't bear the thought of being parted from *him*. But apparently he didn't feel the same way. He considered her as being more necessary as a companion for his aunt. However much she liked Aunt Miranda—and she did, infinitely—she knew that no man who cared for his wife would rather see her with his aunt than himself.

"Well," she said, tipping her chin upward, gathering her pride and turning away from the hurt squeezing her chest, "I don't imagine you'll be much the wiser one way or the other, all the way in Spain."

His eyes flashed at her, but before he could say anything Miranda appeared on the stairs, followed by Sir Robert and Lady Dunlop. The party left promptly, with Sir Robert and Lady Dunlop in one carriage and Felicity, Miranda, and James in the other, making further conversation impossible. Felicity stared out the small window and knew she would behave as if she didn't mind at all what James decided. And perhaps, if she acted well enough, she would learn to believe it herself.

Lord and Lady Wilkington's ball was in full swing by the time they arrived. The mansion was buzzing with a general hum of conversation and the melodic sounds of an orchestra. Felicity paused when they reached the ballroom and took in the scene, the whirling dancers like animated, bejeweled flowers weaving an ephemeral pattern that was constantly being recreated and disintegrating. The room was lit by several high crystal chandeliers, each stuffed decadently with what looked like a year's worth of candles, and producing a glorious glow of soft, sparkling light. She had yet to accustom herself to the extravagance of the moneyed set of people who were James's London friends. She'd half expected his friends to be like Lila, sneering at James's provincial, unknown fiancée, but in fact everyone had been kind.

A tall man of perhaps forty emerged from the crowd and came forward.

"Ah!" he said, a huge grin lighting his thick features, "Collington, this is lucky! The very man I was wanting. Just got back into Town." He winked at James.

She noticed that James looked startled at the sight of the man, but he merely nodded once and presented Mr. William Dover to her and Aunt Miranda. Mr. Dover bowed to Miranda first, and when he got to Felicity, introduced as James's fiancée, his eyes twinkled and he bowed with extra flourish. She then saw him glance at James and wink at him again, and her brow furrowed in puzzlement. Who was this man to James? There seemed to be something other than friendship between them.

Someone touched her arm from behind, and she turned to find Hal, resplendently handsome in a coat of midnight velvet that made a striking contrast with his fair hair. She smiled. She'd not seen him since their carriages had parted ways near London. But ever since she'd arrived, she'd heard him being referred to by a nickname by which he was apparently known among the *ton,* a name that made her smile: Lord Perfect.

"So, I finally have the pleasure of seeing the belle of Longwillow here in London. And I was right—you are by far the finest woman here."

She blushed. "Hal, you are an irredeemable rogue."

"But exactly, my dear," he said with that familiar wicked twinkle in his eyes. Tonight, after hearing of James's plans for her, Hal's insouciance cheered her. "That means I can't be expected to be held accountable for my actions." He spoke teasingly as always, but she knew he was no wastrel.

"Might I have the pleasure of this dance with you?" he asked.

"Me?" she teased. "To dance with Lord Perfect? That must surely be the height of any young lady's aspirations."

He allowed his eyes to glitter at her mischievously, and she laughed, ignoring the sinking feeling that had clung to her ever since James had told her of his plans for the summer.

James was deep in low conversation with Mr. Dover and did not look likely to wish a dancing partner soon. She looked away from him as her heart tightened with the knowledge that he would soon be leaving her so easily. And maybe she wouldn't want to dance with him at all, she thought petulantly, knowing she was being ridiculous and that she would soon get over it. She must simply learn to care less. And Hal was here, the perfect partner for a lighthearted turn around the dance floor. She accepted his invitation.

From the corner of his eye, James watched Felicity dance with his cousin. Lord Bloody Perfect in his element. While Dover continued to gush about the delights of his visit to Tethering, James wondered what the devil Hal thought he was doing, resting his hand on the bare skin above the back of her dress. He didn't like the way they were dancing—Hal was holding her too close, moving her about with the familiar suavity

James was well aware made the ladies swoon. Hal was now closer to Felicity than James had managed to be since they had left for London. Damned waltz. It ought to be reserved for married and engaged couples only. He screwed up his lips in displeasure and tried to focus on what Dover was saying.

"Yes, I am convinced that the Tethering estate will suit me admirably!" Dover was becoming more animated than was wise in a room full of people who delighted in gossip. "I'd like to take possession as soon as possible and get to work clearing out a portion of that lower orchard to make way for a horse track."

James cringed. Pray God Felicity never heard about the demolition of her beloved orchard, never mind how she was going to react now that it was certain Dover would buy the estate. James's plans were otherwise coming together perfectly. She still had no idea, even though the circle of people who did would widen exponentially after tonight, with the garrulous Dover trumpeting it about. Miranda, Hal, and Josephine already knew, though they also knew not to mention it.

He resolved at that moment that he would tell Felicity that night about the sale of Tethering. He would cozy up to her after the ball, find a pretext to be in her room and seduce her into a state of delicious acquiescence before he carefully broached the subject. She needed to know about Granton Hall, what a magnificent old estate it was. Granton would make up for the loss of Tethering. She could establish a bigger, better orchard there, and anything else she liked.

But he couldn't have anyone else hearing about

Dover's imminent purchase before she did. Fortunately, the man excused himself then to visit the gentlemen's retiring room, and James suggested they rejoin in the library to resolve the details of the sale.

Alone, he scanned the room casually, his eyes eventually drawn to a group of dowagers who were unmistakably stealing glances at him. When they perceived his eyes on them, they turned away, though he could tell they were giggling. Sniggering, more likely, he thought with a twist of his lips. No doubt gossiping about the Collington scandal again, now that he was here to remind them of it. Well, soon enough he would redeem the Collington name.

The waltz was over and Hal was bringing Felicity back to where James stood. When they arrived, Hal bowed low over her hand and kissed it, eliciting a girlish laugh from her.

"Hal, you blackguard, that will do," James said in what he meant to be a lighthearted tone.

"Will it?" Hal replied impishly, releasing Felicity's hand. Her cheeks were rosy with the exercise, her eyes sparkling. "I suppose it will have to, for now," Hal continued with a familiar deceptive look of laziness about his lips, a look that had fooled many a man at the gambling tables into parting with his coin. "Though if Felicity were my fiancée, I would certainly not bring her to a ball then spend my time blathering with Dover. Or desert her while I gallivanted about Spain." He sighed theatrically and smiled. "But when you are out of the country, dear cousin, you can rest assured that I will be happy to escort her around."

James clenched his teeth.

Felicity laughed. Had he noticed before how musical her laugh was? The sound of it made him want to smile, though he was not feeling happy at the moment.

What the hell was Hal doing? Dammit, he didn't know now whether he liked the idea of her being in London without him. True, not long ago he'd thought she would benefit from leaving Longwillow and coming to Town. But now, seeing her happy and fashionably dressed, he found he did not like the idea of her being there without him. She was far, far too appealing to escape notice.

Watching her banter and flirt with Hal, he was struck with how easily she moved among society. And as his wife, she would be invited to many of the best parties and balls. He had a strong suspicion that the combination of her beauty and her honest lack of interest in currying favor would make her irresistible. And he would not be there to guard her from the scores of men who loved nothing so much as the challenge of a beautiful, seemingly neglected married woman. The thought made his blood boil.

A young buck appeared then at her side, as if conjured by his imagination, and spirited her away for a quadrille.

As soon as she was gone, James turned to Hal. "What the devil are you up to with Felicity?" he asked.

Hal lofted a single eyebrow. "I wonder why you care, since you are so soon to desert her. Clearly her daily life will be of little import to you in Spain. Someone ought to look after her interests. Why not me?"

James pressed his lips together. "I will look after her interests."

"You? You're practically her jailer." Hal looked remarkably animated, a rare occurrence in a man who cultivated the impression that he did not care too deeply about anything. "How can you in all conscience marry this beautiful young lady and then abandon her to a future of months at a time spent alone in the country?"

"I'll only be gone a few months a year. And she won't be alone," James said firmly. "She'll live with Miranda at Granton Hall. They already get along famously."

"I'm sure they do," came the dry reply, "but she's a young woman. A desirable, vibrant young woman who deserves to be valued and cherished. She shouldn't be sentenced to a spinster's existence. And equally important," he persisted, "have you told her about your plans for Tethering yet? About who Dover is?"

James, whose face had flamed at the word "desirable," was irate. "No, dammit, I'm waiting for the right moment. And who appointed you her champion?"

"Somebody has to look out for her."

"And somebody is doing that. Me."

They were still glaring at each other when Josephine approached them. "Well, and what has the two of you looking like a couple of rams locking horns?"

A muscle twitched in James's jaw. Hal looked away from his gaze at last. "Nothing too serious. Just discussing the couple's plans for the future."

Josephine's eyebrows shot up with interest and she turned to James. "And what are your plans, James?"

"Devil take it, you know my plans. I'm going to

clear the debt and move back into Granton Hall. Then I'll return to Spain while Felicity stays at Granton with Miranda. Once things are settled at the bodega, I will come back and prepare for the election."

She regarded him steadily. "Ah. You will not take her with you to Spain? Have you told her about Granton yet, and the changes it will mean for her?"

He sucked his teeth angrily. Why the devil were his cousins harassing him?

"I see," she finally said, when he didn't reply. She glanced at Hal, who shrugged.

"What is it with you two?" James demanded. "And Miranda too? People get married all the time and live apart. Nabobs. Sea captains."

"Yes, James," Josephine said gently, "but anyone who's in love would never do it by choice."

"Well, I am perfectly capable of making my own choices," he returned, heartily sick of this conversation. Why were they standing here, giving him a hard time and talking about love? Whatever feelings he had for Felicity were completely his own affair.

Josephine regarded him, composed as always. She inclined her head in acknowledgement. "Of course, James. These are your own affairs."

She smiled politely, then linked her arms with his and Hal's, forcing them all to be agreeable. "Let us not quarrel."

Looking out toward where the dancers were coming to the end of their set, James caught Felicity's eyes, and something grave in them tugged on his heart. Confound it all, he *was* growing uneasy. He had not wanted to think about her likely reaction to the selling of Tethering. He'd told himself he had solid plans for a future they could both enjoy, but now he was beginning to wonder about those plans for the very reason his cousins were suggesting. This made him feel as if he didn't know his own mind. He should be thrilled—all that he'd been working toward these last three years was about to bear fruit.

Annoyed and unsettled instead, he left the room to finish his business with Dover.

After another hour and a half of dancing, during which time Felicity saw no sign of James, she sought out Miranda, who was sitting at a small table near the edge of the dance floor.

"Are you enjoying yourself, my dear?" the older woman asked.

"Yes, I am," Felicity replied truthfully. Dancing was great fun, and she'd had no occasion to do it for years. "But it's tiring." She noticed that Miranda looked fatigued.

"Would you like to leave, Aunt Miranda?" she asked.

Miranda looked regretful. "I'm afraid I do feel more tired than I would have expected, dear girl." She flicked a glance around the room. "But I don't believe Robert and Josephine are ready to depart, and I haven't seen James for some time."

"Hmm," Felicity said. "Perhaps if we make for the cloakroom, we will see him on the way."

An acquaintance of Miranda's whom they encountered on the way out of the room mentioned having seen James going into the library, so the two ladies inquired of a footman as to the location of that room.

Felicity pushed open the library door, and there was James, standing over a table with Mr. Dover, both of them looking at something on the tabletop. Behind Felicity, Miranda sucked in her breath.

The two men turned as one to see who had opened the door, and their faces were a study in contrast. Mr. Dover's meaty visage held a look of triumph mingled with pleasure, while James looked… strange. As if something were disturbing him. Mr. Dover's incipient smile widened hugely.

"Miss Wilcox, Miss Claremont, you may congratulate me. I am to be the owner of my very own country estate!"

"Indeed?" said Miranda, her glance going to James.

Felicity looked on with a creeping, sick feeling. One look at James, whose attention was suddenly intensely riveted by the large gold watch he had pulled from his pocket, told her all she needed to know.

"Yes, Tethering Hall, of course!" Mr. Dover chuckled. "Collington and I have just shaken hands on the agreement."

"I see," Miranda said slowly. "I guess we must congratulate you then."

No one else said anything. Felicity stood perfectly still, staring at James, pinning him with her eyes, but his expression was unreadable.

"Yes, yes!" Mr. Dover gushed on, oblivious to the tensions rising in the room. "Won't take possession until the end of the summer, but the deal's been fixed. Mrs. Dover will be happy as a child on Christmas morn when I tell her. She's always wanted a country home, and now we have the very place to establish the Dover line."

James could see that Felicity was upset. "If you'll excuse me," she said in a voice that seemed impossibly small. Damn! Not in a million years would he have wanted her to hear about the sale of Tethering this way. Of course, he was sorry that Tethering had to be sold, but there was nothing for it. And a quick cut was best, would be the least painful. So maybe it was for the best that she knew now.

Except that the way she was looking was making him feel almost ashamed. She was pale, like someone had just died. It was only a house, for pity's sake, he wanted to shout at her as she turned away, refusing to meet his eyes now that he suddenly felt that they must connect. And in the next moment, before he could even assay one syllable, she was gone from the doorway. Forgetting Dover, James began to rush in the direction of the door when he heard Miranda clear her throat.

"James, Felicity and I were coming to see about leaving. But you go ahead now and I'll return with Josephine."

Still striding toward the door, he stopped a moment and blinked, distracted by this mention of mundane details.

"Oh, yes, good idea, Miranda." He turned and bowed to Dover, who, thank God, was such a thick-headed clod he seemed totally unaware of the undercurrents in the room. "As we agreed, then, Dover, we'll have the lawyers sort out the details and you can take possession at the end of the summer."

"Excellent!" James heard as he turned to make for

the door. And then he was down the hallway after Felicity, desperate to talk to her.

He could see her ahead of him, weaving efficiently among the groups of people standing about in the lightly crowded hallway, leaving a trail of men bowing after her with pleasure as she swept past them. She had a head start and so was out the door and down the wide, torch-lit front steps before James could get close to her. A light rain had started, and the steps were wet and slippery so that he had to slow his pace. He called her name but she did not acknowledge him, save to accelerate her steps. He finally caught up with her several yards along the drive, where the guests' carriages—one of them his—waited, their drivers leaning against them or standing in groups talking.

He grabbed her by the elbow and pulled her around to face him.

"Let go!" she demanded, her delicate features screwed up, her hurt and anger evident in the glow of the torchlight. Droplets of mist clung to the curls around her face, making her look dewy and young. She had trusted him. He closed his eyes, ashamed of himself for causing her pain. He should have said something earlier. But now he would apologize and beg her forgiveness.

"Felicity, you can't just run off," he said in a quiet but firm voice. The last thing he wanted to do was put on a show for the coachmen arrayed in the drive around them.

Her eyes blazed at him. "I can and I will," she said, her voice choked. "Let go of me this instant!" She was somewhere between begging and ordering him, and her desperation cut him to the bone. Damn it to hell, he had been a bastard. But he couldn't let her go, couldn't let her leave furious with him. And he knew her—she'd think up something crazy to do. Perhaps she'd go to Dover's townhouse and stir up trouble there, maybe tell her ghost stories to his wife. Or something else devious—his mind supplied a vision of her lying draped across the front steps of Collington House in protest.

"No," he said, and in response she tugged her arm hard, trying to escape his grasp. Her gown was growing damp; he could feel it sticking to her under his fingers. He didn't want to hurt her by holding her too tightly, but he couldn't loosen his grip or she'd be gone. "We have to talk. You have to hear me out."

He began pulling her toward his carriage, which was, mercifully, only about fifteen feet away. She resisted, digging her heels in so that they scraped up muddy pebbles from the drive as they went.

"Stop this!" she demanded in a low, angry voice. "I never want to see you again, you traitor! I'm going my own way!"

He stopped pulling her a moment, glanced around warily to see if their scene was drawing unwanted attention, and turned to look at her. "Oh really, and where would that be?"

"That's not your concern." Her finely defined lower lip trembled, and he longed for her to be simply happy with him again, happy as she had been for the last few days. If he could just get her to listen, if he could soothe her, she would see how well everything would turn out in the end. She would love Granton, he was sure of it. If only she would be reasonable, which at the moment seemed like a big "if."

"It blasted well is my concern what you do, but we're not going to discuss this out here, for all the world to see. Get in the carriage."

"No."

"If you don't come with me reasonably to the carriage, I'll just have to pick you up and carry you there."

She squinted at him, the mist darkening her eyelashes and forming them into little groups, as if she'd been crying. "You wouldn't dare."

"Of course I would." He shrugged. "I'll simply announce that you've taken ill."

She gave him a ferocious look, then gazed away from him. She allowed him to lead her to their carriage but refused to look at him again.

Once he had her installed in the carriage, on the seat facing him, he knocked on the roof and the coach took off with a jerk.

Twenty-four

Felicity stared out the tiny carriage window, oblivious to everything save the occasional glow of the coach lantern lighting the raindrops that gathered on the window as the carriage passed along the dark, rainy city streets. She was wet and wilted, cold now in the late evening air. It echoed the miserable state of her feelings.

James sat across from her but she didn't look at him. She didn't want to see him, handsome, smooth, confident James, so good at getting things accomplished. James, who'd just accomplished the sale of her home. Her chest and throat were constricted, weighted down, making anything but shallow breathing difficult. She closed her eyes as her chin seized up in a spasm of emotion, and she forced it to stop quivering and be still. She would not fall apart. And maybe there was still a chance.

"Is the sale final?" she asked in a flat voice.

"Yes, it's final. You know it's perfectly legal for me to sell my house," he said, hard words though his voice was gentle, kind. His kindness was wasted on her now.

"It looked like a very casual exchange."

He cleared his throat. "We agreed to terms and shook hands on the deal. A gentleman's handshake. We won't sign the papers until the lawyers have sorted out their part. He's to take possession at the end of August."

Her head snapped toward him. "You haven't actually sold it yet?"

"Felicity," he said, his voice a warning. He must be damp too—his hair looked wavier than usual, giving him a wild appearance. "We shook hands on it and he gave me a note. That's as good as a legal document as far as a gentleman is concerned. The lawyers' contribution is just a detail."

She said nothing and returned to looking out the window.

Across from her, he slumped forward and leaned his elbows on his knees.

"Felicity, I'm sorry."

She stared out the window, knowing she would refuse to accept whatever smooth explanation he would offer.

"Lis my sweet," he said, urgency creeping into his voice. "Look at me. We are engaged. We have to talk about this."

"I am no longer engaged to you," she said to the curtains. Velvet curtains, she noticed. They looked to be old but of good quality. Like the blasted Collington family.

He did not acknowledge what she said. "I made a mistake, not telling you earlier about selling Tethering. I'm sorry. But we have to discuss it. You'll see it's for the best. We—"

"There is no more we." She turned to look at him, her anger overcoming her hurt. "I've told you, the engagement is ended. Let me off at Josephine's and I will pack my things and leave in the morning."

He pressed his lips together and inhaled forcefully. "Don't be ridiculous. You can't break off our engagement now. And you haven't *listened* to what I have to say."

James looked at her, delicate and ferocious at the same time, his angry fairy queen, capable of terrible magic.

She said nothing and he took it for an indication to proceed. "I had to sell Tethering, I had no choice. I must pay off a very large debt that was called in much sooner than I expected. That's the only reason I'm in England and not at my bodega. That's why I was gambling with your uncle in the first place. And I risked everything to get Tethering. I had to sell Tethering from the moment I was fortunate enough to win it. Can't you see, my love? I had no choice."

She stared fixedly at the floor, no emotion showing on her face.

"I know about your brother and the debt," she said.

"You do?" How the hell did she know?

"Josephine told me."

He leaned back and crossed his arms tightly, feeling attacked, though it wasn't as if she were accusing him of anything. He didn't like that he hadn't been the one to tell her. And that his troubles were common knowledge.

"I don't know how much she told you, but my brother tricked me into signing for a debt he ran up that I assumed for him on what was to be a temporary basis. He died a few days later, and I was left owing ten thousand pounds. An old family relative, Admiral Beene, paid off the creditors and gave me six years to pay the ten thousand while he held Granton Hall as surety and collected the income from the estate. But now the admiral is dead and his heir has called in the debt. I have only until the end of the summer to pay him or I lose Granton forever."

He leaned toward her again, resting his forearms on his knees and praying she would see reason. "Granton Hall has been the family seat of the Collingtons for three hundred years. Kings have dined there, treaties have been negotiated over our dining table. It's an irreplaceable part of my family's connection to the country. An indispensable part of what we will do in the coming years."

"Tethering was my home, James. It may not have hosted kings and treaty-signings, but it has been no less important to me than Granton has been to you. But I see that this is more important to you than anything else."

Her words stung like a slap. Why was she being so damned obtuse? She was like a dog with a bone, and Tethering was the bone. She just couldn't see past it.

"Felicity," he said with more patience than he felt, "Tethering estate is a sweet place. I understand your reluctance to part from it. But can't you see beyond it, to something greater? Granton Hall is important, significant in a larger way."

"Oh." She closed her eyes and exhaled. "You understand nothing about me."

"What do you mean?" he demanded, knowing he was growing angry, feeling control slip away.

But she didn't answer him. Instead, she lifted her hands up and undid the clasp of the necklace he had placed on her hours ago.

"Here," she reached out and held the pendant between them. He looked at her pale, set features, his heart thudding in his chest. He wouldn't take it back. When he didn't, she simply let it fall to the floor between them.

"It's just as well," she said. "This never would have worked. I'm not from a world where Granton Hall and its trappings mean much of anything. What I care about is a happy home. About the changing seasons and how they affect growing things. About whether my father's proofs have printing mistakes. About whether Simon is happy at school. What's going to be cooked for dinner. I care nothing for dynasties."

Caught in a swirling cloud of whys and why nots, he focused on the one detail that would anchor them. "You can't break off the engagement. You could be pregnant."

He could tell by her stillness that she hadn't considered that.

She shrugged. "So we won't make a public change for a few weeks. But privately, we'll know."

"I agree to nothing of the sort," he burst out. "We are still engaged. You will stay at Josephine's tonight as planned and we will travel together to Granton tomorrow."

She said nothing for a long minute. "Very well," she said at last, coldly. "I'll come with you and stay for as long as I need to. But don't expect anything else. You can't manage me into being your fiancée."

"Oh, yes I can," he asserted, ready to do just that, to badger her, if need be, into submission. But at that moment the carriage jerked to a stop because they had arrived, and then the coachman had the door open and was unfolding the stairs. She was down them in a heartbeat, leaving him to follow.

When he stepped out of the coach, though, determined to catch hold of her, his coachman required his attention. One of the new horses in the team appeared to be going lame. James could only watch in frustration as Felicity swept up the townhouse stairs, the silky length of her gown briskly kissing the steps as she ascended and passed through the lantern-lit front doors being held open for her by a servant.

Inside her room in the townhouse half an hour later, Felicity sat on the edge of her bed in her new chemise. She was listening in spite of herself for the sound of James's footfalls in the hallway as he passed, but he did not come. Perhaps he'd gone out, or perhaps he was somewhere in the house, she thought as she lay back on the bed and stared up in the moonlit darkness at the filmy canopy of her bed. She must learn not to care.

James worried that Felicity would defy him and refuse to come with him to Granton after all, but she and Miranda were both packed and ready by late morning the next day. Though really she had little choice anyway, with the possibility that she might be pregnant and no easy way to return to Tethering without him.

James left the women to themselves in the carriage

and rode ahead, so that when Granton Hall finally came into view he was the first to see it from the wooded rise that dropped down to meet the vast front lawn. Beyond the house he could see the estate's fields and farms, whose proceeds had by the agreement been going to the admiral. No more now, he thought with a growing feeling of triumph.

He stopped his horse to revel in the sight of his ancestral home laid out below him. It was a grand Elizabethan manor, strong and graceful, built in a C-shape with a central courtyard. Ah, home at last. With a happy shout of anticipation, he kicked his horse into a gallop and set off along the path toward home.

The carriage brought Felicity and Miranda to the front door of Granton Hall. Miranda, who'd been a quiet passenger, had pointed the manor out to Felicity from the rise, when it came into view as they passed, and Felicity would have felt churlish not looking. It was grander than Tethering Hall, of course. Handsome, in a closed-off, arrogant way, its precise lines suggesting nobility, its historical appearance proclaiming enduring importance. There was nothing at all welcoming about it. It had a long pebble drive, and fields stretching away behind and to the side, and it gave the impression of dominating the valley.

And now James was opening the door to the carriage and handing them down. He looked searchingly into Felicity's eyes as she descended the few steps, her hand in his for the moment that was necessary before she took it back. His eyes were aglow with eagerness and excitement.

The front door opened and a servant emerged to

meet them, a droopy older man who seemed excited by the arrival of James. His hands fluttered to clasp his wrinkled face in astonishment and then plunged into his white hair.

"Sir!" he burst out. "Welcome home!" Then his old eyes took in the two women. "And Miss Claremont!"

"Partle," James said warmly. "Thank you, it's very good to be back. I've brought my fiancée as well, Miss Wilcox." He indicated Felicity and the servant bowed politely. James glanced beyond the man, toward the open doorway. "Is Mr. Farnsworth in?"

"No, sir, he's from home today. But we expect him back early tomorrow."

James nodded once. "Very good. Have someone bring in our bags." He screwed up his lips. "I suppose we'll all be in guest rooms, at least for tonight, until I've sorted things out with Farnsworth. By Jove, but it's good to be back!"

Twenty-five

Felicity went over to the ornate desk in the chamber she'd been given and ran her hand over its smooth, rich surface. It had obviously been given a cursory dusting immediately prior to her arrival in the room, as dust still lingered thickly at the corners where the swipe of a rag, or perhaps a shirtsleeve, had not reached. She looked around the room, which was handsomely appointed with maroon velvet drapes and bed curtains and several substantial pieces of dark furniture. The decor spoke of grandeur and elegance, though it smelled musty.

She moved to the windows and pushed open the curtains to let in the early evening light. Then she sneezed violently over the cloud of dust she had stirred up, which was evident now in a sunbeam. After some moments of struggle and more sneezing, she got the window open. The view gave onto a terrace dotted with statuary.

Granton Hall struck her as a house that wanted to be important. With its queenly exterior and rooms filled with velvet, rich carpets, and gold-framed paintings, it looked as though it existed to impress, to announce its inhabitants' respectability and eminence. It did not look like the cozy home of a family. Well, what did she care—she was not going to be living here unless the worst came to pass and she was pregnant. In future she'd have all the coziness she needed at Blossom Cottage. She'd long since been wishing for its cheerful familiarity.

She'd taken the dower house for granted all this time when she'd been focused, hell-bent even, on securing Tethering. And that had all been for naught, she thought as she began pulling out hairpins, having decided she would not go down to dinner and asked the maid to send up a tray.

Now her anger over James selling Tethering had cooled to numbness, and she realized that thinking of Tethering didn't bring despair. Instead, what she felt was almost relief. Tethering was as good as gone. Nothing could be done about that, and she was almost grateful, as if an impossible burden had been lifted. Almost, because the only person she could be grateful toward, barring Jonathan's contribution, was James. And she had nothing for which to be grateful to James.

But that was not exactly true, she mused, picking up a brush and bringing it through her hair. She loved James. Knowing him, loving him, had opened her horizons to the world beyond Tethering Hall, as if a breath of fresh air had swept through her life, sweeping away old ideas and opening her eyes to new ways of looking at things.

She thought now of Blossom Cottage, where her father was at that moment, and found that it didn't any longer seem like a terrible come-down. It was simply a place to live in the world, and really a comfortable one at that. She didn't feel defined by it or attached to it one way or another. It was a house, a place to live, which was a perspective that had not been possible before her world had been shaken up by the arrival of James. She didn't need Tethering to give meaning to her life. Gratitude and love gave her life meaning.

Putting the brush down, she went over to her suitcase and found the little box that held her mother's necklace. She took it out and closed her fingers around it as if it were some part of her mother that she could touch, like a hand. But a necklace wasn't flesh and blood any more than a house was, she thought. Tethering wasn't an extension of her mother, some part of herself she'd left behind on earth before fading away in death. And, she realized, opening her hand around the pearl and looking at it fondly against her own palm, that was all right. She didn't need the walls and doors and trees of Tethering estate to feel connected to her mother now—everything they'd ever shared together lived on and grew within her.

Her mother's words to her when dying now had a different meaning. *Take care of Tethering and it will take care of you.* Instead of an insistence on the family being at Tethering at all costs, she now saw the words as her mother expressing her desire for Felicity and her brother and father to be happy, well, and safe. And knowing that, owning it, was so freeing—a feeling that she could relax her hold and live according to what the days brought, whether it was sorrow or joy, fear or pleasure. Hadn't she, in a way, been *tethered* to Tethering? And now the cords had dropped away.

Maybe this was growing up, this feeling of trusting yourself to be able not just to contend with what life brought, but not to be beaten down by it, she thought as she put the necklace away. Maybe it was the power of her love for James; love was love, whether it was filial love, platonic love, romantic love—true love was meant to free us. *Love bears all things, believes all things, hopes all things, endures all things.* She understood these words now in a way she never had before.

But loving him didn't mean surrendering to him, to his plans. Surrendering her dignity. That would be surrendering her own worth completely. And that she would not do. Even though she was finally at peace with the loss of Tethering, she felt profoundly betrayed by his cavalier disposal of it. They'd shared intense closeness, they'd made love and perhaps there would even be a baby, and through all of that he couldn't see that she would be hurt by his secret plans. Or worse, he didn't care that she would be hurt by his betrayal. He didn't love her.

A knock at her door announced the arrival of the maid with Felicity's dinner tray. Once the girl had left, Felicity put the tray on her bed and, uncaring of the crumbs that would ensue, commenced to eat her dinner on the bed.

James came downstairs to find Miranda awaiting him in the drawing room, reading a book on a divan. The room was so much larger and grander than Tethering's funny drawing room with its walkway that he felt startled for a moment by the unaccustomed feeling of its vastness. She looked up when he came in and greeted him.

"Is everything as it should be with your room, Miranda?" he asked.

She bobbed her head noncommittally. "Fair enough. Things have been a bit neglected perhaps."

He nodded. "We had to expect that, I suppose. I think the admiral just stayed here every now and again. The place will have suffered a bit for not having a focused caretaker."

"Well, now you're here I'm sure all can be set to rights."

"Exactly." By Jove, he was feeling excited, motivated into action by being—finally!—back at Granton Hall. Since returning from India three long years ago and finding the family affairs in a shambles, he'd dreamed and worked toward the day when he would return to Granton and begin the process of restoring to the Collington name the respect it deserved, and clearing away the last of Charles's messes. A seat in the House of Commons all but awaited him, and with Felicity by his side—once she'd calmed down and seen reason—he'd have all going as it should.

After some minutes of conversation with Miranda, he wondered aloud what was taking Felicity so long to come down.

Miranda said, "She's eating dinner in her room. She sent me word through a servant."

James frowned. "A message I did not get. Is she ill?"

"I don't believe so. Perhaps she's just tired from the journey."

"Yes, perhaps," he said, going to stand by the window. Outside night had fallen, and through the open window he could hear the chorus of summer insects swelling. It was peaceful here at his home. Granton Hall was such a grand old house, he was certain Felicity would come to love it, if only she would give it a chance.

A servant arrived a few moments later, sent by Felicity to confirm what Miranda had said.

"The devil!" James muttered darkly.

"What's that, dear?" Miranda asked innocently from the sofa.

"Nothing. Let's go in to dinner," he said, coming to offer his arm as gently as he could and concealing his escalating frustration, which was an all-too-familiar feeling where the maddening Felicity Wilcox was concerned.

Outside the windows of Granton night had fallen thickly under a moonless sky. Felicity sat on the bed brushing her hair, dressed for bed in her shift, a pretty, delicate garment that was part of the clothing James had paid for while they were in London. She supposed she ought to give it back at some point, though what would he do with a woman's shift? On second thought, she didn't want to know. She must teach herself not to be interested in him and his plans. But she was a long way from the hope of success, fascinated as she still was with him.

A knock sounded on the door.

"Yes?"

"Felicity," came James's deep voice from the other side of the door. Her heart quickened at the sound. "Are you feeling all right? We missed you at dinner."

"Oh." She'd forgotten what she had told the maid some hours ago. She wasn't really all that tired. She just didn't want to have dinner with him. But she didn't want to confess that. "Yes, thank you, just a touch tired."

"Could I come in to talk for a few minutes?" he asked in a reasonable voice. But coming in to talk was not a reasonable idea. To begin with, she didn't believe that if he came in now, they would end in just talking. And that would only make matters worse.

"No, I don't think that would be a good idea."

"Well," he said, beginning to sound less reasonable, "*I* think it's necessary. We need to resolve some things."

"Really, James," she said sharply, not wanting to be pushed, and then realized how loud her voice sounded in the quiet house. She got off the bed and padded over to the door in her bare feet. "I can't see that there's anything to resolve. We both know what happened," she said in a lowered voice.

"Felicity," he said, clearly exasperated. "I'm coming in."

Her heart raced. She couldn't let him in. She didn't trust herself not to melt at the sight of him. Quickly she reached out and turned the key in the lock. At the sound of its snick, she heard him smack the other side of the door.

"What the devil do you think you're doing?" he said in a low growl.

"Keeping you out there. We can talk perfectly well like this."

Close as she was to the door—she was pressed against it, her ear only an inch or two away from the wood—she could hear the noise he made in the quiet corridor on the other side of the door, a quick inhale followed by a forcible exhale. She could almost see him gritting his teeth.

It was quiet for several moments, and she began to think he'd crept away and she had somehow not heard. But he was still there.

"Sweet," he began in a quiet, tender voice. "What is going on?"

"Nothing is going on."

"I mean with us."

"But I told you, there is no more us. As soon as you are done here, and you said you would only stop a day or so, you must return me to Teth—to Blossom Cottage." There, she had said it, asked for what she needed, even if it wasn't at all what she so dearly wanted.

"So this is all about Tethering. Just as I guessed."

"No, it's not about Tethering."

"Then what? Why break off the engagement?"

Because I don't trust you, she thought. *You have your own plans, you'll do what you think necessary. I'm not part of the figuring, and why should I be? You're not in love with me*. But these were all words she would never say. They had to do with what was too deeply connected to her inner life, to her love for him.

She took a deep breath and prepared to lie, truly grateful that he couldn't see her face. "James, acquiring

Tethering was one of the reasons I agreed to marry you, the other being the way Lila found us. But now Tethering is gone, and in a week or two I can quietly break off the engagement without attracting much attention to either of us."

"But I don't want to let you go," he said, sounding surprisingly earnest, somewhat frenzied even. It must be her wishful imagination. "I want you here with me at Granton. I want...you."

She heard him shift on the other side of the door. "Put your ear against the door," he said.

"Why?"

"Just do it," he said in a tender, irresistible tone. "Please, Lis."

She pressed her ear flat against the door.

"Are you there?"

"Yes," she whispered, feeling the breath of her speech rebound back to her against the door.

"Good. Now listen." She heard a soft rubbing sound, a little muffled by the thickness of the door. "I am imagining this is your skin I am rubbing." More sounds, strangely mesmerizing, a soft shushing that seemed to physically enter her ear and curl down into her. "If I were there next to you, I would put my thumb on your lower lip and rub softly for a bit before I gently inserted it between your beautiful lips."

What was he doing? "James," she said with a note of warning—and panic—in her voice.

"Just listen," he insisted. "You owe me that much."

She listened. After all, she told herself, how much could happen with a door between them?

"My cheek is pressed against the door, and I'm

hoping your soft skin is right on the other side. I love the beautiful bones of your face. And your skin, your luminescent skin. In my mind, I'm feathering my fingertips over your eyelids that cover those brilliant hazel eyes."

His tone was rich and soothing, like a velvet blanket sliding along her body and covering her, as centering as a tuning fork calling all her senses to his voice. She closed her eyes and listened, her lips warm and buzzing, longing for the touch of his mouth on hers.

"I'm sliding my hands down your slender neck now, down over the flesh of your arms. I think you must be wearing only your chemise. Do you realize that just the thought of this fairly unmans me?"

That *was* all she was wearing, and even though they had a door between them, it was as if he had some magical connection to her, an ability to read her mind. Her rational mind squeaked that this was impossible, but her body had its own opinions entirely, and it was loving his voice and the way it was bringing her alive, as if his hands really were on her.

"I'm sliding my hands in front now to touch your breasts, to let them fill my hands." Her head bobbed backward. She was melting, growing warmer inside with each word he spoke. "I love your breasts. They—" he chuckled roughly, "ah, they torment me with their ripe beauty."

"James," she breathed, a note of pleading in her voice. This was growing out of control, becoming a wicked torment. Just as dangerous as having him on the same side with her.

He ignored her and pressed onward down her body,

his words stroking her as effectively as his hands would have done. "I'm indulging myself with the rosy buds at the tips of your breasts, rubbing in a circle—" More sounds of rubbing on the other side of the door, and she found herself moving closer to the sound, so that her ear was directly on the other side of his fingers. Her mind was swirling, her eyes were closed, and the sound of her breathing was loud in her ears amid the silence of the dark room.

Then the rubbing changed, no longer a tight circle near her ear but a sound of long, slow descent. "I'm sweeping my hands along your curves, in toward your waist, out to ride along your hips." Was that his breathing she heard, sounding ragged? She stilled her own breath a moment. It *was* James. She smiled, feeling like a cat, wanting to rub her skin against the door. She slid slowly down, leaning against the door, feeling the vibration of his hands against the wood on the other side as they swept lower too. His voice came from nearby on the other side; he was closer to the floor now too.

"Darling Lis, I'm imagining slipping my hands between your legs, near the top where they meet, where the flesh is soft and satiny." His voice was more of a grumble now, deeper, catching at words. She felt she had become nothing more than an instrument that he was playing. He was caught up in the music too, but it was her body being possessed by him.

"I'm moving my fingers upward, to where you are silky." He groaned. "I want to rub you there." The finger on the door, miraculously already near her ear, took up its slow, sensuous rubbing, and she pressed her ear against the door and absorbed the vibrations, imagining them going to the place he had sent them. She was completely at his mercy, in thrall to him, and she loved it, savored it, even while a nagging inner voice tugged at her attention. Her lips were humming, yearning for his kiss, while every other part of her felt like a stringed instrument, like a cello waiting the master's touch to bring out its music.

"Stop," she whispered, so softly that she could barely hear the word herself. Through the door, she thought she felt the heat of him, though perhaps it was her own heat—she was certainly hot enough now.

"Stop," she whispered again, but more loudly.

"But, sweet, you don't want me to stop," he said in a low, breathy voice. "*I* don't want to stop. You stir me to insanity." An anguished groan. More rubbing, an almost staccato, free-form shushing sound now, broken from its rhythm in a way that spoke of his own fractured control. "I want you," he whispered. "I'll always want you."

She flew apart.

In the midst of the delirious pleasure, she was suddenly pierced by the deepest sense of loneliness she had ever known. She loved him utterly—to the point that, if she let him, he might even be like a puppeteer controlling her strings. She fell away from the door, coming to rest against the wall at the corner while her mind came back to her.

Seconds passed. Waves of pleasure receded, being replaced with sorrow.

"Felicity? Are you there?"

Her breathing slowed, her mind focused. She stood

up and dropped her face into her hands. "Good night, James," she said, hoping he could not hear the note of despair in her voice. "I'm going to bed."

He said nothing for a moment. "I… I so want to see your face now. To share with you—" He seemed unfocused himself.

"Good night," she said again firmly, going over to the bed, the sounds of creaking floorboards announcing her resolve.

"Good night, Lis," he said reluctantly. "I… know you feel the pull between us. We'll talk in the morning."

She got into bed and listened to the sound of his footsteps disappearing down the hallway, presumably to his room.

So he wanted her. He'd always want her, he said. That's what she was to him, a very desirable woman. The thought filled her with despair. She loved him, loved his energy, his sweetness, his nobility, and yes, his body and his dratted charm. He was a good man, even if he could not see how he put his plans above people in importance. If he loved her, she knew they could have resolved the betrayal, come to an understanding about how deeply they must share themselves with one another. But those were the conversations of lovers, and he didn't love her. He wanted her, very much she knew, but that was all. And that was not enough, not by a long chalk.

She tossed in the bed sleeplessly for hours, a heavy weight of churning thoughts pressing on her. Before daybreak she'd made her decision. Staying in the same house with James was madness—that was obvious. It was only a matter of time before she completely debased herself, her principles. Before she traded in her spirit for some gilded birdcage. Before she became the acquiescent prop of James Collington, MP, kingmaker, treaty signer, bodega owner, and whatever else he had in his wide sights.

She had to leave and she could not wait. She got up off the bed and rifled through what she had brought with her. In a few minutes she had packed her small collection of personal belongings into a bag. She put an old mourning gown on over the new shift, which it seemed silly and unnecessary to return, though she left everything else James had bought her or Josephine had lent her.

Taking up the bag, she quietly opened her door and crept downstairs. In the kitchen she found the servants eating their breakfast in the early-morning darkness. A half an hour later she was riding into town with the stable boy. He dropped her at the inn, where it was drizzling. Fortunately, she had only twenty minutes to wait until the mail coach arrived and took her up.

Twenty-six

James had finished breakfast and had a chance to look at yesterday's correspondence, have a second cup of tea, and ponder the likelihood of a ride in the morning rain, and still there was no sign of Felicity. He was not sure what he would say to her, or why he felt so urgent about seeing her, but he was becoming irritated by waiting. It occurred to him that perhaps she had gotten up even earlier than he and gone out, or disappeared somewhere in the house; he had assumed himself to be the first up and had not inquired after her. He rang the bell for a servant who, when asked about whether Miss Wilcox had been down for breakfast yet, blinked several times before responding.

"She left, sir."

"What!" He stood abruptly, though he felt as if he'd just been planted a facer. How could she be gone? With whom? And why, damn it all? "What do you mean, 'left'?" he demanded.

The servant's eyes widened with anxiety. He was a new man whom James did not know, but he must certainly have heard gossip that James was the rightful owner of the hall.

"She—she," he stuttered, then focused himself at a stern look from James, "er, left very early this morning, sir. Got a ride into town with the stable boy, on his way for an errand."

"Alone?"

The man nodded.

"Blast!" muttered James, his mind beginning to race. What the devil was she up to? "Does anyone know where she's gone?"

"Well, she asked us about when the mail stopped, sir. Perhaps she took the coach."

The mail coach. He should have known. And where else would she have gone than back to Tethering, her blasted obsession. If she were to appear at that moment, he thought, he would not know whether to throttle her or embrace her. Definitely both. He sighed in profound exasperation and asked, "Do you know when that is, that the mail stops?"

"Why, about eight o'clock, sir."

James pulled out his watch and scowled at it. It was after ten. The coach would have come already, but it was slower than a horse and rider. He left the room briskly, intent on going to the stables to get his mount and chase her down. In the hallway, however, he was intercepted by a different servant.

"Excuse me, sir, but Mr. Farnsworth has arrived and begs the honor of your company in the library."

James arrested his motion. Farnsworth was there. The heir. How James itched to get the man out of his house, gone, done with any connection to Granton

Hall and the Collington family's debts. His mind calculated options. Felicity was already gone, and if he were realistic in his estimates, probably only a few hours from the Tethering estate by now. If he raced after her now, he would likely only catch her just after she had arrived. If that were the case, it would be better to send a message. If he sent a message, he would have time to compose something more careful, whereas if he went in person, well, he could not predict success. Conversations with Felicity never seemed to go as he expected.

He would see Farnsworth and take care of Granton Hall first. Then he would write a careful note to her and send it by messenger. Satisfied, he fetched the bank draft he'd had made up and went to the library.

Farnsworth was sitting at the library's large desk. In James's rightful place. James clenched his teeth and reminded himself to be civil. The admiral's actions in buying up the debt had bought him three more years than he would have had to come up with the money. Though the admiral had not made out badly, since he'd taken as interest all the rents from Granton's lands. And the admiral had promised him six years, not three, to repay the debt. Apparently, gentlemen's agreements were only valid so long as both gentlemen were still alive.

"Ah, Mr. Collington, welcome," said Mr. Farnsworth, standing up. He was a tall, thin man with a pale, egg-like head over which lay a sparse layer of fine, colorless hair. "I am Wallace Farnsworth, as you will have guessed."

James acknowledged his greeting and got right to

the point. "I have come to make the arrangements for the transfer of the necessary funds."

"Ah," Farnsworth said, indicating they should sit down. "I see. Well, I will be very straight with you, sir. I would not have been disappointed if you had not. This is a grand place. But," he continued with a smirk, his eyebrows lifting with a strange glee, "it is in need of quite a bit of attention."

James bunched up his lips in annoyance but maintained a pleasant tone. "Well, that is perhaps not surprising." Not surprising, of course, that instead of putting some of the rent returns into the house, the admiral had kept them. James had expected as much. Oh well, he thought, this at least is familiar, an old house in need of funds and attention.

Hardly had he signed over the money to Farnsworth—proceeds from the bodega plus Dover's large deposit—when a knock sounded. The butler opened the double doors to announce that the steward, who stood beside him, wished to see Mr. Farnsworth.

Farnsworth smiled, his eyes twinkling sharply. "But no, he doesn't. Mr. Jolett will wish to see Mr. Collington now."

The butler looked confused, but Mr. Jolett, who'd been steward at Granton Hall for two decades, already wore a look of pleasure.

"Mr. Collington, sir, welcome back," he said warmly as he entered the room.

James smiled, glad to see the older man was still there. So much might have changed while he was away. But here was Jolett.

"You are a welcome sight, Jolett."

Mr. Jolett glanced from Farnsworth to James and looked uncomfortable. "As are you, sir," he replied, sounding unsure.

"It's all right, Jolett," said Farnsworth. "The care of Granton has simply changed hands. Reverted back to the Collingtons." He came out from behind the desk. "You need no longer include me in its affairs." And with that he chuckled in his odd way and left the room.

James raised his eyebrows and frowned slightly, wondering at Farnsworth's behavior. He shrugged and made his way over to the desk where, with absolute pleasure, he installed himself in the creaky old chair that had been behind it for years.

"Now then, Jolett," he began, gesturing for the man to sit down. "How are things here?"

Jolett cleared his throat and hesitated. "Well, ahem, they are… not perhaps as good as they might be. Er, will be, I'm sure, once you have addressed the needs, sir."

"Right," agreed James confidently. "And what exactly are, as you see it, the most pressing needs?"

"The most pressing," Jolett repeated, his eyes lofting toward the ceiling as he seemed to weigh the issue. "Well, probably the roof of the threshing barn, which has been leaking these past two years. But there's also the problem of the three tenant houses that are still damaged and unusable from the flood in September—"

"September!" cried James. "But that was last year. What about the tenants?"

"Two of the families are staying with neighbors, but one has had troubles and they've moved on."

"And who is farming their land, I am afraid to ask?"

"The other tenants have taken over some, but it's not easy on them. The farm needs a laboring family."

"Yes, right," James said.

"And..."

"And!" said James. "There's more?"

"Oh, er, I'm afraid, sir, that that's just the beginning. We've got a dead cow poisoning a stream, and the fences are down in a number of places." Jolett's voice trailed off as James's head sunk into his hands.

"Did the admiral do anything, these last three years?"

Jolett cleared his throat. "I'm afraid not, sir. He only came once or twice a year, and he always said he didn't want to be bothered. Very firm he was about that. And he didn't leave any money for repairs. He said the staff should all be grateful to be receiving our salaries, seeing as there was no family in residence."

"I see," said James. He looked up and ran a hand roughly through his hair. "Right. Let's go see those tenant houses first, and then we'll look at the cow and the roof. Just give me a moment to send a message."

He rang for a servant and quickly penned a note to Felicity, asking tersely, perhaps a little sarcastically, whether she'd had a pleasant journey and arrived safely, but he was frustrated with her. He fidgeted with the quill a few minutes, wanting to say so much more, but he finally sealed up the few lines he'd written and gave it to the servant to send by messenger.

As he walked out of the house with Jolett, James could see where all of the future proceeds from the Bodega Alborada were going to be going, at least for a while. So much for his dreams of solvency. He sighed dispiritedly as they walked out over the fields toward the tenants' homes, feeling suddenly very tired. And louder than any of the other troubles in his mind was the voice reminding him that Felicity was gone.

Two weeks later, James sat at his desk in the library and rubbed his tired eyes dispiritedly as afternoon sunlight streamed in the windows. He hadn't bothered with shaving the last few days, and his skin was uncomfortable with unaccustomed whiskers. Despite hellishly long days, not enough had been accomplished to make him feel in any way satisfied.

True, the workers' cottages that had been damaged were being repaired, but it would take at least another week of work before they were habitable. Workmen had been engaged to replace the barn roof. The cow had been pulled, after some head-scratching and muttering by all concerned, from its inaccessible spot in the stream. But in place of these problems many more urgent needs remained, not the least of which was the cellar of the hall, which apparently had been slowly filling with water for some time. The water level was at least three inches deep at the moment and rising, and it was a cause of grave concern.

It seemed to him that all of this would have been so much more bearable if only Felicity were with him. He clenched his teeth whenever he thought of the maddening woman and her foolish flight. He had, as the days passed, thought endlessly over their last conversation, that delirious episode with the door between them. He had felt so deeply connected to her then, and felt sure of her connection to him through the solid wood of the door.

But he also recalled, as his anger cooled with the passing days, her reticence, and that she had said it had nothing to do with Tethering. At the time, he hadn't listened, intent on his own aims. But in the days since, he'd replayed the scene in his mind countless times, and he was coming to see that her departure might have been as much a flight from him as a flight toward Tethering estate.

He had spent the early morning going over the estate accounts, a depressing business. He now stood in his bedchamber, contemplating sending another message to her, something much different in tone than the notes he'd sent before. The first day's message had been answered by her father, who simply acknowledged that she had arrived safely. James had then sent another message, carefully addressed to Miss Felicity Wilcox, but she had not replied. It had been a brusque, pushy missive, his attempt to press her into agreeing that they were still engaged. She had not responded, though he had received a mysterious printed invitation to a summer fete being held at Tethering. Now, several days later, he wanted to say, "Come back, Sweet Felicity, I've been an ass," but that seemed too—too—something, he was not sure what. And he didn't think that would work, anyway. Hadn't he apologized before, in the carriage, and she had still left? He did not know what she wanted.

Life was not the same without her around. He hadn't realized how much a part of his days—and nights—she'd become. He'd seen her every day since arriving at Tethering, and she had become familiar to him. He missed her snappy wit, her resourcefulness, her resilience. He missed seeing her smile, seeing her perfectly formed mouth with its delicate, neatly defined philtrum above, contorting in frustration, in impatience with him, in laughter at his teasing. He missed the flowers in her hair and the light in her hazel eyes, a light that he was beginning to think had been lighting his days, making them come alive. And now of course it was gone. He missed all of her, her face and her wavy golden hair, her slender arms, her delirium-inducing bosom, her skin that when he touched it fired his body while it somehow made him feel more deeply at home and at peace than he ever had in his life. Which made no sense, because he was at home now, at his first and last home—Granton Hall. Only strangely, irritatingly, it didn't feel like home at the moment.

When he tried briefly to explore why, all he could think was that it made no sense. He'd had wonderful times there. A blissful childhood. Until he was twelve, of course, and his parents had died. But even then Granton had still been home—Miranda had come to live with him and Charles. She'd been there when they'd visited from university, a reassuringly familial presence for two boys who did not have much family left. Charles had eventually enmeshed himself in the workings of the state. And James had left for India, to make his fortune with the East India Company. Though, of course, he'd only been there a year before Charles had called him back.

James had seen little of Miranda since they had returned to Granton Hall. When he made it to dinner at night, he often found he was too tired to be much of a companion to her. Glancing out the window now, he saw that she was in the rose garden at the back of the house. He decided to postpone writing the note and seek her out, see how she was enjoying being back at Granton. And perhaps her enthusiasm would help shore up his own flagging eagerness for the work Granton needed.

She was kneeling next to a pale pink rosebush that she was inspecting for pests. She looked almost girlish in a cotton gown and straw hat, a teacup full of ale by her side ready to place the insects in. Miranda, like Felicity, was fond of gardening.

"Here you are, Miranda."

She glanced up, and her familiar, handsome face held a look of relaxed contentment. "James, dear, how are you? Busy, I know." She sat against the back of her legs and looked up, pulling her hat brim lower against the sun behind him.

He grinned and sat down on his haunches, his arms resting on his thighs. He had been devilish busy, but that was just as well. Whenever he had a moment that was not full, Felicity took over his mind.

"I have been rather taken up with all the things that need to be done here, but never so busy, I hope, that I do not make time for my favorite aunt."

She smiled at the familiar old endearment, then her expression turned more serious. "Have you heard from Felicity? I do like her so very much. She will make you a fine wife."

"Mmm," he said. *If* she was going to be his wife. He had explained Felicity's abrupt departure to

Miranda only by saying that she'd needed to take care of something at home, but that James was sure nothing was seriously wrong. Was she pregnant, he wondered for the umpteenth time? He quite wished she were, since that would tie her to him. Not that he wanted her to marry him only out of necessity. But he knew she cared for him, and if only she would give him a chance, they would surely get on very well together. Maybe he should just write that in his note to her.

He picked a few blades of grass, absentmindedly observing their varying heights, feeling the dry juice made by his picking, then tossed them aside.

He could sense Miranda's clear blue eyes considering him and he glanced up from the grass. She fixed him with a penetrating look, and he was reminded of many a sober talk she had given to him as a rambunctious youth.

"James, how did Felicity feel about you selling Tethering Hall?"

He pressed his lips together. He had studiously avoided spending much time thinking about his selling of Tethering, which had begun all the trouble. He shrugged. "Well, she was not pleased when she discovered what had happened, but I imagine you noticed."

"Did you explain yourself to her? She must have felt terribly betrayed."

Betrayed? Hadn't Felicity called him a traitor? "I did apologize about the way she found out. I agree now," he said slowly, "in hindsight, I should have told her much earlier. But of course I knew she wouldn't like the idea—she'd been so focused on Tethering for so long that I don't think she could see there was anything else in the world. And telling her wouldn't have made any difference in the outcome—I had to sell it, you know that. Our engagement changed nothing; I couldn't pay off the debt without selling. Granton is much finer than Tethering, or at least it will be once I take care of everything. Surely in time she will come to realize that."

"I'm not so sure. Tethering is charming, and what's more, it was her home. You can't put a price on that." She sighed rather dramatically. "Is that all Felicity is to you, James, part of your plans, an arrangement?" She shook her head. "You are so used to arranging things, to taking care of things that need to be done."

He rubbed the back of his neck. He felt tense these days, as if something were relentlessly winding him up inside.

"Don't you ever get tired of being busy, James?"

"Tired?" Being busy made him feel invigorated—hadn't it always? "No. I enjoy being occupied. I like accomplishments."

She laughed, but she looked almost sad. "Yes, even as a youth you seemed to have boundless energy. It exhausted me just watching you go from one thing to another, even staying up until all hours studying when you were on holiday from school. But don't you ever feel that you can't always be going here and there in life? That at some point you will want to alight somewhere and stay?"

"But I am going to do that," he pointed out. "I plan to be mostly at Granton Hall, sometimes in London, and sometimes in Spain."

"You have always seemed determined to dominate whatever life might send you through sheer hard work. When you lived with me, you were always doing as many things as possible at the same time. As if you didn't want to leave any room in your life where something you were avoiding might creep in."

The portrait of him that she was painting made him deeply uncomfortable. "But I do enjoy my life," he insisted. "What could be better than accomplishing something, like improving the vineyard, or reestablishing the good name of Collington, which Charles all but ruined?"

"You are right to be satisfied and proud. I am very proud of you," she said seriously. She paused. "But, James, we are so much more than what we *do* in life. The older I get, the more I see that we are meant to be able to just *be*, that that is the greatest gift, to just be who you are fully. But you can't do that, you can't even really see who you are, if you are always moving."

He looked puzzled. "I'm afraid I don't quite understand, Miranda."

She sighed and pinched off a spent bloom near her arm before looking back at him. "No, I can see that. Forgive me, James. Perhaps now is not the time for this conversation."

James held a dinner party the next night for some of the local worthies. A judge, a prominent lawyer, two small landowners and their wives. They seemed very excited by his return to Granton Hall. During dinner they tactfully did not mention his brother, but instead were eager to talk about Smithfield, the local MP whom they expected James to unseat in the next election. James tried to keep the conversation of general interest to the entire party.

The gentlemen toasted him and chuckled about local things, nice enough men if somewhat provincial. After dinner, the men left Miranda and the wives to retire for port, and then his visitors really got down to business, discussing the details of his campaign. But their long list of disagreements with Smithfield added up to little more than evidence of competing business interests. And when James probed them for concrete conflicts with Smithfield that might form the basis of his platform, the issues all seemed so lacking in compelling urgency. He didn't really care where the new road was built, and all their talk of what the newspapers said sounded like a whirligig of opposing interest going round and round. He began to see that getting elected would mean spending a lot of time with these gentlemen.

He waved away the last of the party at a not terribly late hour and stood on his own front steps, looking out across the lawn. The moon was bright and he could see a good portion of the surrounding country. It was familiar, handsome. He knew Granton looked stately among its surroundings, and he had always been proud of that. And inextricably linked to Granton had been his pride in his family, in the achievements of his grandfather, his father, and for a while, his brother. Now it was his turn to take up the mantle of influence.

Miranda came to stand beside him. He looked down at her, and she yawned delicately.

"Well, James, was that a satisfying evening?"

"Mmm," he replied thoughtfully. "Perhaps." He paused. "Perhaps not."

She cast a sideways glance at him. "I never thought of you as a political sort, James. Charles thrived on deal-making, selling ideas to people. He lived to get people to do what he wanted them to do." She shrugged. "It was his talent, whether he used it for good or ill. But you," she said gently, linking his arm in hers so that he looked down at her. "I always thought of you as more substantial. Charles talked about doing things, talked magnificently and confidently and got people to like him and want what he wanted. You were always a doer. You did brilliantly in your studies, while Charles cultivated connections. And you used to be a very good listener."

"Used to be?"

She smiled. "I remember when you were perhaps sixteen, I had mentioned how much I loved cherries. And for my birthday that spring, I found a young cherry tree planted below my window, with a red satin bow tied around its slim trunk."

He nodded slowly, remembering his younger self, all those years ago. "And you find me a poorer listener now?"

"I doubt any of us loses the gifts and talents we were born with, but they can grow rusty from disuse. Perhaps," she said, looking at him ruefully, the moonlight twinkling in her brilliant eyes, "it's simply that your mind has been so taken up with recovering Granton and undoing the damage Charles did that you have not left room for other, quieter thoughts to intrude."

He weighed what she said. "You think I've not listened well to Felicity."

She shrugged, and it struck him how delicate her shoulders were; she looked more fragile with age. "Only you two know all that has passed between you. But if two people are to love one another, they must listen not only to words, but to all the other signs and senses."

He said nothing in reply, and they stood together on the doorstep, looking out across the estate.

Was this what he had wanted and fought for over three long years in Spain? All those days bent over in the fields, learning through his hands what it took to grow good grapes? Those days had been good times, he thought now, satisfying times—and had he ever even noticed, driven as he had been by his goals? He had thought then that his efforts were bringing him closer to restoring Granton Hall and his family's good name. Closer to the respect that would be due him as a Member of Parliament, closer to wiping the scorn off the faces of those who'd delighted in his family's fall from grace.

He looked up to the wide, dark sky above him, brilliant with the specks of the eternal stars. Stars that had looked down on mortals and their choices since before antiquity. The same stars that were shining down on Felicity, miles away from him. Felicity, who'd brought light into his life in a way no house or land ever could. She was his home in a way no building could ever be.

All night in bed he tossed and turned, exhausted but sleepless, wishing every moment that the silence would give way to creaking floorboards that would signal a visit from Lovely Annabelle, even though Lovely Annabelle would never have visited Granton Hall. Well, damned if he didn't want to be haunted by her now. He already was haunted by Felicity. He knew this now: that he loved her. He yearned for her, and she was not there.

The dawn at least brought resolve; he would leave that day for Blossom Cottage. But the morning brought news—a message from Felicity delivered to his breakfast table.

James,

I am not carrying a child. This being the case, I will announce the end of our engagement.

Felicity

His heart plummeted down to his shoes at the news and the cool, bland tone of her message. He called for his horse and left immediately, though not before jotting a quick note to be sent elsewhere by messenger.

Twenty-seven

THE DAY OF THE ANNUAL MIDSUMMER PARTY WAS glorious, a trifle warm, but after all it was midsummer. And who would not enjoy the pure summery glory of the white-blue sky with its puffy clouds, the deep green of the orchard in full leaf, with tiny apples already forming on the trees? It was a perfect day, Felicity thought as she stood at the top of the hill behind the mansion and gazed on the orchard below. It was also a bittersweet occasion—the last time her family would host the party that had been a tradition for generations.

She began walking downhill toward the green meadow, where the fete was being held amid the clover and honeysuckle. In the past few years, the fete had been more of a potluck picnic, with friends and neighbors bringing dishes to pass and a bonfire blazing at night. There had not been funds for much else. But this year, since it was the last that she would organize, she decided to make it a grand farewell from her family. And so the party evolved as a cross between a community picnic and a way to raise funds for the church and school, and she received help from Mrs. Stokely, Mrs. Rossiter, and an entire committee of church ladies.

She smiled with pleasure as the small band of musicians installed in the meadow struck up a lively air whose strains drifted up to her before she emerged from among the rows of apple trees. How good the music sounded. Here, at least, was one benefit of her connection to James. Considering all that had passed between them, she had felt no compunction in directing that all the bills for the annual party be sent to him at Granton.

She reached the meadow, where people had already started to gather. It had been transformed into a glorious fairyland. Tables swathed in yards of rich, cream-colored fabric presented selections of cold meats, fresh breads, fruits, and tarts. A festive cake sat alone on its own table, prettily decorated with delicate wildflowers. A crystal bowl filled with punch sparkled in the afternoon sunlight next to an enormous vase of pale pink roses.

Nearby, a modest wooden platform had been erected for dancing, its sides decorated with garlands of flowers. An area had been set aside for croquet, and already children were running and shouting happily along the course, among them Simon, who was home on holiday. It would be a perfect farewell party. And it was farewell—at the end of the next week, though she had said nothing about it to anyone, Felicity was to join the Carlton family as governess and travel with them to Rome, to teach the children while the family stayed there for a year. She was looking forward to the travel, and to the distraction the whole undertaking would provide. She was very much in need of distraction these days.

She had decided that today at the fete she would reveal the end of her engagement and her plans to leave, not as an announcement, but individually. Gossip would take care of the rest. She had not said anything yet to anyone, in fairness to James, so that he would have time to receive her message. But he would have read it by now, and she would not wait any longer than today to tell her family and friends.

Out of the corner of her eye, she caught sight of Crispin, who was moving a table under the direction of Mrs. Stokely. Felicity knew he must have decided that he could not in good conscience neglect this annual community event. He must have felt her gaze, because he looked up at her as the table was finally placed in the shade of a tree to Mrs. Stokely's satisfaction. She thought he would look away, but he didn't. Instead, he stepped away from the table and came toward her, his dark vicar's suit in perfect accord with the sober set of his features.

"Crispin," she said quietly as he drew close. "I am so glad you came."

His eyes were shadowed as she looked at them, but not as hard as they had been when they spoke in the garden all those weeks before. They hadn't seen one another since.

"Felicity," he said. He inhaled thoughtfully. "I trust that you and your family are well, and your fiancé."

She bit her lip. Should she say something now, reveal that her engagement was over? It was the truth, and she hated the idea of lying to her old friend. But she sensed the truth would only complicate matters between them right now, after that conversation in the garden.

"Thank you, yes," she said. "That's kind of you."

He gave her a faint smile then, a mere shadow of his usual grin, and said, "If your vicar cannot wish you well, things have come to a sorry state indeed."

"Oh, Crispin," she said, reaching a hand toward him.

He shook his head. "Don't," he said quietly. "I do wish you well, but distance is better." And ducking his head in parting, he strode off in the direction of the archery table.

She sighed, thinking that love was the reason for much quiet bravery in the world, something of which she had never been so fully aware before this summer.

Her father found her then, to ask her for the second time if she was sure Miranda had been sent an invitation.

"Yes, and she wrote that she was coming." She smiled at this indication of how much her father was looking forward to seeing Miranda. He wandered off absentmindedly among the guests.

"The fete is magnificent, Felicity! Well done," said Josephine some minutes later as she came toward Felicity.

Josephine took Felicity's hands affectionately and smiled, holding her at arms' length and looking her up and down in assessment. "It is so good to finally see you in something other than mourning colors. Yellow becomes you perfectly."

Felicity blushed at the compliment and the affection

behind it. She and Josephine had grown to be surprisingly good friends. She didn't want to think how the end of her engagement would affect their friendship. They would be unlikely anyway to see each other in the future.

"I must thank you again for the gift of this beautiful gown," Felicity said. "You have been so kind. I feel like a fairy princess." She smoothed her hands against the fine material of the gown, as pale and delicate a yellow cloth as any fairy could dream up. It had a scalloped bodice, cut femininely low and edged in small lace, and it was trimmed here and there, as if scattered, with tiny pale pink rosebuds.

"And so you should," Josephine chuckled. "And you needn't thank me—it was entirely selfish on my part. I've been desperate to see you in something pretty from this century."

Felicity laughed, so glad that Josephine had accepted her invitation. Since she was planning the party in James's name and he was paying for it, it made sense that his friends should be invited. Of course she had sent him an invitation too, out of politeness, but she did not expect him to come. He would be happily installed at Granton Hall, getting his new life established.

She had half wished that he would write back, or simply appear once he'd received the invitation, but she had heard nothing beyond the demanding notes she'd received and quickly destroyed. She hadn't trusted herself not to go running back to him. And he obviously was not coming after her, which was for the best, she had told herself every day, even as her besotted brain continued to hope she might be carrying his child. When she knew finally that she wasn't, she had allowed herself one good, long, sobbing cry, and then she had written to him.

"Ah, Felicity," came a masculine voice from behind her, "you look as tempting as a fairy cake that I might very much wish to sample." She turned even as a hand brushed against her bare arm.

"Hal!" she scolded, laughing, as delightedly scandalized as he always made her feel. He grinned, looking as much Lord Perfect as ever. He was an imp, but a good-hearted one. Underneath all that flirtation beat the heart of a serious and romantic gentleman.

Josephine's eyes were raised upward in dismay at her cousin. "Hal, you are very lucky no one has called you out of late. You become more forward each time I see you. Why, if James were here, I don't doubt he would plant you a facer, cousin or not."

Hal squinted, casting a quick glance around the fete. "And where is Cousin James, anyway? Not going to miss the party, I certainly hope."

"Oh," Felicity said, startled. She hadn't thought about people asking after him, but of course they would. They were still engaged, as far as everyone knew. And that left her to prevaricate. Maybe she should tell the truth now, she thought with a rush of emotion.

But looking at the happy faces of his cousins, at her father, who stood some distance behind them, and at all the guests who were looking forward to a pleasurable afternoon, she knew it would be best to wait until later. She wouldn't spoil the festive mood with talk of broken engagements. Neither did she want to answer questions or be consoled.

She put on a smile and said as breezily as she was able, "He is quite taken up with Granton Hall right now, after being away for so long."

Josephine's eyes lingered on her a moment, but then she shrugged and said, "Just like him to miss all the fun. He can be rather a drudge."

"Well, I'm not," Hal said. "And I believe I see some archery butts over at the far end of the meadow. Tell me, Mistress Wilcox, what is to be the prize for winners of the archery contests?"

"Hmm, prizes," she said, thinking. "There were some little trinkets for the children's games." She pondered a moment. "Oh, yes, I remember, we have some little bookmarks contributed by the church ladies."

Hal rolled his eyes. "That will not do at all. If I'm to compete in a manly contest, I must have a manly prize. A kiss from a maiden would, I think, be a fair prize." He lifted an eyebrow wickedly as he looked down at her. "And since you are by far the prettiest maiden, Felicity, it will have to be you."

"Hal!" cried both Felicity and Josephine together at his outrageousness.

"Done," said a deep voice from behind them. They all turned to stare in surprise at James.

Astonished though she was, Felicity forced herself to remain impassive. Still, his presence and his familiar air of energy worked upon her. He was as devastatingly handsome as ever, the black hair, the perfectly formed features, the muscular, tall physique. And the deep chocolate brown eyes regarding her—no, more than regarding her; he was weighing her reaction, seeking her.

She focused her thoughts. "James, I didn't know to expect you. When did you arrive?"

"Just in time to hear of an archery contest with an irresistible prize," he said, still looking at her intently, as though they were not in the middle of a crowd but somewhere alone.

Hal spoke, breaking the spell, making her aware again of James's cousins, who were both regarding them with different expressions. Josephine looked amused.

"Ah, cousin," Hal said lazily, "you have torn yourself away from the old homestead."

James merely gave him a crooked smile, his opposing eyebrow flicking up briefly, a gleam of challenge in his eye. "But of course. I wouldn't miss the midsummer party for the world, especially if there are to be manly prizes. And most particularly, I do not wish to spend another moment away from my fiancée." He shot Felicity an astonishing look of pure devotion. Josephine gave a small sound of amused satisfaction.

Felicity just stared at him, her mind swirling. He was acting as though he had not gotten her note, as though she had not secretly escaped from Granton Hall. Surely he had gotten the note?

But she had no chance to speak to him, because he and Hal were leading the way to the archery butts.

Two butts were set up side by side at a reasonable distance from a table where stood a cash box and a pile of needlepointed bookmarks. Mr. Pringle, the choir director, was manning the contest.

"A shilling each, please," he greeted them, a jovial grin on his face, his toes tapping to the lively music that was now being played by the orchestra.

Hal and James paid their money and were duly installed in front of a butt each and supplied with a bow and quiver. Alice and Lydia had trailed along behind Felicity and now stood by her, both cheering for James in their little girls' voices as he tested his arrow against the bow. He had removed his jacket and rolled up his sleeves for the contest, and she could not help but notice the outlines of his upper arm muscles straining against the white shirt fabric, the sprinkling of dark hairs on his tanned forearm, the strength of his large hand as it clasped the bow.

"What's this?" demanded Hal in mock dismay as he fitted his arrow to his bow. "Will not you cheer for me?"

"Cousin H-a-a-l," the girls giggled until Alice soberly pointed out that as James and Felicity were engaged, James should have the prize.

"Ah, but it will not be worth bestowing if it's not a challenge to win, eh, cousin?" he asked, turning what Felicity thought was a not entirely jesting face to James. James merely raised a haughty eyebrow to his cousin and gestured for Hal to begin.

They each promptly sent four arrows in their turn to their bull's-eyes.

"Well, gentlemen," chuckled Mr. Pringle, shaking his head with admiration, "I guess it's to be a bookmark apiece. They are very handsome, though starting out like this, I begin to wonder if we'll have enough."

"Move the targets back, please," James said. "Twenty yards."

Hal lifted an eyebrow in surprise but nodded his approval, and a lad hoisted first one target and then the other, carrying them to the very edge of the meadow. They looked tiny indeed now, and Felicity did not see how anyone could hit them at all. Mr. Pringle looked skeptical but amused.

"Very well, gentlemen. You may begin again. As before, four tries each, best score wins."

Hal shot first, dispatching each arrow with a brisk, fluid motion and barely a pause. A small crowd had gathered to stand a few paces behind the archers with Felicity and Josephine. There were soft cries of appreciation from several young boys as he sent his arrows flying. Considering his usual demeanor, he was remarkably focused on his task and did not indicate by any sign that he noticed anything but the targets.

She watched him shoot two bull's-eyes and two of the next highest, red. *Well, I shall likely be getting a kiss from Hal when this is done.* Having finished, he rested his hand atop his bow and gestured with his familiar lazy air for his cousin to proceed.

James took up his position and fitted an arrow to the bow. She thought that on the one hand she would not mind at all giving Hal a kiss in front of James—the familiar urge to needle him was irresistible, even though she kept reminding herself that as soon as they had a moment together she must tell him firmly the engagement was off. On the other hand, there was nothing she wanted more than to be in James's arms, though then she would only stir up the agony herself. If James won, she decided, she must be certain the kiss he claimed was cursory, a quick peck on the cheek.

He took up his archer's stance and focused on the target, his expression serious. His eyes were narrowed with intensity, his angular jaw set in determination. At that moment, the traits that made him successful at whatever he set his mind to accomplish were evident.

But his first shot was a yellow, and she thought, *well good, that's for the best.* He was not as good a shot as Hal—she doubted many people were. He made no comment on his first shot but proceeded briskly to shoot three bull's-eyes in a row.

A small cheer went up from the little crowd, and he turned around after his last shot hit, a delighted grin on his face.

"Well done, James," Hal said affably if with a trace of disappointment, "you've done me out of a kiss to which I was looking very much forward."

"Perhaps you would like a bookmark as a second place prize?" asked Mr. Pringle, finally understanding the alternate prize that was going to be awarded. "I doubt anyone else today could shoot as well as the pair of you."

Hal graciously, if with a deeply wry look, accepted a needlepointed strip decorated with a flower and a tassel. James, meanwhile, had come to stand before Felicity. "And now for my reward," he began.

"James!" she yelped as he reached for her arm. She stiffened as he touched her, but he drew her closer. She started to wriggle away, desperate to keep a safe distance from him. Meanwhile the crowd was enjoying the scene, laughing and shouting encouragement to him to claim his prize. Everyone, it seemed, knew of their engagement and wanted a romantic ending to the contest.

He leaned close to her ear and whispered softly, "None of that wiggling away, Lis. You've already escaped me once. And I must have my prize."

"But—" she began, but could say no more because he was tugging her away from the group near the archery table, toward a stand of apple trees a few dozen feet away. In a moment her back was pressed against a mature tree, the crowd was behind her and out of sight, and James was before her, a palm pressed against the trunk on either side of her head.

"James, stop this. I won't be your prisoner here. You may kiss my cheek, and that will be the end of it. I can see that you must not have gotten my letter. We have to talk."

"I got the letter," he said. "Now, my dear Miss Wilcox," he leaned close and looked intently into her eyes, "I must beg you to be quiet while I unburden my soul."

He touched her face gently with one palm, rubbing her skin tenderly before returning his palm to the tree trunk. What did he mean, "unburden my soul"? She stared at him, her heart turning over in her chest, his nearness having its predictable intoxicating effect.

He shook his head ruefully. "Do you know, after you deserted me, and I had day upon day with no Felicity to cheer me, I began to wish passionately that Lovely Annabelle would come to me at night? God, how I've missed you."

He leaned over and pressed his cheek against hers, the faint roughness of his shaved whiskers sending prickles through her body, stirring her desire. Just as he had always been able to do.

"No!" she said, putting her hands against his chest, a barrier between herself and his beguiling ways, and pushing him back. He allowed her. "My note released you from our engagement. You needn't have come here. I'm going to announce the end of our betrothal today."

"Of course I can't stop you from doing that, but I hope with all my heart that you will not." He closed his eyes for a moment and inhaled once, deeply, as if steeling himself. Then he opened his eyes and regarded her straight from those dark brown eyes she had come to love.

"I love you, Felicity," he said, "utterly and madly."

Her heart tripped at his words. Words she'd so longed to hear. But she forced herself to remain impassive. He was only saying what he thought she wanted to hear. He was so good at arranging things the way he wanted them, and apparently he'd decided he wanted to be betrothed to her. So his words were nothing more than a way to get what he wanted.

When she said nothing, he continued. "I have been pigheaded."

That she could not resist.

"Yes, you have!" she said, her voice sharp and full of remembered hurt. "You've done whatever you wanted, entirely uncaring of who might be hurt in the process. You sold my home because you didn't want to lose yours. And you didn't even have the decency to tell me until the deed was done."

"Yes," he said soberly, his mouth grim. "To all of it. I was incredibly selfish, and it shames me to think of it."

She blinked. Was he truly admitting—truly understanding—that he'd done wrong? Could she trust that he was sincere? And yet, he had dealt honestly with her in every other way. At Granton, before she left, he could have lied and said he loved her, but he had not. He was watching her now with a vulnerability that she'd never before seen in his eyes.

"But you're wrong that I was uncaring, Felicity. I just hadn't planned on love. I thought I knew what I wanted: to save Granton and restore the Collington name my brother had tarnished. I knew the steps that were required to do it. But then I met you and began to care for you. And I realized too late that what I wanted and needed might be changing."

She crossed her arms and turned her head, looking resolutely away from him. "You betrayed me."

James knew he'd hurt her deeply. But was it too late to win her back, had he done too much damage? He closed his eyes, his heart beating a million times a minute, and said, "I know, and I'm so, so sorry. Can you forgive me? I want nothing more than to marry you and love you every day of our lives."

She looked at him now, her arms crossed, her jaw set. His Lis. Oh, how he wanted her to be.

"James, you're not thinking clearly. I'd make a terrible MP's wife," she said. "I didn't even mind that much dressing in clothes from the last century. My family is practically penniless, and my uncle was a grand and public fool. We're very poor on appearances, and what may be worse, we don't really care."

Urgency pressed him. Everything was at stake. "But I don't care about appearances either, I've discovered. I don't want to be an MP, and now I can admit that I never really did. I don't care anymore whether people think the Collingtons are corrupt or worthless or idiots."

"How can that be true? You had such plans."

"Never mind about plans! They won't mean anything, I've come to see, unless I have your respect."

He reached forward and took her hand, not wanting to think how fully she might crush all his hopes—and his heart. "And what I want more than anything, dearest Felicity, is your love."

She looked at him for what seemed like the longest time, her hand unmoving in his, and he thought that he'd failed, that he was not going to be able to make her believe in a future for them. It was no more than he deserved.

But then the corners of her mouth started to wobble. "James," she said in a voice husky with emotion. Her small hand squeezed his and his heart turned over. "All right. I do love you."

Dear God, the release. The instant bliss.

"Then I am the luckiest man in the world!" He pulled her into his arms, both of them smiling like fools. He kissed her deeply, passionately. Her slim arms hugged him to her as she kissed him back, and their love met in the touch of their skin and in the joining of their souls.

They had been kissing and embracing for some time when they became aware again of the world around them through the sound of a voice calling for Felicity. Coming apart and laughing, they ventured out from behind the trees. Fortunately, the crowd had long since dispersed. Miranda, who had come with James, had apparently caught sight of them emerging from the sanctuary of the trees, and was coming toward them from the archery table, smiling; it was her voice they had heard.

Seeing her approaching, James stopped for a moment, so Felicity did too, her face quizzical as she turned to look at him. He was grinning, and he reached into his breast pocket and pulled out a folded paper, which he handed to her with a bow. She opened it.

It was a special license for them to be married.

She looked up at him, her face tipped at a questioning angle, a surprised smile playing about her beautiful lips.

"Darling Felicity," James said, "What do you say to getting married today? We already have an orchard full of wedding guests. And I, for one, don't want to wait another day."

She laughed, her eyes brimming with happiness. "Oh, yes! Oh, James, what a wonderful idea."

Twenty-eight

The surprise news that James and Felicity would celebrate their marriage at the midsummer fete was greeted by their guests with cheers and delight. Aunt Miranda gave a shout of glee that could be heard above everyone else, and Mr. Wilcox didn't stop grinning from the moment he heard the news.

He pulled his daughter into an enormous hug. "Oh, my child, I am so happy for you. And not merely because he is a man any father would be proud to have for a son-in-law, but above all because it is so obvious that you two love one another."

"Oh," said Aunt Miranda, her voice growing thick with emotion, "I've cherished such a secret hope that this would come to pass."

James laughed. "Well, perhaps not so secret. I gathered at Granton that you thought I'd be a fool if I let her get away. And right you were, too," he said, slipping his arm around Felicity's waist.

"Where is our vicar then?" Mr. Wilcox said, looking around. "His services are needed."

Everyone laughed good-naturedly except for

Felicity, who suddenly realized the awkwardness of this otherwise festive occasion. But perhaps Crispin wouldn't feel the awkwardness, because he didn't seem to be present. She was grateful he would be spared this.

"He must have left," she said. "But that is no matter. We can make plans for our wedding to be held soon, perhaps at a harvest fete."

"What?" said James. "I can't wait until the harvest to marry you."

She felt stricken by the one blot on her happiness. Speaking low so only he could hear, she said, "It's just that—"

But Crispin called out then, making for the front of the crowd, to where Felicity and James stood. "I am here. I will gladly perform the ceremony."

"Oh, Crispin," she said, embracing him. "That is so kind of you."

"Yes," he said low but with a hint of dryness that cheered her, "it is."

"Oh thank you, my friend," she replied low near his ear. "What a very, very good man you are."

He gave her a brotherly squeeze before they stepped apart.

James looked quizzical, but Crispin merely said, loud enough for all to hear, "If the bride and groom will join me on the dancing platform, we can start the ceremony."

And so Felicity and James stood on the decorated dancing platform before their guests, and were married by a somewhat sober but still warm Reverend Mr. Markham. Mr. Wilcox and Aunt Miranda stood together nearby on the platform as well, beaming with pleasure. When James and Felicity kissed at the end of the ceremony, a rousing cheer went up.

Nanny Rollins was heard to remark to Lady Pincheon-Smythe that she always knew Miss Felicity would make a fine match, and Lady Pincheon-Smythe graciously said that she could not have wished better for Caroline's daughter.

The picnic celebration turned into the perfect wedding luncheon, and many of the guests remarked that it couldn't have been better than if the wedding had been the original plan. And when, after the ceremony, Mr. Wilcox and Aunt Miranda quietly revealed to James and Felicity that they had become engaged, the newly married couple felt that their happiness could not have been more complete.

Late that night in Tethering Hall, after all the guests had gone, James pulled his cravat loose as he walked up Tethering's familiar battered stairs. He shook his head regretfully; he was really going to miss the old place. But tonight was not for regrets but new beginnings. He had sent his bride upstairs ahead of him while he saw to a few details with an exhausted Fulton. And now he wanted nothing more than to claim her.

All day long as they'd celebrated with their guests, the sight of her had brought him joy. He didn't deserve such a good woman, but he knew he would strive every day to be worthy of her love.

James appeared in the doorway of the candlelit master bedroom, and Felicity's heart turned over with unspeakable happiness. He was her husband, this tousled, gorgeous gentleman in his white shirtsleeves and slim-fitting pants, this beloved, good man who stood watching her where she stood by the window.

Her heart beat faster as they gazed at each other hungrily for long moments, until he came in and closed the door quietly behind him, going over to stand near the bed.

"Come here, Mrs. Collington, and let me take down your hair."

She laughed softly in the quiet house, delight spilling over like a fountain inside her, and went to sit next to him on the side of the bed. His deft fingers began to work her hair, gently sliding out the pins that held it, even their motion against her scalp making her shiver with anticipation. When all the hair was loose, he gathered it in his hands and buried his face in it.

"Ah," he said, lingering there and sighing as with deep satisfaction. Finally he leaned away and adjusted her hair to fall toward her front. He climbed onto the bed and settled himself behind her, pulling her against his chest. He rested his chin on her shoulder.

"So, sweet Lis, where do you fancy to live?"

She turned her head, leaning away a bit to look at him. "What do you mean, James? Won't we live at Granton Hall?"

"Well, that's just it. I didn't know whether you would believe in me when I came to you today, whether you would have me after my abysmal behavior toward you. So I planned a grand gesture to convince you. Only, sweet forgiving woman that you are, I didn't have to say anything."

"Say anything about what?" She looked suspicious. "Darling, what have you done?"

"I've written to Farnsworth to say the funds won't be available after all, as we had arranged. I acknowledged the forfeiture of Granton and wished him well with it."

Her eyes widened. "What! You're going to lose Granton Hall?"

"No, I won't lose it," he said, his face relaxed and as content as she'd ever seen him. "I've chosen not to take it."

"But, James, it's your family home!"

He chuckled, a little sadly. "And you, sweet girl, thanks to me, know all about losing your family home. In part I wanted to make it up to you, what I'd done to Tethering."

She was crestfallen, and he held up his hand for her to hear him out. "I also realized that it had so much to do with my past, with what my family was. But now there's no one left except me, and Miranda, who doesn't give a fig where she lives as long as she can garden. And I realized, when you left me all alone to wallow in my thoughts, that a home is nothing without the woman I love. Wherever we go together, we shall make our own bliss."

"James." She blinked. How had things come to this? They had both set out to save their homes and ended up without either of them. "I am astonished. And moved, deeply moved. Are you certain you won't regret this? Maybe it's not too late. I wouldn't want for you to lose your family home."

He laughed, and again she was struck with how

peaceful he looked, as if the spring that wound him had loosened its coils. At least a bit.

"No, no, it is fine. It was a good business decision, anyway. You see, I don't think anyone has done much about maintaining the house these past years—clearly Charles didn't when he was in charge—and there's a significant amount of water that may have been sitting in the cellars for a while, the kind of problem that could drain away a lot of money. And I can't say I'm not happy it won't be my money."

He grinned, all white teeth and boyish charm, and rested his scratchy cheek against her bare shoulder. "And anyway, we do have the Bodega Alborada, and thanks to Tethering," he said ruefully, "almost ten thousand pounds. Spain is beautiful, and we could have quite a wonderful orchard there..."

She laughed, and tears of joy gathered in the corners of her eyes. "You know, James, I think I would very much like to see Spain."

"And when you are tired of it, my sweet, perhaps we shall take some of our nice money and buy a home of our own somewhere in England."

"That sounds like a wonderful plan."

They were free as larks. Would she ever have dreamed that such a future would appeal to her so much, a future with no Tethering? "And I know all too well that you are very good at planning."

With a playful growl he pinched her bottom and she squealed.

"Ah, sweet girl," he said, his voice a deep rumble now coming from behind her as he fiddled with the buttons on her gown, "seeing you happy has a funny effect on me. Something inside me lets go, and I want to do this to you." He pressed his warm lips to the sensitive spot where her neck met her bare shoulder, the stubble of his whiskers making her shiver deliciously.

"And this," he continued, kissing downward toward the skin he had just uncovered. His breathing was becoming ragged, and it thrilled her.

"And this," he murmured. His hands came from behind her, sensuously conformed to her ribs, and slid along them before coming to rest, possessively, one on each breast. She shivered with pleasure, a jolt connecting from where his warm hands touched her breasts down to the deepest part of her. He gasped, leaned his head against her neck, nuzzling her.

She was sliding into a delicious haze of desire. But tugging equally at her consciousness was fatigue. It had been an incredibly long day. She couldn't help herself then; she yawned uncontrollably.

Her hand flew to cover her mouth. She didn't want to be tired now, not tonight.

Feeling her movements, he raised his head and sighed, his arms coming all the way across her chest to hug her close to him. The feel of his muscular chest, strong and warm against her back, was heaven.

"Tired are you, sweet bride of mine?" he asked in a gentle voice. "Did you get anything at all to eat at the celebration, I wonder?"

Thinking back over the day, she realized it was true; she had been so busy that she had had no more than a cup of punch and a nibble of cake over the course of the day.

He gently separated from her and stood up. "Right then, sweet. Wait here and I'll go fetch something for you."

And before she could utter a word he disappeared out the doorway and down the dark hall.

He appeared a few minutes later, a tray balanced on one hand while he held a candle with the other. He brought the food over and set it on the bed, arranged the pillows against the headboard, and swept her an exaggeratedly servile bow as he indicated she was to sit and eat.

She laughed and climbed up to the head of the bed. He sat next to her and they fell upon the food. He had brought leftovers from the day: some cold chicken, some wine, and apple tarts with thick cream. Until she looked at the food, she had not realized how ravenous she was. All was quiet for several minutes as they ate companionably next to each other.

"Do you eat in bed often?" she asked after finishing her chicken. She could feel the wine they were drinking coursing through her, making her a bit giddy.

He flicked her a glance from the corner of his eye. "Have you never eaten in bed before, then?"

"Just when I was sick. And when I was upset at Granton, and I decided I didn't care if I left crumbs in the bed."

An elegant black eyebrow lifted roguishly. "Stick with me, and I will introduce you to the heights of decadence. From eating in bed, it's just a small step to sharing a bath together."

Her eyes widened at this idea that sounded wickedly delightful.

He laughed and picked up one of the small plates holding the tarts, which he offered to her before taking one for himself.

Finally the little meal was entirely consumed. "Ah, Cook is very good," Felicity said, settling back against the pillow behind her when all was gone. He had tidied up the tray himself, shooing away her hands when she would have helped. It was going to be good to have such a useful man around.

"Well, you recommended her, my dear," he said as he turned toward her, having deposited the tray on the nightstand. He propped himself up on his elbow, all confident maleness.

She laughed ruefully, remembering how she had wanted him to suffer at Cook's hands. "I did rather torment you, didn't I?" she said.

He reached out and put his finger under her chin and tipped her face up to look at him. "You haunted me in more ways than one." He stroked her cheek with his thumb and chuckled softly, a very masculine sound. "And now that I have my very own ghost all alone in my room at night," he said, moving closer so that she could feel his breath against her lips, "she is definitely too much temptation for a poor, honest gentleman."

"Mmm, I hear you're not so poor anymore," she said, drunk with love for him.

He leaned over and pressed a kiss against her cheek. Glancing down at her exquisite bosom, on which he was about to lavish all his attention, he said, "What's this?"

She glanced down too, leaning around his head.

A wayward flake of pastry was resting on the bare, upward swell of her breast. With a groan he leaned over and pressed his tongue against the pastry, and she moaned a little as his moist flesh came against her skin.

"What if I?" she said, pushing him so that he fell over against the bed. She climbed on top of him then and gazed down at him with a look of eagerness that shot a bolt of desire to his groin.

She tossed her laugh back, looking as triumphant as a queen. His queen, who instructed, "Off with your clothes," and never was an order more eagerly obeyed.

Twenty-nine

The roads in Spain seemed bumpier to Felicity than English roads, but she told herself it was just the newness. Even the air in Spain was different—still languorously hot even in late September, and rich with the smell of olives and that orange scent familiar to her from James. Everything was new and different since she had left England: her first sight of the sea, her first time sailing under the stars with her love by her side, her first sight of Spain. For a girl who'd never been beyond Longwillow village, every moment of this trip was a small miracle.

Beside her in the coach, James held her hand. With his other hand he was holding a map. He'd wanted to show her some of the beauties of Spain as they journeyed, and so their trip had included stops in several of the small towns in the hilly region of Cadiz. She'd sampled olives, and tomatoes still warm from the sun, and thin slices of intensely flavored ham on crusty bread. They'd visited stucco churches decorated with bright blue and yellow tiles and been chased, laughing, through a siesta-quiet plaza by an exuberant Spanish dog. Each day only made her smile wider.

She'd also picked up a little Spanish. "*Mi amor,*" she said, turning away from the window. "I'm sure we'll come upon it soon."

"*Sí, mi amor,*" he said, smiling ruefully, "but will it be before we all die of thirst? No sign of anything but road and hills and olive trees for miles."

It was true that they had been traveling for miles longer than they had expected. James had expressed disgust several times with the quality of their map.

She laughed. "We may be out of water, but there's always the wine we bought in Santiago."

With no one but him in the coach with her, she had pulled her skirts above her knees to allow the air to circulate around her legs, and now he put his hand on her bare knee. His touch, as always, made her feel cherished. A prickle of excitement ran along her skin as he absentmindedly stroked the inside of her knee with his thumb. His touch always started a little excitement in her, too.

"I'm lucky that you're not a very proper English lady, or taking the back way to the bodega would be hell instead of adventure. Did I mention that I love you?"

"*Sí,*" she said, smiling and leaning in for a kiss against his cheek, which had gone very tan again now that they were in Spain. He had taken off his lapis-blue coat because of the heat, and his white shirt was putting his darkened skin into relief, making him the very picture of a dashing rogue. *Her* rogue. "And I love you."

After a moment, he said, "Ah. Look up ahead."

Outside the coach window, as the carriage pulled beyond a crowd of almond trees, a vine-covered hillside appeared, row after neat row of plants with dark clusters of fruit. And beyond, more. The estate stretched over several hills, at the top of one of which stood a tile-roofed, stucco building where a man was emerging with what looked like a cask on his back.

"The Bodega Alborada," James said.

She sighed. "It almost puts the Tethering orchard to shame."

He gave a low chuckle. "It's a little bigger, true."

She was searching the hillsides as the carriage pulled onto a drive. "And where will we live?"

"Ah, yes," he said, and she could have sworn there was a smile in his voice. He leaned an arm across her shoulder and pointed in front of her. "There."

She looked and looked, but all she could see was hillside and plants, and at the base of a hill, a small pale thing. "I don't see anything."

"There." He pointed again.

She squinted. "But that's a *tent*!" She turned to look at him and his eyes were laughing with devilry.

"It is, true," he said. "I thought it would be romantic, sleeping together under the stars."

"Romantic," she said slowly. "Well, all right. I suppose that would be romantic." She smiled gamely. "Anywhere would be romantic with you, James. But what's funny?"

He was grinning, and he kissed her and hugged her close.

"You are, sweet. I don't know a single other woman

who would not have handed me my head on a platter if I told her we'd be sleeping in a tent. And I am, actually, afraid that we will have to sleep in a tent—but just for the rest of the week. The workers will be done by then with the renovations to the manor."

And then he showed her, out the other window, the grand white hacienda where they would stay. Surrounded by flowers and climbing vines, with a small fountain in front and a courtyard just visible beyond, it was beautiful and perfect and welcoming.

"Oh! It's heavenly. Oh, James, I can't wait to move in."

She gave him a little push. "Only you'd best make sure it's only a week I have to wait," she said with a dangerously lifted eyebrow, "or you'll be getting a very uncomfortable visit from Lovely Isabelle, Annabelle's Spanish cousin."

"That, my sweet," he said with a rumbling laugh, "I would love to experience."

Acknowledgments

I'm very grateful to all the enthusiastic and talented people at Sourcebooks, and especially to my editor, Deb Werksman. I'm also lucky to have the best agent a writer could want in Jenny Bent.

Writing a book can take about forever when you're just starting out, and I've had lots of help along the way, particularly from the terrific writers at Washington Romance Writers. Thanks especially to critique partners Candy Lyons and Alison Pion, and to Diane Gaston and Sally MacKenzie for their savvy advice. Thanks also to Molly and Nora for reading numerous drafts, and to Abby, Sophia, Jennifer, Terri, Pete, and Jill for being such great cheerleaders.

Watch for the next playful Regency by Emily Greenwood:

Gentlemen Prefer Mischief

Coming December 2013 from Sourcebooks Casablanca

If it hadn't been for the haunted woods, Lily Teagarden would never have spoken to her neighbor, Hal, Viscount Roxham. Known to the fashionable world as Lord Perfect, to Lily he's a man she can never respect… and the careless rogue who broke her fledging heart. But sightings of eerie lights among his trees are causing her trouble, and she needs his help.

Intrigued by this prim beauty who was once an ugly duckling, Hal agrees to investigate, though hardly has he begun when she mysteriously undermines his efforts. The mischief she throws in his path awakens his sleeping heart, just as his touch stirs a passion she can't accept. But Hal is the last man to whom Lily would surrender, and it's going to take everything he's got to win her love.

If you enjoyed Emily Greenwood's *A Little Night Mischief*, then read on for an excerpt from

Lady Vivian Defies a Duke

by Samantha Grace

"Another winning marriage of romance and wit."

—*Publishers Weekly* Starred Review

26 August 1818

Dearest Vivian,

Foxhaven assures me Lord Ellis's visit to Brighthurst House is naught but to pay his respects. Nevertheless, I suspect the duke is sending him to gather information about you. Be on your guard and provide no grounds for Foxhaven to oppose the match.

Our coach is being readied to return to the country as I compose this letter. Send word the moment Ellis departs, and do not omit any details. I must be prepared for the next interview with Foxhaven.

With deepest regards,
Ash

Lady Vivian Worth folded the sheet of foolscap and sighed. Her older brother had always shown a flair for dramatics, often predicting disaster where no risk existed. He had no reason to fret over a nobleman's visit to Brighthurst House. Vivi knew perfectly well how to behave like a lady. She'd had nineteen years of practice. Observing proper manners when no one was around to impress, however, was silly.

She tossed Ash's weekly letter beside her discarded gown, petticoats, and corset, then tore off across the damp grass, her unbound hair flying behind her. The previous night's heavy rain had swollen the spring cutting through Cousin Patrice's property to the ideal depth, and Vivi had always been powerless to resist a good swim.

Reaching the rocky ledge, she leaped into the air with a whoop, drawing her knees toward her chest. She hung weightless for a second, then dropped to the spring below with a loud splash, the water sucking her to the bottom. Vivi burrowed her toes into the pebbled spring bed, then shot upward to break through the surface again as eagerly as a newborn babe bursting into a bright new world.

Ah, sweet ecstasy. This was much better than mindless needlepoint.

Smiling, she stretched out on her back to admire the white clouds soaring like mountains into the sky. Today the sun was brighter, the trees more lush, the birds harmonious in their songs.

Lucas Forest, the twelfth Duke of Foxhaven, was showing interest in her at last, even if he was sending an emissary to call on her.

Vivi had never been a patient person, and waiting for Foxhaven to claim her had been difficult indeed. Yet, she had not faulted him for postponing the final signing of their marital agreement. He had just lost his father suddenly, and she'd understood the magnitude of that kind of loss. By age seven, she was already an orphan and quickly becoming a burden to her brother.

She could also appreciate Foxhaven's shock upon learning of the secret negotiations between her brother and the former duke. She hadn't been consulted prior to their discussions either.

Nevertheless, thirteen months had proven to be a torturously long time for her to exist in a state of uncertainty. She was ready to have the matter settled between them and leave Bedfordshire behind.

When the duke's representative, Lord Ellis, arrived next week, she would give him no reason to find her lacking. She would be everything her brother had promised Foxhaven she would be: a gracious hostess, a proper lady, and an empty-headed ninny with no opinions.

Vivi flipped onto her stomach and swam with the current.

Claiming she had no opinions was perhaps unwise of her brother. Her opinions tended to sprout up like dandelions in a field, and she was often found eager to share her thoughts when others were not so eager to listen. But she would hold her tongue, even if she must bite it in the process.

Swimming to shallower water, Vivi stood and wobbled on the slippery rocks, her hands thrust out at her sides to find her balance. She had best make her way back to the house. Cook was still awaiting her approval of the meals for Lord Ellis's stay. Since Cousin Patrice had taken to her bed with a chill, the task had fallen to Vivi.

Were a gentleman's occupations as mind-numbing as a lady's? Likely not. Their reading selections certainly proved more entertaining. Perhaps she could afford to sneak in another chapter of Sir Thomas Malory's *Le Morte d'Arthur* before addressing the kitchen staff.

She trudged upstream, her mind already preoccupied with the story she had abandoned earlier. She often lost herself in daydreams about handsome knights and being adored by one. It made her lonely days feel less… Well, *lonely*.

She is attending a tournament. Sir Launcelot stops his charger in front of her and declares himself as her champion. Vivi pulls the scarlet ribbon from her hair and presents it to him. Her brave knight holds her offering to his lips, his eyes shining brightly.

"My dearest Lady Vivian, you honor me with your gift. Might I beg of you a kiss as reward for my victory?"

Vivi touched her fingers to her lips. "Yes, my brave knight." She laughed, embarrassed to still be engaging in girlish fancies. Her imagination was rather brilliant, however. She had been so lost in the moment she could have sworn she'd heard the whinny of Sir Launcelot's horse.

The smooth rocks shifted and she landed in the water with a plop. As she struggled to her feet, the snort of a horse—real, not imagined—made her head snap up.

A horse and rider appeared through the tree line ahead and approached the spring's edge.

She froze.

The man sat casually in his saddle, seemingly unaware of her presence, while his horse lowered his head for a drink. She sloshed around in search of someplace to hide, but there was nowhere to go. No bush, boulder, or tree near enough to shield her.

"Damnation!" The gentleman's surprised exclamation echoed off the stone ledge lining the opposite bank.

"Oh, look away. *Please*, look away." She attempted to run for deeper water, but her chemise twisted around her knees. Pitching forward, she landed face first into the water, then came up coughing and sputtering, her hair in her eyes. The sounds of boots hitting the gravel and splashing made her heart leap into her throat.

She staggered to her feet, sweeping aside the curtain of hair obstructing her view. Hastily, she crossed her arms over her breasts. "Stop!"

The stranger drew to a halt, the water up to his knees. Dark brows lowered over the most striking blue eyes she had ever seen. "You aren't in need of rescue?"

She snorted. "Not from swimming."

His intense stare bathed her in heat, making her forget the affront he had just served her. She slowly began to back away. Water dripped from her nose, but she didn't dare expose herself to swipe at it.

If anyone discovered her half-nude in the presence of a gentleman... Well, it would be a million times more disastrous than the situation with Owen, and that debacle could ruin her if word ever reached London.

His gaze didn't waver.

"Will you please stop gawking at me?"

"Sorry." He covered his eyes and his lips twitched upward. "Now that we have established you are in no danger, perhaps you can answer a question. Are you a water sprite or a manifestation of my overactive imagination?"

His voice sounded like he was holding back a smile. He wasn't taking their situation seriously enough in her estimation.

"The second one, so go away."

The gentleman laughed, but kept his eyes covered. "You seem real enough. Perhaps you're a milkmaid from a local farm. Does your employer know you are attempting to drown yourself instead of attending to your duties?"

"I wasn't drowning, and I haven't time to chat with unwanted trespassers."

She continued to ease toward the opposite bank, watching him for signs of pursuit. Her pulse slowed a fraction when he held his position and still didn't peek.

"Are there any other kind?" he asked.

Reaching deeper water, she submerged herself to her neck. "Any other kind of what?"

"Trespassers. Are they ever wanted? By definition trespassing implies—"

"I *know* what it means. Now good day, sir."

He laughed again and dropped his hand by his side. "You're a cheeky one. What is your name?"

Vivi's eyes widened. A true gentleman would have pretended he had never seen her, and if he did by chance discover her half-nude in a spring, he wouldn't insensitively request her name.

"I am no one of importance. Please just go away."

The last thing she needed was a guest of the neighboring estate spreading word of their embarrassing encounter. She would be the talk of Dunstable.

Again.

And Ash would be livid with her.

Again.

The man flashed a grin. "Spoiled your fun, did I? Perhaps before I go, you might assist me."

"I am certain I have no skill in whatever it is you require." She swam backward, putting more distance between them.

"It requires no skill."

He waded out of the spring, stood on one foot to tug off his boot, and poured water from it. "I just purchased these and now I've ruined them coming to your rescue."

"I didn't *need* rescuing." Truly, she was an excellent swimmer. Why wasn't he listening?

"Of course you didn't." His sarcastic tone got her back up, but before she could deliver a scathing set-down, his magnificent eyes locked on her again. "I require directions to Brighthurst House. Do you know the way?"

"Brighthurst?" All the air rushed from her in a whoosh as her gaze swept over him. His expensively cut burgundy coat was dusty and his Hessians—well, they were likely ruined as he had said—but he was attired more fashionably than most gentlemen in the county.

Dear heavens, no!

This gentleman couldn't possibly be Lord Ellis. The earl wasn't due for several more days. Perhaps she had misheard him.

She cleared her throat. "Did—did you say Brighthurst House?"

"I must be close if the blacksmith is to be trusted."

Sweet strawberry jam! He had to be the earl. What was he doing at Brighthurst House this early? And where was his coach? "Uh, I-I don't—"

He frowned as he mounted his horse. "Don't tell me you are unfamiliar with Lady Brighthurst."

She wouldn't say she was unfamiliar with her, for it was best to avoid speaking falsehoods whenever possible. "You might have gone—" She waggled her finger. "Go *that* way."

His gaze followed her wavering finger. "Which way? The way I came?"

"Yes, I think. Maybe."

"Yes or maybe?"

"Uh… Perhaps you should find someone else to ask."

He raised a brow and looked pointedly around the area. "Ask someone else? Who, pray tell?"

"Forgive me, sir, but I really must go." She swam for the opposite bank, reaching her destination and clinging to the rocky ledge.

"Just a moment, I require an answer. Do I go back the way I came or not?"

"Um, yes!" Dear Lord, she had just lied after all. To an earl. Vivi's heart pounded in her ears, blocking out his reply. She blinked. "Pardon?"

"I asked if you would like something for your trouble. A shilling or two?"

"No!" Good heavens, no. She couldn't take his money, too. Her knuckles ached as she fought against the current trying to sweep her downstream.

He walked his horse a little ways into the water. "Are you certain you don't require assistance? You appear in danger of drowning again."

"I *know* how to swim," she said through clenched teeth.

The gentleman rubbed his forehead, appearing to mull over the wisdom of leaving her.

She eyed the steep incline on her side of the creek. It would take a bit of effort, but she could scale the hill. If the gentleman would leave. "Thank you for your concern, but you may go now."

A slow smile eased across his mouth like honey dripping from a spoon. "You are too cheeky by half, chit. Take care when climbing to the top. I wouldn't like to see you hurt."

"I will be fine, but thank you again."

With a shake of his head, he flicked the reins and turned his horse back toward the trees.

Lud! She didn't have much time. As soon as rider and horse disappeared from sight, Vivi levered her elbow against the rock ledge, flopped her leg on top, and then climbed from the water with a soft grunt. Pushing to her feet, she kicked free of the chemise tangled around her legs and grabbed a large tree root dangling down the side of the embankment. She scurried up the hill hand over hand, her mind awhirl.

What was Lord Ellis doing at Brighthurst this early? And why did he have to arrive at this exact moment? She had the worst luck of any person she knew.

Her feet slipped on the dark dirt, stirring up an earthy scent. She held tighter, ignoring the burn in her palms, and continued her climb. When she made it to the top, she dashed for her clothes.

Lord Ellis couldn't reach the house before her. He just couldn't. She needed a moment to think, to sort out what to do before he arrived. She had to find a way to salvage her situation, because she couldn't bear to be a disappointment to Cousin Patrice again.

In the distance, someone called her name. It was her maid.

"Lady Vivian, here you are. I have been searching everywhere for you." Winifred marched through the meadow in her direction. "It looks like another storm is blowing in. You better come back to the house."

A gust of wind sent the meadow grass into a frantic

dance. Vivi snatched up her crumpled gown from the ground. "Winnie! Come quickly. Something awful has happened."

Her maid broke into a run. "My lady, what is it? Have you been injured?"

"No, nothing of the sort, but please help me with my dress." Winnie grabbed her corset and petticoats, but Vivi waved them away. "There isn't time. You may dress me properly once we reach my chambers."

"I don't understand, my lady. What happened?" Her maid draped the undergarments over her shoulder and tossed the gown over Vivi's head, yanking the skirts down her body inch by inch as the Indian muslin stuck to her wet skin.

When her head emerged, she saw a thick cloud dull the bright sun. The air seemed stagnant and heavy. In the distance, foreboding storm clouds hovered on the horizon as if getting into formation to launch an attack. It was moving in quickly, catching her unawares, much as Lord Ellis had.

Before her maid could fasten her gown, Vivi linked arms and dragged her through the meadow back toward Brighthurst House.

"Lady Vivian, what are you about?"

"Oh, Winnie. I'm in a real pickle. Lord Ellis will arrive at our front door in a matter of moments. We must hurry."

"Lord Ellis? But he isn't expected until next week." Winnie planted her feet, jerking Vivi to a stop. Her brow furrowed as she captured Vivi's face and peered into her eyes. "You didn't knock your head, did you?"

Vivi brushed her maid's hands away. "I haven't lost my senses. Let's go."

Fingers of lightning stretched toward the ground, and thunder made the earth below them shudder.

Her maid clung to her arm. "We should hurry, my lady."

"That is what I've been trying to say. Lord Ellis ambushed me at the spring, and he is on his way to Brighthurst House."

Winnie's eyes grew as round as shillings. "Merciful heavens, the earl discovered you in your chemise? Oh dear. This is beyond horrifying."

"You're not comforting me." Clasping hands, they ran for the dower house as the wind whipped through the meadow and plastered Vivi's wet gown against her. The first raindrops splattered the dirt as they reached the house and slipped inside.

Vivi shivered, and her maid put an arm around her shoulders. "Come upstairs, Lady Vivian, before you catch your death."

At this point, death might be the easier solution. "Ash will send me to the nunnery for certain this time."

Winnie squeezed her tight. "Well then, he will have to send me too. I'll not let you wreck havoc on those poor Sisters of Mercy alone."

Vivi almost laughed, but it was hard to find much humor in her complete ruin. "You would do that for me, Win? Perhaps it wouldn't be terrible if you were with me."

"Phoo!" Her maid flicked her hand. "We'll come up with some way to get out of this. But first, let's change you out of these wet clothes."

They ascended the stairs side by side and bustled down the corridor to Vivi's bedchamber. Once the door closed, Vivi wrestled with her damp gown. Winnie hurried forward to assist. With her soiled gown discarded and a dry one donned, Vivi rushed to the window to search for signs of Lord Ellis. The gravel drive was deserted.

"Egads. It's raining like the devil."

A blinding flash and boom caused her to jump back with a scream.

Rain pinged against the glass, deafening with its intensity, and dark clouds blotted out the sunlight.

"Tell everyone we must put lights in every window."

"Yes, my lady."

A deep rumble vibrated the windowpanes. Her heart hammered against her ribs.

Surely Lord Ellis would throttle her for deceiving him.

If he survived.

Lady Mercy Danforthe Flirts with Scandal

by Jayne Fresina

Lady Mercy likes her life neat and tidy. She prides herself on being practical—like her engagement to Viscount Grey, whose dark coloring coordinates very well with her favorite furnishings. But things start to get messy when her best friend abandons her fiancé at the altar, leaving it up to Mercy to help the couple. There's just one problem. The jilted man is Rafe Hartley—Mercy's former husband.

Rafe has not forgiven Mercy for deserting him when they were seventeen. Their hasty marriage was declared void by law, but in his eyes the bossy little vixen was still his wife, even if the marriage lasted only a few hours. And Mercy "Silky Drawers" Danforthe still owes him a wedding night.

One Night with a Rake

by Connie Mason and Mia Marlowe

For King and Country, three notorious rakes will put all their seductive skills to work.

After all, the fate of England's monarchy is in their hands.

Since the death of his fiancée, Nathaniel Colton's polished boots have rested beneath the beds of countless wayward wives and widows of the ton. He's careful to leave each lady smiling, and equally careful to guard his heart. So seducing Lady Georgette should pose no problem. But the beautiful reformist is no easy conquest, and Nate's considerable charm fails to entice Georgette to his bed. To woo her, Nate will have to make her believe he cares about someone besides himself—and no one is more surprised than Nate when he realizes he actually does.

"Deliciously scandalous, with authentic settings, realistic characters, and wicked seductions."—RT Books Reviews, *4 Stars*

"Had me absorbed, entertained, and looking forward to future stories."—Book Savvy Babe

New York Times and *USA Today* bestselling author

by Grace Burrowes

A story that breaks all the rules...

Darius *is a gripping and remarkable tale of desperation, devotion, and redemption from award-winning* New York Times *and* USA Today *bestselling author Grace Burrowes. Her gorgeous writing and lush Regency world will stay with you long after you turn the final page...*

With his beloved sister tainted by scandal, his widowed brother shattered by grief, and his funds cut off, Darius Lindsey sees no option but to sell himself—body and soul. Until the day he encounters lovely, beguiling Lady Vivian Longstreet, whose tenderness and understanding wrap his soul in a grace he knows he'll never deserve...

"Burrowes creates her usual intelligent characters, exciting chemistry, and flowing dialogue..."—Publishers Weekly

"Very compelling... Likable characters with enough angst to keep the story moving along."—Night Owl Reviews *Review Top Pick, 4.5 Stars*

For more Grace Burrowes, visit:

www.sourcebooks.com

A Wedding in Springtime

by Amanda Forester

Her timing couldn't be worse...

Miss Eugenia Talbot's presentation to the queen is spoiled by a serious faux pas—the despicable William Grant made her laugh, right in front of Her Majesty. Now Eugenia is ruined and had better marry—someone, anyone—at once...

And his couldn't be better...

Roguish William Grant has never taken anything seriously in his life. Until he meets Eugenia Talbot, who makes him feel and do things he never thought he would.

Now Eugenia's great sense of humor and kindheartedness may be her undoing, unless William can help her find a husband. To his surprise, that's the last thing he wants to do...

"Engaging subplots involving unforgettable supporting characters make this one a must-read."—Publishers Weekly

"Forester promises her fans a warm, humorous jaunt through Regency England—and she delivers with a cast of engaging characters and delightful intrigue."—RT Book Reviews

If You Give a Rake a Ruby

by Shana Galen

Her mysterious past is the best revenge...

Fallon, the Marchioness of Mystery, is a celebrated courtesan with her finger on the pulse of high society. She's adored by men, hated by their wives. No one knows anything about her past, and she plans to keep it that way.

Only he can offer her a dazzling future...

Warrick Fitzhugh will do anything to protect his compatriots in the Foreign Office, including seduce Fallon, who he thinks can lead him to the deadliest crime lord in London. He knows he's putting his life on the line...

To Warrick's shock, Fallon is not who he thinks she is, and the secrets she's keeping are exactly what make her his heart's desire...

Praise for *When You Give a Duke a Diamond*:

"A lighthearted yet poignant, humorous yet touching, love story—with original characters who delight and enough sizzle to add heat to a delicious read." —RT Book Reviews, *4.5 Stars*

For more Shana Galen, visit:

www.sourcebooks.com

Checkmate, My Lord

by Tracey Devlyn

The stakes are high, the players in position...

Catherine Ashcroft leads a quiet life caring for her precocious seven-year-old daughter, until a late-night visitor delivers a startling ultimatum. She will match wits with the enigmatic Earl of Somerton, and it's not just her heart that's in danger.

Let the games begin...

Spymaster Sebastian Danvers, Earl of Somerton, is famous for his cunning. Few can outwit him and even fewer dare challenge him—until now. After returning to his country estate, his no-nonsense neighbor turns her seductive wiles on him—but why would a respectable widow like Catherine risk scandal for a few passionate nights in his bed?

Praise for *A Lady's Revenge*:

"Devlyn makes a unique mark on the genre with her powerful prose and gripping theme."—RT Book Reviews, *4 Stars*

"Devlyn reveals the darkness of the spy game and entices readers with a talented and determined heroine."—Publishers Weekly

For more Tracey Devlyn, visit:

www.sourcebooks.com

Once Again a Bride

by Jane Ashford

She couldn't be more alone

Widowhood has freed Charlotte Wylde from a demoralizing and miserable marriage. But when her husband's intriguing nephew and heir arrives to take over the estate, Charlotte discovers she's unsafe in her own home…

**He could be her only hope…
or her next victim**

Alec Wylde was shocked by his uncle's untimely death, and even more shocked to encounter his uncle's beautiful young widow. Now clouds of suspicion are gathering, and charges of murder hover over Charlotte's head.

Alec and Charlotte's initial distrust of each other intensifies as they uncover devastating family secrets, and hovering underneath it all is a mutual attraction that could lead them to disaster…

**Readers and reviewers are
charmed by Jane Ashford:**

"Charm, intrigue, humor, and just the right touch of danger."—RT Book Reviews

For more Jane Ashford, visit:

www.sourcebooks.com

New York Times and *USA Today* bestselling author

The Rogue Steals a Bride

by Amelia Grey

A promise can be a terrible thing...

All heiress Sophia Hart's father wanted was for her to marry a gentleman with a title. She promised him on his deathbed she would do just that. But the only man Sophia wants to spend time with is Matson Brentwood, who makes up for the lack of a title by being dashing and decidedly dangerous. Since Matson crashed his way into her life and her heart, that vow to her father has become an awful burden...

Praise for *New York Times* bestseller
A Gentleman Says "I Do":

"Grey neatly matches up a sharp-witted heroine with an irresistibly sexy hero and lets the romantic sparks fly."—Booklist

"Sensual, charming, and touching."—
RT Book Reviews, *4 Stars*

For more Amelia Grey, visit:

www.sourcebooks.com

About the Author

Emily Greenwood worked for a number of years as a writer, crafting newsletters and fundraising brochures, but she far prefers writing playful love stories set in Regency England, and she thinks romance is the chocolate of literature. A Golden Heart finalist, she lives in Maryland with her husband and two daughters.